RETRO

RETRO

SOFÍA LAPUENTE &
JARROD SHUSTERMAN

SIMON & SCHUSTER BFYR

NEW YORK • LONDON • TORONTO • SYDNEY • NEW DELHI

An imprint of Simon & Schuster Children's Publishing Division
1230 Avenue of the Americas, New York, New York 10020
This book is a work of fiction. Any references to historical events, real people,
or real places are used fictitiously. Other names, characters, places, and events are products
of the author's imagination, and any resemblance to actual events or places or persons,
living or dead, is entirely coincidental.
Text © 2023 by Sofia Lapuente and Jarrod Shusterman
Jacket illustration © 2023 by Shania Fan
Jacket design by Chloë Foglia © 2023 by Simon & Schuster, Inc.
Interior illustrations by hobarth/iStock (cassette tape) and me/iStock (musical notes)
All rights reserved, including the right of reproduction in whole or in part in any form.
SIMON & SCHUSTER BOOKS FOR YOUNG READERS
and related marks are trademarks of Simon & Schuster, Inc.
For information about special discounts for bulk purchases, please contact
Simon & Schuster Special Sales at 1-866-506-1949 or business@simonandschuster.com.
The Simon & Schuster Speakers Bureau can bring authors to your live event. For more
information or to book an event, contact the Simon & Schuster Speakers Bureau at
1-866-248-3049 or visit our website at www.simonspeakers.com.
Interior design by Hilary Zarycky
The text for this book was set in Berling.
Manufactured in the United States of America
First Edition
2 4 6 8 10 9 7 5 3 1
Library of Congress Cataloging-in-Publication Data
Names: Lapuente, Sofia, author. | Shusterman, Jarrod, author.
Title: Retro / Sofia Lapuente and Jarrod Shusterman.
Description: First edition. | New York : Simon & Schuster Books for Young Readers,
[2023] | Audience: Ages 14 up. | Audience: Grades 10–12. | Summary: To save her
struggling family, Luna enters a competition offering reward money to anyone
who can successfully live without modern technology for a year, but when this
social experiment turns sinister and her classmates start disappearing, her family's
livelihood might not be the only thing she is in danger of losing.
Identifiers: LCCN 2022039215 (print) | LCCN 2022039216 (ebook) |
ISBN 9781665902755 (hardcover) | ISBN 9781665902762 (paperback) |
ISBN 9781665902779 (ebook)
Subjects: CYAC: Contests—Fiction. | Technology—Fiction. | Survival—Fiction. | Missing
persons—Fiction. | BISAC: YOUNG ADULT FICTION / Thrillers & Suspense / General |
YOUNG ADULT FICTION / Technology | LCGFT: Thrillers (Fiction) | Novels.
Classification: LCC PZ7.1.L3443 Re 2023 (print) | LCC PZ7.1.L3443 (ebook) |
DDC [Fic]—dc23
LC record available at https://lccn.loc.gov/2022039215
LC ebook record available at https://lccn.loc.gov/2022039216

*For anyone who has suffered bullying. And for all
of you who continue to challenge the definition of normal.
Thank you for being so brave.* ♥
—S. L. and J. S.

*Gracias a toda mi familia y amigos, y especialmente a ti, mamá.
All of you have been so supportive since I began my crazy journey,
and you've never doubted that I would conquer my dreams.*
—S. L.

A ═LUNA'S═
PLAYLIST

⏮ ⏪ ▶ ⏸ ⏩ ⏭

rls Just Want to Have Fun"-Cyndi Lau
on't Speak"-No Doubt
tter Sweet Symphony"-The Verve
th or Without You"-U2
se
Don't Need Another Hero"-Tina Turne
Away"-Lenny Kravitz
Will Rock You"-Queen
vin' La Vida Loca"-Ricky Martin
nnabe"-Spice Girls
is Is How We Do It"-Montell Jordan
verybody (Backstreet's Back)"-Backstre
ye Bye Bye"-*NSYNC
se
llstar"-Smash Mouth
asket Case"-Green Day
eedom! '90"-George Michael

19. "Smooth"–Santana ft. Rob Thomas

20. "Wind of Change"–Scorpions

21. "It's Tricky"–Run-DMC

22. "Ironic"–Alanis Morissette

23. Pause

24. "One More Time"–Daft Punk

25. "It's My Life"–Bon Jovi

26. "One Way or Another"–Blondie

27. "La Isla Bonita"–Madonna

28. "What a Feeling"–Irene Cara

29. "Bailamos"–Enrique Iglesias

30. "Enjoy the Silence"–Depeche Mode

31. "No Diggity"–Blackstreet ft. Dr. Dre and Queen Pen

32. "Scar Tissue"–Red Hot Chili Peppers

33. Pause

34. "I Love Rock 'n' Roll"–Joan Jett e the Blackhearts

35. "Iris"–Goo Goo Dolls

36. "Barbie Girl"–Aqua

37. "Macarena" (Bayside Boys Remix)–Los Del Rio

38. "A Quién Le Importa"–Alaska y Dinarama

39. "Higher Love"–Whitney Houston

40. Pause

41. "Oops! . . . I Did It Again"–Britney Spears

42. "These Boots Are Made for Walkin'"–Nancy Sinatra

43. "Africa"–Toto

LISTEN ALONG WITH LUNA:

▶ 1.

Play

You don't know me yet. But here I stand, soaked in mud, blood stained across my diamond disco dress—and I'm not even sure where I am. My heart is splintered glass inside my chest. Un corazón roto.

How I arrived is a story too twisted to believe.

So let me center myself and take in my surroundings. I'm trapped. I was thrown into a sterile white room with no windows, the closest thing to a jail cell I have ever seen. And the maddening silence makes me wish this place came with a minibar and a lobotomy pick. Anything to help me escape my current reality.

But isn't that all the rage these days?

People hide behind an online profile, a facetuned image, or a filter—when, in reality, their face doesn't need a filter; it needs a double cappuccino. Like my mom always said, La cara es el espejo del alma. And how right she was—no matter how much you try to hide, your eyes will always reflect who you truly are. And in my eyes, they found someone who would never back down. I guess I'm difficult. Which is basically why I'm here.

At least they had the decency to let me keep my Walkman. I

press the headphones tight to my ears. It will help me tell my story.

Let me introduce myself.

My name is Luna, but lately I've earned a few others. You might think I'm locked away because I killed someone—or maybe you think I robbed a bank. Assault and battery.

Not quite. But this year we did create a revolution, and I was there on the front page.

Because this year we were invincible.

Or so we thought.

Now my heart is burned by the flames.

My friends disappeared, never to be seen again.

And the blood is dried on my hands.

My music fades out, and I wipe black tears of mascara from my eyes. I don't need a mirror to know that I probably look like a hungry, rabid raccoon. The tape has ended, but the story is far from over—so let's bring it back to the very beginning.

To the first song of the soundtrack of my life.

▶ 2.

"Girls Just Want to Have Fun"
—Cyndi Lauper

I was innocent. She knew it and decided to bury me anyway—silent as a grave. No matter how harmful we know lies to be, each one of us will tell ten to two hundred of them per day. They come in all shapes and colors, from *I love your haircut* to *I have read and agree to these terms and conditions*. Some are white and others stained crimson red. But what they don't teach you is that the most dangerous lies are the ones you don't tell.

Or at least that's what I learned the day I got caught for stealing.

It all went down the last day of summer, on one of those Northern Californian afternoons where clouds threatened darkly overhead. Instead of organizing a funeral for our summer vacation, my friends and I enjoyed one last afternoon of saturated fats, inappropriate jokes, and brand-new clothes. It's not like there was much else to do in our small town anyway.

The Monteverde Mall was always a second home to me, and not just because when I was six I hid in the furniture store until my mom rounded up a mall-cop search party. It was where I experienced my first true deception and mixed all the Play-Doh colors, expecting to get a rainbow and instead got caca brown. I even killed my first gaggle of zombies in the arcade. But most importantly, my family ran the little movie theater in the corner of the top floor, where I had a lifetime supply of radioactive-yellow popcorn.

My mom had given me the day off, so my friends Samantha and Mimi were pretending to be my personal shoppers, though I didn't remember hiring them. Samantha had her mind made up that I was a pop star partying in Malibu, and Mimi, like a seagull, was distracted by anything shiny. A match made in department store heaven.

"Luna, you'll be literally irresistible in this," Samantha said, holding up a microscopic emerald blouse.

"Thanks, but I think it'll fit you better . . . it's too sexy for me," I told her.

Mimi threw an arm over my shoulder. "Like my mom always says, the sexiest thing you can wear are your values."

As wacky as Mimi could be, she was always somehow super wise.

"I see how all the guys look at you ever since you got your braces off." Samantha nudged me. "This year boys are going to be lining up to meet you."

I smiled. "No blouse, no guy could make me feel luckier than having you two."

Samantha grabbed my hands teasingly, making me dance with her. "Come on—love and hormones are in the air."

"Then where's my gas mask?" I laughed.

"Give it up," Mimi said. "The last time Luna had a boyfriend, she was eating sand at playtime, and we all know how that ended."

The rest of our department store experience consisted of Mimi and me pretending that we could afford more than one article of clothing while Samantha spent forever in the dressing room taking selfies in all the clothes. Or at least that's what we thought she was doing.

As we were wrapping things, up Mimi received a call. She hung up the phone, looking concerned. "I have to go. My cat is fighting my iguana again."

I would have asked questions but had learned better by this point. Although I did very much care for the well-being of Professor Meowmington and Juanita.

We hugged Mimi goodbye, and she headed for the exit, but not without winking to a guy in the cologne section. Mimi had no problem hitting on anyone at school, not because she was especially confident, but because she lived on her own planet—and it always blew my mind.

Left to our own devices, there was a weird air between Samantha and me.

"I had a lot of fun today," Samantha said, looking down. "Thanks for inviting me out with you and Mimi . . . you know how my other friends are."

"Don't mention it." I knew exactly what she meant. Samantha and I were well aware that we came from entirely different worlds.

She was the popular one.

And let's just say I was made up of different ingredients.

Her life was about beautiful blond hair, social media

followers, and grades so high, they set the curve. She was the "perfect" friend, and it had always been that way, ever since we were kids on the same soccer team. We never hung out together at school, but I was the first one Samantha called when she won class vice president or became a cheerleading captain. When her grandmother passed away. When she needed to relax and have fun. Because with me, for better or worse, she could always be herself. She didn't have to try to be perfect.

"I have to use the restroom," Samantha said. "Would you mind holding on to this for me?" She extended her orange backpack.

"No problem, girl." I took it and slung it over my shoulder.

While I waited, I flipped through Limbo—the social media app that had devoured all the others. If you didn't have a Limbo profile, you practically didn't exist. My friends and I were always coming up with new dances, having fun with trends, or just killing time. One time Mimi went kind of viral with a kitty-face filter, licking her dad's elbow, which was hilarious.

Anyway, as I stood there in the department store, a scent drifted up my nose. The divine aroma of white chocolate macadamia, coming from CookieWorld, the bakery just next door. I followed the fragrance, drooling like a bulldog. Samantha seemed a little off, and a surprise cookie would put a smile on her face. But as soon as I crossed the exit, I heard an earsplitting screech.

The sound of alarms.

I hovered awkwardly, confused, until a hand grasped my shoulder, spinning me around.

Store security—a man dressed in a yellow-and-black uniform, with the weathered demeanor of a retired cop.

"Ma'am, I'll need you to open the bag," the guard ordered, pointing with his baton. I had almost forgotten I was still wearing Samantha's backpack. I pulled it off and opened the zipper, finding a cheer team sweatshirt.

"Would you mind showing me what's underneath?" the security guard added. No longer so tense, I dug a little deeper . . .

Revealing the sparkle of silver.

A snarl of it—a brand-new space-gray phone, an unboxed smartwatch, a pair of designer sunglasses, and necklaces still with the tags on. There I stood, holding up hundreds of dollars of stolen merchandise, struck to the core with panic.

Samantha was going to steal all these things.

I asked myself *how* over and over again. How the girl who always followed the rules, who never copied homework, was capable of taking so much merchandise—clearly I didn't know her as well as I thought I did, which freaked me out.

"You're coming with me," the security guard growled, blocking the exit. "It'll be up to the store manager to decide whether or not you're going to spend the night behind bars."

"Jail? I can't go to jail!" I wailed, pulling away. I was starting to make a scene. Shoppers circled around.

"This isn't my fault! I didn't do this!"

The guard raised an eyebrow. "Then who did?"

But I couldn't open my mouth to utter her name. I couldn't move. All I could do was stare into her eyes—because Samantha was frozen in place, face blanched, watching the scene unfold from a distance. I waited for her to step forward—for her to take responsibility. But she didn't.

"If it wasn't you, then who did?" the security guard repeated.

Samantha. Please say something! I screamed inside my head.

But Samantha said nothing. She was going to let me take the fall for this. Her eyes screamed *I'm sorry*, and I could see that she'd never intended for me to walk out of the store with that backpack, but everything else about her face told me that this was now my problem. It was her or me, and she chose herself.

▶ 3.

"Don't Speak"
—No Doubt

It was time to welcome back my old friend anxiety, his impossible cousin anger, and all the disappointment that hung around with them. It was all like a nagging pressure, as if an elephant had stepped on my chest, but I didn't want to explode. On this day I needed to be a bottle of water—not a bottle of soda. It was something I had learned whenever I was treated differently because of my culture or because of the tan color of my skin. When others would laugh at me because I had a brain fart in class and just Spanish would come out of my mouth, I'd remind myself that I was a bottle, and inside might be a lot of emotions and reactions, but no matter how much the rest of the world shook me up, I wasn't going to let that pressure detonate. Even if I wanted to scream, I couldn't sell out a friend.

I just wasn't made like that.

And Samantha knew it.

The security guard dragged me through the store to a small door in the back, near the fitting rooms. Then he shoved me inside a detention cell that felt more like the bathroom of an interstate gas station. The door slammed shut, and I was all alone—vulnerable and exposed like a raw nerve.

It wasn't long before I heard the muffled ring of a cell phone on the other side of the door, so I pressed my ear against it. I recognized the voice as the security guard's, but I could only make out some of what he was saying into the phone.

"I've got her here in the back room. . . . I don't know. Charges for a shoplifter aren't pretty."

That sent my mind spinning. Who could he be on the phone with? How could I, *Luna María Valero Iglesias*, the girl who never even took a free pen from the bank, be deemed a "shoplifter"? Sure, I was far from perfect. I always left strands of hair on the shower wall like works of art for the rest of my family to enjoy. And when I texted *almost there* it meant I still had to cross the Great Wall of China, fight a dragon, and find an Ikea exit before getting there. I was someone who hated mugs that tried to force me to be confident. Someone who would love to listen to your life problems—which was why I dreamed of becoming a psychologist. And maybe now those dreams would be shattered.

No college would give a scholarship to someone with a criminal record, and without financial help, my family would never be able to pay my way.

I caught the next sentence through the door:

"That's all fine. . . . All right . . . as long as you've spoken with her family first . . ."

Those words petrified me, because I started to imagine the horror my mother would feel when she received a call from the police—how she would think something terrible had happened, and then how disappointed she would be. What my father would think if he were still alive. The man who'd taught me that my last name, Valero, meant "courage in the face of adversity—coraje frente a la adversidad." Because a crime, no matter how petty, would draw attention to my mother. And the last thing we needed was to be flagged by Immigration when my mother's status was under close review. She was documented, but one crime could start a chain reaction that could separate us. All things that Samantha knew.

"Okay then, you know where to find her. . . . If the owners press charges, she'll be better off in the hands of a lawyer anyway. . . ."

The last thing I heard through the door before the call ended. If I was going to need a lawyer, then I would have to sell my left kidney to afford one.

Time dragged on. Hours passed, and just when I thought I'd never see the light of day again, the doorknob began to jiggle and eventually turn. And when the door finally swung open, I wasn't facing the officers of the law.

No guns. No handcuffs. No SWAT teams in riot gear. Just a woman in a smart business suit, hair pulled back tight. Someone so familiar to me, I could hardly believe my eyes. A woman whose house I had been to a thousand times, a lawyer I had known practically my entire life. And it was then, and only then, that everything began to make sense.

Samantha's mother smiled and gripped the security guard's shoulder, forcing a handshake and speaking in a smooth Southern drawl. "Please thank your store manager for seeing it my way."

"You're lucky she's a minor, or this would be a whole different story," the guard responded.

Relief crashed over me. For a moment I thought I was going to be okay—but Samantha's mother opened her purse and wrote a check to the department store.

For the amount of three thousand dollars.

"Mrs. Darby?"

"This is the fine for a misdemeanor, so this is how much they agreed to let you go for," Samantha's mother explained. "You're lucky they're not calling the police."

She produced a business card and handed it to the guard. "You have a good day now."

Mrs. Darby led me out of the room. Clearly disappointed by the mess her daughter had made. And when I reemerged into the store, my eyes instinctively went to the last place I'd seen Samantha. She was hovering meekly behind a rack of clothes.

If I hadn't been so angry, I would have felt bad for her.

I stared her down, hoping for an explanation, but Samantha never lifted her gaze. Instead, she pulled out her phone. She always flipped through her Limbo feed when she was nervous.

Without a word, her mother led us through the parking lot and straight to her jet-black Mercedes. Then she set a course that would take me home. And though she played her classic post-court zen sounds of birds, waterfalls, and rain sticks, it was the tensest ride of my life. Samantha didn't speak. I kept looking at her, waiting for an apology, waiting for a reason. Ten years of friendship, and she'd tossed me out like trash to save her own skin.

When we finally pulled up to my neighborhood, the Monte Dorado Apartments, the little apartment complex on the outskirts of town, her mother reached back and pushed the car door open, looking disgusted. Then she said something that pierced me with shock. I was expecting her to apologize on behalf of her daughter—or ask to talk with my mother—but as I stepped onto the street, defeated, Samantha's mother rolled down her window and looked into my eyes.

"Don't worry, hon," she said. "You can pay me back later."

"Samantha, please tell her what really happened. You know this isn't fair."

But Samantha turned her head away.

I needed her to be a friend—but what I needed didn't matter to her.

And that's when I realized that I was going to have to pay the price for her silence. Three thousand dollars. It was more than I had in my savings account. After working long nights at the movie theater and being an embarrassing beaver mascot at a water park under the sweltering sun for four summers. Samantha knew I'd broken my back for that money. She knew how hard life was for my family.

And just before driving off, her mother added, "Promise me you won't do it again."

My eyes flooded with frustrated tears.

"Promise me, Luna, and what happened today will disappear."

My lips trembled, and I surpressed the rage that threatened to drown me. "I promise," I finally said, my voice shaking. And like that, the car sped off.

My insides roiled.

I stormed to my house.

How could I be so naive? How could I be so stupid? How could

I be so weak? Instead of pulling me out of the ditch I'd fallen into, Samantha had buried me in it. And I let her! She even allowed her own mother to believe that I was a thief.

We'd started hanging out because her parents would pick me up from soccer when my mother was working late. We even had this little whistle that we passed back and forth to encourage each other on the field. To support each other in important moments, something that always kept us close, no matter how different our lives used to be. We were like the sisters we'd never had. But now that was over.

Since my mom's car wasn't parked in the driveway, it was better to go nuclear inside than freak out the entire apartment complex. I thanked my lucky stars she kept the theater open late on Sundays. If my mother found out what had happened, she would worry herself into a panic. And the last thing a single mother like her deserved was another complication.

I barreled into my room like a tornado, slamming the door behind me.

I didn't want to think about Samantha, even if it was all I could do. There were far too many things in my bedroom that reminded me of her. So I was going to destroy all the evidence. Ten years of friendship erased in a matter of minutes.

I was no longer a bottle of water.

I was pumped full of adrenaline and mixed with disappointment, so that I'd become a bottle of soda—full of explosive Mentos.

I ripped our favorite band poster off the wall.

I mutilated the Cristiano Ronaldo soccer jersey she'd given me with a pair of scissors. Then I shredded a Real Madrid poster that she'd gifted me for my seventeenth birthday. I knew it was dramatic, but I didn't care. I was a heat-seeking missile for everything that reminded me of her. Then, through blurry tears, I scrambled for my phone. I needed backup from the one person who could help me through this. Who would always tell me if I had lipstick on my teeth. Someone who reminded me of the Spanish side of my family—honest, for better or worse, and with all the love in the world.

But when I took my phone and started pouring out my heart, Mimi wasn't surprised.

"Luna, if someone is trying to bring you down, it's because they're already below you," she said. "What Samantha did was really messed up. Crazy. But everyone knows she never had a problem stepping on other people while she clawed her way to the glittery top."

Mimi wasn't pulling any punches, but she was right.

Samantha and I belonged to different worlds, and in hers all the invisible rules of popularity applied—I was just naive enough to think that the relationship we had after the bell rang was the real one. And Samantha wasn't afraid to make enemies at school.

"Samantha's friends have been calling me a freak ever since I got a beautiful cuddly iguana and dyed my hair pink," Mimi said. "But who doesn't want to look like a delicious strawberry gum? Whatever. They're the worst. Everyone knows it."

The more I talked with Mimi the better I felt, until at one point she even had me laughing with her very *Mimi* comments. "Samantha has a bee complex. She thinks she is the queen, but in reality she's just an annoying insect."

For the first time, I was smiling through the tears—convinced that the things she said should be printed on T-shirts, or at least framed in the Guggenheim. Now that I was a little calmer, I went to the kitchen to retrieve my "I give up on life" guilty pleasure: chocolate ice cream and hot sauce.

It wasn't going to solve my problems, but neither would broccoli.

"Samantha doesn't deserve a friend like you, Luna. What happened was a good thing, because now you know the truth."

"Thanks, Mimi. You're so right. I'm already over it."

"That's my Loony," she said, calling me by a nickname she'd given me back in elementary school. Before hanging up, Mimi left me with a few warm parting words. "Don't forget how brave you are. After all, you're the only person I know who cuts her own bangs."

I lay down in my bed and pulled out my phone. It was time to erase Samantha's digital footprint from my life. Whether it was posts on social media, video games we played together, or pictures on my camera roll. But now it wasn't about anger, or rage. It was about my own self-respect. It was about truth.

So I kept deleting. It was empowering. I was no longer going to live in Samantha's shadow. I was on the warpath. But what happens on the internet stays on the internet.

Something I was about to learn in the most hard-core way.

Because in that moment I found the Video.

I didn't even know it existed, but there it was, divinely out of place.

It was the night of Samantha's Halloween party last year,

and because her parents weren't home, she decided to make it a rager. I was never much of a drinker, but Samantha was a pro. She dressed like a Disney princess but was drinking like it was Pirates of the Caribbean. And after everyone had gone home, I was left to take care of the star of the show. I had never in my life seen a princess so wasted. Covered in her own vomit, with her face mushed into an entire greasy meat-lovers pizza, Samantha recorded the wrong video with the wrong phone.

And it was brutal.

In a drunken stupor, she'd trashed her friends and everyone who wasn't her friend: the popular kids, the guy she was hooking up with, the class president, the athletes, and the mathletes. Her teammates on the cheerleading squad. No one was safe. I was surprised she hadn't gone for me—I guess the battery had died before she'd gotten the chance to.

I never was supposed to have that video, but there I was, marveling at it—as if I had my very own Picasso in the palm of my hands. Beautiful and grotesque all at the same time.

The world needed to see this work of art.

If I was going to get scapegoated and lose all the money in my bank account, then the school deserved to see Samantha for who she really was. She wouldn't get to pretend that she was so perfect anymore.

So I opened up my Limbo app and uploaded the video from an anonymous account. And then I finally clicked post, publishing the video to Limbo, releasing with it all the bad feelings of the day. Then I shared it with Mimi, flipped my phone on silent mode, and hopped in the shower. And as I washed the bad vibes away, I reminded myself that tomorrow would be a fresh start. An opportunity to put the past behind me. To kill it on the first day of school. And I told myself that my problems couldn't get any worse.

Little did I know, they would grow into monsters.

▶ 4.

"Bitter Sweet Symphony"
—The Verve

In psychology there's this thing called Maslow's hierarchy of needs. It's the theory that, in order to reach your full potential, you have to have all the building blocks of your life set in place underneath, and like all cool things, it's in the shape of a pyramid. At the very bottom you've got your *physical needs* like food and water; then come *safety*, *love*, and *esteem*. So let's imagine you don't have any food in the fridge. The next day you'll steal your friend's lunch, and then they won't like you. And without their support you'll never accomplish your dreams of becoming president and making Taco Tuesday a national holiday. One by one as the building blocks are threatened, your entire pyramid comes crashing to the ground.

And it was about to happen to me on the first day of school.

That morning I woke up to the disturbingly happy jingle of my cell phone alarm. Past me always had a funny way of torturing future me. I stumbled into a pair of shoes and slathered on makeup. Nothing was going to hold me back—no matter how wounded I felt. I wasn't going to dwell on what had happened yesterday, and I definitely wasn't going to worry my mother about it. That was the last thing she deserved.

"Luna! *¡Hija!* Come drink your juice or it's going to lose its vitamins!" my mom called from downstairs.

"I'll be there in five seconds!" I yelled back, buying myself another five minutes. I cleaned up the fallout in my room from the night before, spritzed my favorite sweet-peach perfume, and flew down the stairs while scrolling through my Limbo feed.

There were the typical first-day-of-school posts: a couple of avocado toasts, a leaping Chihuahua in slow motion set to rap music, and perfect bullet journals ready to be filled. But the whole time I was feeling weird about uploading that video to my spam account—the second account I used for stalking crushes. Even though it was anonymous, I was starting to regret what I'd done.

So I deleted the video, erasing my angry mistake.

My mother suddenly shrieked, making me jump out of my skin. She pointed to my ripped blue jeans. "¡Ay, Dios mío! Why is my beautiful daughter dressing like the walking dead?" She grabbed my face and started scrutinizing. "And those puffy eyes! What are you doing with those bags under your eyes? You didn't sleep well?"

It was clearly residual emotion from the day before—something I hadn't noticed, but nothing gets past a Spanish mother—and mi mamá, Gloria, was no exception.

"I'm fine," I said through gulps of orange juice, then puckered my sour lips. "They're just ideas accumulated in the underneath part."

My mother swatted the air, signaling that she had given up on me. "Well, with all of those ideas I expect good grades, señorita. And don't forget to take your jacket!" Which is something she would say no matter what the temperature actually was outside. In my house, maternal overprotection was an understatement.

"I love you, mamá. Thanks for caring, but I think I'll sweat myself to death."

"I love you too, hija, but you don't sweat. You glisten. Now take the jacket." My mother kissed me all over. I was well aware that the difference between a terrorist and my mother is that with a terrorist, you can always negotiate.

Before taking off, I left a coffee on the table with a pinch of cinnamon and vanilla, just the way she likes it—because mornings are tough for mothers, too. Especially widowed ones. Then I strode out of the house in a puffy coat, looking like the Michelin man, and jumped into my prehistoric SUV, old enough to be "old" but not old enough to be "cool"—like that awkward phase in between haircuts. I gripped the steering wheel, my head up and ready for the day—whether I'd have to face Samantha or not.

I came.

I parked.

I sauntered—down a hall of colorfully painted lockers, where back-to-school banners hung expectantly, eager to welcome us back to the magical world of public education. There was a buzz of excitement as everyone showed off their new outfits and recently developed body parts. The air was thick and full of energy, like Black Friday before the violence. One kid even left his signature on the wall in mucus.

It was chaos.

I went to El Dorado High—which means "golden" in Spanish, but in English it must mean "chronic amnesia," because I'm lost trying to figure out how we have all these planets in our solar system, but all the stupid people wound up here. And the first day of school was no exception, because everyone at El Dorado High had already gathered in their respective social groups—from the athletes to the mathletes—and of course, hanging around the vending machines was the popular crowd: the Goldens.

They were faker than an influencer's breakfast.

I was happy to not be a part of any group.

As soon as I reached my locker, I heard a voice.

"Loony! There you are!" Mimi hugged me from behind like a lemur. "I've gotta say, that video you sent me is next level. All this time Samantha acted like she vomited rainbows, but she's a lowly mortal like the rest of us."

"Yeah, I know, right . . . ," I said, still feeling guilty for posting it.

"You know I'd bite anyone I need to for you?" Mimi smiled.

"Can you imagine if you actually did that?" We laughed, and I threw an arm around her. "Thank you for having my back, but I honestly just want to forget about yesterday."

"I know just the thing." Mimi reached into her pocket and pulled out a bag of assorted jelly beans. "Shall we?"

"Please be a strawberry," I prayed as I reached inside the bag.

Mimi was convinced that whatever flavor you chose on the first day of school would predict your destiny. And although I did not vouch for its accuracy, I couldn't afford to take the risk of not knowing—even Samantha used to join us. But the last few years, I always pulled the same flavor.

Lemon-lime.

That was so me. A little sweet, a little sour, and almost nobody's favorite. Sure, I had friends, but most people didn't notice me. I was smart enough to get into some honors classes, but I definitely didn't have the grades for an academic scholarship— so my only real bet for college was soccer. Though, as I sifted through the bag, I got the feeling that things were going to be very different this year. And that proof came when I pulled my hand out.

"Black licorice," I said.

Mimi gasped and hit it out of my hand.

"What does it mean!?"

"I don't know. But the last time I got one of these I almost drowned," Mimi explained. "Remember when my parents sued the water park, and we got all that money? Let's just say it means anything can happen."

We were on our way to our first class when I heard the sound. The outburst of laughter—and as we walked past the rainbow row of lockers, we realized phones were sounding out all over. Everyone was huddling in circles, whispering, laughing. . . . Only now did I realize that the positive vibes of the morning had been replaced by something less innocent.

I looked at Mimi. "What's going on?"

She seemed as clueless as I was, but then her phone buzzed. It was Limbo.

My body rushed with adrenaline. As Mimi scrolled down, we saw edited pictures and remixed videos of a saucy Samantha, accompanied by all kinds of text:

WHEN U LEAVE HOME AND RUN AWAY WITH PAPA JOHN.

HELP HER! 1-800-555-4357. DRUG & ALCOHOL HOTLINE.

PLS CALL NURSE'S OFFICE. TOO MANY PPL STABBED IN BACK!

FINALLY I'M NOT THE ONLY PERSON WHO HATES ALL OF EL DORADO HIGH.

To be honest, I laughed at first, because a few of the comments were genuinely funny—but as Mimi scrolled and scrolled, I realized that many of the Limbo videos already had tens of thousands of views.

Which stole the breath right out of my chest.

Because Samantha was trending.

"Um, did you share that video with anyone?" I asked Mimi.

"Just some friends from the yearbook club . . . and Miranda . . ." She looked down guilty.

"And who did they share it with?"

"I don't know, their friends, boyfriends maybe . . . ," she went on. "But, Luna, the algorithm picks what it wants. Samantha talked trash about her own friends, and they have tons of followers. Maybe that's what pushed it out."

I looked around. Samantha's friends were huddled over a phone, laughing. And at the center was the undisputed king of the Goldens.

Axel. The alpha social media star. Every school has theirs—some bigger than others. But let's just say Axel was larger than life. He had, like, a million followers. His friends loved him because after he got big, everyone in his orbit started gaining followers too, and the whole town loved him because he put El Dorado on the map. His fans drooled over his little hoop earring and perfectly messy hair, but I could never get past his arrogant smile, and the fact that he and his friends would call Mimi a freak. Like being different from them was a bad thing.

He and his girlfriend, Jade Laurent, were the closest thing to royalty where we lived. She was adored for having led the cheer team to the state championship last year, which scored the school a major sports grant to build a new gymnasium. They were the kind of supercouple that traveled the globe and sold teeth-whitening strips. And they had the power to make Samantha's life a living hell.

When Samantha saw the video, she would know that I was the one who had leaked it. But I hadn't meant for this to happen. I comforted myself, thinking that at least with the truth out in the open, maybe Samantha could stop taking herself so seriously. Samantha had spent her whole life constructing a perfect image, and maybe she could stop obsessing over it so much—she could finally relax and be happy with herself.

But this isn't that kind of story.

▶ 5.

"With or Without You"
—U2

With the scent of blood, the sharks came swimming. There was always someone who was slightly less popular than Samantha. Received lower grades than she did or had less money to flaunt. And because Samantha was anything but humble, every single person she ever crossed wanted to take a bite out of her.

I was in third period when things hit another level.

We were all pretending to be interested in our teacher's love life in order to waste class time when I saw that Samantha was seriously going viral. She even had her own hashtag:

#BackstabbingSamantha.

There were already 1.3 million Limbo posts.

Emotional abuse in more than one language—which meant this was going international. Everyone was getting in on the action.

I tried to report the videos, but no matter how many I flagged, it was no use—they just kept coming. So then I started replying to the assholes to try to make them stop, even if it was a long shot. Sure, Samantha had betrayed me, but this was no longer just a callout. This was a public execution.

I spent an entire class period hiding my phone under my desk, arguing with random strangers, but it was clear that things were only getting worse.

It wasn't until lunchtime that the axe fell.

The world has been a crazy place these last years, and I've learned that one of the greatest threats in any moment of catastrophe is misinformation. An infodemic, they call it. Lies spread and multiply at an alarming rate—eating away at us until we've lost all sense of what is true and what is false.

Mimi and I inched forward in the lunch line.

"Luna, why do we eat cafeteria food, pumped full of chemicals, when soap is made of honey, coconut, and vitamins?" Mimi said, nervously fidgeting with her sleeves and studiously avoiding looking around at our laughing classmates.

I didn't have the crayons or the time to explain it to her. I wasn't doing much better, anxiously tearing a napkin to bits. It was like I could physically feel that Samantha was suffering, but I guess that's what comes naturally after ten years of friendship.

And then I saw her.

For the first time ever, Samantha was eating by herself. She usually hung out with the Goldens, but today she sat in the corner, at a table that was always vacant, near the spoiling trash bins—pushing around peas and carrots, without a single person to talk to.

Samantha was all alone.

It was like the whole school was practicing social distancing all over again, but with her as the virus. There was a tension in the air, so thick you'd need a machete just to traverse the cafeteria. People whispered under their breath and over their lunches, judging from a distance as if she were a specimen to be examined.

Then Samantha looked up and found me—catching my gaze through the passing crowd. It was only for a moment, but that moment was enough. It was a look that screamed, *I'm lost, Luna, and I don't know how to stop this.*

At the center of all the laughter was someone who Samantha knew very well—someone who had once solidified Samantha's spot among the Goldens. The captain of the wrestling team. One of the most aggressive assholes of El Dorado: her ex-boyfriend Vince.

He was one of those kids who'd gone through puberty late and ever since had been trying to prove that he was man enough, even if it meant being a douchebag. You know the scientific theory that we all descended from the same common ancestor as monkeys? Well, Vince was the proof.

His friends were already teasing him.

"Samantha is still way out of your league, dude, even after that messed-up rant."

"I mean, she said you don't have enough muscle to fill out a size small T-shirt and that you shop in the kids' section! Are you going to take that?"

"You know, she said you even have a little—"

"ENOUGH!" Vince screamed. Clearly the teasing was getting to him.

Vince suddenly stood, grabbed his tray of food, and started moving toward Samantha like an ominous cloud before a storm. And it wasn't long until all eyes were on him, his letterman jacket, and the grin across his face.

What happened next played out in a matter of seconds, though in my mind's eye it unfolded in slow motion. Vince headed straight for the trash can. I hoped he would just throw away his lunch and leave it at that. But in that moment he made one of the nastiest moves I had ever seen. No person deserves to be treated like an animal—or fed like one either.

Vince flung his pizza at Samantha.

"Now you get to be as ugly on the outside as you are inside," he snorted.

Samantha was dripping red with sauce.

First the entire cafeteria fell silent. Then chatter echoed across the room.

"Oh. Oops." Vince fought back laughter. "Wow, I really do have good aim."

"Don't be an asshole, Vince," Jade called from her throne at the Goldens' lunch table.

"Well, I didn't mean to do *that*," Vince scoffed. But he was like that—the kind of guy who would break his opponent's arm on the wrestling mat and claim it was an accident. The Goldens hadn't taken a side in the breakup, but today Vince was making sure that the lines were clearly drawn. All eyes were on Samantha to see what she would do next.

She stood up slowly, smeared in pizza sauce, and began to whimper, wounded and helpless. She clamped her eyes shut, so that maybe this would all end. And from that hopeless void, tears began to pour.

Not a single person came to her defense—too afraid to become a target themselves. For the first time in my life, I truly experienced bystander syndrome. *Why take the risk to help, when someone else can do it?* Even Mimi was speechless, motionless.

No one held out a helping hand.

Instead, they held up their phones and started to record.

Samantha took off into the crowd, stumbling for an exit. Tripping and then having to pick herself up. Soon she was swallowed by a crowd so hungry to be entertained that they were willing to film the heartless scene unfolding before them.

In that moment, a switch flipped inside me. All I had was rage. My eyes burned red with tears. Because for once, I felt like I had nothing to lose.

I stormed through the cafeteria until I was standing in front of Vince, staring into his eyes. "You're a monster," I told him.

But Vince just burst out laughing. Right in my face. "No braces anymore, huh? Lola?"

"*Luna,*" I corrected.

"Well, *Luna*, you were a lot prettier before you opened your mouth," he jeered, his friends cackling along behind him. "Go eat your lunch with your loser friends and leave me alone."

Vince turned away and went for his yogurt, which pissed me off even more, so I hit it out of his hands, splattering mixed-berry delight all over his fresh white Nikes.

Now all eyes were on me.

I was officially making a scene.

"No. Not until I'm done with you," I said. But then he did something I didn't expect. This dark look came over his face, and he stepped dangerously close to me. For a split moment I feared for my own safety.

Call it female instinct.

I wasn't sure what to do, but I knew I wasn't backing down.

"Let it go, Vince. It's not worth it." Someone from his crew put a stern, restraining hand on his shoulder. And that some-one was Vince's best friend—the tall, hazel-eyed leader of the Goldens. "I'm not asking you. I'm telling you," Axel warned.

Axel and his friends were always taking challenges, racing cars, partying, or pulling pranks—and often getting suspended for them—so a fight was nothing new. But having been held back, Axel was a year older—which meant a year more devel-oped than everyone else. And Vince was clearly intimidated, because he finally backed down, huffing off.

Axel looked smug, like he was expecting me to clap and thank him, but I think he was just trying to make himself feel better for hanging around with such assholes. Then he turned to me. "Why do you care so much anyway? Samantha talked trash about everyone."

"You don't say things you don't mean when you're drunk? Are you perfect or what? Actually, don't even reply to that one. Nobody deserves what Samantha's going through."

"Well, you'd better get over it. You know she was embar-rassed to have you as a friend."

His words stung, deep. So I stared into Axel's gaze before leaving and lashed out, wanting to hurt him as much as he'd hurt me. "Looks like the rumors are true—the only smart thing about you is your phone," I said. "If it wasn't for all your follow-ers, you'd be alone too."

I turned my back and stormed out of the cafeteria. Mimi was reeling behind me, gushing about how epic that was, but all I could think of was what had happened to my oldest friend. The girl with the bedazzled Pomeranian that I'd help walk, and who I'd then show how to dance flamenco in my room while eating mango chili lollipops. The girl who screwed me over but never deserved this.

And I was thinking that I was no longer uncategorically plain and just lemon-lime.

On the first day of school, I'd unintentionally created my own new category, separate from everyone else at El Dorado High. All eyes were on me, for better or worse.

Because as dangerous as Vince and his friends were, the rules of high school were about to be flipped upside down—just none of us knew it yet.

We always talk about how lethal the click of a gun can be, but no one ever talks about the click of the smartphone. Whether it's a gunshot or a screenshot, lives are altered forever. It has the power to take down your favorite hamburger chain. Blackmail your parent's company. Or trash the reputation of your oldest friend.

I barged into a bathroom littered in glittery graffiti and used gum and kicked open the last stall on the left—where Samantha used to always hide when the drama got too real. But this time every stall was empty. And I could only imagine all the messed-up thoughts spinning in her head. Because Samantha always thought she had to be perfect and successful to make her parents proud, and now, because of my video, that life was over.

I stormed into the science building. The locker halls. No luck. Just before resorting to school security or finding a teacher, I finally realized where she was.

Her car was in the parking lot, in the spot awarded to the

student body vice president. The cute orange Fiat 500, with the black-and-gold cheerleading sticker on the back bumper.

I approached the window, and there she was, sitting in the driver's seat, her head buried in her hands. Broken. I reached out to touch her, but we were separated by glass. "Samantha, I'm so sorry."

She didn't respond.

"I never wanted this to happen. You know me. . . ."

Silence.

Then a muffled sound came from her phone.

It was her Limbo app.

She was receiving a torrent of DMs.

They just kept coming in. And with every one, Samantha's sobs only grew louder and louder. Because those messages weren't texts.

They were more like bullets.

And each one ripped through Samantha's heart. Bombarding a broken girl with every comment imaginable.

UR A BACKSTABBER!

NO ONE WANTS YOU AT EL DORADO.

YOU SHOULD BE ASHAMED OF YOURSELF.

WITH FRIENDS LIKE U WHO EVEN NEEDS ENEMIES?

I pressed a hand against the window, trying to get her attention. "Samantha, this school sucks. The whole world sucks. People are rotten inside. Ignore them." I tried to cheer her up. "They all deserve to get stabbed with sporks! I'll help you!"

Samantha finally pulled her head up, turned slowly, and looked into my eyes. Then she put her hand on the glass, where mine was, so that maybe in another world they would touch.

"Don't you get it?" She smiled weakly. "I'm no better than they are. Maybe I deserve this. Look what I did to you."

With that, Samantha threw her Fiat into gear and took off.

I chased after the car.

But Samantha was already gone. And there I was, standing alone in the parking lot, cursing myself for not having said more. For not having done more. I should have been quicker. I should have forced myself inside her car. What she needed was someone who would look into her eyes with love, hug her, and wrap her up in her sheets like a burrito, like we used to do at our pajama parties. She needed a friend.

It's crazy to think that every year we pass over the calendar day of our eventual death without ever knowing it. Well, that night, Samantha decided to face hers. We wouldn't learn what she did next until later, but it would mark a before and after in our lives. Because upstairs, in her mother's medicine cabinet, was a little bottle of prescription medication—and after her mom fell asleep, Samantha would take a pill for every message she'd seen that day.

Finishing the entire bottle—

Of thirty-seven pills.

⏸ 6.

Pause

I hate to stop the track like this—especially considering what Samantha did, but we will get back to that, I promise. As for right now, I'm bleeding, and bad. And if I lose too much blood, I'll collapse, and you'll never find out why I'm trapped in this sterile white cell from hell to begin with. So let's not be anticlimactic, okay?

I'm going to dislodge the shard of glass from my hip now, and WOW—it really hurts. I'm grunting in pain. Ironically enough, I put the glass there in the strap of my underwear myself, the last time I was face-to-face with them, at El Dorado High. Its edge must have pressed so hard against my skin it cut right into my flesh. Funny, how most tough people in the movies stick weapons in the back of their pants and walk around like total badasses, while I have to cut the tag of the jeans because it itches my sensitive butt crack. As for my little shard of glass, the best part is that nobody knows that I have it. It makes me wonder if I should have threatened them.

Maybe even stabbed them.

Please don't judge my thoughts yet. Wait until you hear the rest. This is just the beginning. After everything they've done to me—to all of us—you would understand, trust me. But then again, I'm not that kind of person. I'm a good girl.

Or at least I used to be.

But the truth isn't always black and white.

Sorry if my thoughts aren't making much sense. I'm dizzy and drunk on nerves. I feel strange in this place. Like that awkward sensation when you sleep over at your friend's house and wake up before they do and share a splendid breakfast with her parents without her.

Wait—

How did I not see this before?! Carved into the plaster wall are notches, tally marks for each day that someone else spent here—someone who wound up just like me. This definitely means something. I'm suddenly realizing that I'm not the first person to be trapped here.

I look to the bloody glass in my hand and go to make my own notch, for my first day here, in silent defiance—so that, in case someone else is thrown in this place, at least they'll know that they aren't alone.

Now, listen up, because what comes next hurt so bad, my voice quivers when I talk about it: the next day we all found out about Samantha's condition.

That she was in the hospital.

Dying.

▶ 7.

"We Don't Need Another Hero"
—Tina Turner

They say the best movie villains are the ones who think they're the good guys. Real life is a lot like that. You're so worried about being the hero of your own story that you don't even stop to realize you might be writing someone else's tragedy. In real life, the bad guys don't come with an ominous soundtrack, and the good ones don't have superpowers or sexy spandex costumes. We're all undeniably human, and we can all make terrible mistakes.

And as the guilty masses realized that they shared some blame, the texts and DMs rolled in like clockwork.

Did you hear about Samantha?

Do you think she is going to make it?

Do you know which kind of pills she took?

And in the midst of my own panic, the house phone began to ring. I walked into the kitchen cautiously, afraid of what I might discover if I answered. So I let it go to voice mail.

"Good morning, Mrs. Iglesias. This is Lucy Chen, Luna's school counselor. We would like to speak to you about your daughter. There was a terrible incident last night, involving Samantha Darby. She's in critical condition. Please contact us as soon as you can."

My chest seized up. My knees shook. I lost my footing, collapsing on the kitchen floor. I couldn't believe this was happening. This was real. I wasn't living in paranoia, but a nightmare.

Samantha had tried to take her own life. And my brain started spiraling with every perturbing image it might have entailed. How she did it. How alone she must have felt. The depths to which she must have sunk to lose her will to live. But I had to keep it together. In order to pull myself up from that cold tile floor, I grabbed onto one fact that I knew.

She was in "critical condition," which meant she was still alive.

Because Samantha was a warrior.

I just prayed that she would pull through—that she could get better. Hope was the oxygen I used in order to carry on. I felt like I was holding that single breath forever, and I would never exhale until I knew she was okay.

I deleted the voice mail. I was in no place to talk with my mother about any of this, not yet. I know it was stupid, but I called Samantha's phone over and over again. She never answered. I called Samantha's mother's number, to no avail. Finally, I sprinted to my car and drove straight to school.

Mimi met me in the parking lot.

"I wasn't sure you'd show up to school today." She hugged me, holding me close.

"I'm not here for classes."

"Then why are you here?" Mimi asked, trying to keep up as I headed toward the one place I knew I'd find what I was looking for.

As I darted through the school, it was clear that the news had spread like wildfire. Some students walked past with their heads down, probably feeling guilty. Others looked around, wanting to share the unthinkable moment with anyone, even if it was a passing stranger. What was once a colorful campus now felt like a wasteland of dimly lit halls. The eerie place where the past and present collided. Because when we saw Samantha's locker, it was being lined in flowers and candles, as if she were already dead. I couldn't tell how many of them really cared, and how many just wanted to be a part of the drama.

I made my way into the administration room, where teachers glided around like phantoms, probably not having slept at all the night before. The principal led students in for questioning, but I didn't care about getting in trouble. I pushed through the double doors of the counselors' office and was instantly greeted by Mrs. Chen, who led me to a partitioned area. The walls were a pleasant pastel blue with one too many motivational posters.

"Luna, please take a seat," she said tersely.

"I need to know where Samantha is."

"Luna, it would be against the law to tell you—"

But that's when I noticed a Post-it note on her desk with an address on it. Her hand went fast to hide it, but my eye was quicker, and I caught a glimpse. "She's at Mission Hospital?!"

She shot me a stern glance. "Samantha's family is going through enough. They're suffering. It's best not to overwhelm them. I suggest you stop your search here."

"I need to apologize," I said, desperate. "You don't understand. What we did to her—"

And what came next caught me off guard, so that my entire body froze up. Because Chen knew everything.

"I know you posted the first video," Chen said.

My brain was screaming *How?* But I was too stricken to ask. Schools always had their ways.

"We've spoken with Samantha's family," she said, her words cutting right through me. "They have talked it over with the administration, and we won't be expelling you, but disciplinary action must be taken. Moving forward, you will no longer be on the soccer team. We'll handle your removal discreetly—we promise. We don't want to create another opportunity for bullying."

In just twenty-four hours, my entire world had imploded.

I dried tears with my sleeve. "I wish I could fix this, but I can't go back in time."

Mrs. Chen put a hand on my shoulder. "I know this wasn't your intention, and right now, you can't help Samantha, but you *can* help the people around you. Promise me you'll remember that. That you'll grow from this."

I exited the office, and Mimi stopped me in the doorway.

So I explained everything. "Mimi, how could I be that terrible without knowing it?"

"Luna, it's not all on you! This is so unfair. You really messed up, but so did everyone else; you can't fix it all by yourself."

"I know," I said. "But when did I ever let that stop me?"

Mimi knew there was no talking sense into me. But I guess being headstrong ran in the family. My mom always said to me in Spanish, *Yo soy madre. ¿Cuál es* tu *superpoder?* Meaning: I'm a mother. What's *your* superpower? Something I never had an answer to—but I was realizing that if I was going to try to help Samantha, I was going to have to figure it out.

Hospitals always give me goose bumps.

It's not just the arctic air-conditioning, or the sterile walls that wind like a labyrinth to nowhere, but the idea that people aren't okay, and everyone knows it. I remember the feeling just before my father passed away. I was young, so my memory is blurry, but I remember the sensation. Both treating him like he was sick and pretending he was going to be okay felt like a lie— uncomfortable. I guess the only true thing was compassion. It was the thought I clung to as Mimi and I approached Mission Hospital.

When we got there, I couldn't believe what was before me. News crews surrounded the front of the hospital.

"What's happening?" Mimi asked as we walked past a nasal reporter from Channel 2 who was standing before a camera and speaking into a microphone.

"Our hearts and prayers are with Samantha and her family, while the larger-scale debate has shifted to Limbo itself. Who's at fault? Those who bullied her into attempting suicide? Or the social media app that let her be bullied?"

This was a hospital. It shouldn't have been a circus. I controlled my breathing, trying not to break down again— watching the hysteria unfold.

Hating myself.

Mimi and I decided to walk along the side of the building

to find another entrance. But then we spotted Jade sneaking out a side door. The queen of the Goldens. The perfectly proportioned beauty blogger who could hide a pimple the size of Mount Vesuvius in a second. Bawling her mascara off, avoiding the cameras at all costs. I always told myself I was nothing like her, but for once, we had something in common:

We were both here for Samantha.

A receptionist checked us in at the hospital front desk and printed our badges. "Phones and anything sharp, like keys, in the bin," she commanded, which struck me as odd, but at the same time made perfect sense. The cell phone was the very vessel that had brought Samantha here. And as I placed mine in the bin, chills crawled down my body.

To the hospital, my phone is as dangerous as a sharp object.

We were led to a room that looked into the intensive care unit, where the main door was locked to both hold people in and keep others out. Then a motherly nurse with an all-knowing gaze positioned herself in the doorway.

"You're here for Samantha Darby," she read off a clipboard. "What is your relationship to the patient?"

". . . She's my sister," I gulped, though it didn't feel unnatural to say.

The nurse's expression softened. She smiled, looking us over—at my name tag, which was a dead giveaway. "I'm sorry, but waiting room space is for family only, unless you're on the list. I promise that the doctors are doing their best to help her."

At least I knew she was still fighting.

That's when Mimi reached in her coat pocket and produced the bag of jelly beans from the day before. "Well, when she's okay . . . you know, give her these for good luck." Mimi wiped the tears from her eyes. No matter how childish the request sounded, it was important. We had thrown out all the bad jelly beans, leaving only positive-forecasting beans inside. Hoping that if she was okay, it could at least make her smile. That she would know someone was there for her and wouldn't feel so alone.

The nurse shook her head. "I'm sorry, no food or beverages are allowed inside."

Mimi stepped forward, crying. "Please . . ."

The nurse looked away, affected. Then gave in. "I'll ask my supervisor," she said, taking the bag. Then she sealed the door of the steel chamber, leaving us alone.

Which was when I had to accept the hardest truth. I was powerless to help her.

▶ 8.

"Fly Away"
—Lenny Kravitz

My abuela used to always say, *Por mayor que sea el agujero donde caigas, sonríe. Todavía no hay tierra encima.* No matter how deep a hole you're in, smile, because there's no earth over your head. But I don't know how she did it, because if I was trapped in a hole, I'd probably be screaming bloody murder and clawing my way out.

Which was why that week I just wanted to lock myself away.

Every day I hid in a bathroom stall during study hall, hyper-ventilating with anxiety at the thought of other people finding out that I was the one who'd posted the video. Paranoid that when they did, they would despise me. And then I started to hate myself for being too focused on my own problems instead of on the person in the hospital. For making her problems about myself. For being selfish.

Every night when I got home, I would lock myself in my room.

And repeat the toxic cycle.

I couldn't let myself think about what my mom would say

when she found out what I'd done. That I was kicked off the soccer team. That whatever chance I had at a sports scholarship was totally gone. It would destroy her. I had been playing soccer since I could walk, and it was one of the ways my mother connected me with my Spanish culture. Plus, she invested a lot for me to be able to play.

I scrolled through Limbo, trying to distract myself, waiting to hear any news about Samantha. First came book-haul unboxings, Yorkshire terrier haircuts set to techno, and five-second pasta recipes that would really take five hours and the help of Remy from *Ratatouille*. And then, after a while, I saw posts from Axel and Jade with millions of likes. Pictures of them training for the next street race in the abandoned forest on the outskirts of town—an El Dorado tradition that the Goldens took to a whole new level.

It's crazy how they could ignore what was happening and post fun content with their friends—people who had all shared and reposted videos of Samantha, helping it go viral.

Their hands were dirty too, and they didn't seem to feel bad.

Despite what had happened, Limbo still hadn't taken down the memes. The algorithm kept pushing them to the top. The more damaging, controversial, or inflammatory, the more clicks it got. There were even remixed versions of Samantha running out of the cafeteria in tears, covered in pizza sauce. The trolling had taken on a life of its own, and now people from all over were taking turns. It's crazy how bad some people can be when hiding behind the screen of a phone.

And all night I was getting news notifications:

Limbo goes public and stocks plummet, with would-be

shareholders hesitant to invest in a tech company facing lawsuits. . . .

Sure, Limbo let this happen.

But it takes *people* to comment.

I was the match, Limbo was the gasoline, and together we'd set Samantha ablaze.

And it was becoming more and more apparent to me just how disconnected we were from one another at El Dorado. I was feeling that tightness in my chest again. That anxiety. Something I've been trying to deal with for some time now.

I once learned in biology class that the human body secretes eleven liters of tears per year, and each type of tear has a unique molecular shape—whether your cat died, you struck gold, or you got lost in an onion patch. And in that moment, I could feel all eleven liters overflowing.

The first tears streamed with sadness. The next were made of frustration, at how complicated she'd made our relationship— how hard she'd made it to be there for her—how I'd failed her. And last came a deluge of anger, for all the terrible things that had been said.

Before I could think better of it, I entered the Limbo help center.

I was about to do something crazy. I could feel it. There was something deeply wrong, but I couldn't fix it alone. We'd all seemed to have forgotten that behind every screen is a human being with feelings, insecurities, and a beating heart. I needed Limbo's help to put out the fire we'd set together. So I stared into the camera of my cell phone, wiped the tears out of my eyes, and pressed record.

▶ 9.

"We Will Rock You"
—Queen

Since I'd been a child, I was never more than an acquaintance to good luck—especially when the odds in life were stacked against me. The chances of my family winning a USCIS immigration lottery green card are one in 185—giving us a better likelihood of getting shot these days. And the odds of winning the SuperLotto are one in 176 million, making you more likely to be struck by lightning. When it came to statistics, the cards were seldom dealt in my favor. I was more of a *Go to jail—do not collect two hundred dollars* kind of girl.

But a few weeks later, my luck totally changed.

On this day I got the news I needed, giving me strength to carry on with life. Because this morning, my mother's shouting was music to my ears. The best way I could have woken up. "¡Hija! She's gonna make it! Samantha is okay! ¡Gracias a Dios!"

I immediately leapt out of bed and started celebrating. I kissed the little saint statue my mother had given me. I shouted. I cried. All the tension exploded out of me. One of these days, my mom would be knocking on the door, wanting to talk all about it—wanting to be there for me.

Though I wasn't ready.

There was far too much to explain. And I love her for respecting that.

But just when I thought the day couldn't get better—the stars aligned to change my life.

Because I finally got a notification.

I had a new DM. And it was from the Limbo help center. It read:

Hi, Luna. We were moved by your message—expect a response soon. A response not just for you, but for everyone ☺

Never in my wildest dreams did I think that a platform with over a billion users would actually hear me—and if they did, I'd already written off the idea that they'd respond. But Limbo saw my video message, where I told them my story. Opened up my soul. Confessed what I had done to Samantha. Begged them for help. For change.

It was nuts.

Random.

I was used to getting my usual lemon-lime outcomes, but I guess all my years on the debate team paid off in more ways than just convincing fast-food cashiers to give me free special sauce. Because after refreshing the app every five seconds for so many days trying to figure out what they meant by a response "for everyone"—I finally got my answer. I saw that there was a new video sponsored by Limbo, one that made it onto every person's feed in El Dorado. Soon it faded in and text sparkled across my screen:

Is there a lack of connection in your world?

Are you anxious, addicted, or apathetic in your current life?

Do you ever wish you could reinvent yourself entirely?

The text was accompanied by retro pop music. Images of people taking selfies with phones dissolved into Polaroid cameras, and a shot of a modern speaker turning into a jukebox followed. Flashes of art drawn on a tablet turned into graffiti, and then California palm trees stood in front of a sunset, with beautiful people roller-skating down the boardwalk, clad in fluo-rescent vintage clothes.

It continued with flashing text:

A challenge of a lifetime. A chance to be young, wild, and free. A year you'll never forget. Limbo is coming to El Dorado High! Because we care about how *we treat one another. We care about you♥*

Disconnect to reconnect.

#RetroChallenge

The video ended, and I was left reeling, staring into the glowing black screen. I didn't even know what I'd just seen— but for the first time in a while, a smile was stretched across my face. This was mysterious. Alluring. I couldn't believe it. I was in shock.

Limbo was actually coming to El Dorado High.

I had no idea when and how Limbo was going to make their appearance at my school. As my mother likes to mistrans-late: I was more lost than an octopus in a parking garage. The announcement was made over the loudspeakers, and the buzz at school that followed could have been heard from space. It was like that exhilarating sensation I got when my abuela would secretly slip me money like a drug dealer, or when someone gave me a french fry, but really it was two stuck together.

Limbo was going to give "the presentation of a lifetime" in the auditorium, and the entire school was invited to join. Everyone was clamoring in anticipation. I hadn't told anyone that I'd contacted Limbo's help center, that I had something to do with this. It was between me and my conscience. I didn't tell even Mimi. But it wasn't out of fear. Fear is what you feel when the cold water attacks you in the shower, and you're helpless, scared in the corner, clutching your shampoo.

That morning I made my way to the auditorium, past rows of withering balloons from the cyberbullying assembly we'd had the week before. Blue and orange antibullying ribbons lined the halls. No matter where you turned at El Dorado, the school was marked by what had happened. There was less laughter since that day in the cafeteria, but at least Limbo's coming was something to look forward to. Something to feel positive about.

"I'm so glad things are starting to look up," Mimi said.

"I heard Samantha's in a psychiatric hospital now," our other friend Miranda added.

"She'll get better—I'm sure," I promised them. "I wonder what she'd think about all this."

"Maybe Limbo is going to expose the trolls," Miranda said, "and then they're going to hack their accounts and show all their dark secrets to the world!" Miranda used to be my go-to forward on the soccer field. One of the worst things about being kicked off the team was not getting to spend time with my friends. And Miranda was a riot. A natural storyteller. The kind of girl who doesn't believe in texting, just voice notes so long they could be classified as podcasts.

But it was Mimi who had the really genius idea. "Maybe it's called the Retro Challenge because they're gonna make us all go paleo and do a focus group where we only eat avocados to see who can get a heart attack first?"

"That's not realistic," Miranda laughed.

We made our way inside the bustling auditorium, and only then did I realize how big the event really was. Limbo had brought teams of workers, all buzzing around wearing purple shirts and lanyards—and they were filming everything with cameras.

For the first time in El Dorado history, it seemed like the whole school had shown up early. There was barely anywhere left for us to sit, and luckily we grabbed the last seats. There was a palpable energy in the air, and it wasn't long until the lights dimmed and the curtains drew upward, heralding the beginning of the event.

But it wasn't much of an event at all. There was no hype. No music, no video pitch, no free shirts or gift cards. Instead, a man and woman stood onstage, smartly dressed, young—maybe in their late twenties. The woman was familiar-looking. She sported a black turtleneck, and he a business suit.

No bells and whistles. Just them. And us.

The woman smiled warmly. "Hello. I'm Elisa Scarlett, CEO of Limbo—the social media world that exists between all others. And this here is my legal adviser, Andrew Fineman. We'd like to thank you for taking time out of your day to come here."

Thanking us? This was Limbo. They were like Google, Amazon, and Meta's cooler younger cousin—and their biggest competition. In fact, all the other companies kept trying to buy them out. These were the people who brushed shoulders with presidents, kings, and the modern giants of our generation.

The auditorium echoed with electrifying applause.

"Adopt me!" Mimi yelled.

I rolled my eyes, laughing.

The CEO pushed up her glasses. "January 1, 1997. The day social media was first launched."

She and Andrew Fineman traded off pitch lines. "The site was called Six Degrees, based on the theory that everyone is connected to everyone else in this world by no more than six degrees of separation. It was a moment that created a schism between the world that was, and the world that would be. Because on that New Year's Day, in downtown Manhattan, the site's creators sent the first friend request ever."

Scarlett picked up where he left off. "Your generation is unlike any who have come before. You all live in a world full of social media, dating apps, and rideshare services."

"And it's changing the way our brains work. Take, for example, you and your peers—electronic interfaces have increased your visual-spatial capabilities, your attentional ability, and reaction times."

"Hell yeah, I'm freaking Superman!" someone from the crowd yelled.

Scattered laughter.

Scarlett chuckled. "Well, you're going to need those skills, considering the world the previous generations are leaving us.

A world stricken by illness. Climate change. Private prisons. College loans. Skyrocketing rates of anxiety and depression. Cyberbullying on a massive scale."

Her demeanor sobered. "We're here because of what happened at this school. A young woman tried to take her own life after being bullied on the platform that we created. After we were contacted by two different students, it became clear to us that you all really needed a way to heal. And we decided something had to be done. We saw that you needed help. So we've made a sizable donation to your school, and the administration has agreed to host this challenge, which we've created just for El Dorado High!"

Contacted by two students? This floored me. I thought I was the only one. I didn't think anyone else cared enough. Everyone broke out in chatter, looking around at one another, speculating about who the mystery people were. I scanned the faces, wondering.

I'm one, but who's the other?

At least they made me feel like I wasn't alone. I finally felt supported and understood.

Fineman continued. "So here we are, answering your appeal for help. See, Limbo isn't just a social media company; it's a social company. Our influence shapes politics, markets, and pop culture. We're a lifestyle brand, and we believe you have to live a life worth posting about. That's why we're here today. To propose to you a challenge like never before." Fineman's eyes glittered like a showman's.

"We want to offer your entire school the chance to take . . . the Retro Challenge!"

The audience was captivated. A smile stretched across my face. I couldn't believe that I was a part of this challenge's origin story. That something good was actually happening. It was like a flower growing through the cracks of the desert.

"And in return, you will be awarded a prize. Everyone who can make it the full school year without modern-day technology will be a winner. We are prepared to offer a full-ride scholarship to the college of your choice. All expenses paid." The lawyer smiled proudly. "In a perfect world, you wouldn't have to make any sacrifices to grow. There would be no challenges."

The auditorium quickly broke into indistinct chatter.

"What?" a boy said.

"No phones? Are you trying to bore us to death?"

Scarlett stepped forward. "Wasn't it a phone that almost killed your classmate? Or was it those of you who stood idly by because you were too afraid to become the next victim? Or was it our fault for not taking down the hateful posts sooner? Your teachers who weren't watching? I don't know. But what I do know is that something has to change, and it all starts with connecting with one another, without hiding behind a profile."

The crowd fell into deafening silence.

"If you choose to take the challenge, everything will be worked out with your teachers to accommodate your new realities. I'm sure you have more questions, and I promise you, soon they'll all be answered," Scarlett explained.

I needed to gain my confidence back. To start from zero.

The Retro Challenge was a chance to reset your life. And it makes sense that in order to reset and reprogram, you need to press the off button first. It all started with disconnecting.

Technology was a beautiful thing that could change the course of elections, connect us to our family during disasters, or crowd-fund a cancer treatment. I mean, it's the reason that Samantha is still alive. Technology can change the world in the most amazing ways.

But I needed to take a break.

Obviously, I hadn't asked Limbo to come here for some secret prize—but now that the idea was being presented to us, I had to admit I was excited. Now that a soccer scholarship was off the table, Limbo's full ride was what I needed—what my family needed. There was no chance we could afford college with just my mother's paycheck. But her sangre caliente, full of determination, was running through my veins. It gave her the courage to start a family in a new land, and it would give me the strength to take this challenge and totally kill it.

But not everyone was as sure about the Retro Challenge.

Scarlett motioned toward the auditorium door. "For those of you who don't want to participate, you're welcome to leave now."

Those were the magic words. Instantly more than half the auditorium began filing out—but in complete silence, as if they knew the gravity of what they were pulling away from.

Miranda stood up.

"You're leaving?" I asked.

"Well, yeah," she responded, clutching her phone. "It really sounds like a great experience, and sure, I want to keep supporting the antibullying campaign, but I have my entire life on my phone. Birthdays. Parties. Exams. My brain doesn't have that much memory. You're really going to do this?"

Suddenly I was hit with panic.

Miranda's question was asked with such conviction that it allowed doubt to creep in. *What am I really getting myself into?* I hadn't thought about the consequences of going without modern technology. But I knew deep down that this was what I needed. It was the only way to begin to correct what had happened. I was being offered a chance to escape this world. A chance to be "young, wild, and free."

I finally started breathing out the pressure that had clenched my chest these past days.

Even if this challenge was some publicity stunt—I didn't care.

It was totally working on me.

"You know I can't say no to a challenge."

Miranda hugged me. "We're going to miss you on the soccer field, but your new competition is this one. Show them what you're made of!"

I looked to Mimi, who grabbed my hand and nodded, as if we were about to jump out of a plane together. Maybe that's what this was: a free fall into the unknown.

"We have to do this," Mimi said, staring down at her mismatched shoes and digging deep. "I need this as much as you do. I always thought that people who made fun of me for being queer or for my awesome pink hair were just bullies with boring taste. But by sharing that video, I became a bully too."

"And if you win? What will you do with the scholarship?" I asked her.

"There's this program in the Galápagos where you get to swim with tortoises, and give them love so they don't go extinct,"

Mimi said. "Feeding them, helping them repopulate, and keeping their ecosystem clean. After all, animals are the only things on this planet that don't judge you."

"I wouldn't expect less from you." I hugged her. Mimi was the sweetest girl I knew, the kind of person who shared the cream filling of her Oreos.

I looked around the room at who was left—what their reactions were. I understood why they'd stayed, whether it was for Samantha or for themselves. When it came down to it, there wasn't much to do in our small town anyway, and this would definitely shake us out of our routines. Sure, being the only person without technology would suck, but this was different. We were all in this together. How hard could it be? There were many people from every social group, but what I didn't expect was to see someone from the Goldens.

Him.

The guy who needed to learn that the earth revolves around the sun, not him.

Axel wanted to be a part of this challenge, and I had no idea why.

Fineman addressed the remaining students, now only a fraction of the seats filled. "Congratulations! You've just made the most important decision of your life."

Scarlett and Fineman met my eyes and smiled, silently singling me out in the crowd.

I was so nervous.

We were about to go retro—without fully grasping what that meant. None of us did. Not even Limbo. And nothing would ever be the same again.

▶ 10.

"Livin' La Vida Loca"
—Ricky Martin

People always talk about what they're worth, but nobody takes the time to talk about what they cost. In my lifetime I'll consume over eleven entire cows, inhale three hundred billion liters of oxygen, and create twenty-six thousand pounds of waste. Until I turn eighteen, I'll even cost my mother something like three hundred thousand dollars. The way I saw it, I was supposed to do something with my life that amounted to more than that. So that's why, if I won the Limbo scholarship, I'd want to go to school to be a psychologist. I figured if I could help others find their self-worth, I'd more than make up for my earthly expenses.

Maybe I could even talk people like Samantha down from the ledge.

Imagining myself winning the scholarship was easy. The hard part was not making a mistake that would get me disqualified. And Limbo had crazy-intense ways to monitor our tech usage.

They would perform random interviews using state-of-the-art lie detectors, with a fancy machine called fMRI. They say when people lie, a special part of their brain lights up on the screen. Its accuracy reaches up to 99.9 percent, which is hand sanitizer level, so you know it's legit. There were even rumors they would use other types of sophisticated technology that we didn't know about to track us, which was pretty intimidating.

All we had to do was follow one rule. And it was simple:

No technology made after the turn of the century.

Because the year 2000 was when the first 3G smartphone came out and changed everything. So any technology with the word "smart" was a no go. QR codes were modern mosaics impossible to decode. And because this was only going to be fun if we really immersed ourselves, retro music and shopping at thrift stores were encouraged.

There were just two exceptions:

First, there were the unavoidables: the pop songs on the radio, the flat-screen TV at the fast-food restaurant, the phone you borrow to call 911 when your friend chokes on a chicken nugget.

And next were the functionals: the new microwave, your mom's car that you steal and race to school, and the X-ray machine you'll need once you've crashed into the science building.

So basically, the rules were airtight. Sure, if you wanted, you could try to use an old boxy computer, but good luck even getting it to load a website. It would be up to you how much fun you wanted to have, but definitely full immersion would make it easier to survive until the end of the year without giving in to temptation. I was just excited to dress in vintage clothes, listen to throwback music on cassettes, and roller-skate everywhere like I was living in a retro movie.

Plus, I was relieved to not be uploading assignments to El Dorado's sketchy cloud drive. Every time I wrote a term paper and added one too many semicolons, the document shifted thirty-seven lines, changed its name, and made a reservation at an Italian restaurant.

The challenge started at the beginning of the next week, which meant I had a full weekend to prepare. Mimi was off visiting her sister at college, to tell her about all the exciting news. And my soul was starting to heal after long nights of crying, after everything that had happened. This was the first step out of that suffocating bed I'd made for myself, and it felt so good to finally breathe again.

It was my parents' dream to fuse business and art together so I could be raised with culture—it's why they opened up our little family theater in the Monteverde Mall. When my father passed away, my mother worked harder than ever to keep his dream alive, to keep at least a piece of him here with us. But no matter how much she tried to hide it, I knew business was going south, which was why I always tried to help out.

Only on this day I was nervous about going to the cinema, because I had no idea how my mother would react after finding out that I was going retro—but even more so because I knew I was going to have to tell her about what had happened between me and Samantha.

I looked down at my phone: *MAMÁ MISSED CALLS (7)*

But I couldn't bring myself to call her back. To reach out to her. Not yet. So I made a detour. I was ready to revolutionize my world, and there was only one place that could help me—where the threads of the past were repurposed and given a second chance to be adored: Sequin's Thrift Shop!

I dragged trash bags of clothes inside and unloaded a heap of shirts onto the counter, hoping they'd pay a pretty penny so I could restock my wardrobe with vintage fits.

"I'll give you twenty dollars," the cashier said. "Sorry, they're out of season."

"Oh no . . . can I even trade anything in?"

And just when I thought I was going to have to give up and wear one of the trash bag to school, my guardian angel descended from aisle seven.

He was wearing a pair of denim overalls and a bandanna tied around his neck, with an iconic flattop haircut—around my age, though maybe a foot taller.

"*Girl*, you're more lost than a penguin in Africa." He smiled boldly and turned to the cashier. "I got this one, Carol."

"Don't blame me. Blame climate change."

He laughed. "Name's Darnell, don't wear it out."

"Luna. Say it all you want" was my counter. I recognized him from trig class.

"You're going retro too, aren't you?" He looked at me, sizing me up. Then he sighed and dropped all his bags as if this was some kind of humanitarian crisis. "Listen, you're never going to survive the entire school year dressing like Lindsay Lohan after leaving the club."

I liked his sense of humor.

He linked my arm in his and guided me down the aisle. I scanned the rows, spotting all types of fun things, from band posters to light-up basketball shoes to lava lamps. "Lesson one:

thrift shops. Our sanctuary from the circus that is the mega consumeristic-capitalist agenda. See, department stores are designed to disorient shoppers to increase impulse purchases. It's also why they put the bathrooms in the back corners. Or intentionally make carts with broken left wheels, so you grip the handle with your left hand, and fill your cart more easily with the right."

After amassing a mountain of clothes, I headed for the fitting room to try some of them on. There's this saying, *Mirrors never lie*—well, thank god they don't laugh, either. I wasn't sure how my body would look dressed in vintage gear. It was hard not to compare myself with the contoured models on social media—perfect people like Jade Laurent. But when I exited the fitting room, it was like I stepped out of a time machine.

As we say in Spanish: *I was in my salsa.*

"Now *you* are a natural beauty!" Darnell said. "Booyah!" He had this sureness about him that made me feel like he didn't care at all about what people thought.

"Next lesson is music." He reached into a box, pulled out an old Walkman, and handed it to me. "The soundtrack of your year," he said, then sorted through the cases of cassettes and stacked them in my already full arms. "You're going to need Britney Spears when you find out all boys are assholes—and then when you're all angry, that's where Nirvana comes in. Oh, and Green Day when you get dumped."

"That's not how I want my life to go!"

"You're right. You're living la vida loca. Here. Take some Ricky Martin."

As much fun as I was having, at some point I started to feel like I didn't have a right to—not when Samantha was still in the hospital. And soon, even Darnell could tell that I was getting overwhelmed. He rested a thoughtful hand on my shoulder.

"You were friends with Samantha, weren't you?" he said. "It's all right to have a little fun, you know, even if you're juggling your emotions. Even if you're crying on the inside. It's okay to not be okay."

"You sound like you're talking from experience."

"Right when I came to El Dorado High, freshman year, I met my first crush. Martin. We started dating, but he hadn't told anyone else that he was gay. But before he was ready, the rest of the world made his private life public gossip. One day, some of the guys on the football team launched a text attack."

"I think I remember hearing about that."

Darnell grimaced. "Martin broke up with me immediately. He moved away, and I didn't see him until last summer, holding some girl's hand at the county fair. He walked right past without looking at me, but I could see that he was so sad."

"That's terrible, Darnell." I felt for him. "I'm so sorry."

"Yeah . . . I just wish I had told my parents sooner. It was hard for them to understand, but they supported me. They're pretty cool."

I thought about my own mother, how I had been avoiding her. And I was beginning to regret that I hadn't opened up yet. It was a distance she didn't deserve.

Darnell looked like he needed some cheering up. So I laced our arms, letting him in on a secret. "You know what they say really helps when you have boy troubles?"

"What?" he asked.

"Take a piece of paper and write down all the damage he did to you. Then fold it six times, put it in a bottle, and break it over his head."

Darnell's chuckles turned into laughter. "Where were you freshman year when I needed you?" Then he sobered. "If I'm one of the winners, I'm moving to a big city where *different* can mean *better*. This town is too small for all the big judgments we have."

Darnell settled on a dusty boom box at the end of the aisle. "Final lesson: when in doubt, listen to 103.7 Retro Radio. It's, like, the best station ever." He turned the dial and cranked up the music—and of course he knew all the dance moves.

We belted out lyrics, dancing wildly down the aisles. It was like I already knew him. We would have never hung out before the challenge, and he definitely wouldn't have been in my recommended friends on Limbo. This was so new.

And I loved that.

Because he didn't just teach me how to combine clothes and kill it in a thrift store—he taught me that I was allowed to laugh and smile, but I was also allowed to be hurt. And both were okay. Because in the end, maybe we're all just perfectly imperfect. Sure, I was never going to forget what had happened, but I did need to learn how to live with it.

I said goodbye to Darnell and walked up the broken escalator to our family theater. It made me sad to see how run-down and empty the mall had become. The closing shops. The forgotten food court. And before I reached the top level, my phone buzzed with a text.

It was from an anonymous number.

I KNOW IT WAS YOU.

I went wobbly with dread. Aside from school administrators, there was only one person who knew my secret, and that was Mimi, who would never tell. I didn't want to believe that it could be Samantha—or even worse, that it was someone who wanted to blackmail me. But just the fact that someone knew damning information about me that I couldn't control made me want to leave forever and hide in a bunker until my personal Armageddon was over. As crazy as it was to say, in that moment, I couldn't have been more ready to take a break from my phone.

When I finally gathered my bearings and made my way through the red-velvety movie theater entrance, I found my mom stressed out in the back office, among stacks of papers and disemboweled film reels. My sweet mamá was trying not to yell into the phone, but I knew that she was getting so pissed off she could evolve into a Charizard at any moment.

"¡No me lo puedo creer! I know we need to bring more customers to keep the mall open, but I'm not going to play a superhero movie with an insect man fighting a robot panther from a different galaxy!"

As soon as my mother and I locked eyes, I knew what kind of day this was going to be. I hadn't returned her calls, and I was sure she had already called a thousand embassies and produced a docuseries about my disappearance. The FBI should create a unit of just worried mothers, with Gloria Iglesias as the captain. And once she's finally triangulated my location, emotional fallout always unrolls in a three-step process:

Phase one: dousing me in sugar. "¡Hija! I was so worried

about you! ¡Gracias a Dios que estás aquí, pensé lo peor!" She kissed my cheeks profusely.

Phase two: patting me down, making sure I still have all my bones. Smelling me, to identify any foreign scent, like weed or some young man's cologne. And once she's convinced that I'm alive and not a juvenile delinquent, she enters—

Phase three: demonic possession. "Luna María Valero Iglesias! You're going to *wish* that they really kidnapped you, señorita!" She shouted so loud, I swear it set off car alarms.

If not responding to her calls was this intense, I only imagined the atom bomb that would explode when I cut the line of communication entirely. But there was only one clear way to explain it to her—by telling the truth.

"Mom, I'm sorry I've been avoiding you, but I have to tell you something. . . . I'm taking the Retro Challenge. Which means you won't be able to call or text me this year."

I explained the rules, but she did not take the news calmly.

"What is this? The new excuse you picked to ignore me? Are you telling me that I won't know where you are? What if someone tries to hurt you? What if you fall and break your hip?" I couldn't tell if she was treating me like a child or a very old woman.

"I understand that you don't like it, but please, Mom, I need to do this."

She took a deep breath. And finally the unavoidable question came. "Luna, why is this so important to you?"

It was going to take all the strength I had to speak the words.

"Samantha wouldn't have been bullied if it wasn't for me. I was the one who posted the video and started this nightmare. I was too afraid to tell you before, but I need this." And then I held out a permission slip. "Since I'm not eighteen yet, I need your signature to take the challenge."

I was ready for her to ground me for life. I was ready for her to never let me see my friends again. I was ready to be sent away to nun camp.

But instead of yelling, my mother responded earnestly. "I'm very disappointed about what you did. But, Luna, I don't know about this challenge. . . ."

She took my hands and sat me down, leveling with me. "It's not smart to gamble with your future. Don't forget how hard your father and I worked to give you this life. The fact that you're mature enough to want to better yourself means you're halfway there. Someday, you'll open up your own psychology practice and you'll help people, but in order to do that there is just one path—and that's getting good grades. Because if the mall closes and we lose the theater, I don't know how else I'll send you to college."

"We won't let the theater close. I'll come and help more often. And I can still work the old films."

"I just want what's best for you."

"Then let me be me, Mamá. Let me do this!"

"Luna, I would die if anything bad happened to you. And without cell phones, everything gets more complicated."

I met her eyes. "You once told me, 'If you don't fight for what you want, it's called losing'—and that's why you decided to fight for a life here. Now it's my turn. What do you think Papá would say?"

My mom pulled me in for a hug. Holding me closer than

ever before. All the while, I was thinking of what my papá once told me, that *telling the truth is the easiest way to sleep at night*.

I knew my mom didn't agree with my decision, but at least now she understood where my heart lay. And there, in her arms, I felt certainty. No matter what was going to happen, I would have to succeed. I was taking the challenge for myself, but I was going to have to win it for her.

⏵ 11.

"Wannabe"
—Spice Girls

This is the day! The thought repeated as I rubbed my eyes awake. I'd barely slept the night before, because as soon as I lay in bed, my brain decided to dance reggaeton. I was so nervous, I accidentally watered my artificial plant. Because this was the first day of the Retro Challenge! Having nerves was much better than feeling numb. It was better than waking up in the morning just to go back to sleep again.

It was being alive—and I was so ready to live my life.

I applied some colorful makeup; then, like a total rebel, I drank from the milk carton because my mom wasn't looking. I sported Converse shoes, jeans with knee holes, a pink crop top, and my super touch: a pair of eight-bit blue-and-red 3D movie glasses. It was an outfit I would've never dared to wear in my old life. Something that lemon-lime girl would have never had the confidence to pull off.

The doorbell rang, and when I answered it, Mimi slapped a newspaper into my hands. "Everyone is talking about what we're doing!" She smiled proudly. I unfolded it to see that our high school had made the front page, a full article about the Retro Challenge.

I extended a customized denim jacket out to Mimi. "Just a little gift, for always having my back. So here's a reminder that I will have yours, too." I pointed to all the patches I had ironed on. We always had this joke about how our friendship ran so *deep*, so it was covered with patches of bottomless things, like black holes and supersized french fries. And in the spirit of our new reality, I'd stuck a Limbo logo on the sleeve. "I've got one too." I spun around to show her my own matching jacket.

"WOW! It's so freaking cool! Loony Toony, I don't care what they say—your big heart is not proportional to the size of your boobs." Mimi beamed, meaning it, which made me laugh.

I felt a wave of gratitude to have her by my side.

And just before we left, my mother crammed a croissant straight into my mouth and attacked me with a Magic Marker.

"What are you doing?" I yelped through a full mouth.

"So you don't forget. No one knows anyone's phone number anymore." My mother wrote hers on my wrist. A part of her was still worried, and another part of her was clearly loving the fact that I'd have to learn to live unplugged—the evil part of her that used to punish me, not by taking my phone, but by confiscating my charger, only to watch the fear in my eyes as my battery slowly died.

She grabbed my hands and stared deeply into my eyes. "Don't forget to be the tequila, not the lime. You're to be chased after, not the other way around."

"You know I will!"

"Oh, and no sex or alcohol!"

"Mom, I'm going to school, not a frat party," I groaned.

• • •

We made our way to my car, and that's when I realized there was a little box on the driveway. A peculiar package, addressed to me.

"There's no return address."

"That's so creepy," Mimi said.

When I opened the box, I immediately felt a strange tingling in my chest, because what was inside had everything to do with that room I couldn't enter at the hospital. In that little box was the last thing I expected.

A purple whistle hanging on around an orange lanyard.

It belonged to Samantha.

Back when we were kids, Samantha and I would pass around this little whistle, an idea we got from our first soccer coach. Whenever one of us was going to play, we'd give it to the other person before they hit the field.

"What does it mean?" Mimi asked.

"It was Samantha's and my way to say 'it's your turn,'" I told her, my spine going stiff. Nervous. *What is she really trying to tell me? It's my turn to do what?*

"She must know about the challenge by now," I said.

"Maybe Samantha's coming back." Mimi looked at me, eyes wide.

I slipped the lanyard over my head, slinging the whistle around my neck. If Mimi was right and Samantha was going to make her return, I would be ready to accept whatever that meant for our complicated relationship. Even if I had no idea what she was going to do next.

• • •

As soon as we pulled onto the main road, something crashed into the back of my car.

Well not exactly *crashed*—more like stuck.

Mimi screamed. I looked through my rearview, fearing the worst—that a vehicle had hit me, or that I'd run over a fire hydrant again—but instead, I saw a person clinging to the bumper.

It was Darnell.

He was on Rollerblades—letting the car pull him along, surfing our concrete wake. His visor sunglasses glinted in the light.

"Luna . . ." Mimi gaped. "Who is that lunatic on the back of the car?"

I smiled. "My new friend, Darnell."

He waved, weaving over rough patches of asphalt until we hit a red light, and then he slipped into the back seat.

"You hardly know each other!" Mimi looked at him. "How do you know we're not serial killers?"

"Oh, don't worry—there's a very low probability that there would be three in the same car," he responded with a wink.

Mimi glowed. "I like him."

"By the way, your ride is off the chain," Darnell said, which caught me by surprise. I was usually self-conscious about my awkwardly old car, about the fact that my family couldn't afford a better one, but now it was suddenly cool.

He pulled a CD out of his Discman and put it into the ancient player in my dashboard. "I know exactly what you two need for the first day of the challenge." He cranked up the volume, playing "Wannabe," by the Spice Girls, an addictive classic we've loved since our shoes were strapped with Velcro. Now our windows were down, and we were singing into the wind.

"Mimi, love the neon fanny pack," Darnell pointed out.

"Yeah. The coolest clothes are the free ones you steal from your parents' closet."

"You two ready for this?" Darnell flashed his pearly whites.

"I was born ready," I said, though I was still not so sure, and pulled into an open spot.

And with that, we stepped out of the car, pushed through the double doors of El Dorado High, and crossed into our new world.

▶ 12.

"This Is How We Do It"
—Montell Jordan

I was no longer invisible. Everyone we passed seemed to be checking us out, up and down—or at least giving us looks.

"Crazy, isn't it? To be noticed, whether you like it or not." Darnell beamed.

"It feels kind of weird," I told him. Maybe the Goldens were used to it, but it wasn't exactly my thing. I was suddenly a new type of jelly bean, the mystery kind with a random flavor—but you have all the hope in the world that it's going to be good.

The others who had gone retro seemed different too. Most had absorbed the guidelines, choosing to embody the vibe or decade they liked the most, though there were still some too skeptical to totally immerse themselves. We all got to play whatever role we wanted. From the girl in the tie-dye shirt and bell-bottom jeans singing along to her cassette player to the boy in the Adidas tracksuit with the Pokémon lunch box. And we were all headed toward the same place. The Limbo launch event in the gymnasium.

It was becoming very clear that Limbo had put their everything into promoting this challenge—on all the lockers were banners painted with racing stripes, on all the doors were neon ribbons, and the floor sparkled with confetti. Everything in Limbo's signature purple.

"You don't think it's funny that Limbo is doing all this, just to make more postable content? A new distraction for the news to talk about," Darnell pointed out.

"It seems like they really want to help," I said. "Or else why go through all this trouble?"

Then, when we passed the front office, I heard the groan of a familiar voice. A voice that sucked me back to that day in the cafeteria. Because the person being led out of the disciplinary office was the reason for at least five of the pills that Samantha had taken that night.

Her ex-boyfriend.

Vince crossed his arms. "This challenge is such a joke. What are all these weirdos doing? I'm so glad I'm leaving this school."

"You're not leaving—you're just being suspended. But expulsion is right around the corner for you." The principal slammed the door behind him.

"Whatever. I'm a state wrestling champ! And with the money I make on Limbo I could drop out tomorrow," Vince yelled at the closed door. "I don't need your stupid school!"

"It looks like the administration finally realized how he treated Samantha . . . ," Darnell said. "Too bad it took them so long to pin the bullying down on Vince."

"Better late than never," Mimi responded.

When Vince realized that we were looking at him, he spit on the floor, by our feet.

"Gross!" Mimi yelped. "It's like you have the same cognitive development as a llama."

"Watch it, freak. Next loogie is for you," he snorted.

"You call my friend a freak again and I'll shove this Rollerblade up your ass until you call me daddy." Darnell stepped forward.

Vince chuckled. "Can somebody tell this gay sidekick to calm down?"

"I'm nobody's gay sidekick!"

I practically had to hold Darnell back from exploding.

Vince was clearly going to be another threat to contend with this year, whether I liked it or not. "Let's go, guys. He's not worth it." I threw my arms around my friends' shoulders.

Just before arriving at the gym, we passed Samantha's locker. The flowers that adorned it looked brighter than ever. Our friend Miranda approached from behind.

"There are rumors that people have seen Samantha around school."

"I heard she was transferred to another school district," Darnell said.

Nobody knew the truth. But the whistle around my neck was the only clue.

As exciting as all this was, the challenge did come with asterisks. Because, just like every other app, Limbo had its own terms and conditions for the Retro Challenge. Fineman stood outside the gymnasium event, in a slick black suit, overseeing a booth of workers who were all passing out tablets to contestants.

"Have you signed the waiver yet?" said a perky Limbo

employee. She extended one of the tablets to me, so I scrolled through. Pages and pages of legal jargon that I hardly understood. I hesitated before clicking *Accept terms and conditions*.

Fineman stepped in. "Need some help, Luna?" he asked. I was shocked that he remembered me. "It's our standard liability procedure."

"As long as I'm not accepting a permanent move to the moon, I'll sign anything," I chuckled as I scrolled to the bottom and clicked *ACCEPT*.

"Good luck this year," he said warmly.

I was turning to leave when a strong force suddenly crashed into me, spilling the tea I'd picked up from the refreshments table all over my shirt.

"What the hell?" My hands and shirt were burning with hot water.

I looked up to meet Axel's eyes. He was clutching his skateboard, after speeding through the hall. I was surprised that he'd left his Porsche behind for a skateboard. Axel wore an elegant white shirt, with a chain dangling from his jeans, and that signature hoop earring of his. It was disgusting how good he looked.

"Oh, you again," I groaned.

He got on a knee to help me pick up my things. "Here, I'll help you. Wouldn't want you to break a nail." He handed me my last book and chuckled guiltily. Axel wasn't exactly famous for staying out of trouble.

"If you want to help me, clean my shirt."

"My pleasure. Take it off." He flashed a cocky smile.

My face flushed red, but it was probably just out of anger.

His attitude was so gallito—that's Spanish for a rooster. Someone who acts cooler than they are.

"Sequin's Thrift is open until late. I'll buy you a new one."

"Money doesn't fix everything. What, you think you can just pay me off?" I said, realizing I'd gone too far, because he was actually being sweet. So I added, "That's nice of you, but it's not necessary."

"You're a difficult person. You know that?"

Before I could answer, Jade Laurent approached—they were on and off, but by the look in her eyes, she was going for the "on" position once again.

"Hey, babe, I have something for you." She sauntered over, pressed a big kiss on his lips, then handed him a bag.

"What is this?" Axel asked.

"You left your jacket in my bedroom last night," she said. Then scanned me up and down, as if I were an object to evaluate. "Who's your new friend?"

"We're not friends," I assured her.

"Well, you missed a spot," she said, sickly sweet, pointing to tea that had wet the crotch of my pants—something I hadn't noticed. Her friends pretended to hold back their laughter. Snidely she added, "You'd have to be pretty clumsy to fall into a guy's arms like that."

I was steaming with anger. And even though my brain knew that staying quiet was best, my mouth decided to ignore me and spit the words out anyway.

"You're so fake," I accidentally said out loud.

"Excuse me?" Jade said.

I doubled down. "You're faker than Barbie's vagina."

Axel burst into shocked laughter. Even Jade's friends couldn't help a nervous giggle, until she silenced them with a death glare and huffed off.

I looked at Axel. "What are you laughing about? You're dating her."

"Difficult," he reminded me. "But I guess that's the reason why I'm here."

"What?"

And then he said something that totally caught me by surprise. "Maybe there was a little bit of truth to what you said that day in the cafeteria," he admitted, biting his lip.

Wait, what exactly does he mean by that?

Axel walked off, leaving me to think. It's so easy for us to create a profile of ourselves online and simplify who we are—but the truth is, we are deeper than the two-dimensional people we make ourselves out to be. And I found myself reeling, wondering if there were hidden depths to the king of the Goldens, too.

▶ 13.

"Everybody (Backstreet's Back)"
—Backstreet Boys

High school movies were always the same. The guys were definitely in their midtwenties, the sex scenes were fast and awkward, and the nerdy boy always somehow got the hot girl in the end. Real life never quite worked out like that, but something about my new reality made me feel like anything was possible, because just seeing my fellow contestants in the gymnasium put me right in the middle of our very own movie. I could feel the exhilaration in the air, as if we were all together at the top of a roller coaster, peering over the tracks right before the drop.

I wondered what Samantha would've thought, seeing all these people here, in a public display of support for her. I looked around, anxious, checking to see if I could spot her face in the crowd, wondering also if the creep who'd sent me that text was taking the challenge too. But maybe I was just being paranoid. After all, I was a girl who was desperately afraid of wiping her face with the same part of the towel that she used to dry her ass.

After long anticipation, Scarlett stepped onto the stage once again, causing an explosion of applause and purple confetti.

"Welcome to your first day of the Retro Challenge! Look around the room," Scarlett said. "Each one of you has the potential to win, as long as you are left standing at the end. This year is going to involve a series of challenges or tests, and your very first one begins right now."

"My legs are turning into Jell-O," Mimi whispered. "Are you ready?"

"As ever!" Failure was not an option—and my least favorite f-word.

Scarlett cleared her throat. "I'd like to introduce you to your school's Limbo representative, and our master of ceremonies!" She stepped down, yielding the stage to a youthful man in a velvet purple suit and matching top hat. His face was powdered white, his cheeks were rosy, and he had a purple mustache.

Like the Willy Wonka of Limbo.

"Hello, Retros!" he exclaimed, twirling a cane. "My name is Andy, and I will be the keeper of your gates to Retroland. I'll be present in your day-to-day, so when you need anything, come right to me. Consider me a big brother." He winked. There was this air of pure pleasantness about him, even though he was about as unnatural as the words "I understand" in trigonometry. "Now, if you haven't noticed, anything that happens at school will be recorded and uploaded to Limbo as we share the Retro Challenge with the world. We didn't mention it before because we didn't want to attract contestants who were just looking for fame. Look around. Do you see the cameramen?"

I scanned the room. Limbo's videographers stood in every corner, all wearing the same purple branded baseball caps.

"Don't ask them questions. Don't talk to them. They're like

those British royal guards. You'll find no movement in their facial muscles. They're *veerryyy* boring. Well now, shall we begin?"

Right on cue, a team of Limbo workers wheeled out a large glass locker lined with purple neon lights. "Every week, when you least expect it, there will be a new elimination challenge," Andy explained.

A pleasant chime played out over the loudspeakers.

"Whenever you hear this sound, you must come for the next elimination round. So . . . WELCOME TO CHALLENGE NUMBER ONE! Please, take out your phones."

Like a towering safe, the glass box glowed in the middle of the stage.

And that's when the whole crowd gasped, because we all knew exactly what was coming. I felt my phone, tucked into my back pocket. The moment had finally arrived.

One of the camera operators zoomed in on us for a close-up. It was a weird feeling, being filmed like that. But at least the world would know what happened at El Dorado.

"Your smartphone is the ticket into this new world." Andy grinned. "And all you have to do is place it right here! Every challenge is designed to teach a lesson, and today's is very simple. You might think you're losing something big right now, but we want you to know that these devices aren't *communication*. They're a *way* to communicate. This is the first step to gaining an all-new type of confidence. No more multiple personas with multiple profiles and accounts. Now you have one single identity. The brand-new you!"

The idea was to store the phones in an off-limits locker, like a time capsule that would mark our initiation. And soon they had us stand in a line, ready to offer up our technology in what felt like a sacrificial ritual.

One by one, each member of the crowd started placing their phones inside. Now, I was aware that human beings have two basic primordial instincts of fight or flight, though clearly there exists a third:

Spontaneous combustion.

While getting in line, a girl frantically etched her class schedule into a notebook. Another ordered a last-second alarm clock online. Others slipped out the back door, opting out entirely.

Amid the panic, one guy stepped forward, totally unfazed.

Someone known for his chest tattoo, a flaming heart that crawled out of his shirt. He was big and tall, with jet-black hair, and a punky leather jacket. He reached into his pocket, producing an old, cracked phone, something that probably didn't have enough memory for even an app. It was like he had been retro all his life without even knowing it.

I'd seen him around school, but he was someone I hardly knew anything about. No one really did, other than his name— Kilo.

Then came the next contestant—a girl with long loc'ed hair named Ruby. I recognized her face because she was one of the people who'd recorded a video of Samantha in the cafeteria. I guess we all had our demons to fight.

The longer I stood in line, the more the implications sank in. My life was really going to change. Our Kim Kardashians would transform into Lizzie McGuires, and selfies would have to be taken with Polaroids.

It was finally my turn.

I hesitated, which made me angry. This was important to me, yet I still couldn't convince my fingers to let go. And then I remembered that moment at the hospital, when we tried to visit Samantha, how I had to give up my phone just to enter. It was about healing, and we all needed that. So my fingers loosened, and I dropped my smartphone into the locker.

My life was officially in permanent airplane mode.

Mimi motioned a *rest in peace* cross with her fingers over the locker.

"You can try to use old technology, but you'll be wasting your precious time," Andy continued. "Old phones and dial-up internet are virtually inoperable on today's networks. And any website you'd even want to use wouldn't load anyway."

Limbo left no loophole unsealed.

Last came Axel, who dropped his phone inside without the slightest bit of doubt. It really looked like he was happy to get rid of the thing. I wondered what he was going through, deep down, what secret side of himself he'd been hiding from his followers.

What was he trying to escape from? Then again, where we were headed, if you have one million people following you, a call to the FBI is in order.

I guess we all had our reasons for doing this.

We stared silently at the towering locker full of smartphones. It was like they were staring back, beckoning us. Buzzing. Ringing. Calling out for attention.

They were all right there on the stage, though the distance between us felt like light-years. Despite our impulses, and as curious as we were, they were clearly off-limits and no longer a part of our lives.

Ruby stepped forward, nervous. "I should answer mine—what if it's my mom? What if she needs to talk to me? What if she needs to know if I'm okay?"

"And why should your mom get to know everything about your life?" Andy asked with a mischievous smile.

That made something click in all of our brains—because what was once shock and uncertainty grew into a current of energy.

A strange, scary excitement.

A taste of freedom.

Though Mimi was still unconvinced. "I know I'm going to experience so much this year and that's really exciting, but I would love to share the things that I live. It's like every memory will just happen and disappear."

"I feel you, girl," I said. "But there's a ton of people here that we're going to share moments with—probably way more than we ever would have met on our own. Come on—this is way better than scratching your belly at home or swiping left on the same people week after week." I leaned in closer. "You wanna show the world just how cool being a 'freak' is, right? Because when this year is all over, what you'll have to share will be *a part of you*—whatever crazy thing you did, or badass risk you took. Plus, it'll all be on Limbo for us to watch after."

"Sure, I get it . . . but don't you feel a little trapped?" Mimi pointed out.

"A year without our parents' annoying texts? Are you kidding me? That's freedom. This would be lame if we were doing it alone, but luckily for us, we're all doing it together." And the more I talked, the more I convinced myself, too.

Mimi started to lighten up. Because it was true.

The longevity of our day would no longer depend on a battery percentage. Say goodbye to annoying spam calls! No more trolls—and exes wouldn't know what you were doing at all times! As basic a difference as this was, it was significant. No—it was epic.

After the ceremony, the crew opened up a set of double doors on the side of the gymnasium, ones that used to lead to an old storage room.

"And now, without further ado," Andy proclaimed, "we'd like to present to you your new hangout—the Retro Lounge!"

We all funneled inside.

It wasn't until then that I realized how powerful Limbo really was.

My eyes sparkled as I took it all in.

Pinball machines all over the place. Vintage televisions and Nintendo games zinged. First-generation *Sonic* and *Super Mario Bros.* A vending machine with all types of snacks. Gumball machines. A lifetime's supply of books, and purple Chester sofas to binge them on. But the coolest thing of all was the giant bulletin board called the Live Feed, where people could tack up pictures or general questions they had. And, like a forum, people could write down their answers. It was like a real-life profile, only without the references to genitalia, or heated arguments that ended with a stranger explaining to you how he was going to copulate with your mother.

Then one student did something impulsive. He snuck back to the locker, sifted around the phones to find his own, and started to compose one last text.

"Hey! You can't do that!" someone yelled, snatching the phone from his hands.

"I was just turning it off." He tried to cover for himself. "No big deal, right?"

That's when Andy snapped and said, *"Him!"*

Bulky Limbo workers swooped in, grabbed the boy, and escorted him to the door.

"What the hell are you doing?" he yelped.

Andy reached for the phone and handed it back. "Keep it," he said coldly. "You're disqualified." The boy was dragged out the gymnasium doors. "As for the rest of you, let this be a warning."

The crowd went quiet. Because we'd just realized that our biggest enemy was ourselves.

▶ 14.

"Bye Bye Bye"
—*NSYNC

My heart was beating out of my chest as we exited the lounge. I was exhilarated, nervous. It would all be worth it. I could already see myself in an Ivy League school. And then as a psychologist, in one of those sofa-bed hybrid things, with a million leather-bound books I'd never read. But most of all, I imagined my mother as a naturalized citizen, rather than with a business visa that could be canceled if work goes bad—and she's lounging by the pool in the backyard of a brand-new home like a telenovela star wasted on horchata.

Darnell and I walked back to our lockers together. Mimi had to return to the Retro Lounge because, as always, she'd forgotten her backpack. I prayed she didn't have dreams of becoming a professional skydiver.

"Are you worried about what it'll be like to not have a phone?" Darnell asked.

"Yeah, but I've prepared myself."

Truth is, I was so freaked out about not having access to the internet that last weekend I started looking up any information I could until I was able to diagnose myself.

"I think it's called NoMoPhobia. No-Mobile Phobia . . ."

"Okay, if I contract it and die, please erase all my embarrassing selfies where I'm lying down and my neck looks like a gobble," Darnell said. "That front camera kills me."

"I've got your back," I laughed.

"And don't trip. I did the same thing as you last weekend, and in my paranoid frenzy I read about this thing called phantom limb," Darnell added. "This weird phenomenon that happens to amputees, where their severed nerve endings can't process signals to the brain, so they're unable to comprehend the lost appendage. Well, I think now I'm having phantom phone."

And it was happening to me, too, because all the way to my locker I kept checking for vibrations in my pocket that weren't actually there. I'd obviously been without my phone before, but it was okay, because I always knew that it would be there when I came back.

This was different.

I felt kind of naked—and we all know that's the last thing you want to be in high school. But the ghostly vibrations were quickly replaced by a more immediate threat. My heart skipped a beat as soon as we got to the locker hall, because someone had left a message in red spray paint:

WHO'S NEXT?

There were just two words, but they left me terrified. Sure, they were written across a dozen lockers, but two of them were Mimi's and my own. *What could it mean? Is this a threat? Could whoever did this be the same person who sent that creepy text message?*

And then I heard him. Standing right there, like a parasite that kept coming back for more blood. Vince was grabbing his last books from his locker, preparing for his suspension.

Then he locked eyes with me. Chills.

Was it Vince? Could he be the one who knows my secret?

Maybe he was just seeking revenge on the place that suspended him. Or maybe Vince had even more to do with Samantha's downfall than I knew. After all, he had shared her video with hundreds of thousands of followers. Others saw a popular jerk, someone rough around the edges, but that day in the cafeteria I had felt his sharp, splintered core.

"The suspension isn't going to work." Miranda joined us. "Forcing Vince to change is like spraying perfume on dog crap. Useless."

Hovering around him were the other Goldens. His friend Chad, with a scarred eyebrow, who once kicked someone so hard that the guy was left with one testicle. And then there was Juan, who everyone called Juan Solo because they were afraid to get close to him. They were always getting wasted and destroying things. The type of guys who somehow passed health class even though they thought the food pyramid was a biblical site rather than a dietary recommendation. And as usual, hanging with them were Jade Laurent and her fan club.

Vince examined the painted threat. "What a surprise we have here! Ladies and gentlemen, place your bets. Who's next?"

The truth was, nobody really knew the magnitude of this bloodred threat. But the tall, tattooed Retro, Kilo, appeared out of nowhere and tapped Vince on the shoulder politely.

"Hey, buddy," he said. "Can I please get into my locker?"

Vince clearly didn't like being called his *buddy*. "Sorry, busy, try again tomorrow."

Darnell leaned in. "Cleanup on aisle seven. This is about to get messy."

"Why?" I asked.

I didn't know what to expect with Kilo, who'd moved here from Hawai'i a few years ago. He had this strong presence about him, but had always kept to himself.

Darnell filled me in. "Kilo just does whatever he thinks is fair without caring about the consequences. One time freshman year, some kids were making fun of me for wearing pink, so he doused them in glue and covered them in glitter."

"Whoa, that's . . . amazing. I like him already."

Vince continued to talk to his friends, ignoring Kilo's polite request.

Kilo, clearly fed up with his attitude, literally picked Vince up and moved him over.

"Wh-what the hell is your—" Vince stammered, realizing this guy was twice his size.

Kilo patted Vince's head, drawing giggles from the crowd. "Good boy," he said, and then, as if nothing had happened, opened his locker to retrieve his books.

Vince's face went all pink and puffy, and looked like it was going to explode.

And as if there weren't enough people gawking, Axel rolled up on his skateboard. "Lesson one. Don't mess with people bigger than you." He laughed at Vince.

"Whatever. At least I'm not friends with those Retro freaks."

Axel brushed it off. "Who said they were my friends?"

"Well, it's not like you're interested in being friends with *us* anymore. We can't even create content together now that you're doing that stupid challenge. You know I can't get that many collabs without you."

"Bro. It's not that serious."

Everyone knew that Vince and the Goldens only got their followers because of Axel. It clearly paid to be a part of his shadow. But Vince wasn't the only person who had a problem with Axel taking the challenge.

Jade pulled Axel aside and grabbed his hands. "Axel, Vince is right. You're hurting us."

"What do you mean?"

"I mean that if I really mattered to you, you wouldn't be going retro."

"Jade, can we please talk in private?"

"No. We're talking now," she said.

"Listen." He lowered his voice. "I've taken tons of challenges, and it never affected us before."

"But this is different! How can we be in a relationship if we can't do anything together?"

It was funny how their online profiles portrayed them as this perfect couple, but without the colorful filters and heart-eyed emojis, spectators were encircling them like a Roman circus.

And I couldn't tell who was the gladiator and who was the lion about to be slain.

"We can't even go to that premier party in San Francisco this weekend now that you're doing this. Being an influencer, partying, and doing crazy stunts are the things you're good at. Now you're going to say goodbye to all of it? That's not who you are."

"Then maybe you have no idea who I am," he told her.

"And you do?"

The audience went silent, except for Darnell, who said, "*Ooohh, that's gotta sting!*"

"Maybe not," Axel said, "but I don't think I'm going to find that person with you."

Jade looked hurt. "But, Axel, this is our entire brand."

"Please, Jade. I don't want to do this here."

"I need an explanation." Her arms crossed over her chest.

"Listen, you're an incredible girl. You're so driven, and focused, but we've just been so distant for so long. I've been thinking about it a lot lately, and I feel like we've grown apart. We want such different things now. Maybe you're right, and we won't survive this challenge. I'm sorry."

"What are you saying?" Jade's lips trembled as she tried not to cry.

His silence spoke volumes.

"This isn't over yet," she said coldly, backing away. That final moment they shared wasn't lovers parting ways; it was something much more ominous. And then, just before she left, Jade's gaze caught mine—staring me down. Who knows what was going on in her head.

Vince slugged Axel in the arm. "Ooh, *heartbreaker*."

"What a show. I think the whole world heard us." Axel slammed his locker and went to leave. "I'm so over this. Vince, you should leave before you get in more trouble."

"One last bet and I'll go."

Axel hesitated. "What?"

"If I beat you at the race this weekend, you'll drop out of

the challenge. You'll forget about all of this, and our lives will go back to the way they were."

"And if I win, will you let this go?"

"Sure."

Axel shook Vince's hand, cementing the bet. I could feel the tension between them.

"Then I'll see you there," Axel said over his shoulder as he pushed his way through the crowd and disappeared. The whole school would be counting down the days until the epic showdown, because the underground street race in the abandoned forest was one of the biggest events of the entire year.

⏸ 15.

Pause

Oops! I think my cassette jammed.

I know this was an interesting moment, but old technology is like that. I guarantee you things will get even more interesting between me and those two. I feel like I'm in one of those torture chambers designed to kill you with boredom. I've tried all the normal things bored people do, like singing, biting my nails, and pretending I'm in an escape room.

News flash: I'm losing.

I use a hairpin to fix the jammed tape.

RING! RING! RING!

What the hell?

RING! RING! RING!

It's been a long time since I heard this sound. Am I losing my mind? Is this real?

I hear my phone.

I follow the sound, running my hand along the cold white walls, tracing my way to the little bed in the corner, and underneath the mattress. I lift it up to find an old friend.

Sure enough, it's my cell phone.

Or at least one that looks exactly like mine—the same zebra-patterned phone case lying there. But who is trying to call me, knowing that I've gone retro?

I move closer, and when I finally see what's flashing on the screen, I want to cry with joy, with pain, and then with abject anger. Because the name that I read is the one person I love most in this world, someone who is really worried about me.

Mi mamá.

Every atom of my body wants to answer that call and tell her that I'm okay—that I'm at least alive and breathing—but I resist. This is too good to be true. This is a trap.

"Hey, you! Can you hear me?" I scream to the walls. "That was a cheap trick. But it's not going to work on me. You'll never beat us!" And with the jagged back of my boot, I smash the phone until its ringing squeals to death.

▶ 16.

"Allstar"
—Smash Mouth

Friends and foes alike took the starting line—igniting the roaring crowd. The El Dorado street race has been a town tradition for generations. Over the years the stakes have evolved. Now winners won bragging rights, brands won exposure, and everyone else got to watch the Goldens go head-to-head in their supercharged sports cars. And what better way to say goodbye to my old world than illegal racing in an abandoned forest with Mimi and Darnell?

"This is going to be so epic," Mimi said.

"I used to live stream the race in a space-cat onesie, elbow deep in a Doritos bag," I confessed.

"This place is so creepy in person." Darnell squinted.

We congregated on the side of a dilapidated forest roadway, at least a hundred people in all. Fireflies glinted in the haze. Deserted lake homes lined the old street, their shimmering reflections staring back from the water below. There was a thrilling sensation that something wild was about to happen. I was just waiting for my mom to pop out of the bushes in full camouflage and ground me for the rest of my life.

"What if we get caught for being here?"

"Don't sweat it," Darnell told me. "If my mom is a private detective and I'm not worried, you shouldn't be either."

"Then if something goes wrong, you're breaking me out of jail," I joked as we sifted through the crowd and claimed a spot right by the starting line.

And that's when we felt eyes on us. "Look, it's more of those Retros . . . ," one girl whispered to another.

"What am I, an amoeba?" Mimi barked, then turned to us. "Sorry, but I feel like I'm being examined."

"Me too," Darnell said.

"Wearing skates in the forest isn't really normal, Darnell!" I laughed.

"And what is normal?" Mimi said. "Who decides what's normal? I think normal is whatever we want it to be."

"That's my little unicorn. A hard-core pony with body armor," Darnell dubbed Mimi, who gave him a playful elbow that almost knocked him off-balance. I was starting to think that he slept and showered in those skates. But what Mimi had said really made me think. Normal was what came naturally. Why should we be nervous, self-conscious, or worried about just being ourselves? Because it wasn't like any of us fit the status quo, something that was becoming ever more apparent.

Moments later, a loudspeaker squealed.

"Racers! ARE YOU READY?" the MC belted from the starting line. It was Kosta, the foreign exchange student from Greece. By the looks of it, he was taking the Retro Challenge too.

"That accent . . . I could listen to him for hours, even if he was just reading an instruction manual," Darnell drooled.

"You should get on that." I nudged him.

"I don't even know if Kosta would like me that way." Darnell looked off, deflated. "Like, maybe he just smiles at me because of his Mediterranean charm."

"Well, there's only one way to find out."

"START YOUR ENGINES!" Kosta shouted.

The crowd roared, waving checkered racing flags. Racers revved the engines of their flashy supercars, which probably cost more than my apartment—but not more than my mother's mug collection. That, she's convinced, is worth millions.

I could smell the gasoline and the envy in the air. All the Goldens were about to race. A crew that was always competing for everything, and this race was just another public forum to one-up one another.

First there was Juan Solo in a souped-up green Mini Cooper, then Vince in an aggressive matte-black BMW. But the next contestant's car totally caught me off guard. A car so badass and retro you'd think it was ripped right out of a movie. Because that's when a vintage Ford Mustang pulled up to the starting line. The red-and-white–striped hood sparkled in the faint sun.

And behind the wheel sat none other than Axel.

He was famous for doing daredevil stunts in his super-charged Gran Turismo, but this new ride was next level. And the crowd was going nuts over it. He even had a fan club.

Vince revved his engine, taunting.

"Vince is someone I definitely wouldn't trust at a hundred miles per hour," Darnell said.

"Yeah, totally," Mimi laughed. "Like, if his brain was a plane, there was no pilot, just crying babies and sweaty pasta . . ."

He and the Goldens had been riding Axel's coattails since Axel had gotten big on Limbo, and they were going to need him out of the Retro Challenge if they were going to keep their following online. So it was everyone versus Axel. Cameras flashed all around the starting line.

Kosta stood atop a car on the sidelines, counting down. "THREE . . . TWO . . . ONE!"

Screeching tires. Burning rubber. The racers rocketed off.

And only then did I realize that half the guardrails were falling apart, which was their only protection from the jagged rocks below.

The crowd was buzzing with electricity. But among all the jumping and screaming, someone static stood out to me. Kilo—dressed, per usual, in all black.

He was sitting alone on a tree stump, eating a sandwich from a brown lunch bag. He counted seconds with a stopwatch and scribbled onto a notepad. Seeing him eating by himself reminded me of Samantha. How her final meal before that fateful night was in the cafeteria. All alone. How people just watched her suffering, too cowardly to help.

Wasn't that why I had taken this challenge in the first place?

"I feel bad," I said. "He's always so alone."

"He's a lone wolf, I guess," Darnell said.

"Well, it doesn't have to stay that way," I proclaimed. "We should go sit with him."

"Are you sure?" Darnell questioned. "He's a complete stranger."

"No way . . . he's one of us now," Mimi said. "Besides, in your old life, would you have just randomly gone and sat with the lord of the underworld?"

"Yeah. Time to do things differently." And before I knew it, my feet were churning.

I took off through the crowd as my friends tried to keep up. We made our way over and sat next to Kilo.

He looked at me, confused.

"Um," he eventually said awkwardly. "I don't want to buy anything. . . ."

"Oh, no, I just wanted to say hi. I'm Luna, and these are my friends Mimi and Darnell."

He glanced at my hand, but instead of biting it off, he shook it. His hand was coarse, but his grip was soft and gentle. There was something authentic about his eyes despite his rough-hewn exterior.

"I already know you," he said in a deep voice. "You're the white 1979 Mercedes G-wagen, license plate 5YEL802."

We fell silent, creeped out, staring at him like he was from Mars.

"Yep," I said, "that's me."

He lifted up his grease-stained hands and cracked a guilty smile. "I have a little garage on the outskirts of town. I like to heal cars."

"Oh *phew*." Mimi laughed. "I thought you were a weirdo for a second. I like to heal shoes." She pointed to her duct-taped Converse.

"That's so cool," Kilo said, blushing.

Darnell and I glanced at each other.

"Well, it's nice to meet you, Kilo." Mimi threw an arm around his shoulder.

"Why are you guys here?" He looked at us strangely.

I jumped in. "We want to be your friends."

"Thank you, but I don't need new friends."

"Even introverts need friends," Mimi said.

"I'm not introverted. I'm just . . . socially selective."

"Like back in ninth grade when there was a flood in Mrs. Kavinsky's science lab, and you saved all the rabbits before the people?" Darnell said.

"Someone had to liberate those poor creatures." Kilo raised an eyebrow. "Your point?"

"I heard about that!" Mimi beamed. "That was you? You're my hero!"

Eventually the crowd started clamoring again. The racers were finally coming back around for their first lap, and Axel and Vince were in a dead heat for the lead.

Juan Solo in his green Mini was behind Axel, almost hitting his bumper. Axel paced directly ahead of it, making sure Juan never found the opportunity to pass. But now they were headed full speed into a massive dead sequoia. And then, at the last second, Axel's Mustang swerved left, and he gassed the accelerator—forcing the car behind him to spin out in a cloud of dust. As much as I hated to admit it, I was pretty impressed.

"YEAH! That's what I'm talking about!" Kilo shouted.

"You're cheering for *Axel*?" Darnell raised an eyebrow.

"I'm cheering for his 1966 Shelby Mustang. I worked on it yesterday."

This close to Kilo, I could see something on his chest through his low-cut shirt—the large flaming-heart tattoo that covered a deep and uneven scar, skin that had been mangled, then healed. It gave me chills for its rawness. It gave me chills for its beauty.

What secrets does he hide inside that tattoo?

After a few minutes, the cars were back around and approaching the finish line. The crowd thundered, because in first place was Axel's Mustang, head-to-head with Vince's blacked-out BMW ramming into its body—a dirty move to take the lead. And with the final bend up ahead, Axel only had one option if he was going to win.

"He's not going to do it," Kilo muttered, rising to his feet.

"Do what?" Mimi reached inside Kilo's bag of chips, but he was too entranced to notice.

In the final turn, the Mustang cranked its wheels, letting the tires slip in a controlled drift—as if it was sliding along ice. And finally, when the tires stuck, the car stabilized, and he launched directly past Vince's BMW, positioning him in first place for the win.

"THAT WAS INSANE!" We all jumped up, screaming.

"That maneuver could have got Axel seriously hurt, or worse, totaled the car," Kilo said.

"He clearly thinks he's invincible," I said. But the truth was that I was really glad that he hadn't hurt himself. Axel may have won the race, though he was going to lose everything else he had that day, because what happened next was ugly.

▶ 17.

"Basket Case"
—Green Day

The Mustang skidded to a halt in a cloud of smoke.

And when Axel emerged from the haze, Vince was shouting. "The only reason you won was because you cut me off!"

"Well, I still beat you, so technically, you lost the bet."

Vince looked like he was going to explode, though he was still trying to save face for the fans on the live stream. But on this day someone else was going to blow up.

Because standing on the road was a familiar silhouette.

It was as if time slowed in the headlights of the Mustang. From that beam of light emerged one person, coming straight for Axel. She'd been waiting for him at the finish line, letting her emotions whip into a full-blown storm.

Jade approached, a bloodred look in her eye, clutching a rock.

And she threw it.

Axel dodged in the nick of time. It collided with the windshield, cracking the glass into a spiderweb. *"What's her name?"* Jade shrieked, eyes black and runny with mascara.

"What the hell is wrong with you?" Axel yelled back. "Whose name?"

But Jade had her own version of the truth. She was too hurt to ever believe that Axel would leave her without having other options lined up. She couldn't live with the idea that having no one was better than having her.

Jade whipped around, pointing an accusing finger into the crowd. "Is it her?" Jade's eyes scanned through each and every onlooker. And with one gesture, she was able to draw the attention of the whole world—singling someone out in the crowd. And that person was me.

I was now the focus of Jade's rage.

A thousand eyes stabbed me like knives. My cheeks went red, and I couldn't tell if it was because I was embarrassed to be thrown into the spotlight or out of anger for having been accused of something so insane. The phones flashed and recorded as they always did, and the elephants that used to step on my chest came back, crushing me until my eyes watered. I felt little. And all I wanted was for the earth to swallow me and spit me out on a Caribbean beach.

"What are you talking about?" I asked. But no one heard—or cared.

"With *her*? Have you lost your mind?" he shouted, seeming ashamed of the mere accusation. It stung, but in truth, I would've responded the same way—or worse.

More spectators started recording the drama to post on Limbo. Exactly what Jade wanted. With a show like this, how could everyone not believe her? Axel looked to Vince to come to his defense. But the opposite happened.

"Is it true?" Vince asked. The rest of the Goldens collected behind him. "Did you really cheat on Jade?"

"You and I both know that she's lying," Axel said desperately.

"I always thought you were such a gentleman, Axel," Vince said. "Can't believe it was just another one of your stunts."

It didn't matter what the truth was, because this was his opportunity for a power grab, and he was taking it.

"You disgust me," Vince sneered, and then stepped dangerously close to Axel, whispering something into his ear. Whatever Vince said pushed Axel past the brink of control. Because that's when Axel's hand pulled back and curled into a fist.

The blow connected with Vince's nose, a shot so heavy that it sent him to his knees. But as soon as Vince fell back, a bloody grin began to form, stretching from ear to ear. Axel had played right into Vince's hand. It was obvious. He'd wanted Axel to hit him. And he'd wanted everyone to see it so Axel would appear guilty on all charges.

Jade got down to console the fallen Vince. "You and I are finished for good, Axel," she declared, making sure everyone heard her words.

"You heard her, so why are you still standing there?" Vince shouted. And soon others were shouting at him too. All the Goldens had taken Vince's side.

Axel was far less useful than he used to be. Now that he was taking the Retro Challenge, there would be no more followers to leech. No more parties. He was being dethroned as leader of the Goldens.

I watched as Axel turned his back on his past.

▶ 18.

"Freedom! '90"
—George Michael

The dead side of the lake was illuminated by an orange sun and an expanse of taillights that wrapped through the forest. The race ended, and the crowd quickly dispersed, filing into cars before the police showed up. The red glow grew blurry as tears of anger collected in my eyes. Mimi, Darnell, and Kilo went to get me a bottle from a water boy. After what had happened, I needed some time alone. I sat on the side of the road by my car, wondering what lies and rumors were being spread about me. Which Limbo hashtags were being used to trash me.

Maybe I really was *NEXT*. Like the spray paint on the locker. Like what happened to Samantha.

I felt the weight of her whistle with each breath as it rose and fell on my chest.

And then a familiar powdered face appeared among the dissolving crowd—almost frightening me as he approached. Our new big brother.

What was *he* doing here?

"Luna, right?" Andy asked.

"Yeah, how did you remember?"

"I keep an eye on my Retros." He smiled. "Listen, it's unfortunate what happened back there . . . but just know that whatever they might be posting doesn't exist anymore, Luna. It's not real for you now."

And he was so right. In Spanish we say, *Ojos que no ven, corazón que no siente*. Eyes that do not see, heart that does not feel. I was safe so long as I was a Retro.

Andy noticed my friends coming back. "You guys should head out soon. The cops will be here any minute now."

"You're not going to tell the principal about the race?"

"Of course not. We're Limbo. Where normal rules don't apply." He winked. "Haven't you heard?"

"Thanks."

"I've got your back—don't worry," Andy said, and then, before my friends saw him, he vanished into the forest of glowing fireflies.

There was something I liked about Andy. Even if he was watching us like a hawk, he was rooting for us to win. The others finally came back after what felt like a week's trip to Niagara Falls. Darnell handed me a bottle. "Fresh water for the bright-eyed queen."

"Thank you, but I know they're red and puffy like tomatoes."

"Rubies," Mimi corrected me.

I couldn't help but smile, until I noticed that Kilo was staring at me.

"Keep looking and I'm going to have to charge you," I joked. But then I realized that Kilo, with his big hand, was holding out a little handkerchief.

"I normally use it to clean engine grease. But now it's for you," he said with an honest, sweet smile. "I promise it's clean. It's just stained." I felt warmer than ever with that dirty cloth in my hand, because now, in addition to my unique Mimi, there were new people in my life to cheer me up—even if Kilo was dead set on not having friends.

"We should get going," I said, realizing that all the other cars were gone.

"Hey, how'd you get here?" I asked Kilo.

He shrugged. "Walked."

"Seriously? We're miles from town. I'll drop you off wherever you need to go, but first we're going to kidnap you to grab a bite of food with us."

"Hm. Okay. I know the perfect place to go." He smiled.

Usually in a moment like this Mimi and I would use a delivery app and cram our faces with orange chicken in my garage, but not in Retro mode. So we piled into my vehicle and put the car in fresco mode, where you roll down the windows and blast the heat. Darnell cranked up his longtime favorite station, 103.7 Retro Radio—the one he'd shown me in the thrift store.

"Tonight's theme song: 'Freedom! '90,' by George Michael!" the DJ announced.

The schoolwork in the back seat whipped up and flew out, taking all my worries with it. Mimi propped her feet on Kilo's lap; Darnell opened the moonroof and stood up in it, screaming the chorus into the wind:

"Freedom!

"Freedom!

"FREEDOM!"

Soon we were all singing along.

We followed the glowing city lights home. All the while, Kilo was pointing out shortcuts, whether it was a fast-approaching turn or paths off the main road. Off-roading. Dust kicked up and clouded around us, forcing me to throw on the windshield wipers, which were so dry and noisy, they did a perfect impression of two cats mating.

We turned left at the last fork, which could only have meant one thing.

"Wait! Are we going to the Roller Derby Diner?"

Kilo tried to hide a smile, found out.

"I thought I was the only one who knew about it!" It was one of El Dorado's local secrets and had been my favorite late-night restaurant since I'd been old enough to sneak out of the house. The old-school diner had neon lights, plush red booths, and a jukebox, which made every day Throwback Thursday.

I looked at my friends in the car as they danced like crazy and belted out lyrics. I was already beginning to see how things were changing. I wouldn't have hung out with these people before. I wouldn't have gone to the street race. But now that my mom couldn't text me, there were no specifics to fill her in on. Fewer little things to nitpick and bother me about. My night would have ended early, and now it had no end.

Like our new theme song, this was a little taste of freedom.

We soared through the night. All we could see were the one hundred feet ahead of us lit by the headlights, trusting that we'd get to where we needed to go. I just didn't know that all paths were leading us right to him.

▶ 19.

"Smooth"
—Santana ft. Rob Thomas

First came the smoke, a cloud of dark gray air that obscured the road ahead. Then the taillights illuminated the woods like we were in a horror movie. And eventually, the entire vehicle came into view. It was parked on the shoulder and steaming from the hood. We recognized the car before we recognized the driver. Axel leaned over the smoking engine with a wrench, more lost than a flea in a teddy bear.

"Stop!" Kilo yelled, and almost dove headfirst out of my car, so I slammed on the brakes.

"Are you crazy?" I asked. "After everything he's put me through?"

He shook his head. "You don't understand. We have to help the car or it's going to die."

Kilo ran to the car and nearly scared Axel half to death.

"Dude, what are *you* doing here?" They did a friendly fist bump before Kilo went to the hood of the car and started fumbling around with its insides. "Thanks a million, man. I have no idea what the hell I'm doing."

Kilo squinted in the glow of our headlights and then stepped back, jaw dropped.

"What is it?"

"Axel . . . I can't believe I'm going to say this, but someone tried to sabotage your car. The engine coolant reservoirs are all slashed and leaking." Kilo got down to inspect the wheels. "They even tampered with your brakes. It's like someone wanted you to crash."

Axel went pale. "I know what you're thinking. Vince is a jerk, but he'd never go that far."

"Then who did this?"

And I just got this strange feeling that everything that had been happening lately was connected in some twisted way. The text message. The writing on the lockers . . . Someone had it out for us, and I wasn't the only target.

"All we can do at this point is call a tow truck. If you run the engine now, it'll overheat."

I knew what was coming next.

Axel stewed in the uncomfortable silence.

"Can I get a ride?" he finally asked, looking straight at me.

"I don't know—maybe you'll need to kiss my feet first." I sighed. "Fine. I guess."

"Loony, are you sure about this?" Mimi whispered.

"Well, we can't just leave him there."

"What will everyone think when they see you two?" Darnell asked.

"I couldn't care less," I said, for the first time actually meaning it.

Axel hopped in the front seat, and we pulled back onto the road. "Well, apparently you know Kilo. This is Mimi. And that's Darnell."

"What's up?"

"History class, right?" Axel asked.

"And science. And English," Darnell added.

"Cool . . ."

There was an awkward air that hung in the car. Because maybe a million people wished they could be friends with Axel, but that wasn't our case. For me, he was the guy who made my life more difficult than it needed to be.

"You want one?" He sucked on a lollipop.

"No thanks."

"Most of my friends vape, but not me. Sugar is my vice," he said with a smile.

I caught him stealing a look at me.

I looked away.

"You're getting goose bumps. Do I make you uncomfortable?" he joked, cocky.

"No. They're just needles so you don't get too close to me."

"Okay. I get it," he said. "I'm sorry about what happened back there."

"Whatever. It's fine. It wasn't entirely your fault."

"It's just crazy that anyone would believe you and I could've ever been *together*." He gave an embarrassed chuckle.

"And why is that?" I leveled him with a glare.

"I don't know." He strained himself to find the perfect words. "Maybe because I was such a jerk and you're so . . . *opinionated*."

"Smart choice of words." We both laughed, though I wasn't going to let him off the hook that easily. "You weren't exactly nice that day in the cafeteria."

"Sure I wasn't. But if you kept yelling at Vince, you would have become his next target. I said what I could to get you to leave. I was just trying to look out for you." His eyes flickered in the passing streetlights, earnest. Meaning it.

"I didn't need your saving."

He let out a laugh, incredulous. "Actually, you were the one who saved me. I couldn't get what you said out of my head, how I was going to end up all alone. I hated you for it, but only because you were right. My friends . . . they weren't good for me."

"So why do you hang out with them?"

"It's complicated. I guess I didn't want to be alone," he said.

"Just because you're thirsty doesn't mean you go around drinking poison."

"Touché." He shook his head. "I never thought of it that way. But I knew I had to stop. To leave it all behind. I just didn't know how. Maybe I was waiting for the perfect moment."

"When someone throws a rock at your head is a good moment."

We started busting up again.

"Me and Jade . . . we were just kids when we started dating. Jade is hurt, and not used to being denied anything. And sure, sometimes she goes overboard, but I still feel bad."

"Yeah, I don't know. I'm still thinking of making a Jade dartboard," I joked, and changed the subject. "I'm not just going retro for myself. I'm doing it for Samantha, too. This whistle I'm wearing was a thing we used to support each other in tough times."

"Thank goodness she's pulling through," he said, then touched the little whistle on my chest. "I think that whistle is pretty cool. . . ."

"Thanks, Axel."

"You know, even though Samantha acted like she was above you, we all knew there was only one picture inside her locker, and it was of the two of you."

"I never knew that," I said, touched, realizing that the tension was easing up between me and Axel. I glanced at everyone in my rearview mirror, and I couldn't help but smile. There was Kilo, this intimidating guy we'd just met; Mimi, who was trying to convince him that the car had broken down because Mercury was in retrograde; and Darnell, air-DJing invisible records. Never in a million years would I have imagined all these people crammed into my car.

After a while Mimi stuck her head between us. "So, Axel, we've been debating, and I'm sure you know better than anybody—what's Limbo really like?"

Axel was ready for the tell-all. "Well, if you really wanna know, their headquarters, Limboland, has fake grass indoors, all-you-can-eat buffets, and bouncy balls instead of office chairs. Basically, Scarlett and Fineman are so rich they could afford a bunch of assistants just to separate out all the red Skittles—the best flavor."

"Whoa! That's crazy. What other juicy stuff do you know?" Mimi exclaimed.

"Remember back when Microsoft released that prototype of a self-aware online chatbot named Tay? It was supposed to learn from the culture of the internet and develop its own personality. Within sixteen hours on social media, the chatbot became a total monster, making hateful comments. It even grew a god complex. Well, I've heard rumors that Limbo has a larger master plan in the works. But that's the side of Limbo that most people don't know about."

Darnell pulled down his shades. "That's so freaky."

"The more you learn about Limbo, the more intense things get." Axel looked down.

"In what ways?" I asked.

"I think that's enough for tonight," he said, turning up the radio. Which made me realize that there was much more to the story that he didn't want to talk about.

We finally rolled up to the Monteverde Mall, which at this time of night was totally closed, with the exception of one magical culinary institution: the Roller Derby Diner, a place where the red booths looked like Thunderbirds from back in the days before seat belts. It was all neon lights and jukeboxes and clearly hadn't been remodeled since it had been constructed, though it was immaculately maintained. We took a booth, and soon our waiter arrived on roller skates—only he was someone we instantly recognized.

Kosta scrambled to tie his apron on, running late for his shift.

"Have fun at the race?" I asked him.

"Shhh. My boss will kill me. Let me take care of you guys. I'll bring you the best burgers. One Retro to another, everything is on the house," he said, before running off to fix an exploding milkshake machine.

I grinned. We Retros really were part of a secret club.

"Wow, his body is made of marble chiseled by the Greek gods," Darnell muttered dreamily. Axel squirmed.

"Oh, give me a break. I have to listen to guys like you talk about boobs all day." Darnell looked him square in the eye. "Get over it. It's not like I said the word 'penis'!"

Axel tried his best not to flinch. "Yeah, sure. My bad, man."

Darnell let out a laugh and slugged him in the arm. "I'm just messing with you." Then he got serious. "Kind of."

It was funny to see Axel so out of his element. He was nothing like the confident, self-assured person he had seemed to be on Limbo and at school. But getting out of your comfort zone is like that.

Axel changed the subject, trying to lighten the air. "This place is so rad. I can't believe I've never eaten here before."

"That's because it doesn't even appear on Google," I explained.

Mimi winked. "Just because you don't see it doesn't mean it doesn't exist."

Then Darnell leaned in furtively. "Y'all hear about that mega fast-food chain that moved in across the street and pretty much stole all their business? Well, they put all types of chemicals in their burgers to get you addicted. Have you heard of E110?"

"Here he goes with another conspiracy theory." Mimi giggled.

Kosta rolled by, delivering burgers, fries, and shakes. "Here's your food, hot and ready." He turned to Darnell. "Those Rollerblades you were wearing today were pretty cool."

"I love your skates too," he said, nervous. "Looks like we have something in common."

"I guess." Kosta smiled.

"Anyway, thank you so much for the food."

"Yeah, sure, dude. Anytime."

"Did you hear that?" Darnell whispered to us. "He said ANYtime!"

Axel rolled his eyes cockily. "If there's one thing that I've learned about getting a date with *whoever* I want, it's that you have to be *a lot* smoother than that."

"Okay, cool boy." Darnell laughed it off. "If you get me a date with Kosta, I'll give you my entire wardrobe."

"I do like your style," Axel admitted. "I'll help you. I'm cool with Kosta. We've got second period together."

"Why can't you be just sweet all the time, without a side of arrogance?" I stole one of Axel's fries.

He winked. "I guess I'm difficult too."

Despite his attitude, Axel was really nice to offer to help Darnell.

"I love this burger joint." Kilo finally spoke. "It's basically always empty. This is where I go when I'm tired of the people at school."

"So why did you bring us here?" Mimi asked.

"I don't know. I guess I don't mind not being alone tonight. Plus, you guys aren't so terrible," Kilo said in a way that totally didn't feel like a joke. Then he inhaled his entire burger in one bite and smiled, like he hadn't just insulted us.

I looked to Mimi, like, *Really?*

But it made me feel so good that we were here together.

"So, Axel, how did you learn to race like that?" Mimi asked.

"Well, I started stealing my parents' car at thirteen, so I've had a long time to practice," Axel explained. "You learn cool tricks. Like, for example, try to balance yourself. Now do it while pressing your tongue to the roof of your mouth."

We all attempted to balance on one cheek.

"See, the pressurized nerve endings send electrical signals that stimulate balance. . . ."

"Wow, it really works!" Darnell lit up.

Mimi tried too until milkshake started spraying out of her nose, which was hilarious. And when the laughter settled, Axel leaned in.

"I just have one question for you guys. Why did you help me back there?" he asked. "I ignored you at school, and I'm sure all of you were the butt of a joke at some point."

I was the one who answered. "Sure, it hurts being laughed at. But I've made mistakes that have hurt people too." I dug deep for the right words. This was going to be very difficult, but I trusted them.

And I had to get this weight off my chest.

"Please don't tell anyone, but . . . I was the person who uploaded the video of Samantha."

Kilo stopped mid-chew.

"That was you?" Darnell asked.

"Samantha really screwed me over and almost got me arrested for stealing, so I got angry and uploaded it anonymously. I was a mess that night. It was stupid. It was selfish. I just thought we would all laugh and move on." I stared emptily into my hamburger. "That doesn't make any of it okay, but it means, more than anyone, I believe in second chances. And if we're going to make it through this year, we're going to have to stick together."

I could see something change a little in Axel. He looked disappointed with me. Samantha had been his friend too.

"Thanks for telling us that, Luna. I mean, that's pretty heavy—but your secret is safe with me." Darnell looked at each of us. "If something goes wrong, whether that be a broken car or a broken heart, I've got all your backs."

"Sure. But no more penis jokes," Axel said.

"Fine. I'll skip the long ones."

Axel playfully flung a gob of fries and ketchup at Darnell. Then Mimi threw a cheesy wad of paper, and before long I was shooting spitballs at Kilo, who was throwing fries at me. And like that, in the dirtiest of ways, the five of us were officially consecrated the most unlikely team that had walked the streets of El Dorado.

▶ 20.

"Wind of Change"
—Scorpions

This year, the scary stuff happened about a week before Halloween—worse than all the possessed dolls and hellhounds on earth. When it went down, I was still buzzing from all the mushy vibes my new friends gave me. I was on a roll, whether it was working hard at the family theater, or finding new songs for my Walkman.

On this particular day, I rolled out of bed in an amazing mood, even though my pinky toe and nightstand have a never-ending toxic relationship. Ever since the challenge started, I'd have three-way calls with Mimi and Darnell on my new candy-apple-red landline phone to debate important concepts like whether you should eat pizza crust or donate it to the birds, or if the person flying in the middle seat really deserves both armrests.

"Does it scare you that Mars is technically a planet inhabited by robots?" Mimi asked me through the receiver—which blew my mind. But before I could answer, a thought struck me.

"Mimi. I should go. Something's up. It's too quiet. My

mother hasn't yanked the cord out of the wall or threatened to make me eat the gross black parts of the bananas yet."

"Weird. Go investigate it, Loony."

It was true. Today my mamá was silent.

The scariest sound you could hear from a Spanish mother.

Loudness was commonplace for her, especially due to her one crippling weakness: historical telenovelas. My mom would become so overwhelmed by plot twists and devilishly handsome evil twins that she was convinced that her life was a lot more dramatic than it really was. But when I walked into the kitchen, I found my mom at the table, head buried in her hands, with an expression I hadn't seen in so many years. One that never brought good news.

"What's happening, Mamá?"

"Absolutamente nada. Go and get ready for school."

"Then what are these letters on the counter?"

One of them was torn open. My mother was wearing a look on her face that was only reserved for large medical bills or Immigration Services.

I started reading the papers until my mother snatched them back. "Por favor, don't worry about that, hija!" she pleaded.

But it was too late. I had already seen what it said. I was totally caught off guard. The letter threatened to tear down everything my family had worked for.

The Monteverde Mall was going to be put up for sale.

It wasn't generating enough business, so the owners wanted to sell. Apparently this big real estate company wanted to buy the land and construct a housing development over its ashes. Some fancy complex with application prerequisites that included having a yacht docked in your bank account.

"What does this mean for the theater?" My voice trembled.

My mom forced a smile. "Sales always improve during the holidays. Maybe the owners will change their mind?"

But I already knew that was a long shot. Our town's mall had been decaying for years, and one by one stores were being abandoned. Soon I was hit with a head rush of emotion so intense that I almost threw my heart up across the kitchen floor. How could the place where my father introduced me to *Star Wars* and *Titanic* be laid to waste? Where, as a family, we used to watch all the soccer games on the big-screen TVs at the electronics emporium, while he and my mom argued over who made better arroz con leche? The mall was also the home to the thrift store where I'd met Darnell, and the Roller Derby Diner.

In moments like these it had always been my father who saved the day. He would have worn his most elegant three-piece suit, charmed the owners to reconsider, or liberated the whole mall by fearless justice-y force. If it isn't already obvious, all my childhood memories included him as Zorro. But since he was no longer here, I was going to have to be the superhero.

Only problem was, I didn't know how.

My mom made me look her in the eyes. "You have enough going on in your life. You have a scholarship to win." She smiled, fighting tears. "Promise me you won't worry about this."

"I don't make promises I can't keep," I told her as she pulled me in for a hug. My mother was my home, and my compass when I lost my way. Holding her so tightly, I realized that my fantasy of winning the Retro Challenge couldn't just be wishful thinking. It had to be a reality. Because my mother wasn't just crossing her fingers for me anymore; she was betting on me to win. And now this challenge was *definitely* the only way I'd ever make it to college.

Sure, I was devastated to hear that the mall could be demolished by some real estate company—but what those developers didn't realize was that they were trying to buy off our entire town's memories too. And that came at a price bigger than they could have ever imagined.

▶ 21.

"It's Tricky"
—Run-DMC

Ever since we'd gone retro, all our classes had changed as we knew them. It's not like Limbo could make our school change the curriculum, but our teachers modified our lesson plans and gave us special assignments to make the challenge a learning experience. For example, in AP World we spent a lot of time learning about the gender inequalities of the past—how in the nineties not even 12 percent of parliaments worldwide contained women, a number that has since doubled. We even learned about badasses like Frida Kahlo, who championed Mexican heritage through art.

So instead of making PowerPoints, we created political leaflets and developed photos just like the suffragettes would have. So much of the Retro Challenge was about trying to enjoy the nuances of the past, but the past was also a tough place, and now I could connect with their struggles. I felt like part of a little movement of our own.

Like they say, *Stand for something, or you'll fall for anything.*

Because of the bad news, this was definitely going to be one of those days when I'd ask my teacher if I could go to the drinking fountain so I could really just take a tour of the whole school and kill time. Plus, hanging with my new group of friends really helped the time pass. Sometimes I picked them up in the morning, which became the best part of the day. And because we were bored without our phones, we always had the worst/best ideas to make our own fun.

Monday was go through the drive-thru backward.

Tuesday was *Can we go off-roading to get to school?*

Then Wednesday: Let's aggressively scream compliments at random strangers!

While the others ran into a gas station to buy coffee for a coffee-guzzling competition, I stayed in the car. But I wasn't alone, because Axel had decided not to move from the back seat. I couldn't figure out why, until I saw who was filling up their tanks next to us.

Vince and a few of the Goldens were messing around on their motorcycles.

"If you're that afraid of them, I'm happy to stuff you in my trunk and throw away the key."

He laughed it off. "No way. I'm not afraid."

"Then what's the deal? Do you not want to be seen with us?"

Axel didn't respond.

Wow. I was right.

"Unbelievable. Did your parents ever teach you that being different is a strength?"

"My mom is always working, and my father isn't in the picture," he said.

"Oh. Sorry. I didn't know. . . ."

"Don't worry about it. He was an asshole."

"That must be tough. Are you doing okay?" I asked.

"I'm fine. He cheated on my mom and left, so we're better off without him."

I was starting to realize why Axel was so rough around the edges. How he could be such a good guy and a bad boy at the same time. And I found myself feeling bad for him, because we had a lot more in common than I'd expected.

"My father isn't around either," I told him. "He died when I was a kid."

"I'm sorry, Luna. That's a lot worse. At least I get to hate my dad. It's easier that way. . . . You're a badass for going through all that."

"You know, when I lost my dad, I learned that the thing I wanted most was to be a psychologist. That way I could help people get through moments like that. What did you learn?"

Axel went to speak, but no words came out. He couldn't answer that question. And I just wished I could show him that wearing all that arrogance as armor wasn't going to protect him.

Suddenly Axel climbed into the front seat, next to me, where his ex-friends could see him.

"What are you doing?"

"I guess my back was hurting in that old car seat." Axel played it off.

"You know, having feelings doesn't make you less attractive."

"Who says I care if you think I'm attractive?" he teased, but he didn't look away. He just kept staring at me. I didn't look away either. My face was turning fire-hydrant red—and luckily, that's when the rest of our friends came rushing back in the car with, like, a gallon of coffee.

"HEY! AXEL STOLE MY SEAT!" Darnell skated over, dragging him out.

"And now for being tricky you get the middle seat," Mimi joked. "Perfect sandwich between Kilo and me."

We parked at school, but instead of quickly slipping off to class, Axel made a point to stay with us. And when we entered the locker halls, it was like we were walking in protest of all those barriers that told us that we couldn't hang out together. That people so different couldn't be a group. For better or worse, we were turning heads. The Limbo camera crew was following us all the time. There was gossip. Whispers.

Maybe all this would just reinforce Jade's beliefs about Axel and me—and there was nothing I could do about that.

As we passed others who were taking the challenge, we could feel this subtle connection—this camaraderie between us all. A silent understanding.

But things were about to get intense.

"Diana Patel, you are eliminated."

I had just sat at my desk in physics when I heard the voice over the loudspeakers. Not even an hour at school and someone was already facing elimination.

Diana froze in her chair. Silence struck the whole classroom.

Limbo workers entered immediately, followed by a cameraman, ready to take her away.

"My sister's phone kept talking to me! I didn't touch it, I swear!" Diana pleaded as she was escorted out. "Siri did it on her own!"

We all looked at one another. I turned to Miranda, sweating.

"I almost peed myself. It's crazy that Limbo knew."

She shrugged. "Good luck this year, girl. You're going to need it."

And Miranda was right.

Adapting to this ecosystem was going to be harder than we'd imagined.

By the time I got to trig, Darnell was already staging a strike. Our teacher, Mr. Kowalski, who was older than Pythagoras himself, had decreed that we couldn't use calculators.

Darnell marched up to the front of the class.

"Not again," Mr. Kowalski groaned. "Darnell, please take your seat."

Instead, Darnell cleared his throat. "The calculator was invented in 1773 by the German priest and astronomer Philipp Matthäus Hahn—therefore, not using a calculator is an insult, because it totally follows the Retro guidelines."

Kowalski raised a bushy eyebrow. "Are you finished? Can we continue class?"

"Yes. Yes we can." Darnell came back to his desk, and I rolled my eyes at him.

"What? If I wanted to take the caveman challenge, I'd already be half-naked and painting gazelles all over the walls."

"Please keep your pants on," I told him. "They say mental math is good for the brain."

"That's what the Illuminati want you to think," he joked.

Darnell would never know just how much I appreciated his antics that day. I'm sure my classes would have been worse without him, but my teachers didn't make it any easier either. Because the real torture didn't begin until the next period, when our AP Lit teacher dropped a big clumsy hunk of metal on the desk in front of us.

"This"—Ms. Heathrow beamed—"is called a typewriter!"

Mimi and I looked at each other, terrified, because I knew that neither of us had a license to operate heavy machinery. It was like our teachers were punishing us for all the times we complained about uploading papers to the complicated classroom cloud.

"Funny to think how good we used to have it," I said.

Mimi leaned in. "I'm seriously starting to regret that time when I compared my science teacher's DNA to a cow's. He shouldn't be mad. We share eighty percent of their genetic code."

"I guess so," I said, twirling my hair with a pencil, still stressed about the family theater.

"Everything all right, Loony?"

"Yeah. I'm just not so convinced you're human." I recovered and playfully threw a wad of paper at her. Though Mimi didn't buy my bluff.

"I've had way too much caffeine today." She offered the rest of her iced caramel macchiato to me. But that's just how Mimi was. She sensed something was off and wanted me to feel better, in any way possible.

That afternoon, the bell sang out that Pavlovian lunchtime jingle that made me salivate all over my three-ring binder. Just before we got in the lunch line, someone ran into the room, accidentally making people drop their lunch trays. Crashing into every corner of every table.

"Pardon me! Sorry! Excuse me!"

It was Kilo. And he was frantic, scared, and sweating like a rotisserie chicken.

I gasped. "Is that a *smartwatch*? Oh my god, he's wearing a smartwatch!"

"Help me! I fell asleep in class and I don't know what happened!"

Axel pulled Kilo to our table. "Calm down. Start from the beginning. What happened?"

"Last thing I remember, I fell asleep in third period, and then after class I woke up with this thing on my wrist, and the clasp is glued shut!" Kilo panicked. "I didn't know who to go to, so I came to the cafeteria to find you. I knew you all would be here because it's Taco Tuesday."

"Smart," I noted.

"Okay. Kilo, breathe slowly, and repeat after me," Mimi said, sitting him down. "I didn't use this piece of technology or any of the amazing and modern applications that it has."

The smartwatch was still beeping like a time bomb.

"Should I cut it off?" he asked.

"Your entire wrist?!" Mimi yelped.

"NO, JUST THE WATCH! JUST THE WATCH!"

And that's when we heard them from the corner of the room. Because Vince, finally back from his suspension, was with Chad and Juan Solo, dying with laughter.

"Eye for an eye, Kilo," Vince snorted, not realizing that our purple angel had just arrived.

Andy stepped through the cafeteria doors.

"Look what we have here." He motioned to his Limbo grunts, who worked the watch off Kilo's wrist. Andy projected his voice. "Who is the owner of this device?" He held it up to the entire audience. Andy scanned the crowd, scrutinizing people's faces. "Nobody? Okay. You had your chance to do this on good terms. Now, it will be done on my terms."

Andy went straight to the Goldens' table. He sniffed them out, zeroing in on Chad's stubbly face as he dropped the watch on the floor. "You know what they say: 'Time is relative.'" Andy winked at us, smiled, and smashed it with his cane.

"Hey, you can't do that! That's mine!"

"Silly boy. Nobody owns time."

Snickers from the crowd.

And it wasn't long until Limbo's camera team came rushing over to record Retros for our reactions.

Vince was practically growling with rage. "We should smack the grin off your face."

But Andy didn't even blink. It seemed like the Goldens regretted not going retro and were looking for any chance to get in front of the cameras. But they weren't a part of the challenge, so it wasn't going to happen.

Andy turned to Kilo before he left. "You won't be eliminated for this, because it wasn't your fault, but you all need to watch your backs."

We were lucky that Andy was on our side, because that day it became ever more apparent that this wasn't just a challenge.

It was a competition.

▶ 22.

"Ironic"
—Alanis Morissette

When we all left the cafeteria, I could tell Axel was fuming with rage, because he was doing breathing techniques just to not blow a fuse. And once Vince was all alone, Axel made his move. Our lockers weren't far away, so I did that thing where I pretended to listen to music, but in reality, I was overhearing all the juicy drama.

"You guys are pathetic, you know that?" Axel said.

"*We're* pathetic? What about the new friends you're hanging out with?"

"At least they didn't sabotage my car. They didn't tamper with my brakes and try to kill me."

Vince shut his locker. This had his attention. "Wait, someone did something to your brakes?"

"Don't play dumb. After that stunt you just pulled, I feel like I don't know you anymore."

Vince laughed, then realized it wasn't a joke. "You really think I messed with your brakes? Wow. First you turn your back on your friends; then you accuse them of trying to kill you. . . ."

"Don't play the victim. Just leave us alone, okay?"

"You wish," Vince muttered, then disappeared into the crowd.

I didn't know what was freakier, the thought that Vince and his friends had put a target on our backs, or that maybe someone we didn't even know was willing to tamper with Axel's brakes and put him in harm's way.

Life as a contestant wasn't going to be easy, especially when people were trying to sabotage us, but there also were some unexpected positive surprises as well. Something that happened one day before school, turning my bitter week nice and sweet.

I saw multicolored necklaces on people's chests, peppered throughout the parking lot. But rather than fashion accessories, they were far more meaningful than any jewel. Because around their necks were little neon whistles.

Just like the one I wore that Samantha had sent to me.

Axel and Kilo were carrying a massive box, with a little group of students circling around them. Darnell held a sign that read CHEER SAMANTHA ON! Axel smiled warmly when he saw me approaching.

"Did you organize all of this?"

"Kilo did most of the heavy lifting."

Axel high-fived Kilo, who warned me, "I just needed a good workout." Which was a lie, because he was clearly still in "friend denial."

"Whatever you say, Kilo." I smiled.

He went off to pass out more whistles, leaving me and Axel to sit on the hood of his Mustang together. Axel touched the whistle on my chest. "I don't think I have to offer you one, because you've got the original, right there."

I was moved that he'd actually remembered my story and cared enough to take it a step further. Axel was really trying to change—or maybe he was just finally showing his true self. It was crazy to think that just the month prior, in the same high school cafeteria, everyone had stood idly by while a girl was destroyed—but at least now we were rallying around her.

"If Samantha was here, she would've loved this," I told him.

"Or she would have painted the whistle orange so it would match her backpack."

"I wouldn't expect less from the queen of fashion." We both chuckled fondly. Samantha wasn't perfect, but she sure tried to be.

"I miss the sound of these things. Whistles always meant game time. I loved that." He'd been a quarterback before he was an influencer.

"I know how you feel. I miss playing soccer," I confessed. "I know this is my new competition, but I miss my team."

"At least you didn't get kicked off the team, like I did," Axel said.

"You'd be surprised." I laughed off the pain. "So, what did you do?"

"I missed a ton of practice because of all the Limbo events I went to, and then I almost burned the field and bleachers down doing a challenge."

"Oh my god, that was you? We ended up training in the dance room for a month."

"Guilty." He laughed. "So, what about you, rebel girl? What did you do?"

"It was my punishment for uploading that video of Samantha. For being a terrible friend."

"You're a good friend who made a terrible mistake," he said sincerely.

And that meant a lot to me.

"Looks like we're both pretty impulsive . . . The way I see it, at least now you're competing for something much larger than before. Plus, look on the bright side. Now you get to hang with an awesome guy like me."

"DING DING DING!" I called. "Oh, sorry, that was my douchebag alarm."

"My bad," he chuckled. "I'm new at this."

"I'll give you a pass, but just because what you did with these whistles was really sweet, and really thoughtful. And I really appreciate it."

"So showing my emotions is working on you . . . ?"

But before I could respond, I realized a cameraman was creeping over my shoulder. "¡Por Dios! ¡Quítamelo!" I screamed.

"Seriously?" Axel said to the Limbo worker.

For legal purposes, Limbo was only allowed to film contestants, but they went overboard in adhering to that directive by filming as much as they could. Supposedly, Limbo was uploading new content every day. It's not like I could see it, but it was out there. Which totally blew my mind.

Suddenly Mimi jumped on my back like a sloth, half tackling me to the ground. Then Miranda caught up and pulled her off with a laugh.

"Hi, Axel," Miranda said, trying a little too hard to play it cool. "I'm Miranda."

"Nice to meet you."

"The Goldens are throwing a big Halloween party this weekend. Are you guys coming?"

Darnell skated over. "Haven't you heard? Retros aren't invited. Apparently, the location is a geo pin drop, so you can only find it with a smartphone."

Axel rolled his eyes. "Which excludes us. Well, who cares?"

The Goldens sat atop their motorcycles—happy to have blacklisted the Retros from their party. I could feel Jade's eyes, like daggers in my back. They didn't know it yet, but the balance of power at El Dorado was about to change.

I went to the bathroom before class, and that's when she hit me. Well, bumped into me, but I knew it was intentional. It was just me and Jade alone in the restroom.

"Oh, thank you," I said to Jade. "I needed to wake up."

"You know, you have such an attitude. You should talk less."

"I can try, but neither my mom nor my doctors have been able to shut me up."

"You better find a way, because you're getting on my nerves. I know things about you."

"Really? How did you know I love to pop pimples?"

Jade stepped dangerously close. "I'm serious, Luna."

What the hell does she know?

Jade wasn't playing.

"I don't know what you're talking about," I told her.

Jade got in front of me so that I couldn't leave the bathroom. I was alone, and she could do whatever she wanted. "Samantha was my friend."

"She was mine, too," I protested.

"You weren't a real friend."

"And you were? Because I know you and the Goldens shared that video all over Limbo," I retorted. "You didn't stop the cyber-bullying. You made it worse!"

"At least I didn't start it!"

I gasped.

She grinned.

"You're the one who sent me the creepy text."

Her icy glare was my confirmation.

"You're the person who spray-painted the threat on the lockers." Now my anxiety was really kicking in. I felt like the neck of my T-shirt was choking me. *What would happen if everyone knew my secret?*

"That video was filmed in Samantha's room. She only let two people inside. And I know you were one of them. The girl from the photo in her locker," Jade explained bitterly.

"You're upset that she kept a photo of me in her locker, and not you?"

"Don't push me, Luna."

"So why haven't you posted about it on Limbo yet? Why haven't you told the world? You could've destroyed me if you wanted to."

"You're not worth my precious time."

"Sure, but there has to be a deeper reason, Jade."

"Taking you down would have been the last thing Samantha would want. At the end of the day, we don't need two broken girls at this school," Jade said, fixing me with a stare. "One was too many."

I didn't know if I should've been terrified that Jade had the power to destroy me or comforted by the fact that she hadn't done it yet. And suddenly I realized that this wasn't only about Axel. It was about Samantha. About what I did.

Then the Limbo jingle chimed out over the school loud-speakers.

"Better go before you lose your challenge," Jade taunted, striding off.

I was struck with both excitement and panic. That jingle let everyone know it was time to pull out their phones and watch more content about the challenge—but for the Retros it meant that today, people were going to be eliminated.

⏸ 23.

Pause

"¡CABRÓN!" My voice echoes in the empty cell.

I always said that I'd never kill another living creature in cold blood. But if there's one thing I can't stand, it's a mosquito. That's why I scream and kill them the first chance I get.

Whatever to pass the time. I'm losing hope.

I've never been locked away before, not even in an elevator. I miss all those day-to-day pleasures of my old life. The taste of my father's chilaquiles verdes transporting me back to summers I spent in Xochimilco, when we'd float on the boats and listen to the music of the mariachis. The simple things, like putting on a two-hour movie only to finish the snacks in a minute and twenty-five seconds.

Wait.

Mosquitos being here means there's another opening to my solitary confinement. My first and only stroke of genius. Now I'm patting down the walls; I need to find a weak spot, something,

No luck. Unless . . . this bug must have come through an opening in the ceiling! So I jostle loose one of the panels, and light finally pours inside, warming my cold little cell.

I peer through, finding an air vent that leads to the outside world. And what I see is a place that feels so familiar, I can't believe I'm here. I've been in this place before.

And now I just want to scream.

▶ 24.

"One More Time"
—Daft Punk

Each week the contestants met in the Retro Lounge to participate in a new challenge. And each week more of us have been eliminated and filmed for content. This week I scanned the crowd with one important question knotting in my brain:

"Who do you think was the other person who sent a video to Limbo's help center?" I asked Mimi.

Not knowing was driving me crazy. And I needed a new distraction. Luckily, there was plenty of that to go around. Today we were given access to exclusive products that hadn't even hit the market yet, and merchandise that had long since been pulled off the shelves—all to make our experience that much cooler.

Phosphorescent soda flavors.

Retro shoes that lit up when you walked.

Chips that tasted like nothing I had ever heard of before.

Whenever Andy snapped, the Limbo team would bring out whatever our hearts desired. He was the Willy Wonka of Retroland, but in a way, he really felt like one of us. He would even ask us questions about how much we liked the cool new gear. He really cared.

"Products like this were wildly popular back in the day, and no one has access to them anymore, except you." Andy opened his arms like a showman.

Axel licked flaming-hot something off his fingers.

No detail was overlooked. The Retro Lounge was decked out with sprawling streamers and dazzling laser lights. And as usual, the camera crews were there, documenting everything.

"Sit still so we can get a close-up," they would tell us.

"Can we get a shot of you on the roller skates?"

"Smile for the camera and tell us what your strategy is to win!"

The colors dimmed, and behind the scenes, we could see Limbo workers bustling about. Something big was happening today.

Andy was sitting on an old Pac-Man arcade game in the center of the room. He cleared his throat. "I have a question for you. How many hours per day do you think the average person your age spends in front of a screen?"

The crowd shouted out, taking guesses.

"Five!"

"Maybe three!"

"I think it's seven!"

Andy shook his head and smiled, almost apologetically. "The answer is thirteen. Most of us spend thirteen hours in front of a screen per day. These days screens are so powerful, they can save lives, but they can also take them." He paused, scanning the room. "And they can also cost you the scholarship of your dreams."

Andy pointed his cane. "Greg McDaniels," he announced,

like a prosecutor before a jury. Limbo guards closed in on the student. "Today during lunch, you broke the rules. And, if I may add, you were looking at quite the naughty website."

"But—I was in the bathroom!"

The entire room erupted into muffled giggles . . . and then fear crept in.

Andy didn't flinch. He motioned, and his grunts pulled the boy from the crowd. "We know exactly where you were."

"But . . . but . . . how could you have known?"

"You'd have to be pretty obtuse to break the rules at school. Look around you—we have a full team supervising this challenge, monitoring if any of your devices are being used."

Clearly, if you wanted to outsmart a tech giant, you definitely shouldn't piss on their territory, and that included the bathrooms of El Dorado High.

"One more down," Darnell said.

Kosta leaned over to us. "You know how three people got eliminated this week? I heard they're doing random lie detector tests now, and they caught someone with a second phone."

"The Goldens are trying to get us eliminated left and right," Kilo warned. "Also, we can't prove it, but we think they cut the hoses and tampered with the brakes of Axel's car."

"Whoa. That's intense," another Retro said, a girl in a headscarf named Nika. Someone I recognized as the smartest girl at school. Nika continued, "Things are getting pretty serious. The other night after school I heard creepy noises in the halls. Like strange voices. I didn't know if it was someone trying to get us disqualified or not, but I was ready to call 911."

"That's so weird," I said.

"Maybe it's the Goldens' next plan of attack. Be careful. None of us are safe," she added.

Andy waved goodbye as the eliminated boy was hauled off, and then he whistled and strolled over to the big bulletin board that acted like a real-time feed. Each contestant had their photo posted so we could track who was still in the game. Then Andy pulled a red marker from his pocket and crossed out Greg's smiling face.

I was thrilled. Nervous. Of fifty-something people, fifteen had been eliminated.

"Congratulations to all of you who have made it this far. It's been around a month since the challenge began. Consider yourselves winners of the first leg. And to reward you for your success today, you will all receive a very special gift."

The Limbo aides entered and started passing around little platinum boxes. When I finally got mine, I lifted the lid to reveal one of the most badass things we had received yet: a holographic Casio G-Shock watch, made custom for the challenge.

It glimmered in the light. The words PROPERTY OF LIMBO were engraved on the back of the watch.

"These aren't just to congratulate you for making it this far, but also to test a new line of retro items. We want you to wear them and give us feedback! Don't worry, the technology isn't new!"

Now that we didn't have our phones, I had to be more accountable when it came to meeting up with people. There was no *let's hang out soon* and then never getting together. There was no room for last-minute flaking, or texting *leaving now* when you were really just getting in the shower. Without my clock app, I was running late to everything, so a watch was going to be super convenient for us— and, apparently, to Limbo's marketing department.

"This is so sick." I showed mine to Kilo.

"They better let us keep these watches when this is all over!" Darnell added.

"I know, right?" Mimi tried hers on and smiled. "I love it when people whisper sweet nothings into my ear. Like 'it's Friday,' or 'it's free.'"

"You should always be wearing these. Always," Andy emphasized. "The watches will not only help others know who is taking the challenge, but it will help you identify the contestants among yourselves. As you've experienced, some people are going to be jealous. They'll try to get you eliminated." Andy playfully messed up Kilo's black hair. "But what's most important is that you stick together and get to know one another."

Then he pointed to the Live Feed—where people could write questions and post comments. With so many faces tacked up, the wall was a massive presence that stared back at us.

"WELCOME TO YOUR NEXT CHALLENGE! This week's challenge is about truth." Andy scanned the smiling faces on the wall and settled on the photo of a girl with long loc'ed hair—Ruby. Then he pulled off a card that was tacked to the wall and handed it to her. "Back before social media feeds, you had to ask your questions in person. So today, your peers have physically posted theirs to the Live Feed wall. Whatever you answer, it must be the truth, or you'll be eliminated," Andy warned, heading for the exit. "Good luck . . ."

▶ 25.

"It's My Life"
—Bon Jovi

The double doors slammed shut, and as soon as he was gone, all
eyes redirected toward the person standing in the center of the
faintly lit room.

The girl with the beautiful locs.

"Hi . . . everyone. Let's do this," she said, playing nervously
with her hair, and read the anonymous question from the little
slip of paper. "'Ruby, why are you doing this challenge if you
don't even have plans to go to college?'"

"Okay. Well . . . my name is Ruby Delgado, which is a little
ironic because Delgado means 'skinny.' A paradox that caused a
lot of bullying. But why should I be punished for not following
the beauty standard just because the rest of the world decided
I should? Maybe I don't want to show all my ribs. Life is not a
barbecue restaurant."

Some people blew their new whistles around their necks to
show support.

"Back in sixth grade, I used to get teased for my size. There
were certain people who were worse than others, but most of

the flak came from the Goldens." She focused on Axel.

He looked down—too ashamed to meet her sharp gaze.

"There was one girl who might not have been the worst of them, but let's say she wasn't the best. She caused me so many hours of counseling. So many lost moments of happiness. So much free time to think about revenge, so when the moment came, I did something as despicable as those who bullied me."

The crowd was silent. Some people looked away, stricken with guilt, while others faced her with compassion. Axel couldn't bear to take his face out of his hands. The whole room was enveloped by a paralyzing wave of discomfort.

"I was one of the ones who recorded a video of Samantha that day in the cafeteria. Remember that Limbo video with the pizza filter? The one that read 'puts out for pizza'? Well, I made that one. And now I feel like the worst person in the world. I'm not going to college next year, so I don't even *have* to win this thing. I just wanted to win myself back."

When she finished, all the Retros blew their whistles in applause. Ruby walked off, her head held higher than before, and went to the board, pulling a card tacked to a certain influencer's photo.

Axel squirmed in his seat.

"I'm sure your life is more interesting than mine," Ruby said wryly.

He smiled to the crowd as he took Ruby's place. Being the center of attention seemed to fit him so naturally.

"'Axel, what secrets do you know about Limbo?'" he read aloud, then paused thoughtfully. "Well . . . years back, Facebook introduced the like button after studies showed it spiked high levels of dopamine in users' brains, like a drug. And Limbo took that technology to the next level. It's why we check our phones like a hundred times a day."

"SPEAK YOUR TRUTH!" Darnell shouted, which drew laughs from the crowd, including from Axel, who grew in fervor.

"The kids of these tech companies don't go to normal schools with computers. They go to low-tech private schools, completely isolated from the outside world. Smartphones aren't even allowed in their homes. Because they know the truth."

Once he had gotten on a roll, it was like he couldn't talk fast enough.

"It only took me five years of dangerous pranks to realize that fact. I feel like I'm an addict and a drug at the same time. It's true that no one forced me to be an influencer. It was my decision. But—I guess I feel like I don't have any control over who I am," he confessed. "And what more can I do than take this challenge?"

When his speech finished, the entire room cheered. We were surprised that those emotions had been dormant inside him all along. The perfect cool guy.

Mimi leaned over. "I didn't know he felt that way."

"I always thought he lived this perfect life," I said.

"I guess everyone has their problems."

Axel walked to the Live Feed, scanned the pictures, and stopped before one that I knew well. A photo taken last summer, when life was so much simpler and far less adventurous. He yanked off a little strip of paper and locked eyes with me. I had known instinctively that he was going to pull my name— whether it was just to put me on the spot, or to give me the opportunity I needed to spill my heart, I was going to be exposed for the world to see.

Axel handed me the question. "Don't worry. If you get overwhelmed, just find me in the crowd. You'll have my silent support—I promise." It gave me comfort. I felt protected, knowing he was there.

So I made my way to the center of the dimly lit room, a living projection of what it would be like to exist in your very own feed. But in this reality, there was no delete button. No time to think up the perfect line. There were dozens of people out in the crowd and even more watching the stream on Limbo, but all I could see were the blinking lights of the pinball machines.

As my mom would say, I was sweating like a pork.

I cleared my throat. "'Luna, you're the girl who stood up for Samantha that day in the cafeteria. You seem so courageous, but what are you afraid of?'"

I swallowed down a dry lump.

"Come on, Luna, you got this!" Darnell cheered me on.

"Well, 'courageous' is a tricky word. Most of you don't know this, because I guess I've never talked about it in public before, but . . . I have anxiety."

Deep breaths, Luna. Deep breaths.

"Like, I'm anxious right now, but I'm learning how to not let it take control. I can learn to live *with* it. Like, I think I've failed every school presentation for getting so nervous that I start to imagine everyone is in their underwear to be less intimidated, and then I feel creepy, so I spend the rest of the presentation trying to subconsciously convince you all that I'm not a perv."

Chuckles from the crowd gave me a little more fuel to carry

on. "So, being courageous doesn't mean you're not terrified, or not anxious. I guess it just means you go ahead and do it anyway. But to answer your question about what I'm afraid of, it's the thought of losing my family. I already lost my dad. And now I think I'm going to lose my mother. The Monteverde Mall is going to be sold off and torn down, along with my family's theater. And if that happens, my mother will be stripped of her work visa. She'll be deported; I won't be able to sponsor her until I'm twenty-one. But only if I'm very successful. Which is why winning this challenge will be the biggest step toward keeping my family."

Mimi stepped forward, shocked. "What? Your family is losing the theater? Please, tell me that's not true, Luna! This can't be happening. . . ."

"We have to save the mall!" Darnell said.

"I practically grew up in that theater," Ruby said, "only I didn't know it was yours. I can't tell you how many scary movies me and my sister used to sneak into."

"My boyfriend and I had our first kiss there," Asha, from my debate team, said.

"I used to eat popcorn until I barfed!" someone else added. "Actually, I still do!"

I laughed through watery eyes, moved that other people had a connection to the one thing that represented my family. Soon other Retros stood up, telling stories of how our little theater had touched their lives. As they spoke, a kernel of an idea began to take form inside me. An answer to the dilemma my mother and I faced that morning when she held me in her arms. This was the beginning of a plan. But making it happen was going to mean breaking some rules.

▶ 26.

"One Way or Another"
—Blondie

I used to be an impossible hyperactive monster. When I was a kid, you couldn't pay me enough gummy bears to sit still. And forcing me to take a nap was like trying to baptize a stray cat. I even used to eat crayons in class—my favorite flavor being the delicious green ones. But I was just understimulated, testing kilometers beyond my kindergarten cohort. So when my teachers moved me up a grade, I kicked and screamed and tried to hex them with thumbtacks and stuffed animals.

Because I would be the youngest in my grade forever. And that sucked.

But one day my mother sat me down and said something I would never forget: *It's better to be the tail of a lion than the head of a mouse.* Because the mouse asks, *What will happen to me?* But the lion asks, *What am I going to do about it?* Which was exactly where my mind flashed back to during the Live Feed challenge.

And that's how I hatched my plan to save the mall.

Every year, the Goldens would throw a big Halloween party at one of their mansions, where they invited the people they deemed worthy. And this year, none of them were Retros. Taking the challenge apparently made you persona non grata to the Goldens.

But not all that glitters is gold.

And we were ready to prove that to them—only bigger and better.

The one problem with my plan was that it was risky and could get us in a lot of trouble, because it involved breaking into El Dorado High in the middle of the night, just a few days before Halloween.

My friends and I had all thrown on dark clothes and whatever ski masks we could find—except Mimi.

"Why are you wearing your mother's pantyhose over your face?" I asked her as we snuck into the parking lot.

"I told you, Loony—it's to hide my iconic pink hair!"

"You look scary," I teased.

Even Ruby had come along. We all huddled to game-plan the break-in.

"Thanks for agreeing to do this," I said. "You're seriously all the best ever. De corazón."

"It's . . . our pleasure . . . but um, Luna," Darnell said, "why is your turtleneck covered in needles?"

I sighed. "After my first period my mom freaked out, and she planted a cactus outside my window so I couldn't sneak out to see boys. But it's okay—I'm used to the pain."

They all laughed in the face of my misery.

I think I would've found it funnier if it hadn't been true.

"Did you bring the supplies?" Axel asked, black paint smeared under his eyes.

"I've got it all right here." I patted my backpack, feeling inspired by the suffragettes who had to sneak into town at night just to hang political signs. My history teacher mandated that we use an old printing press, so Ruby and I had put it to good use, even if it was for our own purposes—even if we were going to hang up enormous, unapproved banners all over school.

I pulled the heavy rolled-up posters from my trunk. "All right. The mission: banners at the entrance of each building. Posters on every wall you see. No matter the color, shape, or size. First, we hit the lockers. Then the science building. Last, we take on the bathrooms!"

"The people that made history were the courageous ones who never calculated the risks—so that's exactly how we're going to be," Darnell said.

Because we were on a mission.

We were going to give everyone the opportunity to go retro for one night. Where every store from the arcade to the thrift shop would be open all night and filled with new customers, so maybe we could keep those lights of the mall on for a little bit longer. A retro night, open to all, that would outshine any exclusive Halloween party.

And tonight, we were doing some guerrilla promoting with our signs.

Soon we were on the move, sneaking through the bushes around the perimeter of the school. But just before we stormed the campus, a muscly school security guard in a tight shirt rounded the corner.

"What happens if we get caught?" Kilo asked.

"They'll chop us up and feed us to the freshmen. What else

do you think they put in the cafeteria burritos?" Axel joked.

"Don't worry—this security guard works less than Tarzan's tailor." Darnell licked his lips.

"Well, I'm glad that he doesn't leave much to the imagination. Grrrrrrrr," Mimi growled, clawing at the air like a wild animal. It was genuinely amusing how fast she could make the tough guys in the group uncomfortable.

Axel leaned into me. "Breaking into school . . . you're not such a good girl after all."

"I haven't paired my socks in three years. You tell me."

Once Axel went off to make sure the coast was clear, Mimi yanked me aside. Then slapped me in the face.

"HEY!"

"Sorry. I had to make sure you weren't dreaming."

"I'M NOT, MIMI."

"Fine. But I see how you and Axel are looking at each other."

"I don't think we're each other's type."

"Type? Geez. It's not like you're going to donate your blood to him." Mimi giggled. "Here. I'll make it easy: try to see dating like interviewing the father of your future dog. If you can see the potential, then you know the guy is a good fit."

I looked at Axel as she spoke, for the first time really considering it. Just the thought made my heart flutter. It felt good. Maybe too good.

Until he caught me staring. "Earth to Luna! Are you okay?"

"Oh, um. Yeah. I'm great," I said, like an awkward stupid human.

"Okay, well, the coast is clear! Come on!"

• • •

We followed Axel to the school's fence, where Kilo boosted us over. I was already out of breath by the time I scaled it. It wasn't easy with the giant banners. I couldn't tell if I was really out of shape, or just coursing with adrenaline. Then Ruby, who'd jammed the lock earlier that day with a huge wad of gum, yanked the door open, leading us into the main halls.

"Who knew after hours at school could be so freaking exciting?" I said to Mimi.

"Last time I was here so late was for detention. So unfair!"

"Mimi, what did you expect? You called Mrs. Perry a *muggle*!"

"What? She is!"

We settled by the lockers, and I hung our magnificent art across the halls of El Dorado High. Old-school posters, converted into modern-day marketing. There were Coca-Cola-style ads but full of color, casting aside the nuclear-white smiles of the "good old days." We made Uncle Sam posters with an Afro and shades. *We can do it!* ads with Rosie the Riveter flipping you off instead of flexing—all advertising our retro Halloween night at the mall. Promising a DJ, bands, and shopping sales until sunrise. And Ruby had created all the awesome designs.

"Your talent is pretty badass," I told Ruby before wandering down the hallway. But then, while I was putting posters up in the locker halls, Kilo came racing out of the darkness toward me, with a perturbed look on his face.

"Did you hear that?" he asked.

"Hear what?"

"Strange noises, by the science building, just like Nika was talking about. It sounded like chatter in the hall. Like a thousand voices at once. I feel like I'm going crazy."

"Don't tell me you believe in ghosts—a tough guy with a tough tattoo like yours." I slugged his arm playfully, but in reality it just hurt my hand. "Maybe someone left a computer on."

"I could have sworn I heard something."

"Maybe you just have low blood sugar."

"Right. Maybe I need to eat another Twinkie." And then my ears were assaulted by the crinkliest, loudest, and most annoying of sounds as he unwrapped the little treat.

"What?" he asked, mouth full.

"Why are all the foods you want to eat quietly wrapped in the noisiest plastic?" He shared a bite with me. "Life is so unfair, isn't it?"

I was realizing with Kilo, it was the simple moments that we treasured most. He was sweet, whether he liked it or not. And although he relaxed a little as we talked, I was growing nervous. Because if he'd heard those mysterious noises too, then it meant they could be real. And nothing good could ever be happening at El Dorado High at this time of night.

The next strange thing that night wasn't what we heard, but what we saw. I found Axel outside the bathrooms, motionless.

"Hey, is everything all right?"

"*Shh*," he said, pointing across the hall. "There's someone in the men's bathroom."

We walked closer to investigate, fluorescent lights flickering overhead.

Then we heard shattering glass.

"What the hell is going on in there?"

It was like the labored wheezing of a wounded animal.

Shadows moved underneath the door. Out of reflex Axel stepped in front of me, but I could tell his heart was pounding. And I didn't blame him—I wanted to hide under a blanket, even though if a serial killer came, it's not like he would say, *Oh crap, she has a blanket. I should leave.* But it always made me feel safer.

We finally reached the men's bathroom door—and only then, in that moment, did I realize that I had been holding on to Axel's arm.

I could hear footsteps—human ones—which ruled out my favorite theory about a raccoon eating toilet paper.

Then the door swung open.

I saw the one person who I would have never wanted to be alone with in the middle of the night. The one who had inflicted so much pain in our past.

Vince towered over us, his skin sweaty and blanched of all color. He was gripping his black-and-yellow wrestling team bag so tight I expected his knuckles to bleed.

What the hell was he doing at school in the middle of the night?

Vince spit, wiped his mouth, and smiled. "Is this a getaway for the lovebirds? Just so you know, the girls' bathroom is a better place to hook up. Always smells better. Trust me."

I let go of Axel's arm like it was contagious.

As cool as Vince tried to play it, something was clearly not right with him. His eyes were sunken in. He swayed, hardly able to stand.

"Are you okay, man?" Axel asked, reaching out for him.

Vince smacked him away. "Don't touch me. What's wrong with you people? What are you doing here so late?"

"I think we could ask you the same question," I said.

Vince had a secret of his own.

He ripped one of our Uncle Sam posters off the wall. "What a joke. You seriously think anyone is going to come to some lame mall party?"

He went to leave, but I stopped him.

"What's your problem with me?" I asked. "What is it? That I was friends with Samantha? Or is it that now Axel has gone retro, no one is giving you the attention you crave?"

"You've made Axel join your retro freak show. I don't know what kind of witchcraft you used on him, but I don't trust you. I don't like you. And I know you're hiding something."

He ripped off another poster, crumpled it up like a gorilla, and marched off.

"Vince is my problem," Axel said. "Please, don't worry about him."

"I won't," I lied.

And then, in the doorway, Axel's body stiffened.

Because in that faintly lit bathroom was a row of broken mirrors. The glass was shattered, as if Vince had tried to destroy his own reflection. It gave me the chills.

Breaking into school hadn't gone exactly as planned. But beyond the creepy noises and the strange interaction with Vince, the craziest thing was yet to come . Because just before leaving campus, we realized that something was wrong.

"It's like Mimi's just vanished," Darnell whispered.

Kilo threw open doors left and right. "She's not in the arts building."

"Let's split up," Axel decided.

I took to the first-floor women's bathroom and kicked open each stall. "Mimi?" I called.

Had she been caught? Or worse, maybe she'd bumped into Vince.

However, I finally found her in the locker hall, standing in the shadows, completely frozen, with this strange look on her face that I couldn't decode.

"What is it?" I asked, approaching carefully.

But Mimi didn't respond. I followed her eyeline to the rainbow row of lockers that stared back at us in the bleak moonlight. I scanned them as fast as I could. The locker that Mimi stood across from wasn't hers. A familiar orange lock hung on a locker I knew well.

Samantha Darby.

The ground zero of our stories.

She was coming back. Her locker had been emptied out, but now she was reconquering her territory. And I had a feeling that she wasn't going to return the same ponytailed princess I once knew. Because no one rises from the ashes of their past without the scars of their story.

▶ 27.

"La Isla Bonita"
—Madonna

Friday after school, my friends and I headed straight to the mall to get everything ready. I made sure to not stay too late on campus because those strange voices that Kilo and Nika had heard still freaked me out. Also, there was the thought of Samantha coming back. After everything, I was elated and terrified to look her in the eyes. And lastly there was my mother, and the hope that if our event was successful, maybe the mall would finally be seen as something worth holding on to. And just the idea made me so nervous my vagina wanted to go to the bathroom every hour.

"Tonight will be *reeeally* exciting!" I told Mimi.

"No judgments."

"No guest list."

"And you don't even have to tag the prince of Dubai to get a VIP ticket!" Darnell joked.

As long as you went retro, you were welcome. And maybe if enough people showed up, we could convince the owners to not sell the mall just yet. That it wasn't some dying relic. The mall cops agreed to look the other way, because if this place closed, they'd lose their jobs too.

We had high expectations for this event to be a success, because many of the stores had agreed to stay open all night—but my mom's theater wasn't one of them.

For her, all of this was going to be a total surprise.

I didn't know how I was going to plan a party for hundreds of people if I could never manage how much rice to make for one person—because I always ended up making enough in case the entire Lakers stadium decided to drop by for dinner at the last second.

The crew and I huddled around the mock Roman fountain in the atrium, and I got straight to it. "Kilo, you're the tallest, so you can take care of the streamers and all the string lights. Axel, make sure Nika and her DJ booth and light show are ready by sundown. And, Mimi, please help Ruby set up her tattoo booth. We only have a few hours to prepare, so let's kill it! Thank you, guys. Seriously. I love you more than drama and nachos."

Mimi unzipped a backpack overflowing with bags of red powder. "I have the magic formula for success! I'm going to pour cherry Kool-Aid into this fountain!"

"You're kidding, right?" I said.

But Kilo high-fived her. "Ambitious, I like it."

"That's my little unicorn!" Darnell added.

I sighed, realizing I was going to lose this battle. "I'm too nervous about the party to even think about how unsanitary that sounds," I said, because who was I to crush Mimi's dreams?

"I have a surprise too." Darnell smiled. "I'll be right back."

He reemerged, sporting a fake fur coat, a crop top, and a

bloody axe through his head and striking a pose in the open doors of the nearby thrift shop. "What? I'm a fashion victim."

We all cracked up.

"Can't wait to find a vampire to bite this juicy body." Darnell had worked out a promotional deal with Sequin's Thrift—we could borrow whatever we wanted for the night, so long as we acted as walking advertisements for the store. We scoured the aisles for finishing touches to our costumes.

Kilo threw on a black vest for his Kiss outfit, I was going as a Day of the Dead Catrina pinup girl with a flower in my hair, but Mimi beat us all.

She was a bloody pink Furby.

Then Darnell painted a lightning bolt on Axel's face and found a light blue suit to transform him into David Bowie. And as I slipped into a skintight corset, I caught Axel staring from the next aisle over.

"Girl, if he keeps that up he is going to sprain his neck," Mimi joked with me.

"I guess most guys will stare at anything that has boobs."

"Including mannequins."

I pulled down my top a little more. Maybe I wanted him to keep staring.

Maybe I liked it.

Darnell busted out the goods. "Who's ready to paint their nails?"

"Do guys even do that?" Axel asked. "It seems girly."

That's when Kilo leapt over. "Did someone say nail painting? Like a rock star! I'll do it. Where do you keep the black eyeliner?"

"You know the scientific community says that it's not possible to put eyeliner on without opening your mouth?" Darnell added.

Mimi laughed. "I can verify that!"

But I was still stuck on Axel's comment. "'Girly'? Are you taking the challenge too seriously, or are you just from the eighteenth century?"

"I'm not trying to judge or anything," Axel said honestly. "I just never imagined myself painting my nails." He looked embarrassed, but he was cute when he squirmed. Immediately after, he extended his hands. "Me first!" Axel declared, in a change of heart.

Darnell slugged him in the arm. "Wait your turn, pretty boy."

"Whatever. Just paint my nails," Axel laughed.

While everyone else finalized their costumes, I looked out the atrium sunroof. As the sun shied away from the earth, my excitement waned with it. It was getting late, and no one had shown up. Mimi looked at her holographic Retro watch. Worry crept in.

I kicked a stray balloon. "Maybe Vince was right, and no one wants to come to some stupid mall party."

"Don't say that," Kilo scolded lightly. "Vince is *never* right."

"I guess I'm just stressed out," I said.

"'Stressed' is 'desserts' spelled backward," Mimi said. "Here, take some chocolate." She reached into her backpack.

"I love that thing. It has everything we need inside."

"Yeah, I normally use it to transport my iguana, Juanita."

"That's so rad you have an iguana!" Kilo said, stars in his eyes.

I halted, mid-chew, just thinking that what I was eating had shared oxygen with a reptile.

"Luna, this is going to work," Axel said. "You and your family deserve some good luck."

But what happened next shocked all of us.

Within moments, the first people started to appear. Behind them came another group, and another—until droves began rolling in through the mouth of the Monteverde Mall. I inched closer to the door, and when I peered through the opening, I was thunderstruck.

In the distance was an army of hundreds storming the parking lot—clad in headbands and bell-bottoms, brandishing tattoos and roller skates, wielding not phones but Game Boys, even if it was just for one night.

They all looked like Retros.

People who weren't taking the challenge, or beholden to any rules—and although they had no chance to win any scholarship prize, they joined in because they wanted to.

These people were something totally new.

Retromaniacs.

I was flipping out.

Mimi grabbed me. "Punch me in the kidney. Do it! I've been practicing astral projection in my sleep, and I have to make sure this isn't a hallucination."

"Believe it!" Darnell laughed, spinning her around on his skates.

Even Kilo was dumbfounded.

I hardly knew any of the Retromaniacs. They must have come from different schools in different towns. Different grades. From totally different cultural backgrounds. Had word really spread that far outside El Dorado? Did that many people want to ride our retro wave?

And then I saw a familiar face.

She clung to the carousel—because Axel had set it to three times normal speed. Her neon aerobics instructor costume and puffy hair were amazing. Then she jumped off, dizzy, and almost fell into the plastic ficus. A smile erupted across Miranda's face.

"Luna! Word spreads fast, doesn't it?"

"Wait, all these people—this was your doing?"

Miranda raised her phone. "Remember this?" She winked. "I made a public group on Limbo and uploaded images of some of those posters you put up around school. Everyone is sharing it! The Retro Challenge videos are blowing up on Limbo!" Her brow softened. "We can't lose your theater! I'm sorry you're going through all of this."

"Miranda, you're an average-sized friend with a supersized heart!" I hugged her.

It was so incredible to see social media being used the way it was intended, to connect people—a much-needed reminder of all the good that was out there. And I was so thankful that Limbo could make all of this possible.

"Wait, do you smell that?" I asked Miranda.

"Oh my god, Luna, it smells like smoke!"

I raced past the karaoke booths and took to the escalators, two steps at a time. "Excuse me! Pardon me!" I screamed. After cresting the second floor, I finally caught sight of the chaos— what looked like a million people all circled around the theater.

I broke the glass of the fire extinguisher and ripped it out, ready for the worst. But as I pushed through the crowd, I realized this wasn't a grease fire—no, for the first time in history, the theater employees were overwhelmed with business, and the old popcorn machines were struggling to keep up, puffing out smoke in the process. This was no panicked crowd; it was a line of eager theatergoers!

"Wait, what . . . ," I gasped. "I can't believe it!"

A high-pitched scream penetrated my eardrums, and it was pure luck that I didn't spin around and spray the whole fire extinguisher on her.

"Pero . . . pero . . . ¡¿*Qué* es esto?! What is all this?!"

"¡Mamá! ¡*Sorpresa!*"

She held her chest, hyperventilating. She clutched a gumball machine, her legs already giving out. But this was to be expected. My mother was so full of love that her heart could burst if pushed to the limit. When I was a baby and said my first words, she nearly fainted, even if I was just saying that my ass was full of caca. She practically had a happiness seizure when I took first place in my elementary school's rock-paper-scissors competition.

"¡Por Dios, hija!" She whipped out a little abanico to fan herself back to normalcy. "We've never had a line like this before at the theater! Did you pay them? Bad Luna! Did you sell my mug collection?"

"No, no. I would never. Es que, they're here to support us, Mamá!"

And soon she was holding me, in one of those motherly embraces charged with so much love you can't help but close your eyes. The ones that make you forget all about force-fed boiled cauliflower and cactus injuries you previously endured.

Her eyes teared up with joy. "They can't destroy our little

town's mall if it's successful and popular again! Your father would be so proud of you—do you know that?"

"Well, I know now," I responded, remembering how much he had encouraged me, even if he wasn't around anymore. "I'm sure he sent me all the strength from his luxurious cloud-based apartment in the heavens."

"Of course he did." She kissed the Virgin pendant around her neck. "Pero, Luna, how did you organize all of this?"

"Well, I didn't do it alone." I smiled as my new friends circled around, paying respects to the godmother of the Monteverde Mall.

Axel stepped forward and handed my mother a bouquet of red carnations. "I heard this was a flower from Spain. Maybe you can put them outside your daughter's window instead."

"No, no, no." She wagged a finger. "¡De eso nada, señorito! The cactus stays forever! But you are a very sweet boy." She smiled knowingly. "Only question is are they really for me, or are they for my daughter?"

"They're one hundred percent yours, Mrs. Iglesias," Axel said, looking at me with a grin.

"Good choice. Chico listo." My mother leaned into me. "I like this one. Pero, hija, what are you still doing here? I'll take care of the theater. You go have fun. Just don't forget to check on the projector or it will overheat."

"You can count on me, Mamá."

Axel sauntered past me. "Don't be jealous," he whispered into my ear, giving me the chills. Being that attractive and charming should be illegal when you're just friends. And that's all I thought we were ever going to be.

▶ 28.

"What a Feeling"
—Irene Cara

I went to catch up with the others when someone suddenly pushed my back, and I was yanked into a nearby photo booth. Mimi had kidnapped me, and now I was sitting inside with her, like some kind of against-my-will confessional booth. "Luna, are you seeing what I'm seeing?"

"Seeing what? Are there bats in the cave? Do I have boogers?"

Mimi lifted the velvet curtain and pointed to Axel, who was already off in the atrium, surrounded by an entire group of girls. "He's playing hard-core. Giving flowers to your *mother*? That's some heavy artillery."

I laughed. "I think he just likes my mom."

Darnell poked his head inside. "The whistles. The flowers. The way he keeps looking back at you. Wake up, Luna! Axel likes you."

My body tingled with excitement.

Every extremity pulsed with hot nerves.

Honestly, until weeks ago I had never even considered it a real-world possibility. Especially after all the false rumors. The mixed emotions. We were so different. But lately I couldn't get him out of my head. I was starting to believe that this *different* was the new normal.

So I took a chance and glanced back at him.

This was a night I would never forget. People crowded the dance floor and hung out on the upper level like it was the mezzanine balcony of a concert hall. Onstage were five girls, dressed in stripes, finishing up a ferocious pop routine.

"Thanks, El Dorado! We're THE ZEBRA GIRLS! What you're doing here is amazing!"

I turned to Darnell. "I can't believe you actually got a girl group!"

"They're European," he bragged, then climbed onstage and grabbed the mic. "Thank you for coming tonight, Zebras, you were amazing! And now, before introducing the next performance, I have to say that I'm seeing so much animal print tonight, I guess some of you thought this was a casting for the *Lion King* musical." He spun, showing off his fashion-victim costume, drawing whistles from the crowd. "I hope you're all enjoying our spectacular event at the mall! If you're here for a naughty time, I've got you covered. Just give me a call!"

Darnell whipped the mic cord around, strutting his stuff.

The crowd went wild.

"Allow me to introduce . . ." Darnell peered down at his notes. "Dark Angel!" He looked around confused, until eventually Kilo poked his head through the curtain and stepped onto the stage with an electric guitar, dressed like Kiss, shirt open, his heart tattoo exposed.

He coughed timidly into the mic. It squealed. "Hi. This is a song that is very important to me. It's called 'Let's Make a Barbecue in Hell.'"

Without warning, he strummed his guitar, sending shock waves through the air. The audience cheered like crazy. The truth was undeniable: Kilo was a total rock star on the stage.

"*DIE DIE DIE!*" he screamed.

"*BURN LIKE A SAUSAGE!*

"*BURN BURN BURN! BLOODY KETCHUP EVERY-WHERE!*"

Mimi shook her head in disbelief. "Brilliant."

I laughed to Darnell, who just shrugged back. I was proud of Kilo, because he wasn't exactly that shy guy who sat all by himself anymore. He rolled around on the floor for an inordinate amount of time, performing his earsplitting guitar solo, until Darnell finally took the stage and snatched the mic.

"Thank you for that, Kilo. That was really . . . special."

Kilo stole back the mic. "ROCK AND ROLL UNTIL I DIE!"

"We get it. Love that energy." Darnell kicked him off the stage with a stiletto. "Thank you, distinguished guests! You're all rock stars as far as I'm concerned!"

He bowed, and the crowd roared. "Now take it away, Nika!"

The mall went completely dark, illuminated only by an enormous disco ball that twinkled like starlight overhead, revealing Nika in the DJ booth spinning vinyl records. Music erupted, and the entire place turned into a multilevel club.

Darnell and I broke out in song and dance, belting out, "*WHAT A FEELING! IS BELIEVING!*"

Mimi sat on Kilo's shoulders, concert style. Even Ruby was

letting loose, locs pulled back, rocking out in her pinup-girl costume.

"That flower in your hair is perfect for your outfit!" I told her.

"Thank you, girl!" Ruby shouted over the music, then held up her red cup. "This punch is great! Is there alcohol in it?"

"By now, probably! The fountain bacteria are already fermenting!" Mimi replied.

Ruby stared into her cup, unsure, then beamed. "You know, this challenge is the best thing that has ever happened to me." And it was something that none of us could deny. This was our time to shine. No one could ever take this night away from us.

▶ 29.

"Bailamos"
—Enrique Iglesias

Before the night ended, he found me on the dance floor. And what happened next, I remember only in flashing moments. A silhouette approaching through the strobing crowd. The lightning bolt across his face. He reached out and took my hand to spin me, making my heart quick-step with the rhythm. There was something different in the atmosphere, the feeling that everything was possible—even things that were forbidden.

"I was wondering where you went," Axel said.

"Don't tell me you already missed me," I replied over my shoulder.

It was like he could read my mind and predict what it told my hips to do. Our bodies were in perfect choreography. I felt his hands and how they advanced—touching my body, gripping my waist, controlling the tempo entirely.

Now we were face-to-face.

His chest was pressed close to mine. Our lips were getting closer. The world was starting to fade away. But the moment was interrupted by a thought. A worry about something I'd totally forgotten to do—and if I didn't run fast enough and fix it, it would probably burn down the entire mall.

But this time for real.

"¡Mierda! I've got to go."

"What, why? Now?" He grabbed my hand to stop me from leaving, and when I looked up into his piercing glare, I realized just how much he didn't want to let go.

"Come with me," I said. I led him through the crowd and up the stairs to the cinema. We flew past the ticket counter and to the first door on the left, into one of the screening rooms that was playing the original *Scream* movie. I tried to respectfully avoid the many couples who were making out and went to the back, straight for the heavy metal door of the projection room.

"Over here." I pulled him inside.

As soon as I entered, I found that the projector was blazing hot.

"This old thing always overheats. There's something wrong with the fan. I just have to switch it out and refeed the film before it sets fire and barbecues everyone."

I quickly interchanged the machines, located the reel mount, fed in the movie film, and slid on the empty take-up reel. The audience groaned when the movie stopped, but that was typical.

All the while Axel watched me, jaw dropped. "I feel like you're deactivating a bomb in front of me. How did you learn to do this?"

"I've been working here since seventh grade. Plus, I had the best mentor." I fired up the projector and dimmed the theater again.

"Well, Luna, tell me more beautiful smart things," Axel said, inching closer.

"Did you know that Kodak was one of the players in the silver industry? Each of these old film reels contains silver halide crystals in the emulsion."

"That's why they call it the silver screen." His eyes sparkled.

"There's also cow fat inside, but that's not sexy."

He laughed. "How can you have such a big and voluptuous . . . brain?"

My face went hot; I was flattered. "In my house the mantra was books before looks."

Axel pulled me toward him, and now we were so close, as if dancing again.

"Smart *and* sexy. I couldn't be luckier."

His warm touch grazed my cheeks, sending goose bumps down every inch of my body. Now the only sound between us was the clicking film reel and our beating hearts.

"Me and you won't be easy, but it will be worth it," he whispered.

I wanted him so bad.

And that scared me.

I pulled away.

He pulled me back.

He pulled me in for a kiss.

And what a kiss.

▶ 30.

"Enjoy the Silence"
—Depeche Mode

I was overwhelmed. But in a good way, like a fruit salad of emotions. Everything happened so fast. I never thought that kiss was a possibility until it happened. I've had crushes before—the lead singer of a boy band, the buff guy in the orange juice commercial—but there was always a limit to the feeling.

This was more addictive than MSG.

But even so, I was aware that these sparks needed to stay a secret, at least for now, or everyone would believe Jade's lies—that I stole Axel out from under her—which wasn't fair.

It was all I could think about as I cleaned up the theater after everyone had gone home. All was dark, apart from the few fluorescent lights that reflected across the marble floor like ripples in a pond. Normally I would've been freaked out to be there alone, but now I needed *me* time—plus my mom promised me that all the confetti and glitter I didn't clean up would be transported right to my bedroom. It was funny how her threats just fulfilled my wildest childhood fantasies.

But that night, I felt like anything could happen.

Because when I was all alone in the mall, I got an unexpected visitor.

First were the echoes of a slammed door.

Even louder were the resounding footsteps.

And when I finally made out her face, I thought my mind was playing tricks on me. After long weeks of obsessively thinking about her return, I was finally face-to-face with Samantha.

Something was different about the way she held herself. Instead of wearing that innocent ponytail, her hair was flowing, the tips dyed orange, like a wave of lava across her shoulders. Heavy liner shrouded her eyes. She stood, waiting for me to talk first.

"Samantha . . ." My voice trembled.

"Hey, Luna."

"I wasn't sure I'd ever see you again."

Silence.

"Neither was I." She laughed ruefully before continuing. "Did you realize that just a few shops over is where I let you take the fall that day? I never said sorry for letting you take the blame. Don't worry—I told my mom the truth. You don't owe her a cent."

"I never said sorry for posting that video."

"Even princesses eat pizza with their hands, but I probably shouldn't have done it while talking trash about everyone I knew." This Samantha could laugh at herself—something she used to be too self-conscious to do. But then, wounds that heal into scars no longer feel pain, especially when you've been dragged to hell and back.

"Still, it wasn't my business posting it."

"I know you never intended it to go so far."

"I promise I didn't, Samantha."

But I could sense that she still didn't trust me.

My eyes were beginning to blur with tears. "You know, there's something I never asked you. Something that keeps running around in my mind . . ."

She nodded, giving me permission to continue.

"Why did you do it?" I asked her. "Why did you steal all those things that day?"

Samantha looked into the shadows. "There's a lot that you don't know, Luna. You're just going to have to get used to that. Things in this town just aren't what they seem to be."

"I think I deserve an answer."

"We all deserve a lot of things, Luna." She touched the whistle around my neck. "I really appreciate that you're wearing this. I truly do." She played with it, her demeanor clouding. "This is your chance to do something big for yourself and your family. This is *your turn*. Like back in soccer when you stepped up to be goalie, remember?"

"I got tangled like a helpless fly and tore the whole net down."

"Well, they can't score if there's no goal."

We smiled.

"Luna . . . if you win this challenge, do it for yourself, because I don't want anybody feeling bad for me anymore."

But that was so her.

"It'll be difficult to do, but I can respect that." I smiled at her.

Who knew what Samantha was going through just coming back here. Just how hard it must have been to step back into the real world.

"I saw your locker. Does that mean I'll see you at school?" I asked.

"Yeah, I'll be returning soon. I already got my old locker back. I'm in an outpatient program, which means I just need to go to the psychiatric hospital for therapy sessions and stuff. My doctors thought it would be best if I get back to normal life step by step."

"And your parents let you out in the middle of the night?"

"I snuck out." Samantha grinned. "But I should leave before they realize I've been gone. I heard rumors that something epic went down at the mall tonight, so I wanted to see for myself."

Then she turned toward the dimly lit exit.

At a minimum I knew that Samantha was okay—no, more than that. She had fight in her. And I wanted to feel relief, but I couldn't. I was proud of her for what she had managed to overcome, but I was still trying to figure out if our friendship had chapters yet to be written, because the distance between us was an abyss.

Then she stared straight at me; her pupils were like saucers. "Luna, one more thing. I heard about you and Axel. Whatever you do, be careful with him. There's things you don't know. Secrets. He's more complicated than he seems."

Her warning hit me like a bomb to the heart.

It's true that on the night of the race I saw a side of him that I'd never seen before. This other side to his personality. Complex and violent. That fight he got in. Only—I didn't know with how much gravity I should weigh Samantha's words.

I just didn't know who to trust anymore.

And that's when the applause sounded.

A figure emerged from the shadows. The man, vested in velvet, jumped down playfully from a bench, wearing a smile so bright, you'd believe it had been copied and pasted right to his face.

"Bravo! Bravo, Luna!" Andy clapped vehemently. "I am so pleased to see the two of you together again." He addressed his camera crew. "Get a close-up, right there."

I put my hand up, vulnerable. The last thing I wanted was to be filmed and posted about on Limbo that night. "Andy, you're here. . . ."

"Forgetting something, are we?" Andy raised an eyebrow, opened his palm, and produced a holographic watch out of thin air.

I checked my wrist, and sure enough it was bare. I must have lost my Retro watch on the dance floor. I clicked it back on my wrist. "Thanks for returning it."

"Don't let it happen again. I'd hate for you to jeopardize your chances of winning."

Samantha took a nervous step backward. "I feel like I know you. . . ." Her voice trembled. "You look familiar. You work for Limbo, don't you?"

Andy went mute for a second, then recovered. "Yes. Welcome back, Samantha. We're so glad to see you here," he said warmly. Then he twirled his cane and strolled away. "Do take care of yourselves. It's not safe for young girls to be all alone in the dark."

▶ 31.

"No Diggity"
—Blackstreet ft. Dr. Dre and Queen Pen

The Retro Challenge had started at El Dorado High, but it swept into my home like a torrent. My life was being upgraded to the next level. I felt like a Pokémon in my second evolution. After the mall party, my mother even stopped asking me where I was, who I was with, and what their driver's license numbers were. Mamá was happily busy now that the mall was becoming cool again, because the theater was packed all weekend.

I'd proved that I wasn't just her little girl anymore. She could trust me.

Which was probably why I started getting away with wearing cherry-red lipstick to school. Maybe it would've been different if she'd known that I was really a giant, walking hormone. I couldn't get Axel off my mind: What it would be like to see him. How he was going to say hello to me that morning. *Will it be a kiss? A hug? A wave? Or will he just act like that night never happened?* But I also couldn't forget what Samantha had told me about him. The side of him that I didn't know. And now I wasn't sure if I could trust my own heart.

As soon as I parked my car that morning, my friends were clawing their way inside, thirsty for juicy information, drooling like bonobos.

"What happened?"

"Did you make out?"

"How long did it go on for?"

"Where did he touch you—boob or no boob?"

"Did you get to second base?"

Darnell slammed the roof of the car. "He was respectful to you, wasn't he?! He better have been! I'll kill him if he wasn't!"

"Chill out, guys! We just kissed. But it was incredible," I told them, my body tingling all over. "It was like, soft and sweet but very hot!"

"Like a freshly baked muffin!" Mimi yelped. "I love those."

As soon as we crossed the threshold of El Dorado High, it was clear that something was very different. It came in a manifestation of vivid colors, the shape of flattop haircuts and boom boxes, break dancing and beatboxing, the formations of flower power and kaleidoscopic tie-dye. There were mohawks and studded chokers everywhere. It was becoming clear that this was a before and after in the world of El Dorado High.

"Are you seeing what I'm seeing?" Darnell's eyes went wide. "How many of us were taking the challenge again?"

Kilo joined us from behind, scratching his head. "Well, I know it was never this many." And he was right. The number of people dressed in retro gear had multiplied exponentially. But only a fraction of them actually had a Limbo watch.

But then what's everyone else doing?

I approached a girl in bell-bottoms. "Excuse me. You're not taking the challenge, right?"

"I wish. Our parents didn't let us, but that doesn't mean I can't go retro too sometimes. I'm cheering for you guys!" She blew bubblegum until it popped and joined the other Retro-maniacs.

Darnell grabbed my shoulders. "Holy guacamole, retro is trending!"

"And it's all because of the mall party—*your* idea, Loony Toony!" Mimi added. "There's even a group of girls who dyed their hair pink." Her eyes went dewy. "All those years of getting made fun of for being different, or some kind of freak, and now people want to dress like me."

I hugged her. "Now everyone wants to be a freak. 'Freak' is finally a compliment."

"Hey, Kilo!" We spun around to see Marcus, the quarterback of the football team. "Awesome performance, man. Rock and roll forever!"

Kilo blushed. Everyone was giving him props, instead of treating him like he was invisible. Finally people were realizing how special he was.

Miranda approached our group. "Oh my gosh, I am *obsessed* with all the behind-the-scenes content. The bloopers of Andy trying to give his cheesy speeches are hilarious. If you were on Limbo right now, you would see just how much this is blowing up."

"Yeah, but what is Limbo winning with all this?" Kilo asked.

"At the minimum, new users," Darnell responded.

And that's when an overjoyed Axel came running over.

"This is nuts—everyone is retro now. Are you guys seeing all this?" He hugged us with those strong arms, defined with veins—which made me think about how easy it would be for him to pick me up and hold me. And then there was that smell. The aftershave on his neck. It was so fresh and so hot at the same time.

My heart was racing.

It wasn't going to be easy to keep my distance.

Luckily, before things could get awkward, some bookish girls congregated around a Polaroid camera and waved us over.

"Hey, would you all, like, take a photo with us? It's for the yearbook club."

I guess this was what it felt like to be popular—but it wasn't about being cool, it was about being accepted without judgment. Maybe that's what the word "popular" should've meant all along. Maybe this was exactly what this school needed. Even though the Retromaniacs' phones weren't locked away like ours, they were also trying to live in the moment. And it was then that I realized we weren't just a part of a challenge—this was unfurling into something much larger.

This was a movement.

I was living a civil war between my head and heart. So, at break, I went to my car to collect myself. I looked in the rearview mirror, debating whether or not I should take off my lipstick. And then someone knocked on the glass. Probably the last person I wanted to see. The person whose name was synonymous with conflict.

Jade leaned against her Audi, parked next to me. She motioned to me, so I stepped out of the car.

"Hello, Luna," she said. Jade was making small talk. Something was wrong. And next she uttered words that blindsided me completely: "You had sex with him, didn't you?"

"You're still making up stories about us?"

"Don't play stupid," she hissed. "You got exactly what you wanted—Axel eating out of your hand. Maybe other people think you're this innocent girl, but I know better."

"Whatever you think happened, it didn't."

She smiled. "That's not what the video shows."

"What?! You recorded me?! How?!"

Jade pulled out her phone. "Go ahead, watch," she goaded. That's when I realized what she was up to. Jade Laurent was a lot of things. Gorgeous. Famous. Toxic. And above all, smart.

But she wasn't smarter than me.

"You know what? Chew your envy well, so it doesn't make you choke," I said, turning my back to leave. "I'm not going to let you get me disqualified for a lie."

But Jade played the video anyway and started to narrate the scene. "You and him, getting hot and steamy in the projector room. The lights go out. He pushes you against the wall. Bodily fluids are exchanged, sounds like a video that everyone will want to see."

I was starting to think that maybe we had not been alone in the projection room that night.

"That doesn't mean we had sex," I said firmly, but the truth was I was getting worried.

"But who are they going to believe, Luna?"

I didn't know what was more frightening, the thought that someone had recorded us, or the fact that Jade was threatening to post it online. But if Jade was betting hard, I was going to double down.

"Post it. I dare you. I don't care about what you or anyone else thinks," I told her. "You wouldn't do it anyway. It would hurt your precious ego too much to blast it to your hundreds of thousands of followers. That a girl with hips twice the size of yours could get Axel."

Jade's finger was pressed to the phone like a detonator. "You can't imagine what I'm capable of—"

And that's when I saw it.

Through the opened car door, I could see something shiny underneath the passenger seat.

"What is that?" I pointed, making Jade put her phone away.

"Nothing," she said almost defensively. An instant tell. And then I noticed that she had a few broken nails. I moved closer to find a greasy wrench and rusty pliers.

"You *are* capable of anything. Including tampering with Axel's brakes before the race. ¡Esto es una locura! I should go to the cops."

"Wait, n-no!" she stuttered. "It's not what you think. I swear I never wanted to hurt him."

"You tried to make his car crash!"

Then she started to cry. "No! I just hoped his car would never start!"

"So he would lose that bet and not go retro," I said with realization.

"That way he and Vince could stop fighting. And maybe

we could all be a group again. Axel and I used to be a *team*."

Jade was drowning in her own tears, and I genuinely felt her pain. I would've consoled her in another world—but in this one she took off running. She was volatile. And I was really going to need to be careful, because clearly the Goldens were capable of anything.

I just wish I had stopped them before it was too late.

▶ 32.

"Scar Tissue"
—Red Hot Chili Peppers

After what happened in the parking lot I needed to relax, so I headed for the Retro Lounge. But as soon as I sat on the purple Chester couch, I saw it. After all the good times we'd had together, it didn't make sense. I wanted to believe it was a mistake, or some stupid prank, but the Live Feed wall told no lies. Because there was a new face crossed off in red ink, and this time I knew the person well.

Ruby had been eliminated.

"Crazy, right?" Mimi said as she, Axel, and Darnell approached.

"I guess she didn't hang out with us last weekend because she was embarrassed to tell us," I said, realizing out loud.

"She didn't seem like the kind of girl that would quit so easy," Mimi added. "And I haven't seen her since we danced together at the mall. Maybe something happened to her?"

Darnell calmed me down. "She's right. If anything serious happened, my mom would have heard about it. She has eyes and ears everywhere, and she would have already interrogated me in my weakest moment before breakfast."

Jade's words were stuck in my head—that I had no idea what she was capable of. So I told them about how she'd tried to get me eliminated. About Axel's car. How unstable she was.

"I can't believe her. I could have died," Axel said.

"That girl needs to get a life. Her insides are uglier than a hippo's hemorrhoids. Seriously. You don't want to see that." Mimi shuddered.

"I think she's just really hurt," I said, "and that's what's scary."

"This is exactly what the Goldens want." Darnell got serious. "They want us to be afraid. To get in our heads. Well, I say no. We're not going to let them win. Right now, there are hundreds of people who want to be a part of this retro wave. This isn't a moment to back down—we need to rise up even stronger."

"What do you mean?" I asked.

"Here, just give me a pen. And paper. I've got an idea." Then he put it to the wall, scribbled something, and folded it in half.

"What are you doing?"

"You'll see." Darnell took off into the hallway and handed the little note to a Retromaniac on a Razor scooter who was gliding across the hall. Within seconds she read it and handed the note to another Retromaniac, who passed it off to a girl with tube socks—who smiled and showed the note to a Rubik's Cube guy, who passed it to his friends. And before long, that little paper would find its way through the halls.

"What did that note say?" I asked.

"You'll find out at midnight tonight. Come to the auto

graveyard in the abandoned forest. Bring something from your past life to burn. We're going to need to protect ourselves from our enemies, right? Strength in numbers," Darnell said with a devious smile. "And all these Retromaniacs need a proper introduction to their new world. Consider it ritual initiation."

And though I didn't know exactly what Darnell had in mind, I already knew that I wanted in—not just because it sounded dangerous and fun. But because I saw, just like he did, that there were only going to be two types of people at El Dorado: those who were a part of the retro wave, and those who were against it.

"See you at the bonfire." Darnell grinned.

Ever since Axel and I met, my life had been a roller coaster with no guardrails or safety belts. I didn't know who to believe. After all, if Axel had ever liked Jade, how could he also be interested in someone like me?

Whenever he tried to make conversation, I ended it. He passed me a note. I didn't read it. But if there's one thing I've learned, it's that guys love a challenge.

Axel caught up with me when my after-school study group let out. The autumn sun was weak in the sky, and we were all alone. "Luna, is everything okay? You've been avoiding me. Is this about the other night?"

I tried to act like I was just listening to my Walkman—but of course it didn't work.

"Luna, please. Pause your music and talk to me."

"Everything's fine," I said. "I just need some space."

"But you didn't care about space the other night. The closer we were, the better."

"Well, I guess things moved too fast," I told him. "Sorry to give you mixed signals."

And even though what I said betrayed everything I felt, sometimes you have to be strong, because as much as crushes come and go, you'll always be left with yourself in the end. We finally entered the main hall, but Axel didn't walk me to my locker. Instead he stopped in the doorway, giving me the distance that I'd asked for.

"Okay, Luna. Whatever you need." He swallowed. "See you around."

It felt right, but I hated what it meant for us.

And that's when we heard it.

Maybe it was just the paranoia of being at school after hours again. Maybe eating cereal with more fiber than recommended was starting to affect me for real. But when I turned to check Axel's face, it was clear this wasn't just my stomach or my imagination.

He was hearing the sounds too.

We were all alone at school, our bones quickly chilling.

It was like tons of people whispering to me at once. The same creepy noises that Nika spoke of, and what Kilo heard the night we found Vince in the bathroom. My anxiety was surging again, so I took a moment to breathe, calm myself down, and stop the rapid thoughts.

"What is this . . . ?" Axel said.

It grew louder as we traveled through the hall, following

the din, until we reached an unmarked door with a tinted-glass window, one I had never paid attention to before now.

"It's coming from there."

The voices mixed and swirled together as we neared. Axel reached for the door handle and quickly tried to yank it open.

But it wouldn't budge.

He grabbed his skateboard from his backpack, ready to swing and break the glass, but the sounds immediately stopped.

Axel shook his head. "We're not alone. . . . We shouldn't be here," he said, backing up. It was the first time I had ever seen him so shaken. "Let's just get out of here."

And we did.

Axel walked me back to my car. We didn't talk. We didn't look back. We wanted to forget what had just happened and pretend everything was okay. But those eerie sounds marked a before and after in my life, and things would only get worse that night at the bonfire.

⏸ 33.

Pause

I had to stop the track to show you something. I was just lying on the mattress, debating whether more people are conceived on firm or on soft ones and counting the tiny cracks that fissure the cement floor—but then I saw something.

A little flower petal.

I know exactly who this belongs to. She was wearing a flower in her hair the last time anyone saw her. At the mall party when she was dressed as the sexiest pinup girl ever. Letting me know who occupied this room just before me.

This is a clue left behind by Ruby.

I pick it up.

And then suddenly a siren rings out; I'm scared half to death.

A little metal slot in the wall opens, and something pours into a trough.

"Are these . . . ?" I step closer, carefully. "Cookies!" I'm already frothing at the mouth. Salivating hard-core. My hungry belly is making a rap beat as we speak. But then I stop myself. Why the hell are they just giving me cookies? The old Luna would have stuffed her face, but this one has survival instincts. They smell like home, but I know they're not from there. I wish they were waffles anyway. After all, waffles are just pancakes with six-packs—and that has to count for something.

I won't accept these.

I don't trust anything in this place. How can you when you were lied to for so long? Every time I think about the night of the bonfire, I can't help but remember the important clues that we found, and the ones we totally missed, because we were not alone—not at all.

▶ 34.

"I Love Rock 'n' Roll"
—Joan Jett & the Blackhearts

Sometimes you can't trust your own mind. Memories are living entities that change every time you access them—like how when you unpack a suitcase, you can never quite repack it exactly the same way. So we always reorganize memories to our own convenience, remembering events in ways that suit us. And since the Retro Challenge left me without postable photos, I was afraid that so many of my memories would become warped.

I went to the dingiest part of my home to find a solution. I knew that my garage was probably inhabited by a family of street jazz cats, so I made sure not to bother them while looking for my mom's old film camera, a precious relic she brought from Europe decades ago.

I also found a roll of film, a flashlight, and a dusty map of El Dorado.

I snuck out of my window and climbed carefully down the lattice, hoping I didn't fall off and get impaled by a lawn flamingo or pricked by a cactus. We were supposed to meet at midnight, but I was running late, and thankfully, Kilo had promised to wait for me if I wasn't on time.

"Thanks, dude! I really don't want to have to go into that forest alone."

"Anytime."

We ventured into the abandoned forest, past the location of the underground street race. Which made me think of Axel. Why did everything have to make me think of Axel? A piece of me wished I was with him, sneaking off into the woods together—but an even larger part of me knew our distance was for the better.

As Kilo and I wandered deeper, the moon twinkled across the lake, softly illuminating the trees. I squinted at my map. "Um, I'm more lost than a fart in a Jacuzzi."

"That's because the map's upside down." Kilo shone his light on it. "Don't worry—we don't need it. I know the forest really well."

"This place is so creepy. They say all the trees have a weird blackish color because some chemical company from Sacramento dumped waste into the lake a long time ago."

"I just heard it was haunted," Kilo teased.

"That does *not* make me feel better. What I need is Mimi to tell me that horses fell into all that toxic waste, creating a flying unicorn."

Then we spotted flashlights out in the distance, all over the place like a search party. I just hoped they were my Retro friends.

It was scary, exciting, and I bet that Ruby would have loved it. So much about Ruby's strange elimination was a total mystery, and it was starting to freak me out . . . but things would only get more bizarre.

Everything changed in less than a second.

"¡POR DIOS!" I screamed like I'd seen la Llorona.

A few yards away was a car, flipped over and enveloped in flames. The smoke was dark and thick, growing into the sky, showing no signs of burning out.

My instincts took over. I raced to the driver's side and started pounding on the glass. It was still steaming from the inside. "Are you okay? Stay calm—we're going to help!"

"Stand back!" Kilo yelled, picking up a rock and slamming the window over and over. But when it finally shattered, Kilo took a step backward, aghast.

"What the hell are you doing? We have to help!"

"There's no one inside." He shook his head and ran his hand along the tire. "This car is coated in years of dust."

"But the fire?"

"Look, Luna." He pointed. There was a trail of abandoned cars, all smoking. And as we approached the clearing, everything became crystal clear.

Darnell saw us from a distance and lit up. "You made it!"

"The whole burning-car production was a little too much, don't you think? I thought someone was inside."

"Welcome to the auto graveyard!"

Spread all over the marsh were disemboweled cars, some stacked like ancient ruins. Rumor was that over the last century, this was where all the crashed racers laid waste to their cars. And in the center of the clearing was a massive bonfire, maybe a hundred people congregating around it, embers licking up into the starry sky.

"Everything about this is dangerous. I love it. Even if I'm the kind of girl who covers her eyes for the last hour of *Titanic* because, as far as I'm concerned, it's a horror movie."

"There was space on the raft for Jack," Darnell confirmed. "We all know that."

"That's why I love you," I told him.

"Are you ready for this?" Darnell asked.

I reached into my jacket pocket, feeling for my item. We'd all been told to bring one significant object from our past.

"I've been preparing my whole life."

"Get yourselves comfortable, because this is going to be insane."

More Retromaniacs emerged from the forest, drawn to the firelight. Some even brought tents to camp out for the night. As we approached the bonfire, music competed over the crackle and pop of the blaze. A song by Nirvana called "Smells Like Teen Spirit."

"Look, everyone is wearing our whistles on their necks!" Kilo pointed out. "I didn't think so many people would actually come."

"I never want to forget where I was when the world went retro. Like every generation has a style or something iconic about them—maybe this could be ours." I pulled out my camera and snapped photos, capturing the atmosphere. But what surprised me most was the number of people who had dyed their hair pink.

I spotted Mimi hanging out on the seat of a rusted motor-cycle with a girl who looked vaguely familiar. "You're quite the trendsetter now!" I said.

"Yeah, I'm already planning to shave it all off," she said, snacking on some food she'd brought from home. "I wonder if then everyone would be bald, too! Imagine all El Dorado look-ing like a bowling alley—wouldn't that be funny?

"You know Nika," Mimi said. "The DJ from the mall!" Then she kissed her.

Kilo was quiet, off to the side. I was starting to get the feel-ing that Kilo was crushing on Mimi, and I think she was starting to realize that a little too. Mimi linked arms with him, pulling him aside. "Everything okay, Kilo?"

"Oh. It's nothing," he whispered. "I just thought you were . . ."

Mimi beamed. "Attracted to guys? Yes, I am."

"Oh, sorry. My bad. I thought you two . . ."

She laughed. "Well, I like fruit. Whatever is nice and sweet, though it's got to be ripe. Mature. I'm into bananas, but some-times I just want strawberries."

Kilo smiled earnestly. "I guess doctors do recommend five pieces of fruit per day."

"Exactly. Thanks for getting me." She hugged him. "But for your information, Nika and I are just hanging out. So, if you ask me out at some point, I'll still say yes." She winked and saun-tered away, leaving Kilo speechless.

Everyone congregated by the fire, waiting for the ceremony to start. Through those dancing flames I saw Axel, standing all alone.

And my heart awoke.

I wanted to call his name.

I wanted him to come sit next to me.

But he wouldn't. He was respecting the distance I'd asked for—or maybe punishing me for it. And soon we found ourselves near each other, at the edge of the dark forest.

"Hey, you," I said. "So, what did you bring to throw into the fire?"

Axel lit up when he saw me. "Nothing that interesting. Just an old laptop. Don't worry, it's dead."

"I know we're retro, but you're a liar if you say you don't drool when you think about a nice juicy Google search," I said to break the ice.

We laughed.

"You're really going to destroy an entire computer?"

"I don't know. I guess it's stupid."

"Tell me why. I want to know."

His eyes simmered with the reflection of the fire.

"This laptop was given to me by some marketing company because of an advertising campaign that I did, saying it was the best thing since microwavable burritos, but it crashed on me the next day. So, I guess it's kind of like me. Messed up on the inside."

"You don't seem so messed up."

His gaze wasn't just burning. It was wet. "There's just a lot going on in my head."

I took his hand. "You can tell me anything. I promise."

"I don't know . . . when Samantha was getting bullied, I was too self-absorbed to do anything to stop it. I got so angry with myself. That's why I dropped everything for this challenge.

That's why I contacted the Limbo help center and demanded they fix this."

"Wait, that was you?"

It was like I had bitten my tongue off and couldn't talk. *We are the two people who reached out to Limbo.* This was the mystery person who'd made me feel like I wasn't so alone, all this time. I stepped closer to him. "Axel, I can't believe that was you."

"We have a lot more in common than you think," he said.

"What do you mean?"

"Luna, I always knew the other person who contacted them was you."

"What? But how . . . ?"

"I'll never forget that day in the cafeteria, how you stood up for Samantha. Not afraid to shout to the world just how wrong we all were. There was no other option for me. It had to be you. You're like me. You're trying to fix yourself. You might feel like an anxious person on the inside, but on the outside, I just see a superhero."

I was starting to feel like I knew the real Axel. But then he gave me a sad smile and turned to walk away. I didn't know if he was playing games with me, or just respecting the boundaries I had set, but I was sure that I could no longer deny our connection.

And that's when I heard the sounds again.

It was like the woods were haunted. But without phones, this far away from other people, if something happened to us, no one would know.

I stared out into the blackness, and I could've sworn I saw moving shapes out there.

Axel sensed it too, because he took my hand, leading me away from the forest's edge. "Luna, I don't think it's very safe out there. Let's go back with the others."

When we got back, the blare of a car horn erupted, cutting the chatter around the bonfire. The sound came from a wheelless pickup truck by the edge of the fire. Darnell climbed on top of it, turned on a flashlight, and held it under his chin, as if telling a ghost story.

"Welcome, ladies and germs! We're glad you all made it tonight, but I want you all to know that being a Retro isn't only about having fun. So, for anyone who's just here for a cool story or something to post about, town is that way." He pointed.

Nobody budged.

"Because I'll tell you what's waiting for you in that town. A life direction that isn't good enough for your parents. A personality that isn't interesting enough, smart enough, or cool enough for your school! Pop-up ads that tell you what you're supposed to think beauty is, profiles that try to convince you that all you're allowed to be is happy! That there's always someone out there more recognized, followed, or liked than you! Better than you!"

It was almost frightening just how much control Darnell had over the crowd.

"The problems begin the moment you start to build your personality—not for you, but for a society that doesn't always care about you. So we stand here today, in protest of those impossible standards! And that starts with taking all the lies and the limiting rules you learned about yourself and throwing them in the fire!" He reached into his pocket and pulled out a photo of a man I didn't recognize. "And when you do, focus on something that you really want—for your new self, your new life, your new present!"

He fingered the photo in his hands.

"Last summer I met the guy of my dreams online. He was mature. Smart. We connected immediately. Only problem? I pretended to be somebody I'm not. I used a fake photo. A fake profile. I became a catfish. Why? I don't know. Maybe I was tired of feeling like the only gay person in this little town, but it doesn't justify what I did. Because if I'm going to find my special person, I can't be hiding who I really am."

Then Darnell tossed the photo directly into the blaze.

"But that's just my story. Now it's time to hear yours." Darnell jumped down from the truck bed, waiting for someone to step forward and not just face their demons, but throw them into the flames.

▶ 35.

"Iris"
—Goo Goo Dolls

I went next. My father used to tell me, *Solo se pueden perder dos cosas, el tiempo y la vida. Una es inevitable, y la otra es imperdonable.* Which means "You can only lose two things, your time and your life. One is inevitable; the other is unforgivable." And it was his words that motivated me to step up.

I jumped onto the pickup truck, reached into my backpack, and gripped the object of my past life, clutching it tightly. Knowing that when it burned, I'd be without it forever. Something that would liberate me from my regret.

And apparently, draw a lot of laughs.

"This is Ashley. And yes. I know, very funny. Why am I about to incinerate some stupid doll? Well, this used to be my idea of beauty. I wanted this to be me. A subzero waist size. Legs like skinny fries, without a single hair or stretch mark. And of course, with a bust like two watermelons. But I'm Spanish and Mexican, so imagine how many lottery tickets my genes would have to buy for me to turn out like Ashley. My tan skin looks nothing like hers. Anyway, on my ninth birthday my dad gave me a choice. He told me I could get the Ashley doll, or we could eat tamales and pozole at my favorite Mexican restaurant and spend the afternoon together. Well, it's pretty obvious which one I ended up choosing. Because at that moment, I admired the doll more than my own father. A few months later he passed away, and I never hated this stupid doll as much as I do now. All those ads you see online never tell you the importance of family, so I had to learn the hard way." My eyes watered before the burning heat of the flames. But I didn't care. I stepped closer and threw that cursed Ashley doll to the pits of hell.

The spectators blew their whistles, satiated.

"That was really brave," Axel said as I stepped down.

"Proud of ya, Loony." Mimi hugged me.

One by one we watched as people stood on the truck and sacrificed objects from their old lives to the Retro gods. An athlete in a letterman jacket threw his old baseball, tired of the pressure to always be the best. A short girl burned her high heels, tired of the blisters.

"Hey, Darnell. Next up is your *crush*," Axel teased. "I know you're hoping he takes off all his clothes and burns them."

"Shhhh!" Darnell laughed.

Kosta waved from across the bonfire, oblivious.

Then Mimi took to the truck, her hands in her pockets. And when she pulled them out, they were covered in what looked like blood.

The crowd gasped.

"Exactly. This is the reaction I got from a group of boys when I had my period at school and didn't have a tampon. I had to run to the bathroom, embarrassed. Well, you know what? This is who I am three hundred and sixty-five days a year. And it's time to make it normal. I shouldn't have to hide it or feel guilty or ashamed for that. Stop making this so complicated, taboo, or unnatural. My point is, being retro isn't about pretending to be from the past. Because history was pretty messed up sometimes. We need to learn from it to make a badass present. So, if one of your friends gets their pants bloody, instead of saying a stupid comment or overreacting, please take off your sweatshirt and tie it around their hips. All of us would really appreciate that. . . . Um. Yeah. Thanks . . ."

And then Mimi reached into a bag and started throwing tampons into the crowd. "These ones are not for the fire. They're for all of you! It's time you all get used to these!" Mimi jumped down onto the onlookers like a rock star, crowd-surfing away.

The last speech was a bombshell.

No—it was atomic. Because it was from someone who I hadn't expected to show up at all. None of us had. We all held our breath as she walked closer, approaching the fire.

"Um, Luna," Kilo whispered.

"Is that who I think it is . . . ?" Mimi said, stricken.

Samantha emerged from the crowd. And as she walked up to the truck bed, people gasped, unable to believe what they were seeing, that she had finally returned.

"Looks like nobody thought I'd show up."

Samantha was back—only this time the crowd gave her the reverence that they never had before. And in her hands was an object that represented the beginning of the end. The catalyst that bookmarked our story.

A little orange backpack.

"Hello, everyone." She smiled, unabashed. "My name is Samantha Darby. You know, the one who failed miserably at her magic disappearing act."

She laughed, but the crowd was straight-up crickets.

"That was a joke. . . . Right . . . Well, I'm here because I used to be a little bit of a bitch. I probably thought I was better than most of you. Well, don't worry, I've learned. Because believe it or not, on the last day of summer vacation, I screwed over my best friend."

She singled me out in the crowd.

"I went shopping with her, though I didn't tell my other friends, because they didn't think she was cool enough, but the whole time, I knew why I was really there. I was going to steal everything shiny I could get my hands on and put it in my backpack."

Samantha was holding it so close to the fire, the straps began to melt and curl up.

"It wasn't my plan, but I let my best friend take the fall when I got caught, and I never even had the courage to tell her why. My psychiatrists tell me not to be so hard on myself, but I'm going to say it. I was a coward. I was too afraid of getting caught. My parents are getting divorced, and I couldn't handle that my perfect life was ending, so I tried to hold on to it in the only way I could think of. So yeah. I was stupid. Selfish. Cold. Materialistic. You name it. . . ."

Samantha unclenched the fist that gripped the orange backpack, dropping it into the fire below. The crowd exploded with a cheer.

Samantha's speech hit me hard.

I never knew she considered me her best friend.

And deep down, I knew I had one more story to tell the world. A secret that I needed to unburden myself of. After all, she had come clean about what she'd done to me.

Samantha hopped down from the truck, and I approached her. "Wait, your parents are really getting divorced? The family with the perfect Christmas cards?"

"Yeah, that used to be us. . . ." She looked down.

"I'm so sorry. Keeping that inside must have been hell."

"It was," she replied, distant. "But I shouldn't have dragged you down with me. I heard you got kicked off the soccer team. I'm sorry that happened. . . ."

"I'm having fun with my new competition," I said, touching the lanyard around my neck. "Well, if you need anything, just whistle."

"Sure. Thank you, Luna. . . ."

Axel approached. "Welcome back, Samantha. We were really missing you." He pulled her in for a hug. She flinched but eventually embraced him back.

"Yeah, I missed you, too. But not too much. Don't get excited."

They laughed.

"I'm glad you didn't lose your sense of humor," he noted.

"They pumped thirty-seven pills from my stomach. I think I deserve to make fun. But you—I'm surprised to see that you're a part of this."

"Well, come around more often. A lot has changed at El Dorado."

Samantha considered it without giving a definite answer. Then she turned to leave, heading off into the dark woods.

"You sure you want to go in there alone?" I asked her.

"Yeah, I'll be fine," she said.

I was so relieved to see her okay, though *we* weren't. Not yet. Our relationship hardly had a pulse. What Samantha and I had couldn't be called a friendship, but at least it was an understanding, and that was a start.

Hours passed, and the sacrificial ritual raged on, as did the fire, which grew larger with every offering, until there was one person left.

Kilo.

He lingered in the shadows, reluctant to come forward. He approached slowly, his hands shaking with fear, holding a brown paper bag—and from it he pulled out a bottle of whiskey.

What could this be about?

I didn't know what to expect at that point.

Because he broke, immediately.

Kilo threw the bottle into the fire with the most tortured scream I'd ever heard—a noise that sounded so raw and pained it reverberated in my bones.

The alcohol made an explosion of fire.

Kilo started to run like there was no tomorrow, disappearing into the blackness of the forest. Without thinking, I raced after him.

"Luna, wait!" Axel yelled, but I hardly heard him.

I sprinted through the forest. Branches whipped and pummeled my body. I stumbled and fell, scratched by thorns.

But at that point my own safety was the last thing that mattered as I ran, because my friend was hurting.

Axel's shouts were echoes behind me.

I was chasing after the sounds in the dark, hoping that one of them would be my friend—that is, until I finally found him.

Kilo paced beneath a wilted willow tree, its branches descending like the long legs of a giant spider. He was gasping for air.

He tried to hide, so I faced him. "What's going on?"

"Just go back," he shouted.

"No! Not until you tell me what you're running from!"

"Luna, if I told you about my life, maybe you would look at me differently. You don't understand." That's when he ripped open his shirt, revealing his tattoo, the one that covered his mangled scar. "Why do you think I have this ugly thing?"

I held out a hand and approached cautiously.

"Maybe it used to be ugly, but now I just see a beautiful work of art." I moved forward, but he pulled away. And then, in that separation between us, the forest got darker. Horrifying. Because what I saw there transformed the abandoned forest into a dead forest.

Kilo saw it too, his face blanching. "What the hell?"

They lay in a small field of grass. Lifeless animals—a family of deer, sprawled across the woodlands, slain. We got closer. There was no blood, and their eyes were still open. This wasn't the work of hunters. It was something else entirely. Because just beyond the fallen fauna was a collection of trees painted with a red X on each of their trunks.

Some kind of warning to not go farther.

"These animals didn't die of natural causes." Kilo's voice shook.

"Luna!" Axel finally appeared, catching up with me. And I let his arms hug me, again, wanting the protection that his touch offered. This time I wasn't going to let go.

"We NEED to get out of here." Axel trembled.

He was right—because the image was so disturbing, it burned into my retinas.

▶ 36.

"Barbie Girl"
—Aqua

After the eerie night in the woods, I couldn't stop my mind from overthinking. But at least the Retro Challenge offered new ways to escape reality—and the next day was the best escape of all. We were going to a mysterious place that few people ever got to tour. Somewhere that would make us the envy of everyone we ever met—and all the contestants of the challenge were invited. A step down the yellow brick road to my full-ride scholarship, and through the proverbial chocolate factory of Silicon Valley— Limbo's top-secret headquarters.

Today we were going to Limboland.

Mimi and I threw on our matching denim jackets and caught up with Darnell in the parking lot. We speculated about what it would be like to see the Limbo headquarters.

"I heard there's a stress-relief room where you can break plates, and a yoga room to center your chakras right after," Mimi said, putting on some makeup.

"I heard shoes are illegal there. So are chairs. They just sit on bouncy balls. And instead of walking, they use hoverboards," Darnell added, stealing her eye shadow.

And though my friends always cracked me up, I couldn't bring myself to join them in laughing. There was nothing more disturbing than those dead deer in the abandoned forest, but I didn't want to scare them.

"Well, I heard there's shrimp cocktail in the bathrooms!"

"That's disgusting, Mimi."

"Not if you flush."

I didn't know where Mimi was getting her information from, but Limbo was mysterious and eccentric. Something known in the industry as a unicorn company. One of those Silicon Valley startups that was so carbon neutral that if you farted, they'd catch it, let it free into the wild, and donate a hundred bucks to make up for your pollution.

We joined the other Retros in the school parking lot and were quickly enveloped by the energy that preceded a school field trip. But this wasn't just any trip. Andy had another surprise for us.

It waited in the El Dorado parking lot, twinkling in the dewy sun, double-deckered like the buses of London, except all covered in peace signs and psychedelic colors. Neon lights glowed underneath the chassis, both futuristic and vintage at the same time. It even had RETROMOBILE painted on the back.

The camera crew swarmed in to capture our reactions. It's funny—at first, we were all a little awkward around the cameras, but now it just felt like a part of our life.

"This is *insane*!" Darnell yelled into the camera.

I hugged Mimi and blew a kiss. "We're going to Limboland!"

Andy descended from the bus and cleared his throat. "Good morning, my dear Retros. Much time has passed since this challenge began, and less than twenty of you remain—so this bus is your reward. May I present to you—the Retromobile! We've donated this bus to your school for all your field trips, and you will be the first ones to ride in it. Taking the school bus is a great way to meet people, and the whole point of this challenge is about connecting."

"Whooaaa." Mimi was salivating. "This bus is freaking magical!"

"Please tell me it time travels," I joked.

"Now, without further ado." Andy beamed. "Your chariot awaits!" He tapped on the doors three times with his cane, and they opened. We practically climbed over one another to get inside. This was like a next-level party bus. Laser lights, graffiti art, a little book where you could sign your name and write a memory. We called dibs on the very back of the top level, which was undoubtedly the best spot—because it was right near booming speakers.

Mimi found a velvet seat next to Kilo. "Mine reclines all the way like a first-class seat!"

And then it dawned on me. "There's even a karaoke booth back here!"

"Wait. Is that for . . . *pole dancing?*"

"No, Darnell, it's a fire pole that goes down to the first level," Kilo laughed.

"Whatever! Let's play fireman! I always loved role-playing," Darnell joked.

That's when Andy hopped onto a seat and grinned darkly, which told me that all of this was just too good to be true. There was a catch.

The Limbo jingle chimed out over the loudspeakers.

Which could only mean one thing.

Elimination challenge.

"I'm sorry to say that not all of you will be coming with us to Limboland today. You must pass another test in order to earn your entrance ticket. Welcome to the shopping challenge!"

The Retromobile stopped before an enormous store with a giant Limbo sign over its double doors. We were swarmed by Limbo cameras as soon as we descended from the bus.

"Where are we?" I squinted in the sun.

"Where dreams come true." Andy escorted us.

Lined up at the entrance were dozens of people, cheering us on. We started walking past the crowd when someone got my attention. A girl in a wheelchair handed me a Polaroid photo of her and her friends swagged out in retro clothes. "Luna, could I get your autograph, please?"

"Who? Me?" I was really confused.

"Yes! It would mean a lot. Your determination really inspires me," she said.

"Of course. You guys look awesome in this pic! What's your name?"

"Xena, like the warrior princess. I hope you win! Good luck!"

It was so beautiful to receive love like this from a stranger. We hugged goodbye, and all the while I just wanted to cry. I couldn't believe that we actually had supporters. That people wanted my autograph. That the challenge was getting this big.

Andy paced before an enormous red ribbon stretched across the doors. "My dear Retros, inside this store is everything your hearts could ever desire. From every decade, country, and universe imaginable. And all of it is yours for the taking. Today, you may each choose one item. The one that defines the new you. Some items will disqualify you, others won't."

"That's it? That's the test?" I was almost underwhelmed.

"That's the test, but you have just ten minutes," he affirmed with a wink, "and if you can't choose your item in time, you will be eliminated. It's safe to look at any of these items, but if you take the wrong one, you're done for." And then he cut the ribbon, letting us sprint inside—through the neon double doors—like kids raiding a candy store. Confetti shot out, and when it cleared, we took stock of our surroundings. The inside was deceptively big, a superstore on steroids, lined with endless rows of items stacked to the ceiling, everything festooned with streamers and sale signs.

"Whoa . . . this is so cool I'm going to have an aneurysm!" Darnell screamed.

"Let's have some fun! Gimme that unicycle—I've got shopping to do!" Mimi yelped, as a cameraman followed after her.

We soared down the rows of candies, signed soccer jerseys, and jungle gyms, hearts racing on a shopper's high. We lost Mimi in the pet supplies aisle, and Axel got stuck daydreaming before the brand-new electric motorcycles.

This place was a showroom for your wildest dreams come true.

And that's when one contestant, a tall kid, found something that made us all gasp.

The next generation of iPhone.

It wasn't supposed to come out until next year. It had to be a top-secret product sample. Rumor was that it had, like, seven cameras. The phone stood in a case, backlit, deified. I could have sworn I heard a harp play and saw white doves fly by.

"It's so beautiful," the lanky boy said, entranced.

Nika joined him. "These Limbo people really know what we like. You could be the first person in the world to have this. . . . Imagine . . ."

"I don't want to give in to temptation," he countered.

"Good point. Let's leave," Nika said.

"Screw it." He snatched it from its display.

The boy made his way to the checkout and handed the smartphone to the cashier to finalize his decision. But as soon as it was scanned, a red-alert alarm rang out—and sure enough, Limbo personnel swarmed in.

"Hey, get your hands off me!"

Andy took a bite out of a large candy apple. "You can keep your product, but I must inform you that you are officially eliminated. If this is the new you, then you haven't learned anything." With that, Andy snapped his fingers, and the Limbo grunts dragged the boy away.

"This is going to be harder than I thought," I said, and turned to Darnell.

"Yeah. I can't believe they actually let him keep that phone."

"I mean, there's a next generation PlayStation here. I hear there's hologram technology," Darnell whispered. "I know we'd get eliminated, but do you understand just how much that kind of thing is worth online?"

It was like they knew our biggest weaknesses, our technological kryptonite—and exactly what items would tempt us most into disqualification. Every couple of minutes we would hear the blaring elimination alarm, which just added to the stress of picking the right item.

Mimi stared into the biggest flat-screen any of us had ever seen, hypnotized by jellyfish on the Discovery channel. "I know I shouldn't, but I want it. I need it."

"Mimi, no—" Kilo said. "Think about the Galápagos. You can do this!"

"This is a whole different type of challenge," I said as I wandered down an aisle and found a bunch of Retros congregating around something. I made my way into the crowd to see.

It was a Tesla.

And I found myself sweating a little bit, actually weighing the pros and cons of driving it home—of taking my mom on all those road trips our clunky cars could never handle—or selling it and soothing my family's financial problems.

But that's when something caught my eye. I walked away from the Tesla. It was love at first sight, because I saw the item that I knew was made for me.

A red flamenco dress, the exact kind my abuela wore at fiestas when I was a child.

It was the most beautiful one I had ever seen, and I knew my mother would think the same. The old me had chosen an Ashley doll over family, but this dress meant family before all else.

Andy spoke over the loudspeaker. "Time is almost up! Please bring your items to the checkout, where the interviews will be taking place."

Time for the cheesy confessionals.

I stepped forward to the Limbo cameras. "I want to see this in my wardrobe, a promise that I'll visit my family in Spain as soon as I can." I held out the dress and blew a kiss.

Kilo came back with a bicycle and explained to the Limbo content team, "I have to walk miles to school. Before, I didn't care if I was late, but now that I have my new friends, all the pedaling is worth it."

Mimi got a terrarium tank to house her iguana. "I've learned that 'freak' is a compliment," she said proudly.

I was surprised by what Axel had chosen.

"Really? A Spanish guitar?"

He only smiled.

We went through the checkout lanes to get our items scanned, and instead of receipts, the machines printed our golden tickets to Limboland.

"Congratulations," said the cashier. "You pass! Paper or plastic?"

"What do you think?" Mimi pulled out a reusable bag from her backpack.

We entered the Retromobile still buzzing.

"There's only like fourteen of us left," Darnell said, taking a seat next to Axel.

But then something captivated Darnell's attention, until he was wearing that melty, glazed-over look again.

Axel took the initiative.

"HEY, KOSTA! Can you hand me my backpack? I left it up front. Emergency, bro."

Darnell put a hand over his mouth. "*Axel*, what the hell are you doing?"

"I promised to get you a date with Kosta, didn't I?"

"Here you go, dude," Kosta said. Axel opened his backpack up and immediately began pretending to vomit. "Hey, um, are you okay? Want some water?"

"Sorry, I just get carsick sitting next to windows."

"Oh, right. *Carsick!*" Darnell was starting to figure out Axel's plan. "Kosta, you can sit with me . . . I mean, only if you want to."

"I would love to sit with you." Kosta smiled.

After Darnell's speech about meeting his person, I was really rooting for him. We were all becoming best friends, the kind you never forget about.

But it's true that with Axel things were more complicated.

He was sitting alone on the bus.

And I felt so drawn to him. It wasn't just about physical attraction. He was the other person who'd contacted Limbo in the first place. We had a connection. This was something I had never experienced before. It was more than just a crush.

The music started bumping, and, as the bus finally pulled onto the redwood forest road, I made a decision. My heart pumped with nerves as I traveled across the aisle and took the empty seat right next to Axel.

His eyes lit up when I sat down.

"So, are you going to get up on that fire pole or what?" I asked.

"You'd like that, wouldn't you?"

"Maybe I would; maybe I wouldn't. Maybe I don't want to

see all the people in the bus drooling. It would be totally unhygienic," I said.

"I just care about what you think," he said as his hand found mine. My fingertips grazed his painted black nails. Just touching him made adrenaline course through my body.

"Difficult, remember?" I said as I looked around, making sure nobody was watching. Then I grabbed his face, pulling him in for a kiss.

Axel didn't resist. And with that kiss I forgot the rest of the world. For a few seconds it was just him and me.

His soft lips parted from mine.

He smiled, looking stunned. "That's the first time anyone has ever kissed *me* before."

We looked into each other's eyes, barely blinking. Addicted to each other. The discomfort was risky. It was hot.

"Get used to it," I told him, all sexy, thinking we were going to have the steamiest ride of our lives . . . but instead I totally fell asleep with my face pressed against the tray table.

"We're here, Luna."

The ride was almost four hours, but it had gone by faster because I had curled up on Axel's shoulder. He'd even given me his jacket.

"Hey, Sleeping Beauty, you should wake up. We're here!" he whispered.

When I rubbed my eyes open and looked out the window, I caught sight of the sign through the misty woods.

LIMBOLAND—3 MILES.

Towering above the forest was the most magnificent campus I had ever seen. The enormous glass building at the center glinted in the sun, everything sparkling purple, as if it was an amusement park.

This wasn't just an average Silicon Valley headquarters, no—it was a metropolis.

"It's like a dreamland." Kilo glowed as the bus pulled to a stop.

"It's so glimmery and yummy-looking; I just want to eat it," Mimi said.

As if in a trance, we got off and approached the massive gilded gates before settling into an outdoor amphitheater. We whispered among ourselves, ready for whatever was to come next.

And there was the CEO, Scarlett, waiting for us. She took the stage.

"Limbo's mission is to connect the world. To make our planet a better place. And you are all helping us do just that. It's so amazing to see your faces, to see who has made it this far, and what beautiful things you've done. Take, for example, Nika, who set up an after-school tutoring program. She's helping so many kids, giving them the tools to build a better tomorrow."

We embarrassed her with adulation. Nika was already blushing.

"Luna, you and your friends have given the mall a second life."

I turned redder than a lobster.

She continued after the smattering of whistles from the crowd. "And, Axel, the way you dropped everything, donating the proceeds of your Limbo account to victims of cyberbullying."

"I had no idea you did that," I whispered, secretly taking his hand.

He shrugged. "Yeah, I figured it was the right thing to do."

It was funny—he could be so braggadocious about racing cars and skydiving, but when it came to being a good person, it was like he totally forgot how to accept recognition.

"*And* he donates to charity? Damn, girl," Mimi whispered.

"Beyond these gates is a place unlike any you've ever seen," Scarlett continued. "Where magic and true connectivity exist. And don't worry about the technology here. As long as you don't touch anything, no one else is getting eliminated today."

We let out a collective sigh.

"Guess I can stop covering my eyes," Kilo joked.

"Okay, Retros! This is the moment you've all been waiting for. Prepare yourselves, because now is the moment that you all cross over into . . . *Limboland*!"

I looked all around, jumping, excited like a hormonal chicken with its head cut off.

Because the gates were opening, reflecting rays of sunlight as they parted, blinding us with splendor, like the entrance to heaven. We were hypnotized. Ready to devour the candy-coated dreams they sold us, no matter what lay beyond those gates.

▶ 37.

"Macarena (Bayside Boys Remix)"
—Los Del Rio

Sometimes I have this dream. They say we forget 90 percent of them, but this one I always remember. I'm at the most epic county fair, and I'm a total pro. The gun games aren't rigged to fail. The ghosts and witches in the haunted house always apologize after scaring me. I make out with the winner of the strongman competition, and I even win a giant red-assed-baboon stuffed animal that I proceed to spoon with all night long. I never understand why I chose the baboon over the guy with the six-pack.

But as crazy as that was, Limboland was ten million times cooler.

Because just like in an amusement park, paper maps were given to us as we passed through the turnstile. *Is this real life?* I felt like my brain was high on Pop Rocks.

Andy guided us through the campus.

Limboland had a timeless quality to it, like an enormous movie set where the walkways were lined with phone booths and vintage streetlamps. Fountains full of coins. Drones flew

overhead like gulls, playing happy music as they delivered pack-
ages. Restaurants from every part of the world. And soon the
sweet smell of churros lured us to a snack vendor.

"I'll take one, please!" Mimi offered cash.

"Money doesn't exist here," the vendor chuckled, handing
her the dessert for free.

"Mimi?" Andy said, looking around for her. "Please stay with
the group. There will be time for lunch after the tour."

"Eek, sorry!"

Andy held up his arms. "Here at Limboland, we believe in
inspired creativity, so everything we do is fun and unconven-
tional. And if you look closely, you might see workers enjoying
the Grand Park!"

Dozens of employees hung out on artificial grass, strumming
guitars. Doing tai chi in lotus gardens. Racing around in little golf
carts. Others rode a Ferris wheel. They were all young, like recent
college grads, with different accents from all over the globe.

"See what's on some of their heads?" Andy pointed out a
few who were wearing medieval jester hats. "It means they're
new to the family, and that way everyone will go easy on them—
or not." He chuckled.

"It's like a hazing ritual," Darnell muttered.

But Mimi was growing somber. "Ruby told me that Limboland has the largest Ferris wheel in California . . . Why would
she let herself get eliminated? She seemed so excited to visit
Limboland a week ago. I just don't understand it."

"Hey, cheer up," Kilo said. "I know Ruby was excited about
winning the challenge—we all are. But actually doing it is
another beast entirely."

The song on the loudspeakers suddenly changed to the "Macarena." Immediately Limbo employees started lining up in front of a kiosk.

I stepped closer, intrigued. At the front of the line was a window that administered little plastic cups. "Are they taking pills?"

"A healthy body is a healthy mind," Andy said over my shoulder, startling me.

"What is that stuff they're taking?" Kilo asked.

"It's a proprietary vitamin cocktail, formulated by the world's leading doctors and pharmacists," Andy said, leading us down the path. "Life can be stressful, which is why Limbo takes care of us."

Kilo inspected one of the pills. "Weird."

"Yeah, I'll pass on those," Darnell said, then turned to me and whispered, "Why do Silicon Valley companies always feel like cults?"

"Because they are," Axel said, only half-joking.

Then we were led to the center of the campus, until we were standing before the central building, which overlooked the grounds like a fortress made of glass.

Andy guided us through an enormous set of crystalline doors. "And here is the most important place in all of Limboland—welcome to our headquarters!"

We entered a cavernous hall, with a front desk, a security booth, and an X-ray machine for our belongings.

We all lined up, but when it was my turn, the security guards halted me. "All jewelry comes off until you leave—including that whistle around your neck."

I hesitated. I couldn't bring myself to take it off.

That whistle meant everything to me. It was the hope that maybe someday Samantha and I could go back to the way we were.

"Let her keep it." I heard a voice from behind, and Scarlett appeared. She touched the whistle around my neck. "These whistles are special to them. No one takes this off her, or any of the other Retros. You understand?"

The guard acquiesced, then waved us forward. "Yes, ma'am."

"Those are some cool denim jackets, by the way," she added. "Have fun on the rest of your tour. We're all family now." Scarlett winked at me.

I was starstruck.

But something was still bothering me about Limbo, and for all the admiration that I had toward its creator, I had to spit it out. "I'm sorry, but I'm still struggling with something. If you care so much about your users, why did you let Samantha get bullied? I reported so many messed-up memes, and your admins did nothing about it."

"Our mission to connect the world doesn't ensure each connection is genuine," Scarlett responded. Her mouth grew stern. "We're ultimately not responsible for what happens on our platforms, but we do try our best to make sure everyone has a meaningful experience. And we always try to right the wrongs. That's why you're here now. Don't forget that."

"I . . . guess I understand." She didn't seem used to being questioned.

We eventually cleared security and began walking down through the ultramodern and minimally furnished entrance hall.

Nika tugged on Andy's purple jacket. "Why are there so many cameras everywhere?"

Which was true—you couldn't escape them.

"We believe in full transparency, because we have nothing to hide," Scarlett responded.

We all walked down the hallway until Mimi grabbed my arm, pulling me away from the group. She stopped before a large purple door. And then she went to open it.

"What are you doing, Mimi? Remember what happened at the crayon factory?"

"Come on. I just have a little bit of crayon left in my brain, and the doctors say I don't need to take it out unless it affects my cognitive ability." Mimi started to push open the purple door. "This is probably the only door that's not all glass! Doesn't that make you curious?"

"Stop! Don't enter there!" one of the guards shouted, sprinting over.

Mimi froze in the open doorway.

And soon a security team stormed in. They quickly slammed the door shut, preventing her from entering. "That area is off-limits!" a guard said. "You didn't see anything, did you?"

Mimi fumbled, freaked out. "Um, no. Nothing. Nothing at all."

"Why don't you go back with the group?" said another guard.

"Mimi!" Scarlett commanded. "Come over here. Now!"

"Sorry . . . Geez, it's not like I'm going to steal the formula to your secret sauce. . . ." Mimi laughed like it was no big deal, but when we rejoined the group, she looked off, caught in a fog.

"Everything all right?" I asked.

"Yeah. Totally fine, Luna." She smiled, changing the subject. "I heard there was an ice-skating rink somewhere around here. I just wanted to find out if the rumors were true. . . ."

Scarlett continued the tour, pointing to a work floor of hundreds of Limbo workers in candy-colored cubicles, operating giant computer monitors with the swoosh and wave of their hands. "Here are our Limboneers, the imagination center of our family. They are responsible for developing trends, challenges, and brand activations."

The next stop was at an enormous white door, sealed with intense biometric-security locks. "Beyond that door is a place that requires the highest security clearance. Somewhere that only myself, our lawyer Andrew Fineman, and a few others have access to. Behind those doors is *Heaven*," Scarlett said proudly. "It's where we keep all our cloud servers. This is the control center for all our information."

"That's so cool," Kosta said.

"And what if we don't want anyone to have our data?" Darnell asked.

"Then you're going to have to bust in there and steal it back." Axel pushed Darnell playfully. I really appreciated his sense of humor.

As we walked, I squeezed Axel's hand, and he squeezed mine back.

Soon the hallway hit a dead end. And like all good tours, it led to the same place.

"The gift shop!"

Scarlett stood in front of the store, facing us. "And now, the grand finale of today's tour. The reason we felt it so important to bring you all here. May I present the fruit of our labor, something that was only made possible because of you—"

She swung open the doors, introducing Limbo's latest campaign.

"The Retro merchandise line!"

It was a wonderland of Retro apparel. Tie-dye hoodies that read #GORETRO, neon-purple Limbo shirts stamped with cassettes and record players.

"Go ahead, don't be shy." She beamed. "Take whatever you like!"

We went crazy, filling little baskets with satchels, candies, and foam hats. It was like a theme park, only we were the principal characters. We weren't just an accessory to the challenge— we were the living, breathing brand being sold.

Because on the back wall was a massive line of clothes. I picked up a shirt that read #TEAMLUNA . . . and dropped it immediately, seized with shock.

Scarlett rested a hand on my shoulder. "Not just shirts, Luna. Mugs, hats, stickers, tote bags! Soon, we'll be launching this entire line in retail stores across the world! You'll be a part of the Limbo legacy forever."

I forgot how to breathe. Nothing like this had ever happened to me before.

"No way! Are these pillows?" Mimi screeched, and read what was printed on it. "'Normal is whatever we want it to be.' Oh my god! I said that!"

It was flattering and overwhelming. This challenge was

getting down to the wire, and they were taking it very seriously.

#GOMimi #WHOWILLWIN? #AxelFANCLUB

Do we really have that many "fans" out there?

Is the Retro Challenge really becoming that big?

Because we were unplugged, we had no idea how famous this thing was getting, or how much Limbo was advertising the challenge. But it was growing bigger than any of us could've anticipated.

And not all of us were feeling okay with that.

Darnell stood by the front door, his brow furrowed. "Seriously . . . ? I knew they were making cash off us, but this is next level."

"Is something wrong, Darnell?" Scarlett asked.

"I don't know how comfortable I am with all this."

"It was all there in the terms and conditions," Scarlett said. "You consented to our use of your image. How else are we even supposed to post a photo with you guys?"

"This is more than a photo—we're, like, products," he said.

"That's a good point," I added, growing concerned.

"Guys, a percentage of every sale goes to antibullying organizations," Scarlett explained. "You're the face of a good cause. Think of all the good we can do together."

"I guess if more people think going retro is cool, we all win." I grabbed a hat with Darnell's smiling face on it. "Come on. This looks great on you!" I put it on his head.

"Maybe you're right." He hesitated, then lightened up. "My mom is going to flip when she sees this."

Axel walked the aisles, unfazed. I guess he was pretty used to treatment like this.

"What do you think about all this?"

"It's incredible, but . . . I left the Limbo app to distance myself from this kind of thing. I guess they weren't going to let me go that easy, were they?" Axel brightened. "Let's do a reset. How about a party at my house this weekend? My parents aren't going to be home, and I *guess* you can be my date?"

"You guess, huh?" I hit him playfully with a stuffed animal. "If we're gonna be *dating*, you need to understand that you are the one that kills the cockroaches."

"Deal," he promised, hiding from the cameras to pull me in for a kiss.

No one knew what was waiting for us at his crazy mansion party. Because the memories of that night would seem more beautiful and innocent than they really were. And by the time I realized that, it would be too late.

One of us would be gone.

▶ 38.

"A Quién Le Importa"
—Alaska y Dinarama

On Friday night my hairbrush became a microphone. My toothpaste-flecked mirror was a glamour studio. And the radio a full-on concert, where every song played just for me. 103.7 Retro Radio was blasting my favorite songs by Alaska. One of the best retro Spanish singers.

I painted my nails with three layers of polish, and after some gymnastic moves worthy of the Olympics, I was finally able to put on my favorite skinny leather pants. I was so excited, I didn't know if I needed an iced caramel macchiato or a siesta.

I was peeling off a green face mask when I heard the sound. *Ping, ping.* Gumballs hit my window, letting me know that Mimi was in the bushes and ready to get going. Which was easier said than done, because first I would have to face the wrath of mi madre.

I found her standing there in the shadows as I left my room, clutching the television remote like it was a deadly weapon.

This was the sixth sense of a mother.

Why do they always have to know everything?

"You look really bonita, hija. What good genes I gave you. But your pants are so tight right now, it should be illegal." Funny how most of my life she never told me I looked pretty—she wanted me to put less importance on the superficial—but now that she had, it wasn't a compliment, but an accusation. The older I got, the younger she wished I'd behave on a Friday night.

Maybe old Luna would have made an excuse, or snuck out, but on this night, I was ready to tell my mother exactly what I was getting into. I was ready to make decisions on my own.

She circled me like I was prey. "So where are you going, dressed like *that*?" she said, her eyeballs practically bulging out of her skull.

I took a deep breath. "Mamá . . . I'm going to a party. There won't be parental supervision, and there will be drinking. Also, tons of boys."

She raised her voice. "¡Para, para! I don't want to hear it. Do you want me to have a heart attack while I'm still in the spring-time of my youth?"

I could feel her recoiling like a cobra, and just as I thought she was going to attack, she proved that even when you think you know everything about your parents, they always have the capacity to surprise you. Because that's when she went into the kitchen and started boiling eggs.

"Mom, what are you doing? Are you okay?"

"So you and your friends have food in your stomachs," she said, then stuffed crackers in my pocket. "Believe it or not, I was a party animal at your age, back in Spain. I know what I'm talking about."

"Thank you, Mamá, for letting me go tonight! No sabes— this means everything to me."

"If anything bad happens, if any boy is mean to you, call me immediately. I'll drive right over, and I will put a leash on them and take them to their parents . . . or to the police!"

I was convinced my mother had a double life as a mob boss.

"You'll be the first person I go to. I promise," I said, truly meaning it. Feeling like, with this new trust, I could start to tell her more things about my life.

I waited impatiently for the eggs to boil.

"Aquí están. Don't forget to take your jacket." She grabbed the ugliest one from the coatrack in a last-ditch attempt to make sure I die a virgin.

"But, Mamá, this is Grandma's coat!"

"And how mature you look in it! So elegant! So vintage! So retro! Y por favor, take care of yourself." She kissed me all over, then shooed me out the door—but I was smiling all the way, because I knew that no matter how much I grew up, some things would simply never change.

I always found myself at the same kind of parties. You know, the kind where all the guys enter with a swagger limp, like a reggaeton star, and every girl thinks she's in a slow-motion shampoo commercial. And at the end of the night the cops always bust in the door like we were running an illegal gambling racket. But this party put all those other nights to shame.

We parked somewhere in the El Dorado Hills. Tiki torches guided us toward Axel's mansion. Neon lights seeped through the trees as distant music rumbled beneath our feet. And for the occasion, I ditched Grandma's coat. Instead, Mimi and I wore our matching denim jackets, which, luckily, I'd left in my car.

Mimi wheezed, out of breath. "This is torture! Axel's driveway is longer than my entire street. Who needs a personal trainer when you have super-rich friends?"

We walked past the elegant naked sculptures that stood in the courtyard—you know, the sexy ones without heads but with abs you could wash your clothes on.

"How does anybody get this rich and save this much money?" I marveled. "I have the guilty pleasures of a queen but the budget of a student after Taco Tuesday."

"True. If a thief broke into my room, I feel like I'd end up helping him look for money."

"Is Miranda going to be here tonight?" I asked.

"No, she said the soccer team had an away game, so they're sleeping out of town."

And for the first time, what I felt when I heard the word "soccer" wasn't sadness.

"I hope they do well," I said.

"I know you miss them, but don't worry, Loony—you're much better at the Retro Challenge than soccer!" Mimi smiled like it was a compliment and gave me a big hug.

I laughed, already feeling better about it. "Hey, look at all the Retromaniacs up ahead. This is gonna be *insane!*"

But then Mimi's face went a little sour. She fell silent.

I figured the incline of the driveway was really getting to her, so I pulled out one of the hard-boiled eggs I'd taken out of my grandma's coat. "Here, Mimi. You need some energy to take on the night."

"Thanks, but why are you giving me an egg?"

"My mom made me take them so that we wouldn't get low blood pressure or something."

We busted up laughing.

"So, do you think mermaids give birth or lay eggs?" Mimi asked, puzzled. Luckily, before I had to actually answer that question, we finally made it to the top of the driveway.

And wow . . .

What a house!

The mansion was enormous and modern, sleek and black like obsidian. Crowds of Retromaniacs partied in the court-yard entrance—many of whom I recognized from the bonfire. Through the grand foyer, dozens more raged to techno rave music on the dance floor. Like a VIP rooftop party, with Nika at the helm as our DJ. Confetti glittered like snowflakes in the air, and beyond it was a glass wall that looked across the sparkling lights below.

It was freaking magical.

"You finally made it!" Darnell came flying down the spiral staircase, handing us red cups filled to the brim. "Some naughty hydration for my ladies."

"Hey, Mimi," Kilo said, watching the people around us with the skepticism of a cat looking at itself in the mirror. I figured this was his first house party.

Mimi wrapped one arm around him to make him more comfortable, messing up his black hair and unbuttoning his shirt a few buttons. "That's better. Don't forget you're a rock star!"

"I won't, thanks," he said with a big smile.

Then she kissed him on the cheek, and he went red.

"Where's the pool? It's getting really hot in here." Kilo fanned himself.

"Let's see if the host can give us a tour. Has anyone seen Axel?" I asked, looking around.

"I think he's over there." Darnell pointed to the hallway, where, sure enough, Axel was talking with some of his celebrity friends, with an entourage of girls all around them.

"I guess he's too busy to say hello. . . ."

Which reminded me of how different our worlds used to be. The glitz and glamour was nothing I was used to. But at least I did feel at home with so many Retromaniacs at the party. Everyone was having fun; couples were playing spin the bottle and sneaking in and out of the many guest bedrooms. Since the bonfire, everyone had warmed up to one another.

"I can't believe there's only fourteen of us left in the challenge," Kilo said.

"No, just thirteen." Nika joined our circle. "I'm going to bow out Monday."

"SHUT UP." Darnell poured his drink in a plant. "Why? You made it so far!"

But Nika seemed pretty sure of herself. "It's just time. My phone, my computer, and my mixing programs—that's how I express myself. I have friends I haven't talked to in months because I met them through gaming. I know this was a challenge, and nobody said it would be easy, but I feel like I've squeezed everything I can from this experience."

"You have all my support, Nika," I assured her. Because deep inside I knew when it was all over, I would be just like her. Retro in my heart. Phone in my hand. And even if she wasn't going to be a part of the challenge, it wouldn't stop her from being one of us.

She was so smart, she would get, like, ten other scholarships anyway.

Mimi gave Nika a warm hug. "You do you, girl. I'm proud of you."

Mimi's face got more serious with the passing time, until eventually she pulled me aside. "Hey, Luna, can I talk to you about something important?"

"Sure, whatever you want."

But before she could continue, something stole her attention. "Wait, is she really here?"

Because next we caught sight of someone who warmed our hearts. One who had changed just enough that she wasn't entirely recognizable, but not enough that I didn't remember her.

"Go talk with Samantha." Mimi smiled. "I'll meet you by the infinity pool."

"But, Mimi . . . is everything okay?"

"Yeah, we'll talk later. Go ahead, Loony."

Samantha was sitting on the stairs, talking with Kosta. It looked like she was finally enjoying herself, for the first time in a long time.

"Samantha!" I hugged her. "You're actually here! At a party!"

"I'm checked into an outpatient program, not Alcatraz." She giggled.

"Of course, do you want a drink?"

"If I mix booze and all these pills I'm taking, I'll probably turn into a leprechaun."

"It's not like I have solid proof, but I don't doubt that

whatever Darnell put inside this cup has so much caffeine you'll probably grow a little red-haired beard," I joked, then sat on the steps next to her, getting serious. "So . . . how are you lately?"

"I'm getting better. Going easier on myself. I'm realizing that the trauma isn't my fault, but healing is my responsibility." She smiled, batting her dark lashes at me. "And what about you, Luna?

"I'm doing better now that I know you're okay."

"And what about a certain boy? Come on—I haven't seen that look in your eye since you were eating sand at playtime."

"You know nothing. My first boyfriend left me for a pair of marbles."

"Okay, well, you're making improvements."

We laughed.

"Listen . . . ," Samantha started. "No matter how much trouble I think Axel is, I see that he's really trying to change. Just please, whatever you do, take care of yourself, okay? I wouldn't want to see you hurt."

"You know me. When it comes to my heart, I'm careful," I told her.

At least that used to be true.

Because I didn't know what true love really was, or if it was even happening to me. But no matter how good it felt to think about Axel, what I did know was that my friends really cared about me. They loved me more than the Kardashians love Botox. Which is a lot. And that's what mattered most. At least now we could be 100 percent open with each other. Something we never had before. So I pulled Samantha in, and we shared a warmhearted embrace.

• • •

I looked for Axel through the strobing dance floor, but it was so dark that I only caught people's faces in flashes. I made my way toward Mimi, who stood by the infinity pool, looking out across the twinkling lights of El Dorado. But that's when I saw two people who shouldn't have been here at all.

Vince and Jade.

They approached us, and just by the look in Jade's eye, I knew she wanted trouble. She whispered something in Vince's ear. They laughed, never taking their gaze off us.

"I know Axel didn't invite them," Mimi said.

"Then why are they here?"

"Who cares? Why don't we just go dance?" She grabbed my hand. But before we could escape, Vince bumped into Mimi, doing one of the lowest things you could do to someone. Because his hand drifted to the butt of her dress.

"Oops. Accident." He laughed.

"Don't touch me ever again. I decide who does, and how," Mimi said, seething.

Up close, I got a better look at Vince. He wore the same woozy expression he'd had the night we found him in the school bathroom.

"Who cares anyway?" Vince scoffed. "I thought you were attracted to everyone?"

And that's when my fun-loving friend totally lost it. "Scumbag!" Mimi screamed, and shoved Vince, sending him stumbling backward into the pool.

He hit the water with a splash.

"Oops. I guess that was an accident too." Mimi smiled.

It was one of those epic moments where everyone cheered. "Finally, the leech is in the water!" Asha, the girl from my debate team, yelled.

Vince climbed out of the pool, drenched.

Samantha joined us, all smiles. "I can't say I didn't enjoy that."

"Revenge is a drink best served bubbly and cold. And I've earned one," Mimi proclaimed. She reached for the red cup that sat on the patio table, grabbing mine by mistake.

Thinking little of it, I took her drink—which was left sitting there—for myself. Then Mimi and I went inside, leaving behind a Vince who was dripping with anger. I could feel him staring daggers into our backs—and I got the sensation that this wasn't over.

▶ 39.

"Higher Love"
—Whitney Houston

The crowd inside was thick.

"Excuse me. Pardon. Sorry," I shouted over the beat.

I pushed through the sea of people, and it wasn't long before someone crashed into me, making me spill my drink all over my shirt.

"Wow. Just what I needed," I muttered.

But when I looked up, it was none other than Jade. I should have known.

"So sorry about that," Jade said, disingenuous. "You should watch where you're going."

"You know *sorority* isn't just a place with custom pillows and cheap mimosas, right?" Mimi told her. "It's about defending each other. And that's what we need, not all this drama."

"Why are you talking to me? Don't you have reptiles to water?"

"Your understanding of biology is shocking."

Jade scoffed and went off into the crowd. Mimi grabbed paper towels from the kitchen, then got down on her knees to help me clean my shirt.

"It's okay, Mimi. Really."

"Well at least now you smell like rosé. That's classy, right?" She blotted me. "Bougie people buy perfumes to smell like this." But when Mimi got to her feet, she stumbled, like she was getting dizzy. "I feel weird," she said.

"It's probably just a head rush from standing up too fast. Here, just relax." I reached for her.

"No, I'm okay. I'm okay. . . ." Mimi grabbed my hands, getting weirdly tense. "Luna, you know I love you, right?"

"I love you, too," I said. "Is everything okay? What's up with you tonight?"

Mimi checked her blind spots as if someone was listening. Her pupils were bigger than flying saucers as she said, "Luna, I . . . I don't know. Forget about it. It's nothing."

"What is it, Mimi?"

"It's nothing. Just promise me you'll have fun tonight, okay?" But as she spoke, I could tell her eyes were trained on the front door. Someone unexpected had entered.

"Um, what is Andy doing here?" Mimi asked, puzzled.

Everyone stopped dancing to watch him. Even Nika's DJ records scratched silent.

"BOOOOO! Party's over," someone guffawed. "Hey, Retros, your chaperone is here to take you home!"

But Andy just took off his coat, strolled over to a corner where some guys were playing darts, and snatched one, throwing a perfect bull's-eye.

"What happened to the music?" Andy said, and tipped his top hat, giving the music permission to drop again. He always had a way of making an entrance.

We blew the whistles around our necks in approval.

"Mimi, what did you want to tell me?" But by the time I glanced over, she was off dancing in the crowd. Swept up by electronica and flashing lights. Mimi was partying hard that night.

Like really hard.

I kept an eye on her as she moved to the beat—just to make sure everything was okay. But whatever Mimi's problem was, she was clearly having fun despite it. And when she was ready to talk, I knew she would open up to me.

I felt someone take my hand, spinning me onto the dance floor. I couldn't see his face, but I didn't need to. My body had memorized his touch.

"I was looking all over for you," I said, feeling his warmth.

"I'm sorry. But I've had you on my mind. I just got a little caught up back there." Axel kissed my cheek with those plump lips of his. We danced in the dark, bodies close. He touched my hips. Caressed my neck. I smelled his cologne. He spun me to face him, and when the beat dropped, he kissed me. Intense, hot, sweet. That kiss was everything and more.

But this time in front of everyone.

Instantly I could feel eyes watching us. This wasn't a secret kiss in a projector room, or a hand searching for mine on the bus—this was out in the open.

I panicked. "Axel, you just kissed me in front of everyone."

"So what? I'm tired of feeling like this is wrong."

It was so hard to say no to him. And it's not like I wanted him to stop, either.

Axel sparkled like jewels. "But you're right. Let me do this in a way you deserve."

He got this crazy look in his eye.

Axel got down on one knee before me.

"What are you doing?"

"Luna, I have a confession to make. Lately, I get dizzy. I don't sleep. I'm even listening to country music duets, my god. What's wrong with me?" He laughed and ran his hands through his hair. "You've conquered me without even trying."

Axel reached into a snack bowl, grabbing a mini chocolate doughnut.

"Are you really doing this?"

"Watch me," he replied boldly as he took my hand.

"So, Luna Maria Valero Iglesias . . ." His voice cracked as he put the mini doughnut on my ring finger. "Will you go out with me, officially?"

But the answer was already shining out of me.

"Absolutely!" I screamed—for the excitement. The nerves. The fear. All of it at once. Axel pulled me into his arms. He bit the doughnut off my finger. I smushed it in his face, and we kissed. Music blaring. He whisked me off the dance floor and into a long velvety hallway.

"Where are we going?"

"There's something I want you to see."

He grabbed my hand, dominant. We traveled through the corridor, devouring each other with our eyes. Kissing as books fell from the shelves. I wanted him so bad.

We finally got to the end of the hall, where there was a single door.

His bedroom.

It was ultramodern and sleek, like the rest of the house. Axel closed the door behind us, rendering the party a faint rumble in the background. The sound of our breath echoed between pattering drops of rain. Axel went to his desk and produced a little box, wrapped in a bow. "I see how you're always listening to your Walkman," he started.

I opened the gift, and inside was a cassette. It sparkled in the starlight.

"So I made you a mixtape of a whole bunch of covers. I played all the songs myself on my new guitar." He smiled sheepishly.

"You're so sweet! So, you actually play the guitar?"

"The Spanish one." He winked.

"All these years, you've hidden your giant heart pretty well—you know that, right?" I jumped into his arms. "Thank you, Axel, this is so beautiful."

"I was avoiding you earlier because I kept messing up the last song, and I had to get it just right."

I ran my hands through his messy hair, pulling him in close until we fell back onto his bed, looking into each other's eyes. We were alone. Finally.

Or at least, that's what we thought.

Clunk—across the room, books crashed to the floor.

And the sound came from the shadows.

Jade was standing there in silence.

I leapt up.

"Spilling my drink on me wasn't enough for you?"

"What the hell are you doing in my room?" Axel was tense. "Here to mess with my brakes again?"

"Don't be dramatic—no one got hurt." Jade rolled her eyes.

"Why don't you go to the kitchen, go into the bottom left drawer. Grab a spoon. Enjoy your reflection and leave us alone." Axel was so over her.

"How did you even get in here?" I asked.

"It's not like I don't know my way around Axel's bedroom."

"What a charming and pleasant person you are. Can you leave now, please?"

"I don't think you want me to do that just yet, Luna." Jade grinned, pulling out a leather-bound journal. "Because I think you're really going to want to know what's inside this diary."

"Axel, what is that?" I tugged his sleeve.

But the sight of that journal made Axel paralyzed.

"I know you put on a good show in public, but why don't you tell her how you really are in private? All the secrets your little diary says that you dare not tell . . ."

"Axel?"

His fists were curled.

Rain barraged the world outside, like glass shattering from the sky.

"What do you think those marks are?" Jade pointed. I followed her finger, realizing there were covered-up holes in the drywall. Damage done by Axel's hands.

As a woman, to see something like that was really disturbing.

Jade sauntered over and stuffed the book in my chest. "Read up, princess. Things get pretty violent in this storybook."

Axel's eyes watered. "I've never laid a hand on you, Jade. I would never—"

"That may be true, but that doesn't mean Luna wants to be with someone who has a violent temper. Don't say I didn't warn you."

"Why are you telling me this?"

Instead of answering me, she walked out of the room.

I was now alone with the guy who I used to think I knew so well.

We were *together*, but who was I with?

I sat there in silence, waiting for him to speak.

Maybe I was blind. But I guess I wanted to be blind with him. I didn't want to see.

"I told you that I'm messed up inside." Axel paced the room. His slid his back down a wall to the floor. "Luna, that's why I have the diary."

I opened up the diary and flipped through the entries, stained with years of anger and anguish. Pages of chicken scratch, strange sketches, bold curse words, ripped pages.

"I never told anyone, but I'm seeing a psychologist."

"Okay . . . that's good."

"She has me write everything down. It looks scary, I know. She calls it a rage book. I'm supposed to use it to express myself in a controlled way."

I placed the book in his hands, very gently. "It's okay to not be okay. No one is one hundred percent fine all the time. . . ."

"You never saw the things that people would say to me online. You don't see the hate. If I read comments long enough, I'd spend days thinking I wasn't funny enough, not cool enough or whatever. I just bottled all the anger up, and I guess after seeing what happened to Samantha, how I didn't do anything to stop her from being bullied, I felt powerless. Like a hypocrite—the same way I felt when my dad cheated on my mom, and then I didn't do anything about it. So, I've just been getting so angry with myself ever since . . . until I finally broke. . . ."

And suddenly everything made sense.

All those warnings about how complicated he was.

The fights he'd get in.

The reason why he pushed his life to the limits of danger, and all the reckless behavior—this was the ugly reflection of Prince Charming that you never read about.

"You know what's funny? Even with all the cars and money, I never saw my mother happier than when she found out I was taking the Retro Challenge," Axel said.

He laughed. He cried a little.

"I guess I'm pretty screwed up in the head, aren't I?"

I was trembling inside, but it didn't matter. I kissed him anyway. "No, you're not. You're a work in progress, Axel. We all are. Take me, for example. Sometimes I get anxious at the smallest things. Like talking to strangers. Or confronting cockroaches."

He laughed. "Luna, day by day, I'm getting better. Ever since the first day of school. And getting to know you has been the best part."

"Wait, when I yelled at you?"

"Luna, I've had eyes for you since that day in the cafeteria. You challenge me. More than any stunt. Any dangerous race. More than any stupid dare. And more than any kind of contest Limbo can think up . . . Luna, I'm falling for you."

I kissed him.

But this time was different. It wasn't sweet.

It was hard.

Raw.

I gave him everything I had. He gave every single part of himself right back until we were on the bed together. I pulled off his shirt. Climbed on top of him. And not just out of lust, but because it was the only possible way to be closer to him.

I didn't even know what I was doing because I had never done it before. My body was so nervous. But with Axel none of that mattered. He respected me, just as he had promised. We needed to connect with each other.

Until we finally did.

In a rhythm that was just ours.

My heart pounded. My forehead pressed against his. The only way to fuse with everything he was. All the romantic gestures and the complications. The gentle pain. The beauty and the ugly truth.

I wanted all of it.

They say it feels like prickling effervescent bubbles popping all over your skin. Like you're an explosive volcano in the moment it erupts. Like a rocket blasting off into space. And now I could say for certain all of that was true, but what was surprising were the sensations that never came—because contrary to everything I had ever read or heard, I didn't feel like any more of a woman for what I had just experienced.

And that was the best feeling of all, a reminder that I was born complete. I spent an eternity on Axel's bed, my head lying on his chest. And though that eternity didn't feel like enough, I knew I couldn't stay there all night.

"We should get back to the party," I said as I slipped into my clothes, pulling Axel in by the belt for one last kiss. As seductive as I tried to act, my legs trembled like chow mein noodles crammed into jeans.

"But I don't want to . . . ," he groaned.

"What if our friends are looking for us?"

"They know that I'm taking good care of you. At least let me make you a microwavable pizza and pour you a soda first, while you find the group."

"I can't say no to that."

He buttoned up his shirt. "Why don't I catch up with you in a bit? I'm going to make sure the lock on the door is actually working so no more vampires get in the room."

"See you in a few minutes." I kissed him goodbye.

I wandered through Axel's home until I finally reached the main wing of the mansion. It was the middle of the night, that strange end to the party where most people have already cleared out. This was definitely the comedown.

And my friends were nowhere in sight.

I pushed past the empty dance floor and started searching the guest bedrooms. Couples melted together. Dudes played cards on a couch. Sticky tile under my feet. Cups and Ping-Pong balls floating in the pool. Evidence of a wild night.

I went for the last room down the hall, but it was locked. Darnell opened the door at my knock but kept the gap slim, stopping me from going inside.

"Have you seen Mimi?"

"Last I knew she was dancing her little ass off."

"Then where is she?"

"Luna, she's not here," he said sternly, and slammed the door in my face. It was strange behavior, because normally Darnell would be hanging out with our little unicorn. Or at least care where she was.

Then Kilo came inside from the balcony. "You're looking for Mimi?"

"Yeah, have you seen her?"

"She was acting really weird. I tried to help her, but she wouldn't let me. Then I heard she threw up and locked herself in the upstairs bathroom. She's not here, so she must have gone home."

"Oh no, poor Mimi! I had no idea she was feeling that bad."

"I'm sure she's fine," Kilo reassured me.

"Maybe I should call her house and see if she needs anything."

"And get her in trouble with her parents?"

"Good point. She'd kill me."

Sure, I was concerned that Mimi had gotten sick, but it wasn't unlike her to go all out. And it wasn't unlike her to leave early, either. So I let it go. But, looking back, I wish I could recall every single second—every movement of that night. Every single face that went in and out of the party. If I had been more clearheaded I would've put together the clues, and I could've stopped the insanity that turned my storybook dream into a nightmare.

⏸ 40.

Pause

Something is freaking me out. I was having a staring competition with the cookies when I noticed it, right underneath the tempting treats.

A little white envelope.

Within is a single folded letter.

My eyes finally find their focus, and I see the words, written on elegant parchment:

> *Luna,*
> *The only way to escape is to make that door*
> *open.*

This is a clue.

Maybe someone here is on my side.

Whoever wrote this secret message is trying to help me get out of this place. And I just realized exactly how to do it. So I take a deep breath.

I start scarfing down cookies.

One after another.

After another.

And only when my mouth is finally crusty do I start choking. I'm gasping for air, falling to my knees. And before long, I'm wheezing in between each bite. I hope this plan works. I want to believe that they won't let me die in here.

Sirens wail.

Flashing red lights are everywhere.

I hear footsteps approaching. They're closing in.

Guards swarm to my aid as I writhe on the floor.

Time for phase two of the plan.

I throw out an elbow, connecting with a guard's face. I hit him so hard, the tooth fairy will go bankrupt tonight. And then I dart through the opening—into the hall, past the guards. This is my one shot. I'm going to make it out of here! Or at least, I think—

A sack is thrown over my head.

They're binding my hands.

And now I'm consumed by my friend darkness.

▶ 41.

"Oops! . . . I Did It Again"
—Britney Spears

I spent the whole weekend daydreaming about the night of the party. My mind replayed snapshots of what had happened, reliving the rush of feelings that had drowned me in pleasure. I was turned on like a monkey in heat. I had to calm myself down by taking cold showers while conjuring up images of the pope in leggings doing hot yoga.

No offense if you're into that type of stuff.

I thought about how all this time that Jade was trying to sabotage my relationship with Axel—maybe a part of her was actually trying to help me.

But most importantly, I thought about what Mimi wanted to tell me that was so important. I called her a million times to make sure that she was okay, but she never answered. And after a while of not hearing from her, I started to wonder if maybe she'd partied too hard.

This was officially the first time in history I was happy on a Monday, because I'd get to see her before class and catch up.

Or at least that's what I thought. . . .

I strode through the halls of El Dorado. After everything that had happened Friday night, I felt different. I felt better. And seeing Samantha back at school was the cherry on top.

"Hey, party animal," she said as I approached.

"Look at you! Back and ready for the jungle." Sure, El Dorado has its own ecosystem, but this school had definitely changed since she left. Because when Samantha opened her locker, dozens of little papers and cards poured out.

"Oh my gosh. What are these?"

"People have been slipping welcome-back cards inside, notes of encouragement . . ."

She smiled, eyes welling up as she looked through them. And I could only imagine what weight those letters held, considering everything.

"Did you know this is the first time that we're publicly talking together at school?"

"That's how it should have been all along," she responded, gazing at the little photo of us she kept inside her locker.

"Let's take a new one!" I said. We took a selfie with my film camera.

"So, you've got to update me . . . what have I missed around here?"

"Oh, not much," I laughed.

"Just the minor detail that you're one of the most popular girls in school."

"Still getting used to that."

"I'm sure you'll handle it better than me," she said.

"Well, it's a lot easier with Mimi by my side. By the way, have you seen her? I haven't talked to her all morning. . . ."

"No, I haven't, not yet. . . ."

Then someone approached from behind and covered my eyes.

"Are you ready?" Axel kissed me. "Let me take you somewhere special."

"Yep. Not sticking around for tonsil hockey." Samantha took her cue to leave.

"Bye, Samantha," Axel laughed. Hands still over my eyes, he guided me through the darkness. "Don't worry. You just have to trust me."

And I actually did. Completely. Even when the creaky hinges of the doorway squealed open and shut. And when I opened my eyes, I could hardly see in the dim red light.

It was just him and me alone.

"Are we supposed to be here?"

He smiled and dangled a key ring. "I did steal the keys. . . ."

The vibe of the darkroom was grungy, but kind of romantic all the same. And just when I went to kiss him, I was hit with a strong, stinging odor.

"Cool, right?" Axel said. "I've got all types of chemicals here. I bet we could survive a nuclear Armageddon in this place. I thought I could show you how to develop your photos, so you never forget this time of your life."

"Seriously, Axel, this place is incredible."

"Here, give me your camera." He reached around me, our bodies close, and slipped it off my shoulder. Then he took out the film.

"Yours will take some time to develop, but check out these other negatives in the enlarger." He guided me by the shoulders to a machine off to the side.

I felt his hand graze my own.

It gave me chills.

I tried to look through the photos, but I could barely think. I could only feel his heat against my neck. My fingers quickly chose a photo of all of us at the bonfire. Axel must have taken it when I wasn't looking.

"At first you can't really see all the possibilities, because they're all in the little negative, but if you just expand your vision," he whispered, focusing the negative, "then everything finally makes sense."

Axel and I looked into each other's eyes as he clicked on the exposure light.

"It's all crystal clear to me," I told him, wetting my lips.

He placed the sheet of photographic paper in the developing tray. "Now it's up to the chemicals." Like magic, the photo began to fade in, sparkling to life—and so did a million tingling feelings inside me. "I know those photos belong to you, but I thought we could make them real together. I never want you to forget them. After all, being able to enjoy memories is like living them twice."

"But what about this moment? I don't want to forget it, either."

Axel pulled me up onto one of the tables and slowly caressed my hips. I put my wrists around his shoulders in the dark. I kissed him hard. He bit my lip. Shirts came off. Red heat pounded against our bodies. We were losing control all over again. But if my life were a movie, here's where the projector catches on fire.

Knock. Knock. Knock.

I was so startled, I knocked over the photo-developing tray. We raced to rebutton our clothes.

"It's probably just the photography club." Axel tried to calm the tension. But it wasn't working. I was silently hysterical. He disarmed the lock. But before he could open the door, it burst inward, giving way to a hyperventilating Miranda.

"Luna," she said. "There are detectives in the cafeteria. And they're looking for you."

My brain could barely process her words.

Since class still hadn't started, many students were hanging out in the cafeteria. Everyone was trying to blend in with their surroundings while a couple of detectives spoke with students and staff. The elephants were back to sit on my chest, but this time they'd brought the entire safari to join the anxiety party.

I found my friends at our usual table.

"I don't like the look of this," Kilo said.

Samantha was on edge. "Is this really happening?"

I had spent most of my life being afraid of anyone with a badge.

Maybe I watched the news too much.

The fear of Immigration always made things worse. In moments when my family was between visas, usually for some stupid paperwork mistake, we were afraid that if someone broke into our home, one call to the police could have my family deported. We couldn't even be witnesses to a crime. Because those who were supposed to keep me safe often left me trembling. But I was hit with relief when I realized that the investigation was led by a woman who must have been Darnell's mother. Darnell looked just like her.

I remembered that she was a private detective, which meant she didn't work for the police.

My chest started to unclench.

"There you are, Ms. Iglesias. I've been looking for you." She stepped forward, smiling warmly. She had beautiful silver streaks in her hair. "I want to ask some questions about someone you know." She extended a photo. On it was a girl who'd taken the Retro Challenge, one who wore loc'ed hair and had sleeves of swirling tattoos. Who had been on my mind lately, because we had been beginning to truly see each other as friends until she was eliminated.

Until she vanished.

"Ruby Delgado ran away last week," Darnell's mother told us. "But since she's been in communication with her parents, sending texts, the police won't investigate it yet. Something doesn't sit right with my gut. So we're asking around to see if there's more to the story. And we think it's important to talk to you, because the last time anyone saw her was at your Halloween event at the mall."

"We all had a really great time—I don't understand why she would take off."

"And you're sure Ruby hasn't reached out to you at all?"

"No, I haven't heard from her. I've been phoneless since the challenge started."

"Yeah. Right," she said.

"I wish we knew more. . . . Maybe Limbo can steer you in the right direction?"

"Thanks. We're already on it—I'm sure we'll get to the bottom of things. No need to be alarmed, just vigilant." She took my hand. "I'm so glad to finally meet you, Luna. My son isn't getting you guys into too much trouble? He did get home at four in the morning last weekend."

"Not at all," Samantha declared. "I went straight home when it ended."

"*Ma*, chill out—it was just a math party." Darnell rolled his eyes.

"You want to be grounded, child?" she joked, then turned to Axel. "Hey, kiddo, could I steal you for a few more questions?"

"I'll do whatever I can to help, ma'am," Axel said, walking off with her.

Although the conversation was kept light, the implications were weighty. I turned to my friends. "I just can't picture that sweet girl with all those artistic aspirations ditching her life and giving up on the challenge, can you?"

Darnell's mother thought there could be more to the story, which disturbed me—and the more I entertained the idea, the more I worried.

"Have any of you seen Mimi since the party?"

Darnell knew where my mind was going. "Luna, don't trip. I'm sure she's fine. And Ruby is probably off tattooing swear words on some biker gang on Route 66. And if she really did run away, my mom is a top-notch private detective. Ruby is in good hands."

"It wouldn't hurt to check in on Mimi after school."

"I agree. I think that's a good idea," Samantha said, backing me up.

"I'm sorry, I can't; I have to work in the auto shop. But I'm sure Mimi's fine," Kilo said, trying to be hopeful. "She probably just got a little sick from the weekend, that's all."

"I have tons of homework tonight," Darnell said. But he was avoiding something beneath his sincerity, which wasn't like him. And now I couldn't help adding up his weird behavior lately— plus, his mother had mentioned that Darnell got home long after the party ended.

Darnell was lying about something.

But before I could follow those thoughts, my attention was snatched away by a certain girl in black-and-gold cheer squad apparel. I saw her out of the corner of my eye as she entered the cafeteria and stopped dead in her tracks. Because as soon as Jade caught sight of the detectives, she took off running.

Which meant, in every language, that she had something serious to hide.

Jade disappeared into a mass of students.

And soon I was chasing after her.

"Luna, hold up! Where are you going?" Samantha caught up with me.

But I had my sights trained on Jade, who was already pushing past people until she finally snuck out of the emergency exit at the far end of the hall.

Close on her tail, I stopped in the open doorway. Samantha grabbed my arm. "Luna, tell me what is going on."

I pointed into the distance, beyond the parking lot, as Jade slipped through a hole in the rusty chain-link fence that separated our school from the abandoned forest.

"What's Jade running from?" Samantha asked.

The only way to find that answer was to follow her.

▶ 42.

"These Boots Are Made for Walkin'"
—Nancy Sinatra

The abandoned forest was like a twisted Garden of Eden.

You could get away with anything in the there. It was where most kids experienced their first wild hookup, their first shot of tequila, or their first cigarette. It was actually a nature preserve, but due to budget cuts a few years back, we no longer had park rangers. A technical no-man's-land. It was like whatever happened there never occurred. So, when a tree fell in that forest, it truly didn't make a sound.

We followed Jade along an overgrown path claimed by greedy gnarled trees. My foot slipped as I ducked under a knotted branch.

But Samantha was there to catch me. "I know you're a tough cookie, but you don't have to do everything alone. Especially if you run like a drunk baby deer."

I chuckled. "My favorite machine at the gym is the television."

"Well, learn to run faster, because we're losing her!"

Jade had picked up the pace and started making erratic turns off the path until we found ourselves completely lost. We were enveloped in fog so thick that we could hardly see each other, lungs stinging as if stabbed by needles in the cold. I was getting nervous. Impatient. And the murder of crows squawking overhead didn't help. But when Samantha shrieked, instinct took over. I ran to her.

"What is it? Are you okay?"

Samantha pointed.

Then a terrible sensation invaded my body, because before her was another dead animal.

A fawn, eyes wide open, petrified. It lay there on the old railroad tracks that ran through the forest. No cuts. No blood. Like Kilo had said, these animals weren't dying of natural causes.

"It's, like, just stuck there."

Samantha lost herself in thought. "Wait—I can't believe I didn't think of this earlier, but I know where Jade could be."

She brushed dirt with her feet, revealing more old tracks. "This railroad means we're close."

We followed them until we reached a clearing with an old train car that must have been here for generations, its wrought-iron exterior now green with moss. Dandelion spores floated to the earth like snowfall. It was a place that would have been magical if it hadn't been defiled.

Bottles of booze. Cans of spray paint. Broken glass.

Vince, Chad, and the rest of the Goldens were there, spray-painting the side of the train car in a storm cell of vape smoke. They were joined by some girls from the cheer team, but even so, Jade didn't look entirely comfortable.

Vince tossed his spray can and approached. "Good afternoon, ladies. I'm flattered that you'd join us."

"Hell no. I won't make the same mistake twice," Samantha growled.

"Then what are you doing here? We don't sell pills. At least not your type."

Chad and Juan Solo chuckled, but Jade socked Vince on the arm. "Seriously, Vince?" And usually he got away with those kinds of comments. That is, until now.

"Xanax," Samantha said defiantly. "That's what I took that night. Thirty-seven pills. And if I had the ovaries to do that, imagine what I could do to you now that I feel stronger." She sauntered toward him. "But you're not afraid of *me*, are you?"

She reached out to touch him. "I used to melt for those muscles of yours. I went wild for these arms."

Vince looked at his friends, starting to get creeped out.

"But if I'm the crazy one, why are *you* the one who takes tons of selfies because no image of yourself is good enough? The one who always photoshops a six-pack onto his body."

Some of the other Goldens began to snicker. I was more afraid that this unpredictable Samantha would pull out a knife or something.

"Don't worry—I will never make fun of your insecurities online. That's the kind of person *you* are. I may be on pills, but I'm not as screwed up as you." Then she looked into his eyes honestly. "What a shame you didn't have the courage to take the Retro Challenge, because you needed it more than anyone."

And that's when Jade stepped in between them, coming to Vince's aid. "Go home, Samantha. Why are you following me anyway? What, are you obsessed with me?"

"What happened to you, Jade?" Samantha said, hurt. "We're supposed to be friends."

It was my turn to speak. "We're here because you two know where Ruby is."

"You're wasting your time. I don't know anything about that girl." Vince shook his head.

"Then why did Jade run from the detectives?"

"I don't know what you're talking about. Maybe the popularity is frying your brain."

"Then what about Mimi?" I demanded. "Nobody has seen her since the party—last thing we know she was feeling sick and went upstairs."

Jade laughed it off. "Honestly, I was so wasted that night I almost drank the water from the flower vase. I can't remember. Don't bother me."

"I don't buy it. I work at a movie theater. I can smell a bad actor from a mile away."

"You're so lost," Vince laughed. "Why don't you go talk to your friend Darnell? I'm sure he would know. He was the only other person upstairs all night long."

Then he grinned darkly and said words that I'll never forget.

"Don't trust everything you see, Luna. After all, salt looks a lot like sugar."

▶ 43.

"Africa"
—Toto

Mimi had taken up residence in the garage after her reptile/cat farm ruined her father's favorite Persian rug. The animals got banished from the house, and Mimi couldn't sleep without cuddling them to death. But she was always like that, generous and full of love, even if the rest of civilization didn't exactly understand.

Which was why Mimi deserved someone to check up on her.

I promised myself when I knocked on the door not to alarm her parents. They didn't need that. And neither did Mimi if she'd just been playing hooky all along. I needed to act calm. To make the situation appear as normal as possible. So I brought leftovers of cocido, a Spanish soup, which was basically kryptonite for Mimi and her father.

Mimi's father answered the door in a full-on suit. He was the town's real estate king and was, per usual, juggling multiple calls at once.

"Luna, what a surprise! What can I do for you?" He noticed

the soup and immediately hung up the phone. "Is that Gloria's cocido?"

"She made it especially for you and Mimi, because she knows how much you love it."

"Wow, thank you! We *need* to have you guys over for dinner soon. Your mother is just a bundle of wisdom. I use some of her lines at my quarterly meetings."

"Well, as she says, everyone is the smartest until they see a sticker on a door that says push or pull."

He laughed. "Great life philosophy. Well, I'm sorry, Loony, but Mimi's not here. She left over the weekend for a climate change protest near San Francisco."

That answer almost knocked me off my feet.

"This has to be some kind of mistake—it's weird that she didn't tell me anything. You know she missed school today, right?"

"I dropped out to start my business when I was about your age. And even if I got a hippie daughter, she has my full support. Not all knowledge comes from books, you know?" he said. "I'm sure Mimi will be back soon with tons of stories to share with us. The best way to understand that girl is to acknowledge that you don't. And love her as she is." He chuckled and shook his head. "Your generation is so funny—you're down for tear gas, but you're too afraid to protest when your restaurant order comes out wrong."

"Okay, then . . . ," I said, starting to calm down a little. But as soon as I turned to leave, Mimi's father added a final comment that made my stomach crawl into a knot.

"She sent me a text message when she arrived, so I'm sure she's fine."

The words "text message" reverberated inside me, multiplying my worries. Something was seriously wrong here. It wasn't like Mimi to just leave without mentioning it to anyone—but even more telling was the fact that I knew she would never consciously break the rules of the Retro Challenge. She wouldn't abandon what we had built together.

Did Mimi take off like Ruby?

Are they together?

Or is something more sinister at play?

I couldn't picture Mimi sending that text message, but if it was true, it meant elimination. I feared that whatever had happened to Ruby was happening to her as well, and all the facts pointed in one direction—Mimi was gone without a trace.

▶ 44.

"Ain't No Mountain High Enough"
—Marvin Gaye and Tammi Terrell

Things were getting out of control.

It was straight-up Retromania.

And everything started the next day at school. It was cool to see so many enthusiastic people, but the sheer volume was overwhelming. There were, like, hundreds of Retromaniacs waiting in the parking lot.

"Where are all these people coming from?" Kilo asked.

The answer was spelled out all over the license plates in the parking lot. These Retromaniacs weren't local like they used to be—they were coming from all over the country. As we approached campus, Limbo workers stepped in quickly to usher us along like bodyguards.

"What are we, a boy band now?" Kilo complained.

We weren't backing down from the challenge, and it was clear that the challenge wasn't backing down from us. The stone pathway that once led into El Dorado had become a red carpet lined with screaming supporters, clad in the colorful merch we'd been shown in Limboland. And the camera lights kept flashing all the way to class. Fans gushed from the crowd:

"Luna, you're my hero!"

"Axel, are you in love with Luna or Jade?"

"I watch every single video!" I recognized that voice immediately. It was Xena—the sweet girl who'd asked for my autograph back at the shopping challenge. She rolled up in her wheelchair, smiling brightly.

"Xena! I can't believe you're here!" I went to say hello, but an arm immediately blocked my path. The Limbo guards made it clear I was to walk a straight line.

All this was too much.

At the end of the hysteria was Andy, face painted white and cheeks rosy, twirling his cane like the leader of a marching band. "Welcome, my dear Retros! How wonderful it is to be so adored," he chortled. "It doesn't matter if you're famous or infamous; all that matters is that you're a shining star now!"

"It does matter to me," Kilo said, pulling his hood up to hide his face.

"I totally agree," Axel added. "It always did to me, even when I first got famous."

"If you don't like our culture, then all you need to do is touch a screen," Andy said through a slim grin. At the end of the day, Limbo lived by its own rules. But my own worries not only made it hard to enjoy this special day, they blinded me completely.

Because as I walked up to school, I saw the outline of a familiar person.

She stood right by our lockers, flipping around her pink pigtail in long, mismatched tube socks. But what happened next was like a bad dream.

Because when I sprinted over and touched her shoulder, it wasn't her at all.

"Hey, Luna," the girl said, a stranger's voice. "I hope you and Mimi win the challenge!" She pointed to her shirt, which read #TEAMMIMI.

It was just another Retromaniac following Mimi's trend.

Inside I was full of contradictions, because I could be feeling warmth thanks to their support, while my worries for my very best friend were only spiraling.

"Sorry," I said. "I thought you were someone else."

"No problem. See you around at the mall!"

I wasn't okay. This just marked another morning without my friend, and all day I felt like I was distant from those I held close.

Especially Darnell.

Because in math class, when he left for the bathroom, he took his backpack, as if he was going to leave school entirely. Acting uncharacteristically shady. Though, just before exiting, Darnell made one critical mistake. He crumpled up a piece of paper and tossed it in the trash.

The lunch bell rang out, but it couldn't silence the words that echoed in my brain.

Don't trust everything you see, Luna. After all, salt looks a lot like sugar.

What the hell did Vince mean by that? Why was he talking in such a weird way? I wasn't going to trust any accusation that someone like Vince made about Darnell. But I needed to know if Darnell really was the last person who saw her, the last person who spoke to her. What did he know about Mimi's absence?

What happened upstairs in those final hours? Even if he was with someone in the bedroom, why was he hiding from his very own friends?

I couldn't believe that Darnell had anything to do with what happened to Mimi. He was our friend, but clearly there was more to the story.

So I peered into the trash to take out that crumpled piece of paper.

Which read:

RDD 1PM

And I knew exactly what that meant, and where I needed to go next.

► 45.

"Don't You (Forget About Me)"
—Simple Minds

Luckily, I was able to get out of my last class of the day. All I had to do was say I was having a girl moment and list reproductive organs to my physics teacher until his head exploded, setting me free into the world. But when I arrived at the mall, I realized there was already a line just to enter. Our town had become a holy land for Retromaniacs from all over. The Monteverde Mall was suddenly a main attraction.

My mom had hired three new employees to keep up with demand—but even then it was never enough, because every seat was filled.

I found her wrestling a massive stack of film reels. "¡Hola, hija! What a surprise! Did you come to help me install the new projectors and organize our new classic film library?"

"Oh . . . I have other things to do, and I'm really tired," I lied, which made me feel terrible. But I couldn't freak her out about Mimi.

"Did I hear you say, 'Yes, Mamá, of course. Mamá, I would love to! Mamá, that's everything I want to do in this life'?"

"Okay, first let me grab our favorite combos from the Roller Derby Diner, and then we'll get to work? We're going to need our energy."

"¡Buena idea! See, you are not tired—you are fresh like lettuce!"

I darted out, knowing that I had only a limited amount of time to pull this thing off. I practically slid down the rails of the escalator and into the diner. And there he was. Sitting all alone. Waiting for someone. I stalked past the red plush burger counter to sit directly across from Darnell—who jumped out of his seat.

"AHH! Sweet baby Jesus, what the hell are you doing here?!"

"Maybe I should be asking you the same question." I unfolded the note I'd found and tossed it to him. "Friends tell each other everything, Darnell. But there's something you're not telling me."

He looked around shiftily. "You can't be here right now."

"Why?"

"I can't tell you, Luna!"

Now I was starting to lose my cool. I stood up, raising my voice. "You were the last person upstairs that night, and the last one to see Mimi! What are you hiding?"

"Darnell was with me that night," said a baritone voice.

An accent that I recognized immediately.

Kosta was dressed in uniform—out of school early as part of his work-study exchange program— holding a tray of burgers and fries. His hands were visibly shaking, and he looked like he wanted to be anywhere but here.

"You don't have to explain anything," Darnell told him.

"It's okay. I want to," Kosta said, then took a seat next to

Darnell, across from me. "Darnell and I are together. At the party, you tried to enter the bedroom, and Darnell stopped you because I was there. He's been protecting me."

Darnell took my hand. "I'm sorry I wasn't forthright with you, but I know from experience that you can't make anyone—"

"Come out of the bedroom." Kosta laughed nervously, finally breathing out. Tears collected in the corners of his eyes, and I hoped they were made of relief.

"It's nobody's right but your own. I'm sorry I pushed this." I smiled.

"Don't be. I've been afraid for so long that my friends could find out at any moment and hate me for something I have no control over."

"None of us are going to judge you—and anyone who does was never really your friend in the first place." I looked to Darnell to apologize, but he was already reading my mind.

"It's not necessary, really," he said.

"At least let me give you tickets to see any movie you want tonight. My treat."

"We accept." Kosta smiled, collecting himself.

After a moment, I leaned in. "Our little unicorn is gone. Mimi's father said he received a text from her saying that she skipped town."

"Are you serious?!" Darnell buried his head in his hands. "This is so messed up. I don't believe it. There were too many lies at that party."

"What do you mean?"

"Listen, I want to know what's going on with Mimi as much as you do. That's why Kosta's been helping me."

Kosta looked around to make sure no one was listening. "My boss told me he saw your friend Samantha here on the night of the party."

"So what? We always come to the diner."

"Luna, she gave a fake name and wore a black hoodie so no one would recognize her."

"That's her new look now," I said, defensive.

"And she ordered a meal for two," Kosta added.

But Darnell had a point that I couldn't deny. "Don't you get it? She lied to my mother," he said. "She lied to a detective about going home as soon as the party ended. But she didn't."

"This doesn't sound good . . . ," I admitted.

I touched Samantha's whistle. I couldn't refute what I had just heard, but I'd made the mistake of mistrusting Darnell, and next time, I was going to ask the right questions before leaping to judgment. And I knew exactly where to start.

▶ 46.

"Rayando El Sol"
—Maná

Every day after school, Samantha would check herself into the Mission Hospital psychiatric outpatient program for group therapy. After I helped my mother out in the theater, Darnell agreed to drop me off—that way Samantha wouldn't recognize my car. And when the long, nervous ride was over, we finally stopped before the hospital's front entrance.

"Good luck. Tell me everything you find out." He hugged me.

"You know I will."

"See you later, girl. You got this."

I ducked out of the car and went right to the psychiatric wing, searching for my friend. But what I saw threw me for a loop. I thought what I'd find inside would be creepy, like a scary movie, but reality was far less intimidating. Patients crossed through the hall, weak and irresolute, carrying trays of apple juice and milk. There was a line at the front counter, where sharp objects were collected before entry. I found myself feeling terrible that I'd anticipated seeing some kind of horror scene. These were real people who were ill, and they were suffering.

"Thank you, see you next week," came a familiar voice from behind me.

Samantha was signing herself out on a clipboard at the counter, taking back whatever sharp or dangerous items she'd had in her pockets. But of all the dangerous things she kept, the most significant were the secrets she didn't tell. Because before I could get her attention, Samantha was already slipping through the revolving door.

I tried to catch up to her.

I had to know why she'd lied to Darnell's mother.

She traveled through the parking lot but suddenly changed directions, walking around the back of the hospital building instead, as if to hide behind the dumpsters.

What is Samantha doing?

I rounded the corner. But what I found beyond it made my blood curdle. Because there, behind the hospital, arguing with her, was the last person who she should've been alone with.

Samantha was shouting at Vince.

They quarreled until Vince punched a dumpster and slid down to his knees. Samantha tried to comfort him, but he swatted her hand away, stood up, and stormed off. Though I couldn't let Samantha leave without getting answers.

She saw me and nearly lost her footing.

"Luna! What are you doing here?"

"Samantha, what was that?"

She answered too quickly. "Vince tried to kiss me. He's a pig. I guess he wanted to get back at me for calling him out in the forest." Samantha was a good liar, because that reaction was exactly what any of us would have expected from Vince—but it simply wasn't the truth.

I'd seen everything.

He'd never tried to kiss Samantha.

She was trying to cover something up.

I reached out my hand to touch her. "What's really going on, Samantha? If you're in some kind of trouble, you can tell me anything, you know that? I can't handle losing you again."

She looked into my eyes, afraid. Apologetic. "Luna, I promise you that I'm okay. But I can't be talking about this. You should just leave."

And that's when we heard two honks of a horn. It was Samantha's mother, ready to pick her up. This was her cue to hurry inside the car and evade all my questions, but her mother gave me a second chance. She rolled down the window and spoke in that apple-pie drawl. "Howdy, Luna. Do you need a ride?"

"Mrs. Darby! It's great to see you. I would absolutely love that, thank you," I said as I hopped in the back seat. Ready to pack on the pressure.

Samantha was caught, unable to protest.

"It's the least we can do after the mix-up at the mall." She stared laser beams at her daughter. There were moving boxes all over the car. It was sweet of her to offer me a ride, considering that the divorce was in full swing, but Southern hospitality ran deep in their family.

"It's really nice of you to come and support Samantha at her therapy sessions."

"Yeah, Luna really respects my privacy." Samantha rolled her eyes.

"Don't be rude, hon." She lightly swatted at her daughter—and with that movement knocked the top off a plastic cup. One that sat in the front cup holder.

A take-out shake from the Roller Derby Diner!

So I gambled. "How was your meal, Friday night?"

Samantha sank in her seat.

"You lied to a detective," I said. "Why?"

Samantha's mother looked down, embarrassed. "Samantha lives with her father now. The courts ruled that she wasn't allowed to live with me until the trial date," she said, crestfallen.

"We have to steal time together," Samantha confessed.

"Please don't tell anyone about this—we just really need each other right now." Samantha's mother took her hand. "Never divorce a divorce attorney, hon," she joked, but I knew there was a world of truth behind those words.

Samantha was afraid to lose her old life. Her mother. Court is expensive, and Samantha's father wanted to take everything.

It made me get all teary-eyed.

In case there was any doubt, in college, I was planning to minor in chugging coffee and obsessive overthinking. As you can see, I had serious skills.

"You don't have to explain anything to me," I told them. "I've got some homework left to do, so why don't you just drop me off at the library, right up here?" I wasn't going to waste any more of this woman's time with her daughter, not after I realized how precious it was.

They both deserved that, at least.

And I deserved the long walk back to the mall, where my car was. I was going to need time to process everything. Because even if I knew why Samantha was lying, there was still so much uncertainty shrouding Vince and the argument they'd just had. If she knew something about Mimi, whatever it was, she was too afraid to tell.

▶ 47.

"Fast Car"
—Tracy Chapman

Fifty percent. Those are the chances of finding someone after they've been missing for twenty-four hours. If they've been missing for two days the number is 40 percent, and after three days that number is halved. But Mimi's chances were unknown because no one was considering her missing yet, not even her family—and it was all because of that text message.

I felt like no one was listening to me. I was getting desperate.

"Are you okay?" Axel said the next day at school, kissing me on the cheek. We sat at the lunch tables before class, and he pulled me close.

"Thank you, I'm fine," I said, which meant that I wasn't at all. Sometimes when I say I'm fine it means I want someone to look into my eyes, give me a big hug, and whisper softly into my ear, *I made enchiladas.*

"I know you're not." Axel could decode me even when I was an enigma.

"We have to find a way to get the truth out of Vince."

"We'll have to confront him when he least expects it." Axel

held me. "Vince is a jerk, but he's not some supervillain. I'm sure there's a rational explanation for all of this. We're going to find out where Mimi is. And we're going to do it together."

Axel was the only thing holding me together at that moment.

Funny how I'd spent years coming up with snotty comebacks to tell off guys because I thought they'd end up making my life more difficult. But now Axel's support was making me stronger, and it was in those moments that I fell harder for him than ever before.

He wasn't just my boyfriend. He was my partner.

My inward feelings were gleaming for Axel, but on the outside all I could do was worry about Mimi. And my life was about to get even more complicated. Because that day, we were summoned to an elimination challenge.

The Limbo chime rang out over the loudspeakers.

Which meant it was time to go to the Retro Lounge.

The lounge really was a wonderland of pinball machines and games, where nostalgia was present tense and magic was a mood we all shared. But as soon as I stepped inside that room, I knew something was amiss. The Retros were crowding the all-knowing Live Feed wall.

"Did you hear about the new eliminations?" Kosta asked.

"Yeah, they got three more just this week," said Asha.

The contestants who were left whispered among themselves. Deep inside I knew what was happening, but I still needed to be convinced.

I needed to see it for myself.

As I stepped forward, the contestants parted. I made no

sound. Tears streamed inside me. I was drowning in that very silence. Because the next photo crossed out in red, disqualified from the challenge, was hers.

Mimi had been eliminated.

And just because I'd known this moment was coming, it didn't hurt any less.

Her dreams of getting into a four-year college weren't going to happen, because her C-plus average would require a hefty bribe/scholarship to pay for school. And before doing that, she would rather move to an animal sanctuary to brush the beards of baby goats.

"My little unicorn would have never dropped out," Darnell said.

"Unless someone pushed her," Kilo added.

"Maybe we're exaggerating. Maybe she just got overwhelmed," Axel began.

"No—there was something important she wanted to tell me the night of Axel's party," I told my friends. "But it was like she was afraid that someone was following her."

No matter what the rational part of my mind tried to sell me, my gut wasn't buying it. So I turned to Andy, who was whistling a tune to himself by the door.

I planted my feet in front of him. "Mimi was eliminated, and I need to know how it happened. Please. I thought you had our backs."

Andy's purple mustache twitched. "She texted her parents."

"But what if it wasn't her?"

Andy grinned, like I was a child asking a stupid question. "You'll get all the answers you're looking for when the moment is right. But I'm sure she's okay." He produced an old Game Boy Color and a fresh pack of Pokémon cards and extended them to me. "You should keep yourself busy."

I batted the stuff from his hand. "Mimi's my best friend, and she's missing. Ruby, too."

"Luna, I'm sorry that your friend has been eliminated, but I didn't make the rules. And I certainly don't know where she is. If she really *was* missing, the police would be looking for her. But if I hear of anything, I promise that I will *make things right.*"

"Okay, I guess. Sorry I freaked out. I'm just really overwhelmed right now."

"It's understandable."

Although Andy had this calming, hypnotizing quality about him, I still felt like I was going crazy. If it wasn't shiny and attention grabbing, it was like Limbo didn't make it a priority. And I was starting to think that I couldn't rely on them for help. So we were going to have to do this ourselves, and I had just the friends for the task.

But before I could game-plan with them, Andy hopped onto a table and opened his arms. "Look around, my Retros. You are the lucky number six left standing!"

"Since when is six a lucky number?" Darnell said.

"In China it is, because in Mandarin it sounds like the word for 'flow.' Meaning things will go smoothly. Don't be so square-minded," Andy told him.

Joviality aside, things were really coming down to the wire.

It was still early in the school year, and there weren't that many of us left. Just Darnell, Kilo, Axel, Kosta, Asha, and myself. I had hoped that we could all last until the end and receive the scholarships together, but considering that contestants were dropping like flies, I didn't see how it was possible.

The lights dimmed. Andy held up a mysterious purple box with the Limbo logo on it, then reached inside, produced a set of handcuffs, and latched one of my hands in it.

"What the hell are you doing?"

"One who is a master of patience is a master of everything else," Andy explained, leaving me more confused than I was before.

"This guy just talks like a fortune cookie," Darnell joked.

Andy addressed the six of us who were left. "My dear Retros! Did you know that ninety percent of information on dating apps is lies? Forty percent of résumés are falsehoods. Thirty-two percent of us even lie to our doctors. However, there is only one place where we can be honest. Do any of you know where that is?" He raised an eyebrow, waiting for guesses.

"The White House?" Asha asked.

"Disneyland!" Kosta yelped.

Andy shook his head. "We are most honest only with our Google search browser, but today you won't be able to hide your truths from anyone.

"WELCOME TO THE NEXT CHALLENGE!" Andy grinned mischievously. "Today you will be taking the handcuff challenge! You can't log off; you can't sign out. You have to live this one. You may be stuck together, but the truth will set you free. Each of you will be handcuffed to a partner until midnight, when the locks will automatically disarm."

He snapped, and his Limbo grunts pulled Kilo forward and latched the other side of my handcuff to him. "Is this some kind

of joke?" Kilo scratched his head, taking my arm up with him—
nearly lifting my feet off the floor, so I balanced on my tippy-
toes.

"I guess we're stuck together," I quipped.

And then I noticed his hands.

His fingers were always weathered and smudged with years
of oil changes, but when his palms turned upward, I saw that the
skin was all cut up and dried with blood.

This was a lot more than just auto grease.

I wanted to ask Kilo about it, but I was going to need to find
the right moment. After the night of the bonfire, I didn't want
to push him.

I was just thankful that being handcuffed to him was a solid
distraction after seeing my best friend eliminated, because the
day was borderline comical. I had to write with my left hand,
turning my notebook into a Picasso. But the most complicated
part was going to the bathroom. I had to pee with my arm
extended under the stall door, while I banished Kilo to the other
side and made him scream the alphabet three times backward.

He even came with me to work at the theater, and I had to
dress him up in a uniform so tight it looked kid-sized, and with
handcuffs we couldn't fit our arms in the sleeve. He was especially good at stopping the kids from sneaking in, because he was
stronger than ten-year-old vinegar.

"You should sell Twinkies," Kilo lectured while eating all the
popcorn. "That's the good stuff. Straight dopamine."

I bet other people didn't have it so easy. It totally cracked
me up to imagine how uncomfortable Axel would feel, stuck
to Darnell while he and Kosta sucked down a single piece of

spaghetti on a romantic Italian dinner date. All jokes aside, I noticed that Kilo was acting a little stranger than usual that afternoon. Even more quiet. I went to help him with the popcorn machine because he seemed uncomfortable operating it with those wounded hands.

When we finished the shift, Kilo took his bike from the rack and caught me staring at his palms. He quickly pulled away. "They're just blisters, from the new bike."

"We really need to bandage them up."

"No no. No time. I have to repair a car in the shop tonight." He pointed to his bike. "You can protest, but I'm stronger than you, so it looks like you're coming with me," he joked.

"You know, Kilo, when a woman has an idea in her head, it's easier to rip her head off than take the idea out. So yeah. I'm putting hydrogen peroxide on those hands eventually."

He bowed, motioning to his bike.

I curtseyed and sat on the handlebars, and we traveled up the mountainside toward his cabin. All the while, I thought about how they didn't look like blisters at all. They were lacerations. Kilo was lying to me.

▶ 48.

"Help!"
—The Beatles

I couldn't stop thinking about what Andy had said about lies. I mean, just imagine all the truths you hide. Like when you open up a birthday card and pretend to care about what's written inside, but really, you're just thinking about how rich you're about to be. Or all the times you ignore a text for days and then say, *Oh my gosh I didn't even see this!* Or when you walk into school acting like Princess Leia, but in reality, your legs are hairy like Chewbacca, because you only shaved the places where there are holes in your jeans.

Basically, the only truth is that we all lie.

And when your friend is the lord of death metal, the secrets get darker and more complex. Afternoon rolled into evening—as the shadows descended upon the forest, so did the overwhelming feeling of isolation.

We traveled almost an hour up the road, and I knew my ass was asleep because when Kilo slammed on the brakes, I basically catapulted off.

"We'll walk the rest," he said.

We stood atop the most beautiful plateau that overlooked the view below. The lush green forest. The golden sun that poured over our little town. I took a deep breath, my problems much smaller from this height.

"It's just a little bit farther," Kilo declared, and after another thirty minutes of gluteus maximus torture, he pointed to a moss-covered shack constructed from different kinds of lumber. Cars were disemboweled around the entrance of the garage.

"We made it. We're here," he said.

"You bike this long every day to get to work?"

"Hell no. Some days I walk."

I slapped my arm, murdering a mosquito. "What a creepy place."

"Thanks," he said, like it was a compliment.

But the strangest things I saw were the mounds of dirt in front of the garage. Although upon closer inspection I realized they were far more significant than that—

These were large, unmarked graves.

Crosses and candles littered the earth around them, and the dirt was moist, meaning they were fresh. I tried to tell myself that Kilo had just taken a gardening workshop and gotten inspired, but it was so unsettling I had to ask. "Kilo . . . what's buried in those graves?"

"I'll explain later," he said, sliding open the garage door. "Welcome to my automobile fulfillment center! This is where I fixed up Axel's Mustang." He smiled proudly.

I saw everything *but* cars. Piles of scrap metal twisted like spires to the ceiling, and at the center was a huge radio system, all tuned to different stations, made up of a hodgepodge of parts.

But if he isn't fixing cars, why are we here?

"What is all this?"

"It's a sound-wave interceptor. It plays music, too." He turned one of the dials up, blasting earsplitting heavy metal. He leaned close to let me in on a secret. "I'm trying to intercept the signal of the noises that we heard at school and in the forest."

"I hope you do. I still lose sleep over that." I examined the contraption's rusted edges.

"And this radio doesn't just catch radio waves; it can emit them."

"So you're creating your very own broadcast station." I tried to hide my worry. "Look at you, you practically have a podcast!"

"I like to think of it as a pirate radio—you never know when you're going to need to broadcast a signal. Besides, I never got cell service up here anyway."

As the hours dragged on, everything about Kilo's garage set off red flags. All over the place were bloody rags, ones that were not consistent with the bike-blister story he'd tried to sell me earlier. My heart wanted to skip. It wanted to lurch with adrenaline. Though I couldn't let it. Kilo was my friend. But if he wasn't a threat, why did I feel like I was in the lair of someone with his own creepy four-part true-crime documentary?

How well did I really know him?

Finally, I saw the missing piece to the puzzle, lying there on the greasy workbench. Partially obscured, as if Kilo had attempted to hide it. Because there, sitting on the table, was the witness to what had happened on the night of *the party*. He pulled his arm, attached to mine, forcing me to turn, but it was too late. I had already seen it.

Mimi's whistle.

I knew it was hers because everything she owned was hot pink.

I was tumbling deep into a panic chamber. That feeling of being trapped inside myself. One of those moments that I wished I was just back at home, feeling safe, sitting on my father's lap while we watched the soccer World Cup.

Why in the world does he have Mimi's whistle? Has Mimi been here all along?

I wasn't going to let myself think that she was in one of those graves. My head was spinning, trying to give Kilo the benefit of the doubt as he worked away on his radio. I was counting down the minutes to midnight.

"I want to go home," I told him.

"Not yet. Could you pass me the hacksaw? It's under the bench."

Ten minutes until midnight—I was about ready to urinate all over myself. "Do you have a phone here?" My voice quivered.

"There's no landline." He sharpened the blade. "It's more fun that way."

I saw on a cop show once how a criminal escaped by breaking his thumb so he could slip out of handcuffs. I considered the possibility.

The clock ticked down—five minutes left.

His radio receiver whined in an eerie cacophony of oldies and lost voices.

I missed my mom, and all the times she told me to take a coat for this exact occasion—in case I was running around in the haunted woods after midnight.

A pounding thundered against the door.

I stood, but Kilo yanked me back down.

"Don't answer that," he said, terse, grabbing the hacksaw to use as a weapon.

Boom. Boom. BOOM.

He crept closer, pulling me after him.

The pounding continued until finally the door was kicked open, revealing the people on the other side. And although it literally scared me so much I started to get the hiccups, I couldn't have been happier to see them.

Axel and Darnell stood on the threshold, in a plume of dust, silhouetted by the moonlight.

"There's something you have to see," Axel said as he dragged Darnell inside.

"*Jeeesus!* Am I crazy, or did I see graves outside?"

Axel took off his backpack, reached inside, and pulled out an article of clothing that I recognized instantly. Something that I'd picked out myself, with all my heart.

The denim jacket I'd once gifted Mimi. It was damp and discolored.

"Where did you find this?"

"It was stuck in the filter of my pool," Axel said, his voice shaking.

"She was taken against her will," Darnell explained. "This isn't a getaway to San Francisco—this is a kidnapping."

The clock struck twelve, and the handcuffs unlatched. Without a moment's hesitation, I leapt behind Axel to pick up a crowbar.

"Luna, what's wrong?" Axel asked.

"Kilo has Mimi's whistle!"

"Wait . . . *what?*"

Kilo raised his hands. "It's not what you think."

Darnell snatched the whistle from the workbench.

"I found it outside, after the party. I was going to give it to her at school, but when she never showed up, I didn't want to freak you guys out."

"The blood everywhere?" I demanded. "The graves outside?"

Kilo pointed to a shovel hanging on the wall. "I cut my hands on splinters. Those poor animals that have been dying in the forest deserve a proper burial . . . the rags are still bloody because I don't have a washing machine. I have to take my clothes into town for that."

"What do you mean you don't have a washer?" I asked. "Wait, Kilo, do you . . . live here?"

He looked down, ashamed, his silence answering my question.

"What about your parents?" Darnell asked.

"My parents died in a car accident. We were hit by a drunk truck driver, and I was the only one who survived."

"That's why you moved here from Hawai'i years back," I said as the truth dawned on me.

"I'm supposed to live with my uncle, but he's bad for me. So, I ran away to live here." Kilo stretched down the neck of his shirt, showing us the mangled scar on his chest. His eyes were bloodshot and bright. "This tattoo, that scares away people, that makes everyone think they can judge me, was an attempt to cover up the damage the drunk driver did to my family."

"I'm so sorry. I swear I had no idea." I took his hand.

He broke down in tears. "I don't have much money, or a real home. It's why I took the challenge, because I figured I could use the scholarship money to make myself a better life. But I found something even more valuable. What's that old line? Friends are the family you choose."

"So, you're saying we're friends now?" I smiled.

"No. We're not friends," Kilo corrected. "We're family. And together, we're going to save Mimi. Whatever it takes."

"I'm so sorry I freaked out at you."

"No one said family was perfect, or not annoying," Darnell added. I gave him an elbow, and we all cracked up, easing the tension in the room.

"I'll tell my mom about all this, so an official investigation can be opened."

"Well, I'm not going to sit around and wait for her to be found," I declared.

"Then we're going to have to do it ourselves," Kilo said.

"We'll find our little unicorn," Darnell promised.

▶ 49.

"Stayin' Alive"
—Bee Gees

There is life after death. It's actually been medically proven—when you die, your brain keeps firing for seven minutes. Maybe it's hallucinations, or how you enter the ever after—I always used to wonder what that would be like when it happened to me. Now I had to convince myself that Mimi's seven minutes hadn't yet come.

It was a stupid, irrational thought.

But stress and anxiety are uncontrollable like that, right?

I always figured it was my brain's way of testing just how far it could handle a certain reality before it broke. And apparently Axel could tell I was struggling, because the next morning, he surprised me by picking me up for school. He knocked on my front door, dressed in an elegant vest with matching black Converse.

I opened the door. "Axel, what are you doing here? Aww, how cute!" I said, seeing that he had brought a bouquet of flowers. "Thank you! Wait, are these artichokes?"

"It's technically a flower." Axel smiled weakly. "Like you. Beautiful and . . . unpredictable?"

I laughed. "Sure, I'll buy it."

"We're running late. Let's hit the road."

But my mother appeared out of thin air. "What a surprise, Axel! How nice of you." She gave Axel a kiss on each cheek before snatching the bouquet. "Perfect for the rice I'm making for dinner." Then she pointed her wooden spoon at him. "Take care of mi hija, okay?"

"Of course, Mrs. Iglesias. Always."

"Good boy," she said, before going back inside. "Don't get used to picking her up in that four-wheel rocket."

Axel took my hands, his gaze dewy. "How are you feeling?"

"I'm doing okay," I said, but in reality, I was a total mess, like that time a pen exploded all over my hands so that it looked like I'd jerked off a Smurf.

Axel started up the car and accelerated onto the main road.

"We're not going to school yet."

"Where are we going, then?"

"Luna, there's something that you have to see." We carved up the golden roads of the El Dorado Hills, full throttle. "Why do you think I brought you artichokes? I stole them from my neighbor's organic vegetable garden!"

"Why couldn't you steal roses!?"

"I don't know! I panicked! I needed to improvise! I had to make sure your mom would let you come with me."

By the time we made our way to the top of the hill, I started to recognize the palm trees that lined the street. We were headed for Axel's mansion.

"The cleaning service is still here, so whatever you do, don't scream. Promise me you won't freak out."

"Okay, I promise."

We parked, and he led me through the grand entrance. Just being there brought back bittersweet memories, tainted by my thoughts of what Mimi's last moments were like before she was taken. Abducted. Axel led me up the spiral staircase to the last place where anyone had seen her.

He threw open the bathroom door.

"The cleaning service found it last week. And I knew I had to show you, but . . . ," he said, but lingered back like he was afraid.

And there I was, alone, biting my tongue to not scream. Simultaneously seeing my own reflection and the last piece of herself that she'd left behind. Because on the bathroom mirror were words full of fear, yet written in her signature happy-go-lucky bubblegum-pink lipstick.

> Don't trust everything you see.
> Salt looks a lot like sugar.

This was Mimi. I was sure. These were her last words, written across the bathroom mirror.

Vince's sharp, crooked grin flashed across my mind. He'd been playing with us. Taunting us. And if I had just listened to Mimi that night, if I'd tried harder to get her to speak, then maybe she would still be here. I felt like I was in one of those nightmares where you scream, but no sound comes out. Helpless.

Mimi was being intentionally cryptic. This wasn't just a message; it was a warning. It's like she knew something was going to happen to her that night.

She was trying to tell us something.

Axel paced the room. He tore down the shower curtain, furious. "That's what you told us Vince said to you, right? He better not have anything to do with this."

I took his fist gently, holding it in my own hands until it unclenched. "Blind rage isn't going to bring Mimi back. We have to use our heads when we confront Vince."

"Let me handle him. You should stay back."

"I'm not that kind of girl, Axel."

"Luna, I want to protect you not because I think you're weak, but because I think you're important—you know that, right?"

"The only thing you can protect me from are cockroaches," I told him.

He laughed despite himself. *"Difficult."*

"To the end." I smiled back.

"Well, I know exactly where we can find him," Axel promised, determined.

▶ 50.

"Zombie"
—The Cranberries

There's nothing more gut-wrenching than spending hours worried about a confrontation yet to come. Building up in your mind how it will go down. And anything works to pass the time. I counted seconds; I counted my teachers' gray hairs; I counted stupid thoughts, like why does water make your skin dry if technically it hydrates you? Which carried on all the way through the last class of the day. And when I got to the parking lot, there was a crowd of Retromaniacs circling my car, whispering among themselves.

Because written in bloodred paint across the side of my old G-Wagen were the words:

STOP

NOW

Chills crawled across my skin. Somebody wanted us to turn back. They wanted us to give up. Which meant we must have been on the right track.

Darnell stormed in like a tornado. "Everyone get out of here. Show's over! Go and pop some pimples! One day, it's going to be trendy to be stupid, and some of you are *not* going to know what to do with all the fame."

Like insect repellent, Darnell made the onlookers buzz off.

"Thanks for being there for me."

"Friends shop with you; best friends kill for you," he assured me.

"Whoever wrote this on my car wants to scare us," I said. "They don't want us to keep looking. Asking questions. Which just means we're getting closer . . ."

As soon as we'd told our friends all about the lipstick, they were pretty much ready to hog-tie Vince and rotisserie cook him, apple in mouth, like it was medieval times.

"I think we all know who did this," Axel seethed. "He's gone too far. This ends now."

"We have strength in numbers," Kilo said.

He fist-bumped Darnell, who responded in classic Darnell fashion. "They say it only takes a fraction of any population to overthrow a tyrant."

"Then it's time to dethrone the king of the Goldens," I declared, if not to convince them, then to convince myself. Because that evening I was going to need all the courage I could get.

Wrestling was one of those sports I never really understood. Why a bunch of smelly dudes would want to publicly battle for their manhood in spandex was beyond me, but Axel explained that it was more like a physical match of chess—a dangerous dance.

Most people couldn't care less about the sport, but today a

crowd had shown up to see the school's shining star. We found seats a few rows back, to keep a low profile.

But not everyone could avoid the spotlight.

We heard a high-pitched shriek, and soon Limbo workers pulled a girl out of the bleachers, down below.

"This is unfair! I didn't inhale!" Asha protested.

Andy led the pack, holding up a little vape pen. "You broke the rules. This is not an unavoidable—it's contraband from the wrong century. Consider yourself disqualified."

Asha argued all the way out of the gym.

"That makes one less," Axel said.

"Only five of us left now," I added.

A buzzer went off, and Axel pointed down to the athletic mats. "Look! There he is!"

Vince was one of the top-ranked wrestlers in the state. And although the match was hyped up to be an epic battle, it only lasted a few minutes. El Dorado's golden warrior didn't just beat his opponent, he obliterated him. Vince hyperextended the guy's shoulder, making him scream until the referees had to end the match.

"That was brutal." Darnell shook his head.

Vince's opponent never really stood a chance. The ref raised Vince's arm, declaring him the winner, but his coaches seemed to think otherwise, because they were already getting in his face.

"Get your ass outside and go run laps!"

"But I won," Vince protested.

"As far as I'm concerned, snapping arms doesn't count," his head coach yelled. "You won in two minutes. I wanted a pin in one. So, like I said, LAPS!"

Vince stormed past his coach and pushed his way out of the gymnasium. We snuck out of the gym and followed him. But instead of heading to the field to jog laps, he thrashed trash bins, punched a stucco wall, and ripped open the locker room door.

"Yeah, um. I'll be the lookout," Darnell said.

"Then I'll block the door, so he can't leave," Kilo added.

Axel nodded to me, and together we snuck inside the locker room. Instantly we were enveloped by total darkness, save for a faint ray of light that glinted against the lockers and illuminated the gilded trophies.

Axel led the way while I clutched his bicep, breath bated. My fingers traced the lockers to keep my balance. Finally, we reached a dead end at the far wall.

We heard Vince before we saw him.

It was a sound that I recognized. That same wheezing that we'd heard the night we caught Vince alone at school. A raw cry, and it came from the corner of the locker room, in a single bathroom stall.

"Vince! Come out!" Axel shouted. His words echoed, colliding with one another. "We know what you've done. The game is over."

The door opened slowly.

But the Vince that stepped into the doorway was no vicious animal. Instead, he was a gaunt, weak person I hardly recognized, with the same lifeless sheen to his flesh that I had seen the night of the party.

"Oh my god. What's happening to you, Vince?" I asked.

He took a silent step forward, swaying. There was something

terribly wrong with him. "You can't be here. Go away—" Vince stumbled to the floor.

Our rage turned to perturbation, and I could tell that Axel was growing concerned. He reached a hand out. "Are you okay, man . . . ?"

"It's too late to care now." Vince struggled onto his knees and then wiped red saliva from his mouth. "So just go away. I said go away!" Vince shouted.

"Not until I find out why salt looks like sugar." I stood over him. "And if you don't tell us where Mimi is, we're going to tell the police what you've done."

Vince staggered to his feet, breaking for the door, but Kilo emerged from the shadows and shoved Vince backward to the floor. He was cornered now.

"I'm going to ask you again: Why does salt look like sugar?"

But it seemed like Axel already knew the answer to that question.

He got down on a knee and grabbed Vince's shoulder, propping him up. "Breathe, Vince."

"I have to lose weight to qualify for the next wrestling tournament." Vince gagged, coughed, and then suddenly threw up.

"Maybe that's true," Axel said, "but you've been purging yourself again, and it's not only for wrestling."

I heard the sentence, but I couldn't fully comprehend what the words meant. Not until Vince looked up. "I didn't see Mimi upstairs that night. Because I was in the bathroom, throwing up, when I saw the words written on the mirror. I guess they just made sense to me."

"What do you mean?" Axel asked.

"Like, even if I see one thing in the mirror, reality could be totally different. Maybe I was really sugar, when all I could see was salt."

Vince's eyes reddened.

Axel smiled, catching his old friend off guard. "Remember all the good times we used to have before I quit the wrestling team?"

"No. Not really . . . you sucked."

"Exactly. You were the talented one. You were the one that everyone admired. I used to look up to you, man. It's also why I quit the football team. I'm just good at entertaining people."

Vince looked into his friend's gaze, transfixed.

Axel continued. "You've been a total douchebag this year. And wrong about a lot of things. But there's one thing you are right about—whatever you're seeing in the mirror is a *lie*."

"Samantha told me she thinks I have something called body dysmorphia," Vince explained. "But maybe she was just trying to impress me with her fancy words."

"Which is why you were arguing with her at the hospital," I said.

"Going there was a stupid idea. That hospital sounds lame. I'm not crazy." He tried to dry his eyes, like this was a moment of weakness. But opening up like this was a sign of strength.

"No," I said, "this is the first time you've done anything smart."

He laughed.

To my own surprise, I took his hand. And I repeated the words Samantha had once said to me. "Trauma is not your fault, but healing is your responsibility."

"I knew we were growing apart . . . ," Axel said. "You were pushing me away. But you don't have to do that anymore, bro. We're not the enemy. This ends here, okay?"

Axel extended an arm, helping him to his feet.

"No more painting threats on Luna's car. You understand?"

But Vince shook his head. "Axel, I have no idea what you're talking about. I didn't paint anything."

"Wait. What?" The words escaped my mouth. And the most surreal part was that I believed him. "Then who did it?"

Vince buried his head in his hands, as though the pressure was crushing him and it was time to cave. "If you want to know what happened to Mimi, go talk to Jade."

"What does Jade have to do with all of this?" I asked.

"Jade's the one who brought the drugs."

▶ 51.

"Believe"
—Cher

All I could think about was Jade. If she'd really drugged Mimi, then she deserved to be caressed with a live wire. I was ready to whip out a water gun and threaten to wash away her eyebrows. Maybe then she would tell us why she gave drugs to Mimi. Getting a real confession from Jade was going to mean outsmarting her—and luckily, Darnell had the perfect plan. Because that Friday was one of the biggest events of the year—

The El Dorado Winter Formal dance.

This year it was to be hijacked by Limbo, who would be transforming the school into a massive roller disco. But most importantly, the cheer team would be putting together a performance all on roller skates—and Jade was their captain.

Only after that would the real show begin.

I heard a honk. They were here.

For the first time in a while, I was excited, because we were going to take down Jade and finally get all the answers we needed. Mimi would be back, and the nightmare would end.

I hurried out of my house in my disco dress as Axel stepped

out of the purple limousine. He looked flashy in a half-buttoned shirt, wearing a glittering silver chain that lay on his chest.

"Luna, qué guapa estás. . . . You're stunning." He glowed.

I slipped my arms around the back of his neck and kissed him. "Gracias, tú también. You know I like you more than sleeping in?" Which, believe me, was the closest thing to love I had ever felt. I couldn't tell what was bigger, my nerves or my hunger. And Axel didn't help when he presented a corsage to me and slipped it onto my wrist.

"This isn't made of cauliflower or something, is it?"

He laughed. "No. Red carnations for my hot-blooded girl. What you are, what you deserve. You know, I seriously thought your mother was going to make you wear that creepy necklace she made out of all your baby teeth."

"She almost did. Sometimes I think she loves me too much," I giggled.

Finally, Axel opened the door of the sparkly limousine, and there was my Retro gang, the people who'd signed up to be my best friends forever without even knowing the consequences. Well, everyone except Mimi. She should've been here with us. But at least it cheered me up to see that the rest of my friends were safe. I was especially happy for Darnell, who was holding hands with Kosta—even though they weren't popping bottles and pouring champagne. The inside of the limousine looked more like a detective's office, with dozens of photographs spread around.

"Hey, everyone, what are we doing?" I took a seat.

"I developed all our film," Axel said, "and look what I found."

Kilo leaned over and handed me a stack. I could tell that

some of the photos were from my camera, others I didn't recognize. Some from school. The mall. Various places around town.

"Check out the ones in the forest and tell me if you see something strange," Darnell said.

I finally settled on the photo that we had developed together, the one that was captured the night of the bonfire. But I couldn't see anything.

"Look closer," Kosta pressed.

And when I did, I finally saw what they were talking about. Above our smiling faces was a mysterious object in the canopy. A shiny, reflective flare among the trees.

"What is that?" I asked.

"We don't know," Kilo said. "But what if it has something to do with all the strange sounds we've been hearing? The dead animals? The red markings on the trees—what if it even has something to do with the threat on your car?"

"But do you think Jade is behind all this?" Kosta asked. "Is she even capable?"

Darnell added, "Something this big would mean all the Goldens were involved."

"To get even and sabotage our shot at winning the challenge," Axel said.

"How does this connect back to Mimi?" I buried my face in my hands. All of this wasn't adding up—but we were onto something.

Darnell broke the silence. "I talked with my mom, and she said that the police are opening a formal investigation into Mimi's disappearance. After the jacket and the writing on the mirror, they decided they have enough of a case to start really pursuing this. At least we were able to make that happen."

"It hurts to see that empty seat. Mimi should be with us," Kilo said, tearing up. "I can't believe there's only five of us left."

But soon there would be just four—because another elimination was about to happen at the roller-disco dance. Only this one wasn't a mistake. Kilo had it all planned.

We heard the beat first.

Then came the roaring crowd.

It was as if the whole town was waiting like concertgoers outside the school. We stepped out of the limousine onto an expansive entrance. Purple balloons festooned the path like a grand archway into our very own disco wonderland.

And everyone was on roller skates.

Retromaniacs lining the red carpet exploded in fanfare. This challenge had resuscitated the dying heart of our small town, putting us on the map as an epic tourist attraction. And in a handful of months the grand prize would be ours, and we'd have full scholarships to any school our hearts could desire.

Limbo cameramen were trying to pull me into an interview when Miranda rolled up to rescue/assault me, clinging to my arms and practically bowling me over. "Luna, you did it! You finally hit five million!"

"Five million?"

"Five million followers on Limbo, baby! You're getting huge—you all are."

I was in shock. I couldn't believe it, and honestly, after seeing how complicated Axel's life had turned with all the fame, I wasn't sure how I felt about it. It's not like I had entered the challenge for the popularity. Our old lives were officially gone.

Limbo was turning us into icons.

And they were squeezing every ounce of Retro publicity for their own benefit.

"Welcome, my precious finalists!" came a voice at the end of the entrance.

I spun around to find Scarlett in an elegant purple dress, smiling cordially. "Luna, is everything okay? You don't look so well."

"I'm just a little overwhelmed, considering everything that's going on."

"Well, whatever you need, know that you can always talk to me. I wouldn't want you to get into any trouble—or worse, lose the challenge. Tonight is all about having fun. Focus on that." Scarlett smiled brightly, then turned to congratulate the other finalists. Limbo was shining the spotlight on us while making sure the disappearance of our friends didn't dirty their image. And that really pissed me off. I hoped they'd take it seriously now that the police were involved.

But nothing was going to ruin this big night for Limbo.

The gymnasium was an enchanted Retroland.

People danced in skates under the brilliant disco ball. The room was decked out in balloons and streamers, with Nika spinning vinyl records in the center.

I climbed into the booth.

"Hey, girl, nice remix!" I hugged her. "Do you know when Jade's performance starts?"

"Eek! I think in a few minutes? Center stage," she answered.

A girl leaned over the DJ booth, holding an alcohol flask.

"Check it out. I take a sip whenever I tie my shoes," she shouted over the music.

"But you're wearing Velcro!" Nika pointed out.

"Well, why do you think I'm so tipsy?" She extended it to me. "You want some, Luna?"

"No thanks," I said—because on this night I wanted to be sharper than ever. "I've learned that a night of alcohol equals a morning of Tylenol. And that rhymes, so you know it's true."

"I'm not drinking either," Nika said over the music. "But it's a personal choice, like how I put my phone on airplane mode and go retro on the weekends."

"Retro mode. Love it! That will be me when all this is over." I climbed down from the booth, smiling.

That night someone unexpected showed up to the dance who would've never been caught dead in a place like this. The original hater of everything we stood for. He was hanging out with a group of Goldens by the snack bar, hair slicked back like something straight out of *Grease*.

It was Vince. And he was here in full retro style.

I skated by, waving hello.

He waved back.

And maybe that was all we got from the interaction. Vince was too cool to put on a pair of roller skates or go to the dance floor, but for the first time we had a silent understanding. If he was humbled enough to show up at the dance, hopefully he would go and get the help he needed.

I always liked that version of the story best.

Then Kilo pulled me in for a bear hug so strong, I suffocated a little in his torso, but it was one of those nice asphyxiations. And I realized it was probably the first time he had hugged anyone in many years. He cleared his throat. "No matter what happens tonight, I wanted to thank you for sitting down with me that day when I was all alone."

I squirmed a little and laughed. "Kilo, you're hurting me."

"Oh, I'm sorry." He unclenched his vise grip.

"Thanks, dude. My life wouldn't be the same without you."

"Likewise," he said, before suddenly checking his blind spots and tying something around my wrist. It was a balloon on a string, like the other ones that adorned the gym.

"What are you doing?"

"Luna, I need you to listen very carefully to me. I have something I have to go do. Something I have to make sure of. If I come back before midnight, I want you to untie the balloon and let it float into the sky. But if I don't come back by midnight, promise me that you'll pop the balloon and read the note that's inside."

"But I don't understand. Kilo, why?"

"I can't explain now—they might hear us. It's not safe to talk. Just promise me you'll do what I say." His smile glazed over with desperation. A look that I had seen before. One that reminded me of the look that Mimi had given me before she disappeared.

"Kilo, I'm not going to let you go until you tell me what's happening." I grasped his arm—but he pulled away, slipping into the crowd. I went to chase after him, but the lights dimmed and the music cued, ushering in the cheer squad's big performance, blocking my path.

Kosta took the mic. "Ladies and gentlemen, may I present

to you . . . the all-star, all-state, all-American El Dorado Gold Diggers!"

It was always funny to think that we had that school mascot.

The squad put on an impressive show, soaring across the gym floor in a blur of gold and black. All spinning and flying in a perfectly choreographed dance on skates. Even the big-headed school mascot was breaking out front handsprings.

And among them was a Samantha who didn't try to fit in anymore. Who didn't try to be perfect. I cheered for her, elated to see her back on the team, as she stuck a perfect double loop and beamed.

But the warm moment froze over as their leader took center stage. Jade was the main flyer and the new captain of the team, having taken over when Samantha left school.

Just seeing her face made my hands curl into fists.

The performance ended, and the entire school erupted in applause—which meant it was time for us to make moves of our own.

As Jade separated from the group to find her friends, Darnell, Axel, and I encircled her. As soon as she realized what was happening, she went rigid. There was no escape route this time.

Jade was going to have to answer to us.

► 52.

"Sweet Dreams (Are Made of This)"
—Eurythmics

We rolled in from every angle, cornering her.

But Jade tried to play it cool. "If you want autographs or something, you'll have to wait until I'm less tired."

I opened my mouth, wishing that fire would shoot out. "I know what you did. Why don't you just admit it?"

"I didn't paint those words on your car, if that's what you want to know."

"You drugged my friend."

And those were the magic words.

Her arrogant veneer was splintering, and soon she was fumbling with her words. She shook her head. "I have no idea where Mimi is. I swear."

"What did you do to her?" Axel demanded.

Jade's lips trembled. "I didn't do it on purpose."

"How do you accidentally drug someone?" Darnell pressed.

"Because I wasn't trying to drug *her*."

"Then who?"

She looked away, ashamed, then mustered up the courage to tell us the truth. "I was trying to drug Luna . . . and I don't know what happened. You must have switched drinks."

And that's when I lost control.

I slapped her across the face. With such force that she stumbled back and her cheek pulsed red. I was struck by what I had just done, half expecting Jade to attack me with her inch-long gel nails.

But none of that happened.

Instead, she stood there in silence.

All I could hear was my pounding heartbeat. I regretted what I had done as soon as it happened, but it was too late. Jade slowly stepped forward, getting into my face. And I was ready for whatever happened next . . . but then she said something that totally caught me off guard. "Hit me again," she demanded, eyes welling up. "Go ahead and do it."

I was stunned.

"I felt terrible about what I did," Jade confessed. "That's why I bumped into you at the party that night and spilled your cup. I realized it was a mistake."

Axel was distraught with anger. With disappointment. "That's low, even for you, Jade. Why would you slip something in Luna's drink in the first place?"

"It wasn't a date-rape drug or anything . . . I just wanted to scare you and ruin your night with Axel. It was stupid."

"Just like how you tried to ruin our relationship by showing her my diary?" Axel cut in.

Jade shook her head and laughed ruefully, wiping golden makeup from her eyes. She was being honest, for once. "I felt guilty or something. And I guess I thought you needed to know what you were getting into."

"Being a good person doesn't count if you only do it once," Darnell said.

"But it's never too late to start trying," I told her. "And listen, I didn't need your help, but I do believe you. Like Mimi told you, we need sorority between us. Not sabotage."

"Girls and fries before guys." She smiled weakly.

That was the closest Jade could ever get to an apology—one that I silently accepted, but it would take time to truly forgive her.

"So can we just let this go?" Jade pleaded.

"I'm sorry." I shook my head. "I can't do that. For Mimi's sake. Your mistake might be the reason she's missing."

That's when Darnell pulled out an old tape recorder from his pocket and clicked the stop button, revealing that he had been recording the entire conversation. Then he put an almost compassionate hand on Jade's shoulder. "Honey, my mother is parked right outside. You don't want to be rude twice and forget to say hello to her. You two should have a talk."

"But—but—"

He held up the recorder. "Consider this a courtesy, or this tape goes right to the police."

"Fine," Jade said. "I'll do it." And then she skated off into the crowd, defeated.

But something was still terribly wrong.

We weren't any closer to finding Mimi.

"I'm sorry, Luna." Axel took my hand.

"I'm failing my friend." I started to well up, and made for the exit.

"Don't say that. We're not giving up," Darnell said as the lights turned on and the music cut out. "Luna, you're more than special. You're limited edition. And we're going to find Mimi."

"Maybe we didn't get the answers we were expecting, but we're going to figure out who is behind all this," Axel added.

"Amen." Darnell dried his moist eyes. "Together until the end."

Suddenly I heard voices reverberate across the concrete campus, out the back door of the gymnasium, luring me away from the group.

"Where are you going?" Darnell said as my friends kept up behind me.

I followed the sound, until I found Andy. For the first time, he wasn't the picture-perfect Limbo mouthpiece. Not the elegant showman. He was angry, and he was arguing with Scarlett.

I tried to read their lips, but it was no use.

And when the conversation was over, Andy stormed off. But I noticed that his stylish cane was no longer a fashion piece. Because now Andy was depending on it to walk. He limped.

"What's the deal with Andy?" Darnell asked.

"I've got a better question," Axel added. "Where is Kilo? I haven't seen him all night."

I looked at the little balloon on my wrist, remembering the promise I had made. It was nearly midnight, and he was still gone. He had told me not to go looking for him, but I couldn't escape my own impulses.

"Maybe he's in the Retro Lounge," I said, wanting to be wrong about my feelings, but my instincts always knew better than my head. And before long, I was running through El Dorado

High, looking for him with more desperation than hope, with more fear than confidence.

We sprinted through the darkness.

The first thing I noticed when we arrived were the lights that had been left on. And the door was ajar, striking me with an eerie feeling, like a home that has been broken into.

Because the whole scene was helter-skelter.

Framed photos lay smashed against the floor. Arcade machines sparked and moaned into oblivion. But most disturbing was what we saw on the Live Feed wall.

Another face had been crossed out in red ink.

Kilo.

I looked at the clock. Impatient. Desperate. Staying true to a promise that maybe I should have never committed to.

And the clock on the wall struck midnight.

I reached for the string tied on my wrist and pulled the balloon toward me. I popped it. There was a little paper inside. A message that Kilo had written before he disappeared.

The name of our enemy.

The reason our friends were gone.

Inside was the name of a parasite that we all had invited into our lives willingly.

So I started to unfold . . .

and unfold . . .

. . . until I saw the truth, which read . . .

LIMBO.

▶ 53.

"Killing In the Name"
—Rage Against the Machine

I was being swallowed by darkness. The walls of the Retro Lounge closed in on me until I was sure I'd be devoured by them. My anxiety was taking over.

"Luna!" I heard Axel call out. Then I felt him catch me. "Stay with me. Stay with me." My woozy eyes reclaimed the world as he read the note that I clutched weakly in my hands.

"Limbo was behind the disappearances . . . ," I uttered in disbelief.

"What? This can't be real life." Darnell was wild-eyed. "If they've taken Ruby, Mimi, and now Kilo, then we must be next."

Axel pulled my hand. "Then we need to leave. *Now.*"

We were in serious danger.

I was sprinting through the halls, barely in control. This was fight or flight. Freeze or fold. The corridors of El Dorado were contorting into themselves until the place we once knew so well felt like a labyrinth that we could never escape.

Darnell stopped.

It was that sound again.

That quiet chatter that had taunted our ears, all those nights ago—when we'd snuck into the school to put up posters for the mall. The din of familiar voices that whispered and blended together, making me think I was losing my mind.

Only now we were all hearing it together.

This was real.

"This is ending. Right here. Right now," Darnell declared. His gaze trained on a door at the end of the flickering hallway. The one that didn't even have a door handle. The only one with a tinted black window in the center, where we'd first heard the strange sounds.

"We have to go! They're coming for us," Axel whispered.

"Always be one step behind your prey and one step ahead of your enemy," Darnell said. And in one of those rare moments in history, he actually took off his skates.

"Darnell, come on. This isn't the moment to talk like we're in a nature documentary," I hissed. "They're seriously going to catch us!"

"Are you sure we're not in the jungle? Information is power, and power may save us." Darnell lifted up the sharp butt of the Rollerblade defiantly and slammed it into the window.

Glass exploded everywhere.

I ducked, and jagged shards rained down, and by the time I looked up, Darnell had already reached his arm through the broken window, unlocked the door, and pushed it open.

What we found was proof of just how little we knew about our environment.

We were rats in a cage.

"It's official," Darnell declared. "This challenge is run by psychopaths."

"This is too much, even for Limbo." Axel's jaw dropped.

"I'm definitely going to need some expensive therapy after this," I said as I stepped inside the room, finding a monolithic wall of computer monitors, all blinking in red and white lights. A complex automated surveillance system. I neared it to get a better view.

One monitor was a live video of a still bedroom, and the familiar voice that I knew better than any other in the entire world.

"Is that my *casa?*" I gasped in horror.

And sure enough, my mother crossed the screen, chatting on the phone in her nightgown, totally unaware of her own surveillance, because the camera's view was from the position her laptop usually was in on her desk.

But that wasn't the only one.

Axel was trained on another screen. "This is my living room," he said, perturbed. "This must be recording from my smart TV."

"Look! Even the Retro Lounge is bugged," Darnell exclaimed.

They were recording *everything*.

Beyond the Limbo cameramen and postable content that we knew about, they had totally infiltrated our lives—I doubted even the school knew about this. After all, they would never agree to something that would invade our privacy to such a degree—the parents would raise hell.

This wasn't real life. It couldn't be. I always knew that our phones were listening, that our computers were collecting data, but the fact that Limbo was behind the monitor twenty-four seven was insane. Just the idea that anyone could have been watching me and Axel together, or spying on me when I thought I was alone in my room, made my flesh crawl.

I was flipping out.

It was here, all along. Clearly an operation this big needed a hands-on, local setup instead of pulling the strings from as far away as Limboland.

"Luna, there you are!" Samantha arrived, out of breath. "What the hell?" She took in the monitors. "Those creeps!" Samantha started smashing one of the computer monitors, until Axel had to pull her off. "Of course they did this!"

"Samantha." Axel gripped her shoulders. "What do you mean by 'of course'?'"

"I was still pretty messed up when I left the hospital, and Limbo's lawyers were already trying to make me sign paperwork. That's why Andy seemed so familiar. . . ."

"This is very important," Axel said. "Why did they want you to sign paperwork?"

"Limbo wanted to bury everything and make sure I wouldn't sue them. To clean their image. To deflect any responsibility for the damage that was done to me on their platform. I was bombarded with all kinds of nondisclosure agreements, but my parents made sure I didn't sign anything. If the pills couldn't silence me, then Limbo wouldn't either. And when they offered this challenge, I thought they were trying to genuinely do the right thing. But I was wrong."

We had been living a lie, day in and day out, adorned in flashy fun colors to distract us from what this challenge really was.

"Do you hear that?" Darnell asked.

It was the pitter-patter of a cane.

"Look at the screen." Axel pointed. "They know where we are."

And sure enough, I saw a pixelated image walking down the locker halls.

"Don't turn around, unless you want to scream . . . ," Darnell whispered.

Because there they were, emerging from the darkness—Scarlett, backed up by Andy in his plush purple suit and two burly Limbo guards. We were cornered—stuck in this surveillance room—and Limbo was blocking the only exit. Out of instinct, I picked up a shard of glass—anything to defend me and my friends. And just when I feared that we were going to end up like Kilo—or worse—they totally caught me by surprise.

Scarlett stopped just feet away, smiling brightly. "Congratulations. You have all exceeded our expectations," she said. "To watch you grow has been spellbinding, to say the least."

"Captivating," Andy chimed in. His eye was red and puffy, which meant Kilo hadn't gone down without a fight. Good for him.

"The drama of your lives is real. It's raw." Scarlett sparkled at the thought. "Darnell, how you lifted Luna's spirits after she was ridiculed at the street race. Axel, how you fought so valiantly for love. And Luna, how much you care for your mother. How bravely you've been searching for your friends. The tenacity. The drive. The love. You're simply remarkable."

Her adulation was repulsive, like she was some kind of fan.

"You've lost your minds!" I shouted.

Darnell shook his head. "How could you do this?"

But rather than answering, Scarlett took a step toward Darnell and snatched the tape recorder that was protruding from his pocket. The red light was blinking, still recording.

"I could ask you the same question," she said, and handed the recorder to Andy, who smashed it with his cane.

"What's wrong with you, Andy? We trusted you!" Darnell cried out.

"This is for your own good. Trust me, guys," Andy said with a residue of remorse.

"You're smart, Darnell, but let's just hope you're smart enough to not end up like your friends Ruby, Mimi, or even poor Kilo," Scarlett taunted.

Suddenly I realized I had been squeezing the shard of glass so hard my hands were dripping blood. I was so numb I never felt the pain. I tucked the shard into my waistband—just in case.

"What have you done with our friends?" I demanded.

"You can't possibly think you'll get away with this," Axel said.

"Don't be silly. Of course we will. You all signed our terms and conditions at the beginning of the year. You all agreed to twenty-four-hour surveillance. You all agreed to random focus-group testing. Which is exactly where your friends are right now—volunteering themselves for our research."

I remembered that first day of the challenge, scrolling all the way down to the bottom of the screen, just so I could get it over with.

"But nobody actually reads the terms and conditions," I said.

"Nor do we expect you to."

There was a sick part of me that still admired her. She had

created a magical world just for us—a dream that none of us wanted to wake up from.

Scarlett continued. "We can all agree that this challenge has gone too far. None of you were ever supposed to be able to live without technology this long." She checked her watch, bored. "And I think it's fair to say that now you all know far too much."

"Why the hell are you doing all this? What do you want from us?" I needed answers.

"Well, the right question is what we want from *you*, Luna."

"Me? What could you possibly want from me?"

Scarlett smiled cordially. "You're the star of the show, Luna. The reason we've gained an unprecedented number of new users. And now we want you to tell the public that you can no longer continue with the challenge. That you miss Limbo too much. Because you love us. And if you cooperate, we will still give you the scholarship." Scarlett motioned to the surveillance monitors. "And of course, you all will forget about everything you've seen tonight. It'll be our little secret."

"And what if we don't? I have a good memory," Axel said.

"Who's going to believe you anyway? We're Limbo. We can have all this evidence taken away in minutes."

"I don't want your dirty scholarship money." I shook my head. "I want my friends back."

"We've made you famous. We've given you a new world. We've given you purpose! What else do you want?" Scarlett's expression grew stormy. "Don't be ungrateful."

"Do I look like somebody that wanted to be famous?" I snapped. "I'm the kind of girl who blushes when the barista at Starbucks calls me by my name. Maybe you don't know us as well as you think. Maybe our values were something your spy cams couldn't capture."

Deep down I was terrified.

Because Scarlett was one of the most powerful women in the world, and she was about to make that very clear. "Luna, we would *hate* for everyone to see the confession you sent to Limbo's help center. The whole world will know what you did to Samantha. And, Axel, once your secret is revealed, the people of this town will hate you."

I turned to Axel, but he wouldn't meet my eyes. "What is she talking about, Axel?"

He didn't answer.

"And as for you, Samantha, do you really think you're strong enough to go through it a second time? We program the algorithms, remember?"

I hated her for talking about Samantha like that. But just when I thought I was at a breaking point, it was Axel who made a move.

He threw himself into the guards, sending one of them toppling backward—at least for a moment—creating a small window for our escape.

I tore through the opening and into the hall, but as soon as I turned around, I saw that his attempt hadn't been enough. The guards had outmuscled Axel, detaining him.

Samantha looked at me. "Truth is, I have far less to lose than you," she said. "No matter what happens, promise me you'll *run*."

If it wasn't for what Samantha did next, we never would have gotten away. She walked toward the guards boldly, getting in their faces, derailing their attention. And then it happened.

Samantha saved all of us.

She grabbed the little whistle around her neck and started blowing.

This was an SOS.

"What are you doing? Stop that!" Scarlett commanded.

But Samantha didn't stop—not even when her face went red. Not even when the Limbo guards went to shut her up. That distraction was enough so that we could all escape.

We sprinted down the hall toward freedom.

And soon we were pushing through the emergency fire escape door—disappearing into the abandoned forest.

▶ 54.

"Thunderstruck"
—AC/DC

We were lost in every meaning of the word.

Lost in life.

Lost in our beliefs.

Lost in our thoughts.

And definitely lost in the forest.

We didn't know where we were running, but it didn't matter, because no one place felt safe. I ducked and dodged under the arms of twisted trees. Thorns slit gashes across my legs. Icy rain-drops were daggers in my back.

I heaved, losing strength, falling over again and again.

But Axel was there to take my hand and pick me up, even if I could hardly see him, even if we were too exhausted to speak. At least we all had one another.

"You're okay, Luna. I've got you," Axel assured me, with a kiss on the cheek.

"Keep your head up, girl," Darnell added.

"Thanks, guys." But by the time I rose to my feet, I realized that I hadn't tripped over a branch, or some divot in the mud.

When I looked down, I found two black eyes staring up at me.

A fox, lying lifeless on the ground.

"Another dead animal . . ." Axel's breath caught in his chest.

"Wait—what are these cables?" Darnell pulled black electrical wire from the earth.

"I think that's what I tripped on."

Darnell walked around the pond, following the cable, until finally he pulled back a branch that revealed thousands of snaking electrical wires, thick and coiled around the massive roots of the forest and feeding into the murky pond.

"How did we not see this earlier?" I asked aloud, incredulous.

Before Darnell could travel any farther, Axel held up his arm, stopping him. "Don't step in that water! These are live wires. You could have just lost your life, man!"

And it was true. I thought I had smelled something strange, but it was actually familiar—similar to the burnt rubber on the day of the street race. The electrical cables were slit, stripped, and skinned. Sparking in the sleeting rain. Those animals hadn't been hunted or poisoned.

They'd been electrocuted.

"This is what's been killing the wildlife. Without leaving a single trace," Darnell said. He followed the cables deeper into the underbrush, at a cautious distance, until he came across a group of trees that had been marked in red paint. I recognized them immediately. A warning not to go any farther. But we were pretty beyond threats at this point.

A path led into a little forest clearing, so we ventured ahead to find a camouflaged electrical box, much like a transformer.

The wires fed into its side, with a giant antenna that protruded from the top like a spire.

My jaw dropped. "It's official. My life is a sci-fi movie."

"Is this real, or am I high?" Darnell asked.

The enormous power generator had previously been shrouded by tall pines. The machinery was massive, but one little detail caught my attention immediately. A label. I inched closer, carefully, and brushed away flecks of dirt, revealing the truth shrouded beneath.

PROPERTY OF LIMBO

I was still in shock, but Detective Darnell was one step ahead of me, because he was already standing at the base of the red-marked trees. "Guys, look up there. Cameras!"

Peppered all over the forest canopy were flashing red lights that glinted in the moonlight. "They're still watching us," I breathed.

Axel stared up into the treetops as if in a trance. "I get it now. This must be those strange reflections in the photos I developed . . . this is what has been in the forest all along."

I was aware that so few rules applied in the abandoned forest. I'd just never imagined that a company like Limbo would use it to their advantage.

"We have to get out of here," Darnell said. "Come on, let's move!"

"Where?" Axel shouted. "What's the point? They have eyes everywhere."

Darnell shook his head and smiled. "Not at Kilo's cabin. It was so far up the mountain that he couldn't even get a signal, remember?"

▶ 55.

"Entre Tú y Mil Mares"
—Laura Pausini

The rain had let up, but I was still soaked to the skin.

After an hour of hiking up the mountain, we reached the dry plateau that overlooked El Dorado, a beautiful place that I had last seen from the handlebars of Kilo's bicycle. Where we experienced that golden moment when the sun kisses the horizon as streetlamps began to glow. Where all my problems, from a distance, felt microscopic.

But there were no liberating feelings tonight.

I smelled the fire before I saw it.

Then I tasted its rancid sting in my mouth. When I finally crested the ridge, smoke was mushrooming ominously above our little town, like a bomb had been dropped on the lives we once lived. The blaze was out of control, burning to the ground the most precious place on the planet.

The livelihood of my family.

"Is that . . ." Axel gulped.

"The Monteverde Mall." Darnell finished his thought, stunned.

Axel pulled me close, although I was too petrified to react.

"No—" I pushed myself away from him. "This isn't real. This can't be happening." I fell to my knees.

"Could Limbo have actually done this?" Axel uttered.

I cried and I cried, until my tears were stolen by the wind.

This couldn't have been an accident. Especially after such a rainy night. It was disturbing to think that Limbo could've set fire to the Monteverde Mall—the very heart of the Retro movement— in an attempt to make us surrender. To destroy everything that we'd built, everything that we'd fought for. But all I could think about was my mother. Our theater was gone forever, and if she didn't have a job, that would be a surefire deportation.

I knew, at the exact same moment, that my mother was thinking of me—agonizing over the fact that her daughter had never returned home. That I'd gone missing too. Or perhaps even worse, that I was trapped in that deadly blaze.

"I have to go back!" I screamed, scrambling to my feet and taking off running down the hill. But my friends stopped my stride. "I'm leaving! Let me go!" I shoved Axel and tried to peel away, but he and Darnell outmuscled me. I threw weak fists into their chests, and then into the air, losing what strength I had left.

"But my mother . . . I have to go back . . ."

"Luna, you know you can't do that yet," Darnell told me. "When this is all over, I promise, you'll be able to go back, and we'll all be there for your family."

Axel seemed even more destroyed than me. "Luna . . . there's something I have to tell you." He ran his hands through his hair as he spoke.

"What is it, Axel?" I asked him. "What the hell is going on?"

"I can't keep living, holding this secret inside—the secret that Scarlett threatened to expose. And I get the feeling you'll find it out sooner or later—and maybe you'll hate me forever, but I love you, Luna, and you need to know this."

I waited with bated breath, expecting the worst. The closest thing I've felt to premonition.

Because what he said next destroyed me.

"My family is the one that has been trying to buy and tear down the mall."

There was a delay between the delivery of his words and their reception into my brain. Just when I thought my entire life was a lie, just when I realized that my future was gone forever, I learned that the person I'd opened my heart to had been pretending to be someone he wasn't all along. The person I was falling for had been lying to me since the day we met.

"The mega apartment complex?" I said. "That's *you*?"

"But please—listen—" Axel stammered. "I know it sounds like an excuse, but it wasn't my idea. It was my family, not me. They've been trying to buy that land for years. But I told them to back out of that deal a long time ago—as soon as I learned how much the mall meant to you, I fought to keep it standing. And we turned it into something great."

"Something great? You think this is great? The mall is burning to the ground!" I shouted. "You lied to me. All along, all the times you let me cry on your shoulder, you knew the truth and you decided to hide it from me."

"I didn't know how to tell you," he argued, "but it wasn't a total lie."

"Half-truths are lies."

He grew frustrated and threw a fist into a tree. "Why, when anything is going bad, do you have to be like this?"

"And why, every time life doesn't go your way, do you have to punch something?"

"My god, why do you have to be so damn difficult?"

"I thought that's what you loved about me." I looked into his eyes. "We're done, Axel. You win. Limbo burned down the mall, so now you can buy it all up and finally play house with your new buildings. But please, just make sure it's far away from me."

"Luna, come on—we'll make it work together."

"That doesn't change the fact that tomorrow you're going to get richer off my misery. I'm going to lose my family while you'll get the world on a golden platter."

He tried to grab my hands. "I'm sorry. I know I'm not perfect—"

I laughed through tears and shook my head. "Love doesn't have to be perfect. It just has to be sincere." I turned my back on Axel and on the blaze that was obliterating my past—the burning film reels that had kept a piece of my father alive.

Everything about him was now officially dead.

Darnell had been frozen awkwardly in place. "Sorry to interrupt the drama, but they're coming for us."

"Wait, what do you mean?" I asked. "Coming for us? Where?"

Darnell pointed behind him at a convoy of gunmetal trucks that were speeding full throttle up the mountainside. "RUN!"

He didn't have to tell us twice. We sprinted up the hill, stumbling, running for our lives.

Limbo was on our tail.

▶ 56.

"Welcome to the Jungle"
—Guns N' Roses

They say that when an intense life experience happens, you go through a couple of stages. First comes the impact, where you're thunderstruck by shock. Next is stage two, total denial. And eventually you enter the recovery phases, where you come to terms with what happened. You adjust and learn to deal. But they never tell you what happens when you're stuck in the relentless void between stages. Unable to deny the truth, yet powerless to accept the reality.

I was going to lose my mother.

I might never see my friends again.

There was no more family cinema.

The love I thought I had was a lie.

Everything Retro was dead.

There was no challenge.

I was so numb I could hardly feel the cold, even if my toes, soaked in my boots, were clenched by the frostbitten grasp of hypothermia.

We finally reached Kilo's cabin.

Darnell wrestled the flimsy front door open. Strewn everywhere were car engines and exhaust pipes, the dusty couch he slept on, and that pirate radio of his.

Axel immediately slid a bookshelf in front of the entrance.

"Let's not panic. Let's not panic," Darnell told himself, sifting through Kilo's workbench for anything that could get us out of this mess.

Amid all the hysteria, I noticed a corkboard over Kilo's couch-bed. And tacked up there were Polaroid photos of each of us—his friends.

"Check this out . . . ," Axel muttered, not meeting my eyes. Not meeting anyone's. He had found Mimi's jacket, still resting on the sofa. "We're so stupid. All the answers were right in front of us." He threw it across the room in a fit of rage.

I picked it up, examining the patches. There was one missing—the most significant patch of all of them. The one I'd sewn on in honor of the challenge.

"Mimi tore off the Limbo patch," I said. "She knew it was them all along. I'm sure that's what she wanted to tell me that night."

Darnell searched through items on the workbench, blowing dust off a leather notebook. "Hey, guys, you're going to want to see this! There's a note here that says 'read me.'"

"Are you serious?" I asked. "He knew we would come here." We crowded around to see what Kilo had written. All chicken-scratch instructions, with diagrams of his pirate radio, illustrated in such detail that we might be able to figure out how to make it work.

"This is how we're going to get out of here!" Darnell

frantically turned the knobs and dials, setting the frequency to 103.7 Retro Radio, just as Kilo had prepared. "Maybe if I can figure out how to broadcast, someone will hear us, and they'll come for us."

Darnell's moment of hope was interrupted by a rattling sound.

Truck engines. And they roared outside the cabin.

"How could Limbo know that we're here?!" Axel was frenzied. "This makes no sense!"

But Darnell kept tinkering with the radio while syntonizing something in his own head. Because if there was any way to understand the system, Darnell knew that you didn't just have to challenge it. You had to deconstruct it entirely.

"No, it all makes perfect sense." Darnell shook his head. "The constant surveillance. The challenges. The questions on the Live Feed about our feelings, about those new snacks and experimental flavors. The shopping challenge. Scarlett said they took our friends to do a focus group. But I think we've been in a big focus group all this time."

"I know this is a played-out saying, but it's true," Axel said. "If you don't know what the product is, it's you."

It did all seem too good to be true. . . .

Once the words left his mouth, I was overcome by a paradigm shift. It all made sense:

Limbo was always present. Whenever a contestant had broken the rules, Andy appeared to make an elimination. He was there at the mall the last time we saw Ruby. And he even showed up for Axel's party the night Mimi went missing. We trusted him completely—though, like a magician, Andy had tricked us all, and made our friends disappear.

"Hey, you hear that?" Darnell said. "They're getting closer—we're running out of time."

"But how did they find us?" Axel asked.

I looked down to my holographic Casio watch—the one that glimmered in the moonlight. The thing we were forbidden to take off. The thing that read PROPERTY OF LIMBO.

The label wasn't referring to the watch. Those words were meant to label us.

"We were never out of the system. We were below it," Darnell said. "Well, I'm nobody's property." He ripped off his watch, and Axel and I followed suit, throwing them to the floor, where we all stomped them beneath our feet.

One final, desperate attempt to declare ourselves free.

But Limbo wasn't going to let us go that easily.

BANG—something collided against the wall outside.

Axel and Darnell pushed the workbench against the door.

They were coming to get us. To claim our lives as a part of their sick experiment. We were trapped, and we knew it.

Boots stormed on the roof, trying a new point of entry, making dust sprinkle down.

We were surrounded.

Darnell picked up Kilo's pirate radio and delivered one last message out into the universe.

"If anyone hears this, if anyone is listening—please remember everything I'm about to say. We've been taken advantage of. Used. And Limbo is behind it all. . . ."

Soon the rattling hinges of the front door gave way, and the entire room erupted in a plume of smoke. This was the end.

I can't even remember what happened next. I don't know if Limbo used chloroform to knock us out, or if my brain blocked it from my memory. Maybe I just fainted, because one second I was there, in my skin, breathing, and the next, my entire world went black.

⏸ 57.

Pause

Well, congratulations, you're officially up to speed.

I hope you've enjoyed the soundtrack of my intense biopic, because right now the guards have me pinned to the floor in my holding cell. Fake choking worked to get them in the room, but not so much to get me out. And as if that wasn't enough, I'm blindfolded. Hanging out with my friend darkness.

Awesome.

My hands are bound behind my back with handcuffs, and then I'm being walked through the halls like a lab rat. But the sloppy kind, with smeared lipstick, who needs to take a shower with boiling water, a slice of lemon, and a dash of cinnamon to mask the smell.

I just hope there is a cheesy surprise at the end of the maze.

They finally shove me inside a room, and I know I'm not alone.

Like when you're stopped at a red light and you can *feel* that someone is staring at you, before you even turn to look. It's a psychological phenomenon called "gaze detection," a sixth sense we developed when humans used to be prey.

The cuffs are taken off. The door slams closed. I can't see anything, but I feel the crunch of fake grass under my feet and hear the zips and zings of pinball machines. Is this another one of Limbo's games? A test?

"LOONY!"

I recognize that voice right away.

And immediately I feel at home.

"Mimi!" I shout, sprinting blindly toward the voice.

"Let's take off that blindfold before you smash your pretty face into a wall. I know from experience," she says. My world comes into view as Mimi pulls me in for a hug.

It's actually her. It's Mimi!

I hold her tight, and my arms refuse to let go. I can't stop crying. Every obstacle that we overcame was suddenly worth it because now I've finally found my best friend.

"Poor thing . . . what did they do to you?" Before I can reply, she's sniffing my pits. "Don't worry, girl—you smell better than you look!" Mimi smiles brightly.

I'm laughing through tears. "You can't imagine how much I've missed you."

Someone approaches from behind.

"Ruby!" I embrace my friend. "I was so worried about you. Thank god you're here. We never believed that you would run away without saying goodbye. You're strong for surviving in this place." And when I think my heart can't take anymore happiness, I hear another familiar voice.

"I was afraid they threw you into the moat with the crocodiles!" says Darnell.

346

"Darnell!" I scream, and he's pulling me close.

"I'm so glad you're here right now," Axel says, stepping forward.

I want to hug him so bad, but instead, I pull away.

How can something that's supposed to feel good hurt so freaking much?

And then Kilo is lifting us all up like a forklift until we topple over. "Go easy, big guy!" I laugh.

It's all like a dream.

I finally have them back. Like my mother would say, some friends come and go, like ocean waves, but the true ones stick to you—like a starfish sucking your face. Though when the hellos are over, desperation follows. I look to my friends, at the bags under their eyes, clearly destroyed by whatever Limbo has been doing to them all this time.

I scan the room, taking in my surroundings. I'm in a massive workspace. A fun zone for adults, imagined in classic Limbo fashion: rainbow walls with bouncy balls abound, ornate chocolate fountains, and a massive slide in the middle of the room that leads to a ball pit; and in the corner is a home theater. At the far end of the wall is a giant two-way mirror—something I know because shadows move on the other side. Then I notice that the ceiling is made of the same observational glass.

And our only way in or out is through a shiny, candy-purple door.

"What is this place?" I ask.

"The focus group center," Ruby explains. "They offer us all types of snacks that haven't been released yet. We just drink experimental energy drinks all day and night to increase productivity, so we barely sleep. And the only way they feed you is if you answer their questionnaires and comment cards." She fingers her locs, nervous. "I have to get out of this place soon or I'm going to lose it."

We were subjects of some kind of sick experiment.

"Ruby, how did *you* end up here?"

"Well, this is where I've been for all these weeks. It all started when I saw all the creepy cameras at school that night when we were putting up posters for the mall—but when I confronted Limbo, they threw me here . . . and that's when Mimi found me."

Mimi's hands shake as she points to the entrance—and I don't know if it's the energy drinks, or if she's just traumatized by all of this. "Remember the off-limits room from the tour? The room with the purple door, that Scarlett and the guards stopped me from entering?"

"Yes, of course I remember."

"Well, I saw Ruby that day. I'm sorry I didn't tell you—I wanted to say something the night of the party, but I was afraid Limbo would hear. I didn't talk because I didn't want to put you in danger. That's why I wrote on the mirror. It's why I cut out the Limbo patch on my jacket. I even tried to leave you a note, but they stopped me."

I feel so stupid.

How had I not realized this earlier?

"When you were all here on the tour, I heard your voices and tried to shout," Ruby explains. "I pounded on the door. Anything. Mimi was the only one who heard."

"I can't believe we were so close. I'm sorry, Ruby," I say, millions of questions spiraling in my head, so I turn to Kilo. "And how did you know?"

Kilo wraps an arm around Mimi. "I intercepted Mimi's radio messages."

"And I'm so glad he did," Mimi says. "Other than Enrique Iglesias, Kilo is basically my hero." Mimi gives Kilo a kiss on the cheek, which makes him literally melt into a puddle on the floor. I've never seen such a rough-hewn guy get so mushy.

I had missed a lot in such a short amount of time.

"You have a radio? How did you get a radio?"

"*Shhh*, I'll explain later." She points to the mirror. "They might be listening."

"So we're trapped, and that big purple door is our only way out?"

"No, we are not trapped. The door is unlocked," Darnell says, heavy-eyed, sipping on a yerba maté like a zombie. "We are here of our own accord. We can leave whenever we want."

"What? Then what are we waiting for?" I go for the door, but Kilo stops me.

"Scarlett made it clear. If any one of us leaves, they'll release all the dirt they have on the rest of us. Our search history. Our footprint on social media. All our secrets."

"The psychological help I received on the internet," Axel says. "They'll even make my private diary public."

Darnell steps forward. "How I catfished on that dating site."

"The video I sent to Limbo," I groaned. "My confession."

"The world will hate us all," Mimi sighs.

Limbo is winning this war. I'm desperate.

"So how do we actually leave this place?" I ask.

"We sign those." Axel points to a stack of documents on a nearby table. "Nondisclosure agreements. We forget everything that we've seen, and then we can go."

Darnell swims through the ball pit. "They can't keep us here forever."

"Well, they own the algorithms. If we disappear, they have the power to bury all the news," Axel says. "Even when our parents search for us, no one will know that we're here. For most people, since going retro, we've been totally off the grid."

Ruby lies on the slide, dejected. "And then we'll just become another statistic. Another unsolved case."

"Scarlett wants to buy me off and grant me the full scholarship without you guys," I say. "But I promise I won't give in. I won't sign those documents. And I won't do a public campaign about why Limbo is the best. I won't be an accomplice."

"I wouldn't expect anything less from you, Luna," Darnell assures me.

I put my hand over the whistle that hangs from my neck, swearing a silent oath. Thinking about why we even started this retro wave in the first place. And then each of my friends puts a hand over their chests, taking the same oath—because even though the challenge is now over, we aren't done being a team.

► 58.

"Wonderwall"
—Oasis

There is no time in Limboland.

No clocks. No windows. No metric on life. We are trapped in an eternal fun zone where all real fun is sentenced to die—and at this point, I can't even tell how many hours have passed since this nightmare started.

We really are stuck in Limbo.

Traditionally, it's the place where souls are trapped before getting assigned to heaven or hell. Limbo is forcing us to do the same activities in this room for all eternity, giving us two choices: go crazy or give up. Isn't that the definition of insanity? Doing the same thing over and over again, expecting a different result?

The others went to sleep, but I can't.

And I guess neither can he.

If there is any connection left between me and Axel, it's in our shared misery. I sit alone in the mini theater, watching the same repeating *Friends* episode where Ross finds out that Monica and Chandler are together. My mind looping—my poor mother is probably mounting a search party while the theater lies in ruins, having lost her daughter and her future in one day.

The agony is heart-wrenching.

"Hey," comes a voice from behind.

I try to hide how much he startled me.

"Do you want any popcorn?" he asks, taking a seat next to me.

"No thanks," I tell him.

"I thought you loved popcorn."

"I used to. Now I don't. Not since the theater burned down."

"We have been through a lot." He swallows. "I get it."

"Some of it was your fault," I say sharply, standing to leave.

"Hold on," he says. "I know, I'm an idiot. Seriously, believe me—"

I keep walking, but Axel stops me. "Here, let me show you," he says, and then pours all the popcorn over his head—which almost makes me smile, but not quite.

"You are a total idiot," I agree.

"Great. We're getting somewhere." He laughs nervously. "At least now I have your attention. Please, just hear me for one second, and then you can continue to be mad at me. I know I screwed things up with you. That I wasn't honest with you. That you probably don't even want to look at my face right now. But I don't think you'll feel that way forever, and I'm going to find a way to make it right," he promises me, eyes reflecting the light of the projector.

The way they had the first night we kissed.

"The only way is to turn back time." I plop into a theater chair and run my hand against the grain of the velvet. "Funny, the arms of these chairs used to feel like a warm hug. Now they just feel like defeat."

"What do you mean, defeat? We're still fighting," Axel says, taking my hand—and I'm too weak to stop him. I know that what he feels for me is genuine. I can trust at least that, no matter how selfish he was.

"We can't continue like this. I don't know how, but this has to end. I think I'm going to make a deal with Limbo," I confess. "Maybe holding out for what we believe in isn't worth more than the pain this is causing those who care about us. Maybe just being here is selfish."

"If there's one thing I've learned, it's to never make a deal with the devil," Axel says earnestly. "Scarlett has made you whatever deal she's made you because she knows what you're capable of. Luna, she's afraid of you. And she has every right to be, because you're the strongest person I've ever met. If you want to add this to the list of things you hate about me, go ahead, but I don't recognize this version of Luna. This Luna is a coward. The girl that I fell for doesn't roll over. She finds a solution. Even if it's not the best one, at least she tries."

I bristle. "Maybe we should stop the conversation here, before this theater burns down too," I say, so overwhelmed I'm ready to just leave.

But then comes another voice. "Luna, he's right."

It's Kilo.

Mimi steps into the theater room too. "Luna, remember that time in soccer when you scored that game-winning goal with your head?"

"Um, Mimi, I scored with my face."

"Well, you didn't give up."

"I lost three teeth!" I yelled.

"Which your mom added to her baby-teeth necklace."

"Your point?"

Darnell steps in to clarify. "I think what she's trying to say is that you won the game and you got some dope limited-edition jewelry, all because you didn't give up."

Ruby appears and takes my hand. "That day in the Live Feed challenge, you said that being brave doesn't mean you're not afraid, it just means you fight through it, in spite of those fears. Well, those words are the only reason I'm standing with my head up right now. Or else I would have totally broken a long time ago."

"I don't know . . . I guess you're right. I don't want Limbo to win," I confess.

"Besides, we have time on our side," Mimi says. "There are only so many text messages they can send to our parents, pretending to be us—only so many photoshopped pictures of us on a beach they can post until someone realizes it's all fake."

"Which is why they *need* you to cooperate," Kilo adds. "You hold the cards here."

I'm pacing, shaking my head. "But why me?"

"Because, Luna, you *are* the soul of this challenge." Axel meets my eyes. "Scarlett needs you to admit that you love Limbo, that you need their technology, because all those Retromaniacs out there are looking to you. Listening to you. You have the power to destroy Limbo, which is why Scarlett fears you the most."

"So, yes, you little whiny brat, you're stronger than you think you are," Darnell says.

And it's in these moments I'm reminded of just how much my friends are worth—more than anything else in the entire world. Their safety is more important than my pride. More than my anger—or even my own fate.

And without knowing it, my friends gave me an idea. Something risky that just might work. So I stand tall, with a terrified confidence. Fighting my anxiety with more strength than ever, because this feeling isn't going to control my actions. Not today.

Maybe the old Luna would have frozen up.

But this one fights through it.

"I think I know what I have to do to get us out of here," I say. Then I march across the fun-zone purgatory toward the large purple door—our only way to escape this place.

And I turn the knob to open it.

"I'm ready to cooperate," I say to the guards in the hall.

"Luna, no! What are you doing?" Mimi pleads.

"I'm giving up," I tell her as I extend my hands so that the guards may secure them with handcuffs. "But that doesn't mean I'm going to give in."

Which makes Mimi smile, because in our language that means I still have fight left in me. I hold my head up high. I finally have a plan. And it better work—because from now on, there is no turning back.

⏵ 59.

"Smells Like Teen Spirit"
—Nirvana

I'm led into an executive conference room made of glass. Right away, guards attach me to heart monitors that plug into some kind of lie detector. Which hadn't been in my plan *at all*. I'm sitting across from a team of well-coiffed lawyers, but all I really want to do is talk with Scarlett. Face-to-face.

I wonder where she is.

Before me is Scarlett's lawyer, Fineman.

He sighs, exasperated. "Luna, you've been very defiant."

"Sorry about that."

The polygraph meter starts to go wild.

"Oops." I wink at him. "I guess I lied . . . sorry, not sorry."

Fineman pushes his glasses up. He has a familiar look—a familiarity beyond our few interactions at the beginning of the challenge. I think I'm officially losing my mind.

"I'll only talk with Scarlett," I say.

And just as the words leave my mouth, I hear footsteps.

The queen of Limboland is near.

The door unlocks.

Scarlett enters wearing her iconic black turtleneck with a smile faker than an infomercial. "Good evening, Luna."

I should be terrified just to see her, but there's no reason to be afraid when your life can't get any worse.

"Well, I'm glad you've finally come to your senses," Scarlett says.

"Aren't we all."

"I hear you're not eating much. Do you have a problem with our cookies?" She slides a tray forward to me.

"Everyone here is so obsessed with the cookies. What is it, a fetish?"

"You're a funny girl." Scarlett chews. "So you know, my offer won't stand forever."

"You burned my entire life down. You spied on us. You used us. . . . I should have never taken your sick challenge in the first place."

"No, you should be proud of yourself, Luna. Sure, things got out of hand, and the challenge went too far for all of us. But during these last few months, you made your town—and definitely your high school—a much better place. Also, you helped us get something very powerful—pure, virgin data. We will always be thankful for that."

It feels like I'm being violated, and there's nothing I can do to stop it.

Scarlett continues to bloviate. "What you eat. What you buy. What you wear. What you think about. How you learn and grow. Invaluable information, and we have all of it, thanks to you and your friends." She takes my hand and looks into my soul. "Here at Limbo, we're trying to create a more connected world—a better world. But for that, we need to know all about the people we're connecting."

"A better world for *you*! It's one thing to recommend which show to binge next, but it's something else entirely when you manipulate us until we don't have any opinions of our own."

"This new generation is not ready to handle hard decisions. So we need to utilize our algorithms to influence *how we all think*, in order to make the world a better place."

Scarlett holds a compassionate hand to her heart as she speaks.

I can't believe it—she *actually* thinks she's some kind of savior.

"It's true that we're inheriting a messed-up planet with a ton of problems, and it doesn't come with an instruction manual. But controlling us will never be the solution. People like you are liars, and you and your shareholders just want to play with our brains for your own personal benefit," I tell her. This was Limbo's plan all along. The end goal of the largest social media platform is to seize power over all of us. Mind control.

They want us to wear their smartwatches, buy their smartphones, use their apps, no matter what the human cost. They want us to need Limbo just to breathe.

I lean forward. "Okay, Scarlett. I'll accept your offer. I'll give you what you want. I'll go in front of the press and tell them we all came here of our own volition. I'll tell them that I love Limbo and can't last one year without it. That I need it. I'll even propose that you be canonized as a saint. Whatever you want."

The polygraph machine keeps steady. She knows my word is gold.

But I have one last trick up my sleeve.

Scarlett studies me. "What's the catch?"

"You're not going to give me the scholarship. Not a penny. Instead, you'll award it to each of my friends—a full ride to whatever school their hearts desire. And then after that, you'll let them go home. Immediately," I explain. "But most importantly, I need you to make sure that my mother has enough time to find another job in this country."

Scarlett doesn't blink. She shakes her head haughtily. "Why would I ever accept that? Why would I accept conditions like these from a girl like you?"

Which is when I realize that I'm going to have to sacrifice everything to save my friends. Scarlett is pushing me to the limit. And now it's time to close my eyes and jump.

"Because I'll give you the rights to my privacy—my data—forever," I tell her. "Whatever you need from me. And let's be real, you need a deal as much as I do, because I think it's safe to say that we're both running out of time. I'll even make sure my friends sign whatever nondisclosure agreements you need so this entire mess disappears."

She tilts her head, intrigued. "Why would you go through all this, just for your friends?"

"You'll never get it. Your heart swims in subzero liquid nitrogen."

The polygraph meter never wavers.

"Very well," she says. "Shall we make this official?"

Fineman takes his time drawing up the new terms, then walks over and slaps a stack of legal documents before me. Scarlett extends me a pen. I take it. I can't believe this is actually happening. She smiles victoriously, setting the stage for me to voluntarily hang myself.

But at least the ones I love will survive in the end.

Ruby could go to art school and be a badass tattoo artist.

Axel, with his horrendous grades, could turn his life around.

Darnell could move to a big city, where he can flourish and be himself.

Mimi could take that one-year program to study tortoises in the Galápagos.

Kilo could someday have an actual home. A real future in the outside world.

My mother will have a second shot to stay in this country and build a new future.

I know my friends would never sell themselves into complicity, so I have to do it for them, even if I promised otherwise. No matter how angry they'll be with me, I'm sure they'll be okay.

I press pen to paper, making the first stroke of my signature.

But I stop. Because as Fineman returns to his chair, I notice that he's walking strangely. He can no longer hide his struggling gait, and I recognize that limp. Before I can entertain the thought further, something rips my attention away.

A familiar noise.

It's growing louder and louder with every second. My hand instinctively travels to the plastic whistle hanging on my chest. Something that costs so little but is worth more than gold.

Scarlett shifts in her seat. "Someone stop that terrible noise!"

But I know it as the sound of salvation.

Whistles—hundreds of them.

And the melody of an infectious song, blasting in a cacophony of distant car radios. One that epitomizes the beautiful disaster Limbo created, our anthem since the night of the bonfire. "Smells Like Teen Spirit." A hymn that represents chaos—that reminds me that even though Scarlett created the challenge, we were the ones who championed it into our very own revolution.

"Let's get this over with. Sign the papers now, Luna," Scarlett commands, her tight smile betraying the silent panic on her face.

Instead, I rip off the nodes and wires that connect me to the polygraph machine and run to the glass window that looks down across Limboland. I can hardly believe my eyes. Because below, clanging against the pearly gates, is an army.

But not just any army. This violent crowd is led by the one person who deserves, more than anyone, to shake the foundation of Limbo until it comes crashing down.

Samantha Darby has arrived.

She's standing on the hood of a muscle car, wielding her whistle, leading the battle cry—letting me know that she has my back and is ready to fight until the end. But what catches me off guard is the guy by her side, on a motorcycle. Vince and his crew are all gripping baseball bats and tire irons, looking nothing short of lethal, like a full-on biker gang from another era. Jade is even there too—and considering that she's clutching a big sharp rock, I guess she has my back.

Samantha sees me standing in the window and flashes a smile.

We have a shot at winning this.

Things are about to get crazy, and for the first time, I want to be a part of the madness.

"On second thought . . ." I turn to Scarlett. "You know what your problem is? You've totally underestimated our generation. We're worth a lot more than our data." I take the pen in my hand and press it into the contract, ripping it down with all my strength, gutting it of every controlling lie it contains—stripping away the power Limbo has over me. "I never really liked those tricky terms and conditions anyway."

The alarms start to sound out, flashing red lights.

They're coming.

And everyone in this room knows it tacitly. Which is when I make my move.

I sprint toward the door. I have the advantage of surprise. But just before I can escape, I'm ripped backward by the armed security who guard the entrance.

And that's when they're both clocked over the head.

With a cane.

The guards stumble to the floor, knocked out cold.

"Wh-what in god's name are you doing, Andrew?" Scarlett stammers.

Andrew? I forgot his name was Andrew. . . . I start piecing it all together—but could it be true? All this time Fineman was Andy, and Andy was Fineman! Only now he isn't wearing a three-piece purple suit or top hat, face paint, or purple mustache—just a boring blazer and glasses.

Then he winks at me.

It's crazy how much a filter can conceal.

I can practically see smoke coming out of Scarlett's ears. "Have you lost your mind?!"

Andy hops up on the table, looking down on her, spinning his cane menacingly. "'The world is a dangerous place, not because of those who do evil, but because of those who look on and do nothing,'" he recites.

Andy really is like a big brother in the end. Most importantly, he kept his promise that he would always watch out for us. Because just when another security guard lunges for me, Andy pushes the cane into his chest, sending the guard to the floor.

Andy presses his fingers on the biometric lock and bows. "After you, madam."

► 60.

"(I Can't Get No) Satisfaction"
—The Rolling Stones

My heart is soaring as we run through the halls.

"That was really you all along?"

"Andrew Fineman, Esquire, at your service," he says, as we sprint through the glass labyrinth of Limboland. The echo of whistles crescendoes. I know exactly what's out there.

"You must be the one who gave me that clue with the cookies! Who was trying to help me escape! But—why were you in disguise all this time?"

"I wanted to lead the challenge, firsthand. And Limbo wanted legal to keep a close eye on what was going on," Andy explains. "But as you can see, my advice was disregarded."

I glance through the glass walls, catching sight of the artificially enchanted domain—and the retro army scaling the castle walls. They've come to break us out.

The scene is total chaos.

I hear an explosion. I duck and cover my head. I can hardly see through the black smoke.

Cheers and applause roar.

"Smells Like Teen Spirit" is blasting louder than before. It's coming from inside—they've taken over the intercom!

Down below, the Retromobile has crashed through the main gates. Retromaniacs pour out, storming the Silicon Valley compound. Golf carts are hijacked and crashed. Vending machines are mutilated. Files and documents are set ablaze. Rocks shatter the glass houses.

"Come on! Your friends are this way." Andy pulls me down a corridor with a million transparent doors to nowhere. He's moving as fast as he can despite the busted-up leg. "There are guards all over the place. Quick, over here!"

We cut down a different hallway, finally arriving at the big purple door. I pull it open.

"LUNA!" Mimi sees me first. Her face lights up. "I was so worried, I was going to start biting my toenails."

And soon all my friends come racing to the door. Darnell wraps his arms around me. "Thank goodness you're okay—we heard explosions! What's happening out there?"

"We're getting out of here," I tell them.

"Long time no see, Andy." Mimi and he do a secret handshake.

"Wait. Andy? Is that you?" Axel says.

"At your service," he replies sheepishly, leaning on his cane.

"Thanks for slipping me the radio transmitter," Mimi says. "I don't know what I would have done if Kilo hadn't been listening on the other side."

"What? You're the one who gave Mimi the radio?" Kilo asks.

"It's what I was trying to explain to you the night of the dance, in the Retro Lounge. But you didn't allow me." He rubs his bruised leg. "I knew that if Mimi contacted you, you would tell your friends the truth behind the challenge—but what I didn't expect was that you would eliminate yourself to be with her."

"I'm still lost," I say. "Why didn't you defend us in the surveillance room at school?"

"I wanted you to take the deal to save yourselves—before Scarlett did any more damage to your lives—to mine." Andy looked down. "She has control over my secrets too."

And suddenly many things start making perfect sense.

He was protecting us.

Andy has to be the one who wrote STOP NOW across my car. Maybe all this time, someone wasn't trying to threaten us—they were trying to scare us out of harm's way.

"Looks like they found us," Darnell says.

The hall behind us swarms with security guards.

"Well, what are we waiting for?" Ruby goes to leave. "Let's blow this joint!"

We emerge from the corridor as a nearby window shatters, sending shards of glass flying everywhere. A gang of Retromaniacs bursts into the hallway and overpowers the guards, hog-tying them on the floor.

Andy points to the glass doors at the end of the hall. "So, are you guys ready to be free from Limbo once and for all?"

Hell yeah.

We follow Andy down the corridor, glass walls shattering all around us. Total mutiny is breaking loose on the floors below. Limbo workers collect documents and escape with precious folders, scrambling to save the company's ass. Then there are the others, who join the Retromaniacs to stoke fires, burning files and desks. Even an artificial ficus erupts in flames. This is total pandemonium.

Not to mention the police sirens that wail in the distance.

Darnell grins. "My mama is coming, and she's gonna be *piiiiisssed!*"

"Time to get our lives back," I say. "We need to destroy those files."

"Before they throw me in jail, let me take you to the cloud. But the only way is through the gates of Heaven," Andy says.

I know I've heard about this place before—straight from Scarlett's mouth, on the Limboland tour. This is where precious information is stored. Not just about us, but everyone with a Limbo profile. An enormous digital cloud full of videos and stolen recordings.

We finally halt before a celestial-white door with a placard that reads:

HEAVEN

Andy disengages the lock, and like a safe room, the door hisses and depressurizes, swinging open. I take a deep breath and enter, relishing the moment.

I'm blinded by white neon lights.

"What are we doing here?" Kilo says over the echoing alarm.

I smile darkly. "Up until this point, we were never out of the system. We were below it. But today we're going to come out on top."

"Yeah, on top is my favorite position!" Mimi says.

I shake my head and laugh, taking in my environment. This epic moment. The room is enormous, glowing with infinite rows of massive servers that stretch as far as the eye can see. Lights blink and purr, emitting heat as if they were alive. My friends take in the grandeur, jaws dropped. Just the sheer magnitude could give anyone chills.

Andy and Kilo dart down the ethereal hall and step up to a massive control center.

"We need silence so we can concentrate, because if this doesn't work, you'll never win your freedom back," Andy tells us, as Kilo helps initiate a massive delete on all the files, manipulating three giant touch screens at the same time.

"Seems like a fallen angel finally made it back to Heaven," I hear someone say from behind. Samantha appears in her flame-tipped hair, spinning a baseball bat like Harley Quinn.

"Took me long enough," I say.

"Samantha! What you've done—this is incredible." I embrace her.

Miranda, Kosta, and Nika are here with hundreds of Retromaniacs at the entrance, all giving me their silent and unconditional support—watching Andy and Kilo, hoping that their plan works.

"How did you pull this off?" I ask.

"It all started with your pirate radio broadcast, Darnell," Samantha explains.

Darnell is obviously touched by this. "I wasn't sure that anyone was listening. . . ."

"I wasn't the only one," Samantha continued. "After all, you did hijack 103.7 Retro Radio. And your new family is bigger than you think—I just mobilized them. If we were going to beat Limbo, the more the better—but it was Jade who made things go viral."

Jade comes forward and takes my hands. "I posted and told the world what they did to you guys, and called for every Retromaniac to come break you out. And by the time Limbo took my video down, it had already gone viral."

"You know that Limbo could cancel your account and you'd lose all your followers?" I say.

"I don't care anymore." Jade smiles. "I've decided that we're friends now. Whether you want to be or not." Which is a very Jade comment—one that I love to hear.

"How did you know it would go viral?" Darnell asks.

"I guess you could say I used their algorithm against them."

It's true—Limbo's algorithm only promotes the most incendiary, controversial content to get maximum engagement. And what's more incendiary than a freaking revolution?

Vince steps forward in his "Greased Lightnin'" tee, taking her side. Taking our side. For the first time in history, I'm overjoyed to see him. And even more so to see Jade and Samantha together again, to see that there are no Goldens anymore. There are just people. There is just *us*.

The whine of police sirens nears.

So I step up to the screens, joining Andy. "You know the cops are coming. They're going to arrest you. . . ."

"You should leave," Kilo warns him.

But Andy keeps typing away, his fingers commanding the grand control center. "I know, but this is the only way to be sure that your data belongs just to you. . . ."

Andy was going down with the ship.

Even though he was complicit in so many terrible things, a large part of me has already forgiven him. "Our work here is done," Andy says as he extends his cane to me. "Now, will you do the honors?"

Jade pulls out her smartphone and starts to live stream. "This is growing fast. We've got half a million viewers and climbing."

"Go get 'em," Samantha encourages me. "The world is watching."

So I jump on top of the desk, looking out over all my Retromaniacs—over all my friends. People who have looked to me for answers. People who have followed me into the dark, no matter how impossible the future seemed. And all this time I haven't been telling them the truth about myself.

I'm tired of letting my secrets own who I am.

It's time that I own who I am.

So I stare into the camera, and I speak my truth.

"My name is Luna María Valero Iglesias . . . but I'm not who you think I am. I'm not the heroic leader of some retro movement. I'm just a girl. A really imperfect one at that. I'm the person who posted the video of Samantha Darby. Of my own best friend. And I'm the one who really screwed up her life." My vision goes fuzzy with tears, but I can make out Samantha's face in the crowd—and I know that she's proud of me.

Nothing is going to take her away from me now.

"Over one million views and counting," Jade calls out.

"I messed up. And since then, I've figured out who I am, and who I'm not. We are not the worst version of ourselves. And we are not always the people we are online. Ditching technology doesn't solve all our problems, but it helped me see that, all along, behind every single screen, is a person with a story, with feelings, and with a beating heart."

Then I turn toward the giant computer screen.

"Jade, record this . . . because, Samantha, this one's for you."

I wind back the cane with all my might and take a swing, smashing in the massive monitor. The hollow crash echoes through the room. Then I rip out the motherboard, as if pulling out the heart in a sacrificial ritual, lifting it up for all to see.

The mob erupts into total mayhem.

Computer towers are pushed over, one after another like

dominoes. Retromaniacs take pieces of those hard drives, reclaiming their own data.

Today we are taking everything back.

What we like to watch.

Our favorite frozen yogurt flavors.

The dumb photos that we posted and instantly regretted.

The conversations we've had with our friends about our insecurities.

All our different religions, controversial politics, and our unique sexualities.

Every piece of data that could be used against us or sold to the highest bidder.

Vince offers Axel a menacing-looking pipe. "Are you ready to pull off one last crazy stunt with me?"

Axel cracks his knuckles. "I'd like nothing more in the entire world. Thanks for having my back, man."

"You know I'll never turn down an opportunity to break stuff." Vince smiles deviously.

Next thing I know, Samantha is pulling the fire alarm, activating the sprinklers, while Mimi sits on Kilo's shoulders, middle fingers up like the badass unicorn that she is.

I would love to see Scarlett's face right now. I wonder where she is.

I look across the white cloud of the room. The beautiful hysteria. The sparking, smoking, defeated processors lie in ruin. Fire retardant rains all over the room, liquid that feels like freedom. And then there are the faces of my friends in the crowd. People who I never gave up on, and who never gave up on me.

These are the people I love all the way to heaven and back.

A place constructed by algorithms has missed something vital—we're more than our profiles. We're complex people who feel real emotions.

Andy starts down the hall.

"Wait, where are you going?" I ask.

"To turn myself in," he says, and then leaves me with final parting words. "People in this life will want you to do well, but never better than them. And they'll always have their opinions about you. Just know that you're a lot more than lemon-lime. You're Luna. A unique flavor that just belongs to you. And don't let anyone make you feel otherwise."

I run and give him a hug. "Thank you. For everything." My eyes are welling up with tears, so I hardly even see him go.

I feel someone take my hand, and I know by his touch that it's Axel. So I grasp his hand tightly, and we smile as we look out across Limboland. The chaos.

But then the world starts to vibrate.

The floors tremble. The glass walls shake. Something rips past the building, so loud that I have to cover my ears. We all do, taking cover.

It's a helicopter.

My sight returns, and I see that inside sits the queen of Limboland. My heart sinks with the knowledge that she will escape into the sky and disappear over the horizon.

With no remorse.

This battle is far from over.

Companies like Limbo get away with everything, and even though they're sure to be embroiled in legal battles, I know Limbo isn't disappearing anytime soon. They'll pay a fine lower than the taxes that they pay—which is zero.

A fat juicy nothingburger.

But I can only hope that our story sets a precedent, doing justice in the name of my newfound family, who are far too weird to fit in the outside world, yet mean everything to me on the inside—who cry victory and dance like baboons beneath the showering skies of heaven. Because even though we may have lost the challenge . . .

We sure felt like winners.

▶ 61.

"Heaven Is a Place On Earth"
—Belinda Carlisle

I snap awake to the insanely happy jingle of my alarm.

I'm basically nocturnal now, because ever since what happened at Limboland, I barely sleep at night. Sometimes I just go retro and play a game called nap roulette that consists of passing out without an alarm, not knowing if I'll wake up after twenty minutes or two hours.

It's risky, and I love that.

Months later and my life is still a carnival. I have to manage spring midterms, my mama's job hunt, and national news interviews, which bring tons of tourists to El Dorado ever since our town started appearing on every "top ten places to visit" list in the country.

And of course, there's my future, which stares at me all the time, uncaring whether I'm ready for it or not.

But just like Darnell says, *My stress is chronic, but my ass is iconic.*

My psychologist tells me that after everything that happened, I should try to see beauty in the little things in life. And I totally get what she means. So now I'm looking for a little yacht, or a little mansion. But seriously, seeing her is really helping. Truth is, you don't need to have a breakdown or get kidnapped to see a psychologist—something I wish I'd known before my life totally exploded. I always thought that because I'd be a psychologist one day, I was too strong to need one. But I'm really glad I took Axel's advice anyway. Actually, we all did—it's the only way to move past the trauma.

This evening my phone is blowing up with notifications, calls, and text messages—but instead of answering, I stick to my new personal routine. I don't even check my phone until after I'm properly enjoying my evening. The old Luna would have replied immediately, but this one makes a point to live in the present. It gives me time to relativizar my life—a word in Spanish that means you give perspective to what really matters and maybe find out that so many of those little worries aren't even worth your woe.

So now it's time to roll out of bed, touch up yesterday's makeup, and drink water from the bathroom sink like a golden retriever. Then I poke my head into the hall. "Moooooooom!" I yell, and get no response, so I add, "I'm pregnaaaant!" just to make sure she's not home.

That means I can punch play on my boom box and blast my favorite mixtape.

I'm assuming my mom is out applying for whatever jobs she can. We're running out of time before her next immigration appointment, because she lost her business visa when we lost the theater, and hiring an immigrant is a big commitment for any company, seeing that they might have to sponsor her green card. Plus, the government makes it extremely difficult and doesn't give any incentive to companies to hire people like her. So whatever time I used to spend at the theater is now going toward helping Mamá practice her interview skills—which largely consists of differentiating between the pronunciation of "beach" and "bitch."

Luckily for us, the insurance settlement from the fire is at least putting food on the table. Sure, my mom has debated moving back to be with my abuela in Spain, which has universal health care, beautiful Mediterranean beaches, and enough paella to give any gringo a full Spanish accent—but just the thought of being separated from her hurts my soul. I can't imagine a world where I have to choose between my mother and my life here. Which is why I've already kissed the hope of a four-year university goodbye. After high school, I'll work and take some night classes, and there's no shame in that.

Anyway, let me update you on everything.

If you can't already imagine, I didn't win the Limbo scholarship. For obvious reasons, no one has. The Limbo app itself has been suspended until the date of the trial. And I can't be happier—at least we won the first battle of the war. Even though Scarlett escaped and no one knows where she is, I hope the next time I see her it's face-to-face in court.

The funny thing is, Limbo keeps coming back for more. They've been leaving me voice mails and sending me baseless legal notices every single day. Which leads me to phase three of my daily ritual:

My little DIY project, where I glue all their threats to my bathroom wall so I can laugh at them while I sit on my porcelain throne.

I take today's letters from the kitchen table and start sifting through them. But that's when I realize that the envelopes are all different sizes and colors.

These are different. No legal threats. No junk mail.

The first one is red and has a fancy stamp and seal in the top right corner.

It's a letter from Southern California University—the top private school in the nation. One of the universities on my wish

375

list, with a great psychology program. I open the letter with bated breath, my heartbeat pounding in my ears.

```
Dear Ms. Iglesias:
After the extraordinary acts of courage
you displayed this year, it is our
pleasure to invite you to attend
Southern California University . . .
```

Wait. What?

It drops out of my hands and floats to the floor.

"This is a freaking acceptance letter!" I'm screaming aloud, jumping up and down, but I'm more confused than a chameleon in a bag of M&M's. How could I be accepted into a school that I've never even applied to? I sift through some of the other envelopes to investigate, my hands shaking with exhilaration. Pacific University. Columbus University. Even a prestigious school in New York. I tear open more.

```
We are overjoyed to offer you our annual
Excellence Scholarship . . .
```

```
Congrats! The Dean's Scholarship
is yours! Courage in the face of
adversity . . .
```

```
Luna, you are the recipient of the
Distinguished Student Scholarship for
bravery . . .
```

Full-ride scholarships.

I start to cry.

I can't stop.

Releasing all the late nights of studying, all the times I helped out my mother at work. The dream that my parents had for me. All the hope that burned with the Monteverde Mall. The pain I felt when my friends were taken from me, and the disappointment when we realized there was no challenge at all. I release all of it as I break down.

But I'm not alone. Because they've just arrived.

"LUNA MARÍA VALERO IGLESIAS!" familiar voices call out, honking the car horn.

I dry my eyes with my sleeve, and that's when I see Axel's red convertible Mustang sparkling in the sunset—a retro work of art that he would never trade in, not even for the fastest supercar in the world. And the best part is that all my friends are packed inside.

Darnell opens the door. "Ms. Iglesias, put your seat back and your belt on. It's time for your surprise. Wait, your eyes are screaming 'I just cried'—you read the letters, didn't you?"

"How did you know?"

Mimi gets dewy with joy. "We've been trying to reach you all day, Loony! We're all going to college! We're actually going to college!" She pulls me in for a hug, and soon I'm sloppy crying all over again.

"This can't really be happening. Mimi, slap me—I'm dreaming," I say in disbelief.

"Believe it, girl!"

And now that my friends have their acceptance letters too, I can finally let myself feel the joy.

"Since all these universities learned about our story on the news, the mail just keeps coming," Axel says as I sit in the front seat, taking his side. He puts his hand on my leg. "Whatever university you choose, I know you'll make a difference."

"If I go to that college in the Galápagos, promise me you'll visit," Mimi yelps.

"I can't wait to see you in your native environment." I wink.

Mimi crawls up onto Kilo's lap, and he smiles, holding her close. "And I can't wait to visit you," Kilo says.

Mimi's eyes light up. "We can be naked on a beach in paradise!"

"I totally support that," Kilo tells her, laughing. I've always admired Mimi for knowing exactly who she is, even when that someone is so free-spirited.

"Hey, guys? Is today a map day or Google Maps day?" Darnell says as we all laugh nervously. "Just kidding, I know exactly where we are going!"

And then the rest of us pull out our phones.

"Let's go retro today," Mimi says as she disconnects.

We all throw on airplane mode.

Our fun little way to escape the world and enter a new one.

"So, I heard the word 'surprise.' . . . Where are we going?" I ask.

"There's something we have to show you." Axel smiles in that alluring way that reminds me why I was so moonstruck in the first place.

And then he takes my hand with his black-painted nails, rings on his fingers, and a little artichoke tattoo on his wrist—questioning the definition of "normal"—or the definition that someone really boring made up a long time ago. But we're like that now. Sure, these days the challenge is just a distant memory, but that doesn't stop us from being who we've become. We're Retros, and we'll forever have one another's backs. And even if life takes us in different directions, our bond will always keep us close.

Because we aren't just friends, we're familia.

The car accelerates like a roller coaster into the sunset. Tingles tickle inside my stomach. I close my eyes, putting my hands up, and I can feel my fingertips touch the sky. Darnell cranks up our favorite Retro Radio station, which plays the perfect final song of my soundtrack—"Heaven Is a Place On Earth"—and I'm falling in love with my world all over again.

We belt out lyrics, screaming and dancing into the wind.

Axel turns left, past the school. I start to recognize the area, the way the setting sun glimmers along the trees, the way it warms my skin as we round the corner. Traveling to a place that my heavy heart hasn't allowed me to brave in many months. Where magic used to exist.

"Why are you guys taking me back here?"

"You told me the only way to win back your heart was to turn back time." Axel beams. "Well, that's something we've all become pretty good at this year."

And then I see it.

In the empty lot where our beloved mall once stood is a sea of cars, buses, motorcycles, many of them retro makes and models, all parked around an enormous movie screen.

Darnell shouts like a showman. "May I present to you—your new theater!"

A full-on drive-in theater, booming with life. Retromaniacs all around. And so many recognizable faces in the crowd. Samantha and Vince on motorcycles. Ruby and Kosta waving from afar. Miranda helping Nika at the DJ booth. Even Jade is here for moral support. At the end of the day, the Retro Challenge really brought us together— we've learned that although life is a race, it's not a competition. And everyone's invited. The Roller Derby Diner has a stand, with waiters on roller skates serving food. There's even a Sequin's Thrift pop-up.

My jaw is on the floor.

"We couldn't go off to college unless we knew your mother was okay," Mimi says.

"All of this is for you and your mother," Axel tells me. "I convinced my family not to build on the land, so this portion of it will forever be for your new theater, and all the other small businesses."

For the first time in the history of ever, I can't talk.

I'm drowning in emotion.

The euphoria.

The nerves.

I don't know what to do, so I grab Axel by the face and pull him in for a kiss. A kiss that has been building up inside me for so long, one that makes me lose track of time. And when our lips part, I know that before me is a guy who, in all his imperfect perfection, will always be there for me.

No matter where life leads us next.

"Thank you, thank you, THANK YOU!" I jump into the back seat and pounce on all my friends before finally seeing the most important woman in my world standing by the projector, managing the whole show.

"¡MAMÁ!" I jump out and sprint down the rows of cars, running into her arms.

My mother gives me a big kiss, painting my cheek with lipstick. She's more beautiful than ever, wearing her favorite pearl necklace, which I haven't seen in years.

"You see all of this, Luna? I can't believe it! It's a dream come true," she says, squeezing me so tight. "Your friends are so sweet, I'm going to get type two diabetes!"

"Look at you, a boss jefa again! It fits you well!"

"It fits me perfectly. Everyone in El Dorado is here to support us, even the mayor! De corazón, what I've learned from you, hija, doesn't have any price. If it was up to me, I would put a statue of you in the city hall plaza!"

"I love you, Mom, but seriously not necessary." I laugh.

"I'm sorry, hija. I need to go check the film. We don't want another fire so soon." She giggles. "Enjoy tonight. You deserve it!"

I turn around and spot my friend in the concessions line.

"Samantha!"

She hands me a tub of popcorn. "Hey, you! Here. It's drizzled in hot sauce to keep the fire in your veins. Not that you need it." She extends a gift. "I also got you this."

I start unwrapping it really fast. I always get excited when it comes to presents. Samantha knows this well—after all, she was my very first friend.

It's a framed newspaper article with a black-and-white photo of us, together, exiting the gates of Limboland, chaos all around. Funny how Samantha used to hide a photo of me in her locker, and now we're standing proudly together, front and center.

"We really killed it, didn't we?"

"Looks like it. And don't forget, if you need anything, just whistle." She winks. We laugh.

"You know I will. Now come hang with us—the movie is going to start soon!"

The summer sun glows through the palm trees as the film reel sparkles to life across the silver screen. And just the sound brings to life the image of my father waltzing with me down the aisles of our theater. In full technicolor, and as vibrant as they day we lived those moments.

Because recollections may fade, but nostalgia never dies.

And the future will always barrel on.

Sure, we'll go back to normal lives, full of apps, games, and profiles. We'll all move away and attend different colleges, and nothing will ever be the same. Because we are not the same. And even though we have so many amazing new ways of expressing ourselves, maybe the next time you look up from that screen, you'll see life with different eyes—through a retro filter. A timeless world that exists forever inside all of us. Where every sunset is eternally golden, and all the nights are lined in neon lights. A place where the present moment is more valuable than the past and future combined. Where you may just fall in love with life and touch heaven on earth.

Acknowledgments

Retro is a labor of love that would not have been possible without the friendship and support of everyone at Simon & Schuster—particularly Justin Chanda, Kendra Levin, and our wonderful editor Alyza Liu, for all her hard work on *Retro*. Also, we must thank Amanda Ramirez for believing in the story from the very start!

But there are so many people at S&S who have made all of this possible! Alex Kelleher, Nicole Benevento, Emily Ritter, and Chloë Foglia, to name just a few.

And thanks to Shania Fan for that fantastic cover! Sensational!

A special thanks to our literary agent, Andrea Brown, for everything she does and for having guided us through this process from the very beginning. Without your wisdom, enthusiasm, and patience, none of this would be possible! We must also extend our gratitude to our phenomenal entertainment managers, Trevor Engelson and Josh McGuire; our agents, Steve Fisher and Debbie Deuble-Hill, at APA; and our contract attorneys, Shep Rosenman and Jennifer Justman.

We're so excited for the international publication of *Retro* and want to give our appreciation to Deane Norton, Stephanie Voros, and Amy Habayeb in S&S foreign sales, as well as to Taryn Fagerness, our amazing foreign agent.

Jan De La Rosa, your notes were so valuable. ¡Muchas gracias por todo! And Cam Montgomery—your insight was so important to us. We are so grateful to you!

ACKNOWLEDGMENTS

A big warm thank-you to Neal Shusterman, for not just being a supportive mentor, but also for being a compass whenever we got lost and overthought our brains into scrambled eggs. You are a treasure trove of invaluable, expert writing wisdom!

Thank you to Elaine and Ed Galvez for reading *Retro* and being so supportive of our creative endeavors!

A huge thank-you to our dear friend Javier Ruescas, who has been there for us emotionally and professionally. You have been so generous with your support. You are one in a million! ¡Gracias de corazón amigo!

Gracias Vico, mi mijita, for saving our butts a million times over when it came to digital art and design! You are an incredible person and friend, but everyone already knows that. Thank you, Pati and Paula, for reading, giving notes, and investing time in us without expecting anything in return. You're both the real deal! And Elias Gertler, you have been there since this idea's conception and have been crucial in its development. We can't thank you enough!

Reconocimientos adicionales

Especial gracias a las mujeres fuertes que me han guiado desde que nací, porque sin vosotras todo esto no hubiera sido posible. Mamá, Amparo, Marta y Susana, sois auténticas guerreras y mis personas vitamina.

Y también especial gracias a mis amigos, que sois la familia que elegí. A "estas" vosotras, Bárbara, Claudia, María, Marina, Patricia, Raquel, Yolanda, por estar conmigo desde siempre y hacerme sentir todo vuestro cariño en cada momento importante de mi vida. Por recordarme que la distancia es solo un número.

Gracias a Paula, por ser mi apoyo día y noche, por ser mi norte pero sobre todo mi sur, por no dejarme olvidar quién soy. Amiga, no sé qué haría sin ti. A Nerea, por tu corazón enorme, por ser mi bicho especial y alegrarte por mí como nadie. A mis Carlistas por creer en mí y apoyarme en todas mis aventuras sin dudarlo. A "las niñas", porque los años pasan, pero siempre os tengo cuando vuelvo a casa. A Nuri y a Cris por dejarme ser y enseñarme que diferente es mejor. Sois muy bonitas. ♥

Gracias a toda la Spanish Mafia por ser "LA familia" y estar siempre en lo malo para animar y en lo bueno para celebrar. A Patri y Fran por ser un ejemplo de mujeres fuertes y siempre haber estado a mi lado. Sois lo que nuestra industria necesita. A May y Pablito por ser mis *partners in crime*, porque estuvisteis conmigo desde el principio y siempre me impulsasteis a seguir luchando.

Thank you to my amazing American girls, Mindy and

ACKNOWLEDGMENTS

Bobbie, for your sugar, spice and everything nice! Your kindness always warms my heart. Gracias a Lau por ser la hermana mayor que nunca tuve. A Luci por ser alguien en quien poder confiar y perrear. A Pepe por tu pasión y por siempre perseguir nuestros sueños juntos. A Alex porque sé que puedo contar contigo siempre. A Diego por tu gran corazón y por querer escucharme. Y a Dieguito por siempre ser mi compañero de locuras.

Por último, y con todo mi corazón, te doy las gracias a ti, Chris, porque empezamos este viaje juntos, y me has seguido acompañando y cuidando desde arriba. Lo hemos conseguido, amigo.